HEARTSNARE

HEARTSNARE

Book One of THE UMBRAVERSE

STEVEN B. WILLIAMS

HEARTSNARE: Book One of *The Umbraverse*

Published in 2016 by Lethe Press, Inc.
118 Heritage Avenue • Maple Shade, NJ 08052-3018 usa
www.lethepressbooks.com • lethepress@aol.com
ISBN: 978-1-59021-262-2 / 1-59021-262-2

Set in Carre Noir, Mason, and Eveleth.
Interior design: Alex Jeffers.
Cover art and design: Eran Fowler.
Author photo: Leanne Fox/Gingersnaps Photography.

*

Library of Congress CIP data on-file at LC Catalog Online.

FOR JASON.

ACKNOWLEDGMENTS

HEARTSNARE has been with me in one form or another for the better part of six years, and in that time I've made a fair few people suffer by incessantly talking about it. To that end I would like to thank Dad, who, when I first started this book, kept me in tea and television and didn't complain even once; my loving fiancé Jase, whose insight has helped me shape this story into what it is today; my dearest friend Katy, who has been my Saturday night therapist for over a decade; my cousin Sue, who wouldn't let me off the hook until the damn thing was published; my writing partner Dina, whose unconditional support has helped immeasurably; and fellow author Ann, whose quiet encouragement has seen me from the very first days of this idea right through until publication.

There, now you all know who to blame.

CHAPTER ONE
Then

"So, your nana's not allowed to drive anymore. Mind you, I'm surprised they'd not taken her license before now. Remember when she took out that police horse?"

"Nah, seriously?" Tim laughed, loud and throaty.

"Oh aye. I was so shamefaced going down to the police station to pick up my own mother, let me tell you." Jhardine peered into her packet of cheese and onion crisps. "There's bloody getting less and less in these." She took out one measly wafer and crunched while she looked at the game of cards between them. "Eric, here, it's your go."

Eric, a convergence of wires and drip-lines nestled there on his hospital bed, didn't seem to have heard. Actually, his eyes were glassy, his breathing slow. Looked like he was having to concentrate just to stay awake.

"Mate?" Tim prompted, reaching over a brawny arm and giving Eric's shoulder a gentle squeeze. "Just because I'm winning, yeah, no need to play the sick card." No response. Tim looked to Jhardine, but he found no comfort.

Her incult curls slipped down around her shoulders and hid her face as she reached to take her son's hand. "Eric? Are you—"

"Here you are! A nice fresh jug of water for you," Nurse Lesley trilled as she bustled into the room. "How are you doing, my lovely?" she asked of Eric as she put the tapered plastic jug on the table by Eric's bed.

"He seems a bit, I dunno, out of it," Tim said.

Jhardine scowled at her son's best friend. He noticed and ducked his head. "He'll be fine though," Jhardine hurried as she picked up the cards and shuffled away the Joker she hadn't meant to leave in the deck. "We've probably worn him out. Just needs rest, doesn't he?"

"Oh, of course." Nurse Lesley smiled. Casual as you like, she took off a white hair-tie from around her wrist and attempted to bind her meandering and buttery hair. "Well, we've all had a long day round here," she said. "We had a right palaver earlier with the meals. Everyone complaining they tasted right bitter. You know, I'll just check...." Quick like a wasp to a discarded cider can, Nurse Lesley's fingers landed on Eric's wrist to take a measure of his pulse.

"No, there's no need, I...."

"Oh, Jhardine, you're right, love. I'm just going to get Doctor Smith to bob in when he's on his rounds, all right, darling?" she said, giving a tight smile as she left the room.

"What a cow," Jhardine grumbled when she was out of earshot.

"Mum," Eric piped up, as though waking from a sterile dream.

"Aw, welcome back, mate," Tim said, hand rubbing at Eric's shoulder.

Eric reached up and with a slow hand removed the tiger-shell of an oxygen mask from over his nose and mouth. "Don't be hard on Nan, Mum. She doesn't mean it. She's," he coughed, "even older than you. Prehistoric."

A razor vine of air barked out of Eric's mouth. Another coughing fit.

Tim stood, eyes wide. "Is he okay? What can I do?"

"Oh, it's nowt," she said, pouring a cup of water and holding it to Eric's lips. "It's just what he gets for cheeking me off."

Eric drank and spluttered. Eventually, the agonising spasm in his throat softened to a more manageable squirm. "Sorry," he wheezed in Tim's general direction. "Nothing you can do for me this time, meathead."

Tim smiled, glad Eric still had it in him to joke about Tim's gym obsession.

Jhardine, not so humoured, clamped the oxygen mask back on Eric's face. "Keep that on, you." Eric winced, screwing up his watery eyes. "And for the record, your nan *does* bloody mean it. She might blame everything on the dementia, but let me tell you she's only doolally when it's convenient." Silence threatened to cool the room then, something Jhardine simply couldn't abide. "You know," she started, "your nan would never let me get away with anything when I was growing up."

Eric dared hazard a few words around his mask. "She let you get that tattoo on your—"

"Eric!" Jhardine folded an arm over her chest.

Tim raised an eyebrow and laughed, scratching at his long nose. "What's it of?"

"Never mind you. Did she tell you that?"

Seen through the prism of his oxygen mask, Eric's toothy smile looked stretched and wrong. She tried not to notice. "Oh, that evil old witch." She settled back on the hard plastic chair. "Well, I'll have you know that she didn't like it at all. In fact, she held me down and tried to scrub it off with one of those kitchen pan scourers. If your granddad, God rest his soul, hadn't been there, I'd have been scraped to death."

"I don't understand why you got a tattoo. You," and again came the need for breath, "hate needles."

Jhardine's voice emerged low and hurt. "Your dad."

The absence hung between them, Eric's dad's non-presence a lazy, rotten fart.

"I reckon we'll have you out to watch the rugby final, mate," Tim said as a means to perfume over the moment.

"Maybe," was Eric's reply.

A curt tap at the door and in padded a stout doctor with horn-rimmed glasses atop sinking features.

"Good evening," he said, his wiry hair dancing in the draft that funnelled through the open door.

"Doctor Smith, how are you?"

Doctor Smith stood looking at Eric's charts like they were written in some alien language. "I am fine, thank you, Mrs Mayfair," he said after what felt like hours.

"Ms Mayfair," Jhardine corrected for what must have been the hundredth time. "I've never remarried. I guess no poor bugger will have me." She laughed to a snort and then sat down again, embarrassed and sore from her self-inflicted wound.

Doctor Smith, as sour as though suffering an unexpected prostate exam, admitted, "I always get that wrong, don't I? Apologies." He cleared his throat. "Now, Eric, I hear you're having quite a bit of difficulty breathing."

Eric seemed to wheeze a little louder in response.

"It's probably our fault, Doctor Smith, we've been tiring him out," Jhardine repeated.

Tim nodded too. Then he added, "He's a bit spaced out too, you know, like, doesn't always hear you."

"He will be. The cocktail of drugs he's on is fairly aggressive. Eric? Eric, I'm just going to listen to your chest. Is that okay?"

Eric gave a slow nod.

"Could you help prop him up for me, please," Dr Smith asked of Tim.

"Oh, yeah, mate, sure." Tim slid his thick arm under Eric's back and, supporting his head, lifted Eric up.

Doctor Smith began his game of listening to various regions around Eric's back and front. "Are you in pain, Eric?"

"My chest," Eric rattled.

"Okay. We'll see if we can take care of that for you. Now, Eric, I need to know if you remember that conversation we had the other day. Do you remember what I said about if the infection came back?"

It was the darnedest thing. Eric broke out in a slow, soft smile. "Yes."

Doctor Smith nodded. "That's good, Eric, thank you. And thank you," he said to Tim. "You can lay him back down now. Ms Mayfair, could I speak to you privately a minute, please," and, so there was no mistaking his meaning, he pointed a finger toward the door, "outside, if you don't mind."

"Oh," Jhardine's mouth stayed open a few seconds too long. "Yes, of course. Unless...." She looked to Eric. "Unless you need something, chick?"

No reply.

"Eric?" Tim prodded.

"No, that's right. He's tired," Jhardine said, and inched her way toward the door. Then she came back. "I'll get you a snack, Tim. One of them nut bar things, yeah?"

"Yeah, that'd be nice, cheers," Tim said, never taking his eyes off Eric.

"And Eric, you need more, er, water." The near-full jug on the table by Eric's bed seemed to flare in the light. "I'll just have a word with the doctor and then I'll get you sorted, all right? You'll be right, won't you love?" Eric didn't answer. Then Jhardine whispered a "You'll be fine," as, wringing her hands, she followed Doctor Smith out of the room.

"HI, MATE," TIM said a few minutes later when Eric looked up at him and smiled like he'd just noticed his best friend was in the room. "Here, has that nurse been round again? Him what fancies you?"

"No," Eric said low, a little curl of devilment on his lips. "I reckon it's that aftershave you gave me. Put him off, hasn't it?"

"Listen, I'll have you know that was expensive," Tim laughed. He stole a glance at his watch. Eric's mum and Doctor Smith were taking ages.

"Got somewhere to be?" Eric asked.

"No, sorry, I just was thinking I might get a workout in before the end of the night but all this doing nowt is tiring. Don't know how you manage it."

"Aye, it takes it out of you," Eric agreed. "I—"

"But I don't understand!" came Jhardine's voice leaking in from the corridor.

"So," Tim said, loud. "Have they said when you're coming out, eh? I want to go to Ibiza with you this year, yeah?"

Eric wore that same smile he'd had with the doctor earlier. "I'm not," he coughed. "Water please."

Tim lifted the cup to Eric's lips, his other hand sliding down over Eric's close-cropped curly hair to rest on the back of his neck. To steady him. To steady them both. "What do you mean you're not? Can't stay in here your whole life."

"Want to bet?" Eric answered. "This pneumonia's not shifting Tim. There's no fight in me anymore."

"What? What are you saying?"

"The doctor, he's telling Mum. Telling her—"

It was true that since being admitted to hospital eight months ago, Eric had lost a lot: over two stone in weight, science magazines by the van-load, days and days to infections, fevers and medications, and yet through it all the bitter fact was that his hearing remained defiant and strong.

So neither he nor Tim could ignore the conversation filtering in from outside the room. "But he was better yesterday! He was better!"

"Yes, but today he isn't." Doctor Smith's thin voice sounded like two knives being rubbed together. "This tends to be how it happens, I'm afraid. They rally and then, well, they burn themselves out. It's as if the body tries to give itself one last kick start. But his heart, Ms Mayfair. It's his heart, you see. And with the infection. He's winding down, Jhardine. It's—"

A surge of voices in the corridor and the conversation was lost.

Tim was looking at Eric like Eric was about to detonate. "It's okay, Tim," Eric started. "Mate, listen—"

"Shit," Tim said, backing away. The beaker in his hands slipped to the floor, the water spreading far and fast. "Shit."

"You said that already."

"Shit!" he repeated again.

"It won't be bad, Tim. Like sleep. Well, not sleep. Not sleep exactly. Sort of drowning, but—"

"No, don't start Eric. Don't start with your damned facts!" Tim shook his head. "I can't. I can't No! We was supposed to do stuff, me and you. We were supposed to—"

"We've done this before, this conversation, Tim. We've said all this."

"But our holiday. I thought we had more time."

"More time for what?" Eric said.

Tim's face was screwing up. "No, I don't...." He sucked in a breath and drew close. His hand was on Eric's cheek. "I don't want you to go. I want—"

"He's not going anywhere," Eric's mum said as she stepped back into the room. Her face was grey and cold looking, and tired. Yes, she looked *tired.*

"It's okay, Mum, I already knew." This made her stop. "I'm ready—"

"No!" and a wild, furious look took up on her face. Her corkscrew curls flapped back and forth. A cudgel of fingers rose to guard her lips. "We aren't talking about this, do you hear me?"

"It won't make it go away," Eric said, small, defeated. "I'm dying—"

"I won't let it happen." She ran a hand over the gold cross hanging around her neck. "God won't let this happen."

"I don't think God has anything to do with this," Tim spat.

"So," Jhardine said, ignoring them both. "I'm going to get your water and your snacks and then, when I get back, we're going to sit here and talk and, and, and hate this until the bloody sun comes up!"

She fled the room. Silence followed, such a heavy friend.

"Just sit with me Tim," Eric said, holding up his hand. "Just be here with me."

"I'll, er, go make sure she's all right," Tim said, pulling out of Eric's reach.

"No, please," Eric rasped, beginning to cough again. "Please, just take my hand. Just—"

"I can't. I'm not strong like you, not strong enough, I...." Tim turned away. "I won't be long!"

"No, please...."

And with that, Eric was left to die alone.

CHAPTER TWO
NOW

HE WALKED THE length of Spartan's car park, under the arch of the metal and chrome of the gym's grinning frontage. It was far too pleased with itself, if you asked Eric's opinion. *Though at least it's something interesting to look at,* Eric sniffed. You didn't get much of that round Willingsley.

A vibration shot down his leg. Eric fished out his mobile phone. A text message.

"Do you know you could be owed thousands in compensation? Text...."

And delete.

White numerals of a clock meandered about his cracked phone screen. Now half seven in the morning and still no word from Tim even though they'd agreed to meet at six. No call, no text, nothing. Not. On. And to make matters worse, because Eric couldn't stand the dodgy looks he was getting as he waited outside the gym, he'd been forced to go in and, *horror*, exercise.

A tut. A rubbing of his downy chops. The pale morning cuffed him in the face with an acrid squall. Eric's mum was always telling him that rather than sitting inside on his laptop or reading his books, he should go out and get some fresh air. Problem was in Willingsley, with a belching chemical plant over on Reynaud's Walk at one side of the city and the slurry works on Griffin Road at the other, the air had never seen fresh. Eric coughed. Oh, it got you right in the back of the throat. And to top it off, yep, it was starting to drizzle.

Marvellous.

He pulled his hooded jacket tighter. No way was he going back in the gym, though. He'd probably end up in a Pilates class or some nonsense like that. *And there aren't enough fitties in Yorkshire to ease that pain.*

Just to beggar that thought, though, a young blond lad with a solid frame and flushed cheeks exited the gym with a sports bag over his shoulder and a swagger in his step. When Eric realised he was in the feller's path, he adjusted his Jobcentre tie, smoothed down his shirt a bit.

"You all right mate?" the lad croaked as he walked by, his cloud of after-shave following a few seconds later.

"Y-y-yeah," Eric stammered. The guy smiled and went on his way, leaving Eric to his embarrassment. *Stammering? Seriously?*

It was the early morning workout that had thrown him. Gyms were weird places. A venue for collective sweating, gas release and, if you were lucky, muscle hypertrophy. For Tim, though, an aspiring bodybuilder, the gym was his religious temple. So much so he'd turned it into a verb: gym-ing it. "It makes me feel alive, Eric," he'd said. "Makes me feel connected. I am this body. I am me."

That was about as poetic as Tim ever got. Made Eric a bit jealous, actually. And tumescent. The closest he'd ever come to feeling alive was when he was dying.

Maybe Mum's right, I am a drama queen.

And speak of the she-devil: Eric heard his clapped-out excuse for a car wheezing down the road even before he saw its dirty black shell and cloudy windscreen trundling into the car park. A glance at the back seat as the car rattled to a stop in front of him told Eric his mum wasn't alone.

Wonderful.

"Careful of my bloody window!" Eric shouted as his mum used her shoulder to pop open the always stiff driver's side door.

"Well, how else am I supposed to get out?" she said. "This thing's a death trap." She pulled her trailing cream shawl tight around her shoulders and dashed for the car's passenger side.

"You're not even supposed to be driving, so the question's moot," Eric reminded her.

"Oh for the love of.... You're worse than my mother."

"Here," Eric said, hand to chest. "Words can hurt you know."

Eric's mum gave a rosy smile. "Here, say hi to Chanterelle and Sarah," she said as she slipped inside the car.

Well, I could hardly miss them, could I?

As Eric stepped ever so delicately into the car, because to do otherwise would mean him putting his foot straight through the wafer-thin floor, he duly breathed a hello, turned and gave a blink-and-you'd-miss-it wave to their passengers.

"You all right, Eric?" Sarah asked in her Bradford swaddle. As usual, she'd scraped back her raven hair so tight it seemed she was hoping to induce a thrifty face-lift. When coupled with her avaricious nose, which was taking up more and more space with every passing year, she had quite the magpie charm about her.

"Aye, not bad. You?"

"Chanterelle, if you don't stop playing with that door handle I'm going to unclip your seatbelt and let you roll out onto the bloody road."

Where Sarah was a thin slice of a woman, her daughter, the eponymous Mushroom, was a double helping of delinquent seven year old.

"I hate you!" the pudgy kid screamed, her fat cheeks flushed with defiance.

"Oh, believe me you little brat, the feeling is mutual."

"I want Daddy!"

"Well, if your dad had come home last night, he'd have been welcome to you!" Sarah bit back in a bruised voice. And then, "Sorry."

"What?" Jhardine breezed. "Oh, I wasn't listening, love," she said. She put on her seatbelt and, as she did, caught Eric's gaze and raised her eyebrow in a way that said: *Can you believe that?*

"Where am I heading?" Eric tried to smooth over the moment. "The school, yeah?"

"If you don't mind," Sarah answered. "Chanterelle, if you don't stop nipping me I swear to God I will put you up for adoption."

"Tim all right?" Eric's mum asked, tuning out the drama on the back seat.

"Wouldn't know," Eric said, flicking on the car indicator and waiting for his chance to join the traffic.

"What you mean?"

"Never showed, did he?"

"Oh." Jhardine ran a hand through her curls. "Are you still meeting him at the pub tonight?"

"Can't really afford it. Spent a fiver on my gym pass," Eric huffed. "I proper don't know what's up with him lately." She had no comment. Which in itself was suspicious. *She knows something.* Eric narrowed his eyes. "All right, Mum, what—"

"Here, have you got my board money?" she asked.

He knew she'd just ended the conversation on purpose, but there was no getting around it. "Er, I've not had chance. I'll get it for you tonight," Eric chirped in his sweetest tone.

"Well, I need that money, Eric. The bog's naffed again."

"What's wrong with it now?" Eric was forced to brake hard as a man on a mobility scooter darted across the road with no mind to oncoming traffic. "Fucking hell—"

"Eric!" Jhardine tutted and touched the golden cross on the chain around her neck. "You're a miracle. Miracles shouldn't swear. And it's the flusher. You've probably worn it out. Your bowels are like a bloody steam train."

"Mum!"

"Oh, give over, you," his mum laughed. "Sarah knows I'm only messing. Now, what are you doing this afternoon. Jobcentre?"

"Well I'm not wearing this synthetic shirt and trouser combination for fashion, am I?"

"Right. Then what?"

"Well, looking for a job I suppose. I would have gone down to the library but they've frigging closed it down."

"Eric, language!"

"Fine, Je—"

"And don't you dare start swearing in French." She saw him opening his mouth. "Or any other language, you chuffing little know it all." She was grinning. This was all good-natured banter. "Reason why I ask is, will you take a tenner out of your board and get us some milk and eggs. I've no idea where it all keeps going." She stuck a hand in her oversized silver handbag and set about rummaging until she found a cigarette packet. She was only a social smoker. Had practically given up. She opened up the squashed carton. Empty. "Oh hell, get me some ciggies as well."

"Really don't think I should be enabling your habit."

"Eric...."

"Fine! But when you get cancer, I—"

Mushroom chose this precise moment to kick the back of Eric's car seat. The chair shot back, crushing the poor fungus child. She gave a terrible cry. Her mother only chuckled.

"That serves you right, that does."

In all, it took half an hour for a journey that should have taken five minutes. Willingsley had outdone itself this time, it really had.

The stone building of the school sat like an angry lobster, its red arms spreading out in either direction while the crest of the building's head, which happened to be home to the school's music department, rose high with row and row of mean little windows that glared down at all who entered its gates. The place had given Eric the creeps when he used to attend, and it was no different now. This wasn't helped, either, by the horrible scratching and wailing of violins that came crashing down on them as Sarah opened the car door. She stopped. "Oh, I just know I'll have to listen to that come the Autumn Festival. You know, this one got homework to write something up for it. She's seven! It's not on, is it?"

"Why can't they just let kids be kids?" Jhardine said.

"Because kids are as dumb as rocks," Eric chipped in. Both women looked at him with severe disdain. Clearly, the Cult of Motherhood disapproved.

"Anyway, I'm going to have to go, Jhardine. I'll see you later. Thanks for the lift, Eric. Say thank you, Chanterelle."

"Daddy calls you a bender," Mushroom told Eric. Eric's mum cackled.

Sarah's face grew pale. "Chanterelle! I'm so sorry Eric."

"Don't worry. I call Jim a fair few names behind his back as well, so...."

"Don't we all," Sarah tutted. "Right, come on, you little slut bag. I said come on!" The door slammed shut. The silence in the car was so wonderful it made Eric sigh. "Right," he said to his mum. "To work for you?"

"Aye. Can't put it off any longer," she said. "Here, don't check your phone while you're driving."

Eric glanced at the screen. "I'm just seeing if I have any texts." Nothing. "I swear to God—"

"Don't blaspheme."

"I'm gonna have a right go at Tim when I see him."

"You never do. All that boy has to do is smile at you and all is forgiven." She sighed. "I was the same with your father."

"Me and Tim are just friends, Mum."

"If you say so." She rubbed at her forehead. "Oh, just the thought of seeing Barry today is already giving me a headache."

Eric felt a pang of guilt. If he could just get a decent job his mum could quit working at the café. Then she'd never have to see that god-awful man she called a boss ever again.

Simple as, Eric groaned.

THE ONCE FRESH green signage plastered in the Jobcentre window, around the window and on the street outside had all faded to a queasy mushy pea colour but nothing, *nothing,* could quite diminish the posters' grinning models. All of them had an insane gleam to their eyes and a jaw-aching hook to their smiles. It was as though Her Majesty's Government was trying to beat unemployment in the North through sheer force of antidepressants. But into that happy hell Eric had to tread.

Entering through the stuttering sliding door, which always gave such a shaming squeal, Eric took his place in line before the island-like circular staff desks in the middle of the room.

Once confirmation that he had kept his appointment was duly logged with the lumpy blur of a woman behind the cordoned-off desk, Eric was told he could now take a seat and wait. Take a seat? That was a feat in itself. The chairs surrounding the desks were all pink and angular, the stuff of a designer's wet dreams but murder if you actually wanted to sit on them. Perhaps, though, the jobless were meant to infer that they'd done far too much sitting already. Eric did his best, perching on a corner near a woman with a rat-like dog on her knee. Both had a bit of a constipated air about them. Eric was sure the chairs weren't helping.

Today's appointment was for Eric to talk about his job search. It was one of the many bullshit-smeared hoops through which he must jump so he wouldn't have his government allowance snipped off. On a normal day, he would have to wait out on the tenderising chairs for at least an hour. Not today, however. Just as he was sniffing his pits in case of offensive whiff: "Eric, there you are sweetheart," came Jobcentre Dee's voice from the far end of the corridor. Short, she wasn't easy to spot among the pot plants and rotating stands of binge-drinking awareness leaflets, but Eric managed to catch sight of her hand waving above the sea of green and chrome as she beckoned him over. He found her in the midst of the jungle fumbling with her keys as, with her delicate arms full of folders, she worked at unlocking her office door with just one hand.

"Are you late or am I early? Never mind, we'll call it even. Come on in. And morning!"

"Morning," Eric returned as he crossed the threshold into the positive-energy prison that was Dee's office. She'd filled the small room with miniature Zen gardens, climbing plants that Eric wasn't sure you should have inside because when nudged they gave off an eye-watering stink, and an inexplicable hoard of ornamental birdcages.

"So, how are you this week?" She took a seat on her plush office chair. In comparison, Eric's wonky-legged buffet seemed a bit of an insult.

"Good ta, you?"

Her eyes filled with azure life, her dewy skin brightening. Even the blurry scar that crossed the side of her cheek looked pleased.

"Oh, aren't you lovely to ask how I am. Well, I'm very well. Plans for the wedding—have I mentioned the wedding?"

"Once or twice."

"Well, they're shaping up nicely. Just sending out my invites!" Then without warning, but with plenty of zest, Dee sank beneath her desk.

"Er, Dee?" Eric asked after a few seconds. "You all right?"

"I'm fine!" she said from somewhere behind the desk. Quite possibly Narnia. "I'm just looking for my...ahah!"

She sprang back into view with a small watering can that had on its front a toothy sunflower. "And how is your mum by the way?" she asked as she tended the room's succulents. "I keep seeing her at church but she's always very busy. People there love her, she can hardly keep up with all the clubs and what not, can she?"

Eric worked a slither of toast from between his teeth. "Yeah, she's good, thanks. Seems to be doing all right healthwise now."

"Ahuh, ahuh, ahuh." Dee set the watering can back down below her desk. She made a sad face. "Still no job for you though?"

A surprise attack, that.

"No," Eric admitted.

"Yes, well, it's not for a lack of trying at least." Dee turned to her computer, somewhere there among the climbing vines, and started clicking away. "And you're still helping out at your mother's café when they're a person short, but not for pay?"

"Yeah."

"Because you have to declare if you're being paid." *All right, keep your bloody shoulder-pads on.* "Okay, well, I see you've had a lot of knock-backs from offices, haven't you?"

"Er, yeah. I try to say, you know, why I've not had a job before, but—"

"Ahuh, ahuh, ahuh. Right." Dee began typing again, then came another series of mouse clicks. That same manic grin he'd seen on the posters outside stretched out across her narrow face. "It's just that an office assistant job has opened up at Cook's down the road. You know, the IT firm?"

"Not really."

"Well, it's just down the road."

"Yeah, you said."

"Ahuh, ahuh, ahuh."

Eric was mulling over whether you could kill someone with a miniature garden rake and make it look like an accident when the sound of a computer printer churning out inked pages cut his murderous plans short.

"Hang on." Dee slipped below her desk again. When she scaled her way back to conversational altitude she had in one hand a wad of printed pages and in the other an aggressively large stapler.

"A bit short notice I know, but I've already fired off an email and told them you're coming down to see them today. They're desperate, you're desperate, it's meant to be! There's a map here, see, on the back page of this information pack. It shows you where their office is, but you can't miss it, it's—"

"Just down the road."

"Just down the road, yes! Are you psychic? I think you must be psychic!" A loud crunch and his fate was stapled together. "Now, it's a formal interview." She looked him over, her smile transmuting into what Eric imagined new parents looked like when confronted with their first shitty nappy. "Well, I suppose you'll do."

"Thanks."

"Not at all! It's my pleasure," she said as though she'd just bestowed blessings upon him the likes of which should have earned her stigmata. Then she turned her attention to a small square sticky label by her computer and, picking up her blue sparkler of a pen, wrote down Eric's name and then next to it a definite, and apparently near orgasmic, tick. Seconds stretched. When the fog of ecstasy had cleared and she realised Eric was still in the room, her right cheek gave a bit of a spasm. "Well, shouldn't you be off, poppet? Don't want to be late."

"JHARDINE?" CAME A silky voice from the doorway of the church.

Uncoiling her aching knees, she rose from her place before the altar. "Hello, Vicar."

"I didn't expect to see you here today, Jhardine." The priest came gliding up the narrow aisle between the honey-coloured pews and the white face of the wall. "You're normally busy on a Tuesday."

"Well, I thought I'd stop by and check in with Him upstairs while I'm on my lunch."

"You do right. I always find a quick prayer can get you through the day."

The vicar, David Jackson, was everything you could want from an educated man in his forties. Kind of heart, intelligent, and *unmarried*. Though not for want of being physically attractive, either. From the saintly curve to his cheekbones to the modesty of his black cassock, which hugged his broad chest like a sheet of liquorice, he was marked out as fanciable. *Very* fanciable. Unfortunately, he also had a way of using long silences to extract things you'd otherwise rather not say—a trait that was less pleasing.

"To tell you the truth," Jhardine said, clearing her throat, "things are a bit slow at the café. Not many people in, you know."

The priest's tawny eyebrows convened to express their concern. He pointed a pale hand to indicate a nearby red pew. They were like fibreglass to the cheeks, but Jhardine felt the burden of the vicar's kindness and, with a begrudging flutter of a smile, took a seat.

"Don't get me wrong, we have our busy days. Do we! Sometimes my thighs are rubbed red-raw from all the walking around I've been doing." She blushed at having said the word *thighs* in church. "But, erm, that's when everywhere else is closed or when there's something going on at the Grand, you know, a show or something. Or with the football."

"It sounds like it's quite distressing for you, not being able to rely on a steady flow of customers."

"It's since they changed Blezzard Road to a one-way. Flipping council. I've had to start keeping the place open until after midnight some nights so we can get the drunks coming in. Oh, that isn't against Jesus, is it? Using people's alcohol troubles to fuel my business?"

The vicar gave one of his baritone laughs. "Not at all. Why do you think we offer the wine?" He reached out a hand and placed it on the back of the pew on which Jhardine was sitting. "But I will say, I am a bit concerned you might be in danger of overdoing things."

Jhardine had an urge to rummage in her handbag but, no, she wouldn't be *that* kind of woman. She looked him straight in the eye. "I've been a bit worried about money lately, what with things being so slow at the café, and Eric's not looking like he'll be able to get a job any time soon. Well, I've got no choice but to work all the hours I can, have I?"

"Oh dear, I didn't realise things were so bad."

"Well, not bad. Not bad exactly. Eric gets his dole money. Then again, a tin of beans and some toothpaste and it's half gone. And I won't go on benefits. I just can't." Jhardine felt a growing ache, like she'd got a mint stuck in her throat. "And the café. There I was making something a success, you know? After Eric's cure, thank you, God, I felt blessed. And my job was going well. I just can't understand why this is happening now."

"I understand, of course I do," the priest soothed. "Those are all admirable things you are talking about: your work ethic, your wanting to do well, and it's understandable given how much of your twenties and thirties you gave over to caring for Eric that you would pursue the success you deserve, and with gusto. But, even in these difficult times, it mustn't come at the expense of other things—like your health. We both know that's not God's plan, don't we?"

She looked to the life-sized wood cross suspended above the altar. St Anthony's was bequeathed it after the courts forced the spiritualist church at the other side of Willingsley into closing. One too many dodgy exorcisms, apparently. The plaster figure of Jesus had fallen off a few years ago, which ended concerns among some parishioners that the thing was dangerously Catholic, though a few among the congregation then wondered whether re-crucifying the Lord was the proper thing to do so as not to offend any religious sensibilities. This spiritual conundrum kept the parish council busy for many a night. For her part, Jhardine had always thought the buggering thing was an eyesore, Jesus or no, but no one had asked her. At any length, the shadow of Christ could still be seen. It was like a smudge of ash after a fire. "No, of course you're right," Jhardine said as she stared at that shadow.

"And could I make a small observation?"

She let her silence answer for her.

"I think you might concentrate on your work not just because of your money situation, though it is a very real concern, but also, erm...." He bit into his lip. "How do I say this."

"With your gob," Jhardine said. "It's never been shy before, Vicar, no need to start now."

This was why she liked the vicar, actually. More than his good looks, there was something refreshing about his candour. She liked straight-talking people. Thought it one of her own strengths, actually.

"Quite," he smiled. "Well, I think you perhaps work so hard because, well, you have little else to, er, fill your life." Jhardine felt the accidental touch of the vicar's holy finger as it settled on her back. "Forgive me if that was rude. Of course, I didn't mean to—"

"I have Eric," Jhardine said.

"You do. *For now.* But Eric is a young man. He will leave you, if not soon, then one day. And, for instance, how often outside of CC's do you see your workmates? The girls, Tania and, who's the other one? Wears too much perfume?"

"Ruth."

"Yes, Ruth. And your friends here at St Anthony's. How often do you see them outside of these walls?"

Jhardine stood. "I better go, it's getting to the end of my lunch."

"Oh, Jhardine, I do hope I've not upset you."

"Of course you have." Her policy of always being honest in church was a real pain in the arse. "But the truth's upsetting sometimes, isn't it?" she said.

The vicar placed his hand on Jhardine's shoulder. "Before you go I'd like to administer Communion. I always find it brings me peace and, well, clarity."

Jhardine glanced at her mobile phone. The time was getting on, but how could she refuse? For one thing, a man was offering her food and alcohol. "All right," she said, and begrudging though she was, she did her best to smile.

"Oh good God, I've bust a lung," Jhardine wheezed as she flailed to a halt outside of CC's Café. But she'd made it, that was the important thing. Now all she had to do was not keel over.

Bent at the waist, hands on her knees, she peered up and down the street as she tried to catch her breath. No sign of Barry, the dreaded and pungent boss. Then again, no sign of customers inside the café either. Ruth must have needed to close up.

Great.

CC's was a converted terrace house sandwiched between an ironically damp dry cleaners and an accountant's office. There's nothing funny about accountants. Jhardine had managed the café for two and a half years now. She'd rescued it from almost going out of business, in fact. Now though, times were lean and to make matters worse Barry had developed a particular liking for being hands-on with his all-female workforce. It made going to work each day a challenge, to say the least. But she couldn't quit. With Eric not working they needed the money. That wasn't to say her working hours were completely devoid of pleasure though. The last time Barry had tried something she'd kneed him in the groin; it was a particular highlight and the memory got her through the rough times, it really did. In fact, thinking about dealing a deathblow to Barry's fertility lifted her mood enough that, with one long intake of breath, she found the energy to push open the door, ready to do battle. She just needed to get some customers in before Barry turned up for the afternoon, and he'd never even have to know. The perfect crime.

A hand landed on her shoulder. Soon after came the smell.

BARRY, HOLLOW CHEEKS and a nose that put the deviated in septum, peered over his cheap glasses and leaned back in his squealing office chair. This made the bottom of his grey shirt gape and exposed a triangle of hairy stomach. Vile. Jhardine was already feeling queasy. *Bloody church wine.* Now she was worried she might soon upchuck the body of Christ. *Mind you, it'd only improve this tangerine carpet.*

"These figures won't do, Jhardine."

"It's that time of year, Barry. People are starting to save for Christmas, and they've just come back off their holidays. They don't have the money to spend. We're still getting a decent turnover, though, we just need to sit this out."

The room Barry reserved for himself, down a small corridor along from CC's kitchen, was in reality a glorified coat room and, due to its close quarters, seemed to intensify Barry's onion-like aroma to paint-stripping magnitude.

"Turnover's not as good as last year, though. Mind you, I'm not surprised with you and your staff taking such long lunch breaks," Barry sniffed, his pond-scum hair flopping about as he shook a hand through it. Flakes of dandruff scattered across his desk.

"Barry, I was here on time. And it's not my fault Ruth had to leave. It can't have been closed long. Half an hour at most."

"Well, what about the lack of customers?"

"There's no through traffic anymore. They're all going round the outside of the city because of the one-way system. Mind you, I can't blame the council. You've barely got room to fart out there. I've said this is a bad area for a café."

"Yes, you've made your feelings about our location quite clear." Barry had a habit of talking with an Oxbridge butter to his accent. He'd never made it further than the county border and she knew that for a fact. "I took you on to turn this place around. Now, you've had some success. I can't say you haven't. It's not the gold mine we wanted it to be, though, is it?"

"I told you then and I'll tell you now," she said, stabbing the desk with a pointed finger. "You've got no chance of this place being a gold mine. I wouldn't care but you took out two grand from the account last week, Barry. Two grand! Going on about profits! I had to go and buy more potatoes out of my own money because the bank, geniuses they are, thought someone was stealing from us and froze the account."

"May I remind you, this is *my* business."

"And may I remind you, yeah, that you had nothing before I came here. Just a café named after your trooper of an ex-wife and an empty bloody till. People doing my job are earning twice, no, three times as much."

"Well, there's no money, is there?"

"No, because you keep damn-well paying yourself!" Jhardine was shouting now, and before he could stop her she decided to go right on ranting. "Don't you dare put this on me, Barry. I can't make people eat here. You need to do some advertising."

"With what? We have no money!" He slipped what appeared to be a new mobile phone under the lip of his desk, presumably in an effort to hide it from her—like she was blind!

"Right, that's it, I quit!"

"No, Jhardine," Barry said, his voice all northern and sympathetic. "Let's not get emotional, love."

She stopped trying to untie her apron strings. "Oh, you did not just say that, you sexist mother f—"

"Jhardine, no, that's not what I meant! How about...." He searched for something then and, because altruism wasn't among Barry's natural repertoire, he kept searching for quite some time. "How about I give you total control of the menus?" Jhardine's lack of elation soon prompted an improved offer. "Not just the menus. Er, of the promotion, I mean. All that side of things, yes?"

She stood before him looking as dignified as one can while wearing an apron depicting a bikini-clad supermodel with a glistening jumbo sausage between her fingers. "Say more stuff like that."

Barry winced, "I could pull some money from my delivery business. We could maybe afford to hire another girl too, so you aren't working as much."

"You could always take on Eric."

"No, you know what I've said. I just don't get on well with other men. I don't mind him coming in and helping out when I'm not around, but I don't want him full-time, Jhardine. It disturbs my calm."

It disturbs your perving, more like. "Fine, but I want the girls to have a pay rise—"

"Now, Jhardine, be fair—"

"Let me finish." She shielded her eyes from the light blasting out of the energy-saving light bulbs—takes days to even reach mood lighting and then goes straight to burning through your retinas. Her head was throbbing. "I want those girls to have the promise of a raise if our figures go up. And I want it before you pay yourself. No! Hear me out. I'm not talking about me, but they work damned hard. You know Tania, she's in here six days a week, Barry. She's offered to come in on Sundays. I said we don't open on Sundays. She says she doesn't mind being in on her own, she'll just make sandwiches."

"Yes, well, she is a good worker is Tania. Shame about the...." He pointed a vague finger at his over-groomed eyebrows.

"Well you aren't exactly an oil painting yourself, Barry. None of us is." Jhardine drew in a big breath, rubbing her tingling hands together. "Can we wrap this up, Barry, I need to get on."

"All right, all right. You have a deal. But I want to see some big improvements round here. Six months, that's all you've got. I'm sorry, but I'll have to think about letting you go if there's no pick-up in business. That understood?"

He held out a clammy hand. When Jhardine reluctantly met it with her own Barry tightened his grip. His thumb rubbed the valley of her palm.

"All right, Barry, that's enough. Now you're just copping a feel. And you know how I deal with that."

Barry's eyes narrowed. He angled his crotch away.

"You always misinterpret my friendliness, Jhardine. I don't know why."

"It's because," she gulped, "it usually comes with you sporting a stonking er...erec...." She slapped a hand to the desk to steady herself, but too late. Her legs buckled. She was falling.

"Jhardine, are you all right? Jhardine!"

ERIC WAS FEELING sour. The burp that had slipped out during the written portion of the interview hadn't exactly got him off to the best start, and now he had the distinct impression that the immaculate Mr Godwin Daniels really didn't like him.

Positivity, Eric! He heard Jobcentre Dee's voice chime in his head. *All right then,* he thought. *If you want positive, here it is—with knobs on.*

"As you can see," Eric said, hoping to look bright and employable. It was rather dispiriting how easily the Jobcentre shtick came to him. He thought he could feel the manic grin emerging, too. "I've been on a lot of job interviews. Even though I've not found the right thing for me yet, you know, it shows I'm not lazy."

Mr Daniels took out a sports drink from his desk drawer. It was a clear bottle with a peach-coloured liquid inside and promised to caffeinate and elevate his performance. He took a sip, then put it down. He looked down at Eric's paper, his smooth hazel eyes unimpressed.

"What are your shorthand skills like?" Mr Daniels said, as though Eric hadn't spoken at all.

"I don't.... I mean...." *Positivity, Eric!* "I type really fast so you don't need me to do shorthand. Look, my typing speed's down there. Fastest the Jobcentre had seen, Dee said."

Mr Daniels smiled. He took up a perfectly sharpened pencil and scored a thick black line through part of Eric's application. "No point asking about that then."

Eric fumbled to keep above his rising anxiety. "And I'm, er, really, like, motivated you know? Yeah. I wouldn't ever leave until all my work was finished. I mean, I'd stay extra hours. Anything you need. And—"

"But it says here that you didn't even finish school?" Mr Daniels' eyebrows lifted.

"Well, no. I had some problems. Health problems."

"Yes, I *can* read," as though to imply that Eric, perhaps, could not. "You don't say what though."

Eric's fingers grazed the fist-sized lump under his shirt. "It was a heart problem."

"Would you care to elaborate?"

Not particularly, no. "A congenital heart defect. But it's fixed now and, besides, I know everything school would have taught me. I had loads of time to read. I...." He tried to remember what Dee said about maximising his strengths. "I read fast and I've got a really good memory. A great memory in fact."

"But you don't actually have any qualifications."

"No," Eric said, and then for some reason found himself adding: "But I do have my driver's license," which wasn't technically true because he didn't actually have the money to take the damned test.

"A driver's license," Mr Daniels smiled again. "That will be helpful if I need you to drive up to accounting on the fourth floor." Another thick black line for Eric's application, then.

Eric's cheeks grew hot. "I…."

Call him a dick. He deserves it.

"I…."

"Yes?"

He's an arrogant ass-twat. Oh, that's good. Call him an ass-twat.

"M-m-maybe—"

"You have a speech impediment too? Perhaps not suited to taking phone calls, then. Shame."

"Maybe," Eric managed at last, "maybe I should go."

Mr Daniels folded his arms and sat back in his executive-sized chair. "Oh no, Mr Mayfair, you've applied for this job and so if you're going to waste my time I'm going to waste yours. You will sit here until this interview is over or I will report you to the Jobcentre."

Eric fixed his eyes on Mr Daniels' sports drink. *Stay calm. You don't want another incident.*

"People like you think that you can just waltz in here and get a job at this prestigious company when you have…." Mr Daniels banged the desk with the flat of his hand. "No qualifications." Bang! "No experience." Bang! "No prospects." Bang!

Eric rubbed his temples. His chest felt tight.

"You, Eric, are what is wrong with society today: always take, take, take!"

Thud.

That sound. That unmistakable sound. Then a dazzle of colour spiralled through Eric's left eye, followed by a shadow that raced across Mr Daniels' desk. Eric looked about. Nothing seemed to be wrong. Perhaps this time everything would be fine.

Oblivious and oh so happy with his oration, Mr Daniels reached for the sports drink and, with his fishy lips pursed, took a sip.

Eric felt the patter of water bubbles running down his tongue.

Please, no.

The sports drink Mr Daniels was guzzling ran through with a shock of black, like someone had added in a few drops of ink. It took Mr Daniels a few more gobfuls before he detected the change. His face soured. His cheeks blew out and he spat the liquid all over his desk. He coughed, spluttered and with a flailing hand knocked over the bottle. The syrupy fluid leaked out over the desk, a black and goopy mess closer to crude oil than water.

Mr Daniels, red of face and still choking, glared at Eric. "Just get out. Go on, out!"

Well, that went well.

Safe in his wreck of a car, Eric let himself stew in the cold failure of the interview. It had happened again. That feeling. That sound. He touched the middle of his chest, feeling the rise there under the fabric of his shirt. He rubbed at it. Rubbed harder. Not caring if people on the street outside saw him, he undid the top four buttons on his shirt. The black mass that protruded between his chest muscles, an organ the size of an avocado with black veins spiralling out across his skin and down his stomach, seemed to peer back at him. He touched it.

"Ah!"

The sounds of the road all turned up. He flinched, putting up his hands so he could cover his ears. The noise died as soon as his fingers left the mean growth, but the dizzying sense of reality being fractured went on. *This isn't possible. It can't be. You can't make things like that happen. You just can't.* Eric prided himself on the truth, on reality. This defied everything he knew about the world. Never mind the fact that, no matter who he flashed the growth at, they all claimed they couldn't see it. And he'd tried everyone. There were some parks he could never go back to.

He buttoned his shirt back up and stuck the car key in the ignition. A sharpish turn, foot down. The car moved a couple of yards only for the engine to conk-out.

"I do not need this!"

Two more attempts before Eric managed to swear and smack his faithful junk-on-wheels back to life. A man standing in the doorway of the betting shop across the road, who had been an audience to this most epic of battles, clapped as Eric pulled away. "Yeah, do one, mate," Eric said out the window. "Tosser."

At the end of the road, while waiting for the Brainless of Britain driver in front of him to realise the traffic lights were in fact on green, Eric switched his mobile phone on and let it drop into his lap. Maybe Tim had finally got in touch? Fat chance. He cleared the traffic lights and drove down the road, his anger and frustration beginning to build. He'd done it again. Ruined another chance.

Eric's phone buzzed in his lap. Four missed calls.

"Oh, will you just choose a lane!" Eric shouted as the car in front dithered on the dividing line. As he rounded the bend for the road up to Hainsworth Estate and home, Eric's phone chimed the doom music that meant his mum was calling. He pushed the button to put her on speakerphone.

"Ma, right," Eric said, squinting against the low sun. "You'll never guess what just happened—"

"Mr Mayfair?" came a voice that wasn't his mum's. "Eric, love, it's Nurse Abigail Lesley from the hospital." Eric's head filled with static. "Are you there?"

"Yeah. Yes."

"Okay, good. Listen, love, I'm calling about your mum."

CHAPTER THREE
THE BODY

ERIC LET THE car rumble to silence. He rubbed his clammy fingers around the top of his ear lobe, a childhood habit he'd never been able to shake off. She was getting better. She was *supposed* to be getting better!

All thought buckled as he caught sight of his mum walking out of the hospital's sliding double doors. No wonder she hadn't wanted Eric to rush over: seemed she was having herself a little religious experience. Eric sighed as he got out of the car and slowly approached his mum and the ever smiling vicar.

"You all right, Mum?" Eric said in a cheerier tone than he felt.

"Oh, course I am. They just did scans and stuck me with needles again. My arm's like a pin cushion. Won't find owt though. They never do."

"I could have been here for all that."

"There's no need. They had nowt new to tell me. Besides, the vicar was with me."

"Hello, Eric."

"Hi," Eric offered, and then realised that might be a bit curt. "Er, thanks for staying with her."

"She can hear you, you know," his mum chipped in.

"I was here at the hospital anyway, so it was no bother at all." The vicar used to read to Eric when Eric was in the hospital. It seemed he still couldn't pass up the opportunity for a captive audience. "Anyway, I should dash. I have a meeting to get to." He placed his hands on Jhardine's arm and gave a little squeeze. "Now take care, both of you."

"Thank you, Vicar."

"Yeah, cheers," Eric interjected so as to put a wedge between their loitering, otherwise this might have gone on for another half hour. The vicar bowed his head—*who does that?*—and began his walk across the car park toward the main road. Eric took his mum's elbow and led her to the car's passenger-side door. "Let's get you home."

"I'm not a doddering old dear yet, you know," she said, yanking her arm back. Eric opened the car door and stared at her. "Oh, bloody hell, fine!" She gave up and got in.

Swinging the car in a long arc, Eric pulled up to the car park's exit and signalled for the turn. Checking both ways, he could see the vicar walking down Hitchens' Road toward St Anthony's, the church spire defiant in the air like a middle finger. Eric was driving in the same direction as the priest. His mum had noticed too.

"You could have offered him a lift," she said as they sped by.

"Off to a meeting, weren't he?"

"Oh, you can be a right mardy git sometimes. Is this because he spilt that drink on you that time?"

"He was trying to baptise me against my will!"

"It was orange juice. It'd take bloody battery acid to get you clean of your sins!" She looked out the window. "Filthy to the bone, you."

"To the bone," Eric repeated, laughing to himself. She tutted. They drove on.

Eric slowed as they approached the roundabout and the looming dark of Jodie Woods. The mass of trees split the road in two, one half going back into the city's centre, the other taking the traffic along the border of the city and out to the surrounding suburbs and countryside. It was possible to get back to the estate going either way, but Eric chose the quicker of the two and signalled for the vein to take them toward the city centre.

"Well?"

"Well what?" Jhardine fiddled with the radio. *Good luck,* he thought. Eric could never get a signal.

"You know what. Do they know why it keeps happening? Those pills were supposed to sort you out."

"No, they don't. I've got to go see the doctors again when I get the test results. It'll just be more pills, mind. I suppose they'll get it right eventually."

"The fits aren't just happening random though, are they? It's when you're stressed. Did you tell them about the stuff at work?"

Jhardine looked out through the drizzle-laved windscreen. "It's cold. Winters seem to come faster these days. Mind you, Eric, when you get older time goes by quicker. It's science, that."

"You didn't tell them, did you?" Eric said, ignoring her dubious factoid. "Mum, you've got to—"

"Look, I'm fine now." The chop of her tone made him grind his teeth. "I was just having a slanging-match with Barry. You know how he winds me up. Like you said, there's a pattern. I mean, it all started the night you were really ill."

"Going to die. You should learn to say—"

"It was never God's plan for you to die Eric, or else he wouldn't have healed you, would he?"

"He didn't heal me. He—"

"Remember what happened that night, have you?" It wasn't quite checkmate, but Eric's queen was definitely in trouble. "Look, ever since that night they've said to me I've got to avoid stress. Avoid. Avoid. Avoid. But doing that's easier said than done, isn't it? Maybe if I lived underground or, I don't know, I was invisible or sommat. God, that would be nice."

"You've got to promise, yeah, that you won't cover it up. If you're getting worse, I mean—"

"I'm not getting worse. I've been praying on it, and this is just a blip. Now shut up about it."

Eric didn't know how to answer that without getting into a debate on the efficacy of prayer. The silence between them swelled. *I'm right, but am I being a dick about it? I'm being a dick, aren't I? I shouldn't be badgering her after what she's been through. God, Eric, you can be such a tosser sometimes.* A deep-fried olive branch was in order. "Do you, erm, fancy a takeaway?"

"Oh, yeah!" she smiled, but it soon slipped. "Aw, no, though. We can't really afford it."

"I didn't have dinner because I was in this dumb-arse job interview—don't ask—so yeah, we can."

"Aw, lovely. That's just what I need, that is. Right, I want rice and chips with a side of sweet and sour sauce. And we're going to the Phoenix, aren't we?"

"Yeah, I'll nip in now on our way back."

"Right, well, tell them to make sure them chips are crispy. Last time we got an order the chips were limper than your wrists." She chuckled to herself, folding her arms across her chest and putting her head back against the seat. Two minutes on and Eric could see her fighting to stay awake, her head bobbing up and down like a cork on water. By the time they reached the flaming yellow and red of the Phoenix takeaway, Jhardine was snoring in a way that would make even the most ardent of bugle players feel outclassed, and she was still dozing when Eric returned to the car a half-hour later.

"Chippies!" she cheered with a groggy lilt. "Oh, it always smells so good, doesn't it?"

"Aye. Put it on the floor though. Last time you got cooking oil all over my seat. How did you not feel it?"

"I just thought I'd wet myself. Didn't want to say owt," she said, still rustling in the bag. "Right, Jeeves, home!"

Easier said than done, though. The roads had been clear before, but as Eric drove the last leg of their journey they hit a snarl of standing traffic. Turning onto the long and narrow belt of Harris Street, Eric found himself locked into a worm of cars that stretched as far as the eye could squint.

"This food better not get cold," Jhardine complained, eating a gobful of rice.

"Mum, you're getting it everywhere!"

"As if you can even see with all these fast food cartons about. It's like a landfill in here," she bit back. When the bag of food was also a few chips lighter, she added, "Oh, will you look at all these shops what have closed down. It's not on, Eric. Government thinks that England stops at effing Birmingham. Where the hell am I supposed to buy clothes now? I mean, I never actually went to any of the shops, but that's not the point, is it?"

Eric wasn't looking at the abandoned retail outlets. "'Ere," Eric said, pointing to a police officer stood at the side of the road talking to people in the cars in front.

"Oh, I wonder what he wants?" Jhardine said, unable to keep the intrigue out of her voice.

With the policeman approaching, Eric tried to roll his window down. It lowered about four inches and then seized up, so he was forced to push the window down the rest of the way, a horrible sound grating the air as he did. The indignities a man must suffer!

"Hi, sorry, mate, it's a bit stiff," Eric said.

"Careful Eric, you've only just met the man. Don't want to scare him off," his mum whispered.

"Mum!"

"Evening," said the adolescent-looking police officer, oblivious to Eric's distress. "We're setting up a diversion. Sorry for your wait."

"Right, cheers." Eric didn't want to keep the man. He also had to figure out if he could pull the window back out of the door compartment seeing as how the button was doing bugger all to move it.

"Here, love," Jhardine said, clicking her fingers to grab the officer's attention. "What's going on?"

The young policeman, who had an offensively prominent bum-crack chin, declared he was not at liberty to say. Eric watched his mum give the officer the roving eye.

Oh, no.

"'Ere, don't I know your mum Linda? You're Linda's Simon off of Ridgeworth Lane, aren't you?"

"Er, yeah," he said, a nervous static creeping into his voice.

"Oh, I talk to your mum all the time when she comes into CC's. She's right proud of you, being a policemen and all that," Jhardine said, smiling. Then that smile twitched. "I'd love to say how nice you were to me when I next see her."

She had the officer by the curlies now, no mistaking. If he didn't tell all, she would make sure his mother knew he had refused a friend some information, which was a cardinal sin. As it turned out, Jhardine was a bit of an evil genius.

"Well," he stuttered. "I shouldn't say owt really."

"I would, mate," Eric said rolling his eyes. "It gets this over much faster."

"You'll keep it schtum, right?" he begged.

"I go to church," Jhardine announced, "and it's a miracle he's even here. You couldn't hope to find a more trustworthy pair than us, love."

"Right," he said, blinking through that information. "Well." He leaned in a bit closer. His breath stank of kebab meat. "They've had to close off the road at the top of High Street." His bum-chin rose high as he folded his bottom lip up over his lower teeth and, with a dextrous tongue, licked. "They've found a body," the officer said. "Well, parts."

"AND THIS is an exclusive: One eyewitness told me she saw a figure who appeared to be eating the body parts. I spoke to the attending officers, none of whom would give an official comment, but I have reason to believe that, yes, teeth marks were found on some of the bones."

"What?" Jhardine asked when Eric stopped feeding his face. "If that's put you off your food, I'll have it. I'm famished."

"No, and no, you won't," Eric said. "For a minute I thought I.... Oh, I dunno." He rubbed at his left eye. He'd been complaining about his eyesight for months but he never did anything about it. "But, er, it's bloody awful, isn't it?" he said as he picked up his fork and resumed troughing.

Jhardine shook her knife at the television.

A lamppost, the old shoe shop in the background, the glassy cobbles. She'd walked by there so many times, never even given it a thought. Now, it was where a man had been strung up. It was where someone's life had bled away. Different, always different now.

"It stops you feeling safe, doesn't it? I mean, I—" A piece of green pepper almost stuck in her throat as she tried to suppress her surprise: "'Ere, look who it is! Turn it up!" Jhardine snatched the remote and turned up the volume until the television gave off a menacing rattle.

"I don't know what to say," the vicar said, looking ghostly and good. His eyes were pained and his face seemed tight and cold. "I was just on my way to a meeting and I, I don't...." The orange-tinged reporter grunted what Jhardine thought was a nonsense question. "Well, of course I'll be holding my church services as usual," the vicar said, the glint of the floodlights they'd placed around the crime-scene making him squint. "But I would like to offer that anyone affected by this, even if they're not religious, they can come along to the church just to talk or, of course, pray. I will make sure I am available all day this week. I'm sorry, I can't say much more. I'm just, well, saddened and shocked that this could happen in our quiet little community."

"Saddened, shocked that this could happen. Thank you, Vicar, for summing up what no doubt everyone will be feeling in the wake of this awful tragedy. Grace Richardson reporting, back to you, Mike."

"Oh, she winds me up, she does. That's not even her real nose you know." Jhardine used her teeth to break into a fortune cookie and proceeded to eat the lot, her future and all. "Did you see how she was draping herself over him. What a disgrace, I—"

The clatter of Eric's fork interrupted her rather marvellous character assassination. "Here, is that clock on the TV right?"

"Yeah, they stream it direct from wherever *decides* the time."

Eric blinked. "No one decides the time."

"Someone must have else we wouldn't have twenty-four hours in a day." *Ha, got you you little know-it-all!*

"N-never mind that," Eric said. "I forgot about meeting Tim and the lads. I better ring him and tell him I can't make it tonight," Eric said as he slid his phone out of his pocket. "Though I've half a mind to just not turn up."

Jhardine went back to finishing Eric's chips. He let out one of his weary sighs.

"Oh chuffing hell," she said, "it was only a handful of chips."

"Not that. Tim's phone's off again. I'll have to text him. Hope he'll read it before he gets to the Richies."

"What are you talking about? You always go on a Tuesday." A sneaky burp popped from off her lips. "Oh, *excuse* me." Oh Lord, she was turning into her mother.

"I can't. Not after the day you've had."

"Will you bugger off and stop fussing around me."

"No. And I don't see why I should be at his beck and call all the time, either."

"Eric, you have to keep your friends. You have to because, well, I didn't and now look at me. I've got no one," she said, the vicar's words striking a gong next to her ear.

"But it's Tim, Mum. He's being weird."

Well, Tim had been weird before. She'd been able to get him off of the weird once, but there was no getting through to him this time. "No, I don't want to hear it. He's been good to you, has Tim," she said. "He was with you all that time you were in the hospital."

"Not all the time," Eric bit back in a little bird's voice.

"Look, whatever this is, you owe it to him to at least hear him out, don't you?"

Eric grew sullen. "I don't need a lecture."

"No, I don't suppose you do," she said. Jhardine wasn't exactly a saint in this either, was she? "Besides," she smiled, "your nan'll be ringing me soon, so you're better off out of it."

Eric's eyes widened. That point had landed. "Well, all right. But we'll just have one drink, okay?"

"You better. It's dead expensive at the Richardson's Arms. You can have as much tap water as you like though."

Eric crammed his feet into his battered trainers and put on the hooded top he'd slung over the back of the sofa a few days before. The entire house was Eric's walk-in wardrobe.

Then, another sigh. "No, I can't go."

"Oh, out! I've had enough. Out I say!"

"Mum!"

She pushed Eric out the front door and slammed the bloody thing in his concerned face. "And get me my rent money!" she shouted through the letterbox before shuffling her way back into the living room. Sitting herself back down on the sofa, Jhardine happened to glance over at Eric's plate there on the tea-stained coffee table. She was on a diet. She couldn't possibly.

Oh hell, why not?

Though she didn't like oyster sauce, she made short shrift of Eric's remaining fried rice, even licking the plate clean. *Saves on the washing-up.* She sat rubbing her stomach and licking her lips like a cat who got the wasp. She flicked through a few television channels, but there was nothing of merit on. "I don't know why I pay the license fee, I really don't."

Jhardine gathered up the plates and waddled into the kitchen. As she put the plates in the washing-up bowl, the white totem of the fridge gurgled. A bar of cooking chocolate sat on the top shelf, didn't it? It was probably getting close to its use-by-date. Well, it was definitely getting *closer,* anyway.

The phone started to ring as she popped bitter square five into her mouth. It rang again as she finished the entire sixteen-piece bar. When the wrapper was empty she was about to close the fridge door when the light seemed to put a halo around an iffy block of white cheddar she'd been meaning to throw out. The ringing became a near-constant drone as she crammed the last of the mouldy wedge behind her teeth. Wiping the smeared cheese from her face, her hands trembled.

Okay, this might not be normal.

She briefly wondered if she could be pregnant, but that was ridiculous. Experience had taught her that the male population of the world had agreed an embargo on her ladyparts. Even as she thought this, her hand opened the blue egg box on the middle shelf. One lonely speckled egg sat in its cradle as though waiting for her to give it a home.

It was difficult to get the thing halfway into her mouth but, oh Lord, was it worth it when she bit down. An explosion of shell pieces. The clear fluid slid down her chin, a liquid delight. The crunching sound as she chewed, like pulverising bones, became a glorious orchestra of noise.

The phone went on ringing.

"YOU ALL RIGHT, Eric?" chirped Dennis, the Richardson's Arms' craggy-faced barman.

"Aye, not bad. Tim here yet?"

"Not seen him, mate," Dennis said as he ran his dishcloth over the bar. His scaly arms caught the light.

"Right, well, I'll have a pint of shandy and a cider please. Whatever it is Tim has."

"Coming up."

Eric propped himself up at the bar as he tucked away the money he'd taken out from the bank. Had to go into his overdraft to get his mum her board money, but so long as Tim paid him back tonight everyone would be square and he could put the money back in the morning. He reserved a tenner for the drinks and stashed his wallet away in the inside pocket of his jacket.

Glancing around the pub, he noticed all the regulars seemed to be in, including Jim, next-door neighbour Sarah's husband. With his receding pan-scourer hair and his love for clinging blue and lavender shell-suits, which in all honesty made him look like an over-stuffed sausage, it was hard to see what Jim used to attract Sarah; difficult, too, to see what made other women syrupy over him, but sugar they did. At least, most nights. Jim's current companion, however, seemed somehow able to resist his hypnotic girth.

According to local gossip Christina, a red-haired beauty wearing a plunging silver chiffon dress, was an experienced lady of the night. Or day. Whenever you wanted, for the right price of course. So when Jim lay a hand on her back and she threw it off without missing so much as a single beat, Eric wasn't surprised in the least.

"I told you no. I don't want to go. Why would I?"

"Let me be there for you. Come away with me, Chrisy—"

"There you are, mate."

"Ah!" Eric'd been so intent on the conversation he'd forgotten about his drinks order.

"You all right?" Dennis asked as he served up Eric's shandy and let it join the bubbling cider already waiting.

"Yeah. Bit of earache is all," he said. He realised then that Jim and Christina were too far away for him to have possibly heard their conversation. Right at the other side of the bar, in fact. Yet he had heard them.

In a hurry to leave that queer moment behind, Eric headed for his and Tim's favourite table, the furthest from the whiffy loos. He sat down and tried to make himself as small as possible so as to avoid being subjected to a random punter's inane chit-chat, a talent Eric had cultivated in the hospital and really mastered since getting out. Taking a sip of his lemonade-heavy shandy, because Eric didn't have much of a stomach for any kind of booze, Eric occupied himself by flicking remnants of pork scratching off the table while every so often looking at the crowd. After a few minutes, his mind started to wander.

They began doing Tuesday nights shortly after Eric got out of the hospital. It'd been Tim's way of introducing Eric to some of his mates so as to get Eric a bit of a social life—but Eric never knew what to say to strangers. Especially not people his own age. When they were out living life, he'd been in the hospital. He couldn't talk about holidays or music festivals because he'd never been. In essence: they'd lived, he'd just survived. When faced with a bunch of Tim's friends Eric would smile and try to follow the conversation but, when put upon to contribute anything, his mouth would only produce stammering sentence fragments. One by one the lads had dropped away like flakes of Dennis's dead skin, until it was just Eric and Tim again. *As it had always been.*

THREE YEARS OLD and only recently having wowed the world with his ability to stand upright, Eric was flung into a world of ear infections, warm and somewhat dubious milk, and the delightful freedom of splashing poster paint wherever he pleased.

"Well, it's not my carpet," his mum said as she let Eric loose on the so-called *creative area* at Toadhall Nursery.

Eric did enjoy the paints, but now he had a new favourite. Plasticine. It could be anything you wanted it to be. And it tasted nice when chewed. Always important, that.

He was just rolling out a fat blue worm to munch on when a boy, more candle factory than human what with the amount of snot dribbling over the crest of his top lip, came up to the table and, without manner or mind, snatched Eric's plasticine away.

If Eric had known how to glare he would have but, unable yet to hold a grudge, he turned back to the plasticine block in the middle of the table and decided to cut himself a new slither. Besides, fresh plasticine tasted nicer anyway. Just as Eric leaned in with the plastic knife though, Snot's grimy hand descended on the block.

"Mine."

Eric felt something in his eye twitch. His eyelids were narrowing. Glaring was close. Glaring was happening.

Then a boy, taller than Eric and bulkier than either he or Snot, sat down at Eric's side. He cut off a wedge of plasticine from the large block, said not a word to either of them, and began rolling out a vague disk into which he began to prick a smile. Inevitable, like a Jehovah's Witness at the door as soon as you've taken off your trousers, Snot wobbled over, hand on the table to guide him, and attempted to snatch for the plasticine treasure.

"Mine."

The larger boy shoved Snot and sent him to the ground. "No," he said, before going back to his play.

Snot, already somewhat viscous anyway, sat a moment in stunned silence before letting rip a scintillating wheeze that soon turned into an outright howl.

Within seconds Miss Halfpenny, the nursery teacher who coincidentally always struck as being half-a-penny short, bustled over. "Timothy," Miss Halfpenny scolded, "you will not shove!"

Tim looked at her as if to say he would shove whomever he pleased.

"What am I going to do with you, aye? And don't you get mixed up with him, Eric. He's a bad lad. Come on, Stephen." Miss Halfpenny tugged a still blubbering Snot away, promising him first pick of the small bottles of milk if he shut his whining hole. She was nicer about it, but only just.

The boy called Tim watched them leave, then went back to playing with the plasticine. After a while he rolled a somewhat sticky ball over to Eric.

Eric picked up the plasticine, put it in his mouth and chewed. Never had anything tasted finer.

ERIC TOOK A sip of his shandy. Sweet Mother of Sin, it was vile. He couldn't drink anything heavier or he'd be sick, but he couldn't stick to orange juice either. Not on Hainsworth Estate. He'd never live it down. Only thing Eric could drink, weird enough, was mulled wine. Just a glass, mind. It took the edge off Christmas.

"NO, HE'S NOT real," Polly Thorn said, smiling as she broke this most devastating of news to the entire ensemble of Class Three while they sat on the rough carpet eating their soggy packed lunches to the beat of the June summer playing out beyond the classroom's glass wall, which is to say it was pissing it down.

"But my mum says Father Christmas is real," Eric said, confused.

"Yeah, she does," Tim nodded as though this was one of Newton's laws.

"No. *My* mum says that it's just a big conspiration—"

"Conspiracy," Eric corrected.

"—to make mums and dads have to spend their hard-earned monies on their children. It's why my mum and dad live in different houses. Well, that and because mum says dad's a twat fish."

Santa, a big fat fib? Eric pondered this grave news. The reality of the season, not peace on Earth and mercy mild but bankruptcy, acrimony and divorce? The lies that grownups tell!

"What's a twat fish?" Tim asked, offering Eric one of his cheesy puff crisps.

Eric took it. "A shubunkin?" Nana had shubunkins. Like her, they always looked like they were about to die, but they never did.

"Who the hell has been outside?" the caretaker, Mr Dixon, grumped as he walked through the classroom door. "I know one of you little hellions has! That door is to stay locked at all times." As though drawn by gravity's inescapable love, his eyes settled on Tim. "Was it you?"

Maybe it was because Tim looked so much older than the rest of the children, but the caretaker always seemed to point his arthritic finger of blame Tim's way. Tim went on eating his crisps. "No."

"Well, none of this lot is tall enough to unlock the door so it must have been you."

"Maybe it was you and you're so old you forgot," Tim said.

Silence.

Mr Dixon loomed over Tim. The young boy put down his crisps and stood, staring up into Mr Dixon's face. Mr Dixon raised his arm. "Just admit it."

Tim remained blank, except: Eric saw it. Just the smallest curl of a smile in the crevice of his right cheek.

Mr Dixon's arm swung up higher, ready for the stinging drop. "So help me, I'll tan your hide!"

"Is there a problem here?" Mrs Walters, just back from her most recent nervous breakdown, jittered from the doorway.

Mr Dixon seemed to remember where he was. He folded his green jacket closed, zipped it up and griped, "These kids are supposed to be inside. Keep them in."

"Yes, yes, of course," Mrs Walters said, papering herself to the wall as Mr Dixon stormed out.

"You got in trouble," Polly Thorn sang at Tim.

"You've got a big head," he said.

Polly Thorn never spoke to Tim again.

Eric groaned as, for the fourth time, he heard the end of the ringtone and the start of the automated voice telling him to leave a message. He put the phone down, then picked it up again and tapped out a text message.

Where the bugger are you?

Tim had been flaky lately but, together with missing the gym that morning, this was something else. Beyond a joke, in fact.

Wait, what actually is beyond a joke?

No, never mind that, Tim had gone too far this time. Too far. Eric raked a hand through his hair, feeling his small curls catch around his fingers. He let out a long, tired breath. *Who am I kidding?* Eric had never stood up for himself. He always needed other people, always needed Tim, a fact that was enshrined the day when Eric first fell ill.

"Kick it, you dick! What are you doing?"

"Enough of that language Shane," Mr Cardwell shouted. "But, Shane is right, Callum, don't just tap it like a puff, yeah? Give it a wallop."

Eric was in goal. He was always in goal. Namely because he was *bad* at football. Unkindly bad. His team had found out, though, that with Eric in goal and Tim defending, Eric couldn't do much to lose them the game. That was because Tim hardly ever let the ball past him. This was one part talent and one part the fact that Tim, even at thirteen, was in possession of a near-adult body, full muzzle of stubble and, there had been rumours, a full crop of pubic hair. This was an exaggeration, Eric knew, but not by much.

Suddenly though, a striker from the Oakenshaw Millers, a team so blond one had to suspect some kind of Aryan plot, skirted past Tim with a bit of flashy footwork and took a run at Eric. The boy kicked the ball, and something unusual happened. The ball slapped Eric's flat palms and ricocheted away. It was a bad kick, true, but this was a good save—even if it was unintentional. A cheer went up. The rest of Eric's team ran at him, slapping him on the back, and even hugging him. He didn't like that. But then Tim was there, chest pressed to his, lips on his forehead in a celebratory kiss.

Then a pain. Not like fire, not like ice. More like metal. Like wire being drawn through Eric's chest. He couldn't breathe.

As Tim pulled away he saw the panic on Eric's face. "Mate?"

Eric fell to the floor, tingling into unconsciousness.

Next thing, Eric found himself strapped to a stretcher as a couple of paramedics fussed over him. Deputy Head Mrs Worboyce, a woman with suspiciously uneven shoulders, emerged from the din. "No, he's going to be fine. He just needs to see the doctor. Tim, no. Timothy!"

"Get off me, you daft cow, I'm going with him."

"Timothy, you will not address me in that manner!" Mrs Worboyce said in her most uppity of tones. "Timothy, you get back here this instant!"

"You all right, mate?" Tim asked as he stood over Eric.

"What's all this fuss about?" Head Teacher Mr Taggart said as he joined what had apparently become a convention for the school faculty.

"Yes, well, Mr Taggart, Tim is refusing to do as I tell him and he's preventing—"

"Actually," said the female paramedic as she pushed her way through the circle of gorping kids, "you're the one preventing us from going. You've got all this lot standing in the way and we can't load him into the ambulance."

"Well, I never. I will be ringing the Royal to make a complaint. What is your name, young lady?"

"Abigail Doesn't Give a Fuck Lesley. Now if you don't mind, we need to get him to the hospital. Move. Move!"

Whether it was due to shock, or the fact that she felt the twinges of the aneurysm that would kill her just two weeks later, Mrs Worboyce did move. She also didn't notice Tim as he crept into the back of the ambulance with Eric. By the time Abigail D.G.F Lesley spotted him, the doors were closed and they were about to start rolling. "I'm already going to get a rollicking so you might as well come along for the ride," she said to Tim. "Just ring someone as soon as we get to the hospital, yeah?"

"I will," Tim said, giving a charming grin the way he always did when warmed by kindness. Then to Eric he said, "Us cartoons will be on soon."

Eric finished his pint of shandy.

"Another one there, Eric?" pub landlord Dennis asked, swooping in from nowhere to take up the empty glass. Caught off guard, Eric said yes. *And that's another three pound down the pisser,* he counted. Oh, money! He texted Tim again:

I need that cash I lent you. It's my job seekers. Mum will go spare. Where are you? And then, betraying the pang he felt, he added: *Just let me know you're okay, yeah?*

Eric wasn't sure if Tim knowingly traded on Eric's feelings, or whether it was kind of an instinct. He suspected it was the latter. Tim was simple like that. Straightforward. Except when he wasn't.

"You're quiet," Tim commented, his eyes bright in the low sun. He bent and picked up a piece of stone. It had a vein of quartz running through it, a relic of the railway line that used to run beneath the bridge. After looking at it a while, Tim let the stone drop through his fingers. It fell in a blaze of white and then, when it hit the ground, became dull and uninteresting. He repeated the process a few times, watching the fall. The light. The end. "You were at the doctors today, weren't you? Have they said what they're going to do next?"

"No," Eric said, all sparrow.

"What?" Tim hugged his own chest. "I mean, they said a heart transplant, didn't they?"

"They," Eric breathed. "Here, did you catch that game last night? Weren't the Reds shit?"

"Eric? What are you saying? The transplant—"

"Not tonight, mate. I'm tired."

"No, what is it? Tell me."

Eric hadn't wanted to do this so soon. He'd hoped for a few more months of pretending. It'd probably be a slow decline, after all. He could hide it for a while. Still could. He could lie. He looked into Tim's indigo eyes, how they became deeper yet more innocent in the sunlight. They were like the eyes you find on a baby. Too blue. Too pure. But Tim's body was thick with muscle now. He was barely sixteen, but the way he moved, the way he spoke, it was all sex. Both barrels of the gun loaded, and you couldn't lie to that. "They can't do the transplant. I'm not strong enough for it."

"What you talking about? You can take it."

"No," Eric said at last. "No, I can't."

Maybe it was the tone. Maybe it was the way Eric ducked his head as if sad to burden Tim, but Tim didn't fight him. "Oh." He looked away. "How long?"

Weird, though, that the details were easy. Facts, they'd always been something Eric could work with, even then. "I could have a few years if they can find the right drugs," Eric said.

"So there's a chance, then, that a treatment could, like, be invented?"

Eric saw the hope in his eyes. "I don't think so—"

"No, that's good, there's a chance!" Tim looked hopeful. "Because me and you, we're.... I need you here. You're my mate. So you can't die, yeah? I need you."

"It's not how it works, Tim. You can't just *not* die. I'm going to, and there's no use pinning my hopes on some treatment that—"

A fierce, hard kiss that rattled their teeth and cut Eric's lip. A rolling change in the sky as the sun turned to hail. At least, that was how Eric remembered it. "I know you want this," Tim said. "Fight it, and I'll do anything for you. I'll *be* anything you—"

"You proper shame me," Eric said, pushing Tim away.

"No, I mean it," Tim said, holding Eric's cheek.

Eric tried to pull back, but Tim was too strong. "You're hurting me."

"If that's what it takes," Tim said. "Anything. I'll do anything. Just promise me you'll fight."

Eye to eye, Eric found something that he did want. "My mum. I'll fight if you promise that, if I do die—"

"No, Eric," Tim shook his head. Now it was Eric's turn to be strong. His hands clamped around Tim's shoulders and somehow he had strength enough then to stop the man from pulling back.

"Swear to me that you will look after her!"

"I—"

"Swear it and I'll last. I'll drag this out as long as I can. Just *swear* it."

Finally, Tim nodded. "I swear. I'll do it. I'll find a way to protect her, always," he said. "And I'll protect you too. I'll be strong enough. I will. Strong enough for both of us."

ERIC FINISHED HIS second pint of shandy. Feeling the buzz of alcohol in his system, Eric felt bold and mad. He took up Tim's pint of cider—well, he'd paid for it—and drank it down in one, the fizz and burn of the sour apple raking his throat. There was another taste in there too. Something dark and earthy, but he couldn't name it. *This was bound to happen,* Eric thought. It was inevitable Tim would outgrow him. Without a job, without any money, and without a vagina, what could Eric offer? A final check of his phone, but the battery was so low it was close to turning itself off. He'd run it out of life checking, checking, checking. *How pathetic.*

He stood, swayed, and then set off, pushing his way through the smokers gathered at the door. "Watch where the hell you're going!" Eric groused as a drunk woman nearly knocked him over, her barely-contained bosom jiggling long after the aftermath of their collision.

"Tosser!" she shouted after him.

Across the road and down the small, steep stairs into the subway, Eric was grateful the council had seen fit to dot the walls with little yellow lights so that the journey through to the other side wouldn't be made in the pitch black. To Eric's surprise, the subway wasn't empty: Christina, the woman Jim had set mind to charm at the pub just an hour and a half before, was there texting on her phone.

"You all right, love?"

"Do I look it, aye?" Eric griped.

"Oh, darling, you're not old enough and not ugly enough to be carrying that kind of attitude," she said, her full lips curling into a demure smile. "Get home and sleep it off."

"I'm not exactly going to take advice from the local bike for hire, am I now?"

She smirked, turning on her finger what was obviously an expensive diamond ring. Those who cycled paid quite well, apparently.

"A bit of advice: Don't knock what you haven't tried, yeah?" With a swing of her hips she stepped toward him.

About to argue, Eric opened his mouth—then a sharp turn of his head and up came the night's libations.

"Oh," she said. "Try not to get any on those lovely trainers, darling," Christina sang as she made her way to the other end of the subway and out into the night, laughing as she went.

EIGHT IN THE morning, he'd finally drifted off to sleep two hours ago, and now his phone was ringing. Slowly, cracking the crust on his eyelids, he let the world back in. Through the white onion slice of this first look at the new day, Eric saw something that made him sit bolt upright. A shadow.

A shadow *standing* at the foot of the bed—not lying against the wall as shadows should. And then, of course, it was gone. Eric rubbed at his eyes and it became a passing decal, a shadow from outside cast by something long gone. Apparently, he hallucinated when hungover.

Eric picked up his still ringing phone, fumbling over the keys to answer. "Hello?" he mumbled, rubbing at his long stretches of eyebrows to try flatten out the headache that was already threatening him.

"Eric, it's Dee from the Jobcentre." He groaned. If she heard, she didn't care. "Listen, I need you to come back down today. I've just heard of a job that might be perfect for you."

"Is it better than yesterday's?"

"Well, I should hope so. They weren't impressed with your application at all. In fact, from what I hear, Mr Daniels had to go home. You made him ill, Eric!" *He should count himself lucky that's all I bloody did.* Before Eric could chip in with a few choice and slyly cutting words, Dee told him to be at the Jobcentre no later than ten, and then signalled the end of the call: "Ta ta!"

Eric seethed. The grey walls of his bedroom looked back at him, boring and smug. He glanced around his little coop. The blue threadbare carpet, the dingy windows that had misted over because the seal on the double-glazing had bust, and the desk by the foot of the bed that was full of drawings never quite finished; life was like this before he went into the hospital and it was much the same now he was out. A disappointment. He glanced at his phone again. No messages from Tim either.

"'Ere, who was that?" his mum asked from outside Eric's bedroom door. *Ears like a fucking whale.*

"Jobcentre. Have to go down again."

"Right, well, I'll fish your shirt out of the wash. It'll just need some spraying and it'll be right."

"Cheers." Eric yawned, scratching at the arrow-head of hair below his navel. "I'll get a shower and then I'll drive you into town if you like?"

"Aw, that's nice of you. But you'll want to hold on for ten minutes. The plumber's in there fixing the bog." A bang. "Oh hell, look, there's water everywhere!" he heard his mum shout. "If you had half a brain you'd be dangerous, you!"

Eric's straining bladder would just have to wait its turn.

"So, I've cut out carbohydrates and I'm doing two gym sessions a day. It's CrossFit in the morning and then whatever dance class they have in the evenings."

"Right," Eric nodded as he tried to look interested while perching on a wonky buffet. Dee's glazed eyes vibrated back and forth as she talked, and he could practically smell the fumes of black coffee powering her sharp-edged multitasking.

"Though I have to be a bit careful," she went on. "The other day I went in and it was pole dancing. Now, I'm not averse to it on moral grounds, Eric, but I just don't like wrapping my legs round something that might not have been properly sterilised, you know?"

Eric didn't know whether to pounce on the joke or seize on the small gap in her gob-shittery to give her a nudge. He chose to play it straight, and then reminded himself that there was a first time for everything. "You said you might have a job offer going?"

"Ahuh, ahuh, ahuh. Right." She typed a quick line into her computer and started the familiar mouse-clicking frenzy. All stop. She looked sideways at Eric and, spreading her hands in the air like she was about to do a turn for a kiddy's magic show, offered: "How do you feel about house clearance?"

A bit philosophical, that, for so early in the morning. She was looking at him expectantly though. Was he, so bowled over by the genius of this idea, supposed to ask her to bend over so he could kiss her ever diminishing rear?

"I'll do anything."

"Yes, I know, you've said." She looked a bit sour, like he'd pissed all over her new cerulean wedding shoes. "It'd mean early starts, you know?"

"I don't mind. I've not been sleeping right anyway, and—"

"Ahuh," she said and squinched at the computer screen. "Says here they've been looking for a while now. Had a lot of turnover. The people they've been sent before haven't got on with the existing staff, apparently. That's why they're only offering a trial period."

Eric, though it took a sizeable dollop of willpower, refrained from rolling his eyes—or, for that matter, clobbering her with her gigantic stapler. "You mean I won't be paid?"

"Not at first. After they've seen you working though, they'll decide whether to keep you on."

"Is that legal?"

"It's a job," she said with a shrug. "The boss Paul, Paulo or something, he seemed very genuine on the phone."

Eric wasn't about to argue. If he refused the interview they could, by law, threaten to cut his jobseeker's allowance and, even though it was a pittance, the Mayfairs needed that money. *Mouth shut and look grateful.* He plastered on his his best Big Boy smile and held out his hand to take the collated, highlighted and anal-all-over information pack Dee had just finished putting together.

"The interview's today at half-twelve. Now, I've not mentioned about your, you know, past troubles," she whispered, like they were bartering over the sale of foreskins. "Probably best not to say anything in case they think it means you can't do any heavy lifting."

"No," Eric said, "I wouldn't want them to think that."

THE COMPOUND'S TOWERING steel gate emerged from an equally large stone wall. It gave the impression of a mid-medieval keep. Surrounded as it was by abandoned mills and old shopping outlets, this was the business district that time had clean forgot.

He deliberated for a few minutes about how he was supposed to gain entry into this fortress of drudgery, then spied a promising looking electronic box embedded in the wall to one side of the gate. He pushed the red-ringed silver button. Long seconds of static eventually transmuted into a human voice.

"Yes, what is it?"

Eric told the disembodied gatekeeper that he was interviewing for a job.

"Ah, Eric Lanefair?" *Well, close enough.* "Peter's expecting you. Once you're through the gate turn right toward the office and knock. Do not go anywhere else. This is a potentially dangerous environment and you've not signed any release forms. Thank you."

A beep, a click, and the gate pulled away from the wall—but at a crippled slug's pace. "Oh, come on," Eric sighed. Once Eric could just about squeeze through the gap, he did as instructed and turned to the right. Trudging along the heavily pitted ground, and trying to avoid the slaking mud and puddles of water dancing under a fine percussion of rain, Eric let his eyes track over a row of white vans and a haphazardly skewed forklift truck, and then, finally, the blue hut he assumed was the much hyped office. He knocked.

"Come in," said a raspy voice.

Eric stepped into the damp, warm little room to find at the far end a red-faced, middle-aged man wearing blue overalls and an offensively low cut vest. He sat squinting in Eric's direction from behind a grubby desk. At his side, and in stark contrast, was a young man just a little older than Eric. He had a shaved head, clean skin and a solid build. Eric had seen the man before, he realised, feeling a warm panic growing in his chest.

"Hi. Er, I'm Eric Mayfair. I'm here about the job trial," Eric managed, peering out from under his brow as he walked toward the odd couple and handed the older chap his Jobcentre forms. Eric could smell the younger lad's aftershave like electric to the nose.

"Ah, right, lad," said the man. "Yeah, yeah, that Dee phoned from the job office. Said you was coming down." The man knocked his taped-together glasses down from off his head and onto the bridge of his nose. He gave the papers a quick scan. "Well, I'm Peter. This is Grant. No, he's not special, he just always looks like that," Peter laughed.

"All right, bud?" Grand held out his hand. "You look familiar?"

Eric didn't so much as blush as turn to sweat. "I-er-the gym—"

"Here, Grant," Peter cut in, picking up the empty cup on his desk, "go make this lad here a cup of tea. I could do with one myself as it happens."

Grant gave Eric a displeased look that said the tea might come with a large dollop of saliva, and then clomped out of the office, his mucky yellow high-visibility jacket flapping seductively as he went.

Silence. Peter scanned the papers in his hand. "Well," he said, with an apologetic hiss. "I...er...don't...."

"No," Eric said before he could stop himself.

"Pardon?"

Not again.

"Peter, right?" Eric fought hard to keep his mouth from clamping shut. He needed this job. His mum needed him to get it. "I know I don't have much experience and stuff, yeah, but here's why: I was sick for ages when I was younger. I had this heart trouble, but then I got better. I haven't been able to get work even though I'm fine, and the doctors will even sign a note saying it. Just, no one will take me on because I don't have the experience or the qualifications, but I want to work. And I would work hard, you know. Please. I do really, really want this job."

Peter chewed on this. "You," he said, shaking a finger in Eric's direction and scratching at his fuzzy chest with his other hand. "You're that kid, aren't you?"

Oh, no.

"Mayfair. I remember now. The *Willingsley Gazette*, page thirteen, last October. Photographic what's it, me," he said, tapping the side of his head. "You was dying and then, poof, you got better."

"Not poof. Not exactly poof. I mean—"

"Right. Well, I've never believed in miracles myself." Peter sighed.

"No, I don't either."

"And I'm sure there's a perfectly reasonable explanation for how you got better, right?"

"Yes, I'm sure there is." It wasn't lying. Not exactly. There *could* be a perfectly reasonable explanation, just Eric was damned if he knew what it was. But on this one, sorry, Peter, he could not budge. So, Eric sat and let the silence do its work. Before long Peter gave a friendly grin.

"Ah, it isn't much fun being a legend, is it, mate? I know, I've been there." Peter spread his fat hands out on the desk. "Captain for the Under Eighteens five times in a row. Finished when I was twenty-six. That takes some skill, that, lad. Made me quite a news item." Peter leaned back and then, as though showing off a fridge on a game show, he used his hands to frame a picture that was propped up on the small filing cabinet behind his chair. The grubby photo showed a young-looking Peter standing with his foot on a ball, the lush green of Clementi Park as a backdrop.

"You were twenty-six there?"

"Nah, only twenty-four in that one. Had to shave everywhere twice a day though so as not to arouse suspicion. And I mean *everywhere*. Terrible, terrible rash."

Eric didn't know what was more impressive: Peter's grand deception or the innumeracy of Willingsley's amateur football clubs.

Fortunately, before Peter could regale Eric with any of his football stories, the door opened and in swaggered Grant with a clinking tray of teas, a packet of ginger biscuits, and something in his pocket that Eric hoped meant Grant was pleased to see him.

"Here, boss," Grant began, sliding the tray onto Peter's desk. "Denny's back. He says that there's that old git following 'em again. Wants to complain about the collection van parking at the other side of his road."

"The house what we're clearing is there. Where the flipping hell else is it supposed to go? Over the rooftops?" Peter sighed. "I'll have to see to this, Eric. Help yourself to a biscuit and I'll be back in a bit. Grant can walk you through what we do and how we do it. He'll see if you're up to snuff, won't you, lad?"

"Aye, boss." Grant gave his best grin and Peter thudded out, mumbling under his breath some newly minted curse words.

With Peter gone, Grant sat back in the boss's chair and put his feet up on the desk. A clod of mud fell from his sole into one of the cups of tea.

"I won't bullshit you. There's gonna be some changes round here," Grant said, fixing Eric with a look. "This ain't Peter's firm. He runs it for this other guy who doesn't like getting his hands dirty. Long story brief: this'll be my office soon. Do you know what that means, Eric?" Eric could guess. "It means that if you want a job, some loyalty might be a good thing." Grant bit a chunk out of a ginger nut and crunched. *Ah, a good-looking dick head. Rare, that.* "You get me?"

Grant, who obviously enjoyed the sound of his own voice, didn't wait for an answer and instead proceeded to tell Eric how the firm went into repossessed homes, cleared the place from top to bottom and sold on anything they had salvaged. He informed Eric that if Eric got the job he would start on three days a week to see if he "gelled" with the lads, with the possibility of more days if he was found to be suitable. He'd start on office work, and might progress to the collection teams at a later date if he found Grant's favour.

"Does that suit?" Grant finished. Before Eric could answer Peter returned to the office, still barking at someone outside. Grant leaned in. "You'll think on, won't you? About what I said."

Jobless or working with this tosser? Eric resigned himself to his answer. "Reckon I will, yeah."

"How's it going, lads?" Peter asked, leaning over Eric to pick up his cup of tea and, in the process, pressing his round stomach down the side of Eric's face. For this, Eric didn't warn Peter about the clod of mud swimming in his tea. As it happened, Peter didn't seem to notice and didn't even flinch when he took a swig. "He going to fit in here?"

Grant pinned Eric with a pressured look.

"Don't reckon he'll cause any trouble whatsoever, boss."

"NINE AT NIGHT, would you believe it?" Jhardine shouted, rattling through the door. Then, in what she condemned as being typical *her*, managed to drop a whole bag of tinned food over the hallway floor, taking off a great line of paint from the banister to boot. "Oh, flipping heck."

"Mum?" Eric called from the living room. Fat lump, of course that's where he'd be.

"Aye, it's just me. I've dropped my tins."

"You're late," Eric commented as he came through to her and began snatching up the cans. "You should have phoned me, I'd have come up to collect you." Before she could say anything else, Eric had all the tins back in the bag and was carrying it through to the kitchen. "You been at the church all this time?"

"Since finishing CC's at four, yeah," she said, following him. Was his hair thinning at the back? She'd have to be careful next time she got the clippers on it. "The vicar's prayer meeting lasted hours, you know, because of the murder, and then we had this church council thing afterwards about helping the kiddies somewhere abroad where they've got nowt but polio. Anyway, we wanted to do some fund-raising but it turned into a right farce. In the end I got cross and said I'd do it. We're doing a tinned food collection, obviously."

"Mum, you shouldn't have," Eric said, spraying water from the tap down the nozzle of the kettle.

"Oh God, Eric, it's only some tinned ham. I know we're hard up but—"

"No, I mean, it's just another thing for you to do, isn't it?"

"I suppose."

"You shouldn't let them take advantage."

"Don't," she said, trying to get a hand through her curls. *Bloody hell, Jaz. When did you last wash your hair?* "I know, I'm doing too much. You don't even know the half of it." She slumped down at the kitchen table. "And I've had Sarah up at CC's crying all afternoon about Jim. Turns out he was at the Richies last night talking to that prostitute again."

"Aye, I know. I saw."

"What! And you didn't tell me?"

"Sorry, I didn't see you last night and I didn't think to say anything this morning, what with us paddling about in the bathroom. He fixed the leak then?"

"Aye," she said, giving Eric the eye to tell him that, when it came to gossip, he'd failed in his duty as her son. "Anyway, turns out Sarah's known about the affairs. Says he's been doing it for years, she's just never got round to throwing him out."

Eric nodded along with this as he went about brewing Jhardine a cup of tea and shaking her out a small bowl of cereal.

"So yeah, she's on about giving Jim the boot as soon as his next pay-cheque is in the bank."

"Well, that's good sense, isn't it?" Eric said, nursing his own cup of tea. She noticed then that he had on a bit of a smile.

"You look pleased with yourself. What have you done?" She brightened. "Oh God, have you had sex? Who is he? And, more importantly, does he have a slightly—only slightly, mind—older and devilishly handsome brother?"

"Mum!" Eric rolled his eyes.

"What? Well, one of us should be getting some. Is he dishy?"

"It's not a bloke."

"Oh," she slurped her tea, losing interest rapidly. Then a thought. "It's not a woman, is it? Cos I've told you before, biggest relief of my life when you pranced out of the closet."

"Can you just be normal for once?"

"Well, I'm beginning to think I'll die before you get your end away."

"Are you going to let me finish or what?"

"Is that what you said to him?" she cackled. Then, "Fine, fine. Tell your boring story."

"Well," he started, drawing it out just that bit longer, "gone got myself a job, haven't I?"

"You haven't!" This was better—way better—than sex! *God, that's a sad commentary on my life.*

"It's a trial thing, so don't get too excited. Doing house clearance though, you know?"

"Oh, with the council?"

"Private."

"Well, I bet that will pay better."

"Hope so. I have to do two or three weeks of trial, I forget, and then they'll decide whether they're taking me on. I don't know what wage I'd be on, but Grant—this no-neck that works there, pretty fit though—he said he was on a good salary. I start on Monday, and it's, erm, three days to begin with."

"Fantastic!" Jhardine rattled the table. "Come here!"

"Mum, no."

"I said, come here." She pulled him into a hug. "Aw, this will be really good for you."

"I know," he laughed.

"Might be our luck's about to turn round!"

OH GOD, THIS *is going to shatter him.*

Jhardine paced up and down the hall outside Eric's room, still clutching the phone to her chest. They'd called two hours ago, not long after Eric had gone up to bed. She'd come straight upstairs intent on telling him, but how?

How?

More pacing.

Jhardine had never recovered from Eric's dad leaving them. This? It was as bad. Worse, even, in its own way.

The cross she'd stuck to the wall just above the stairs caught her eye. It looked wonky and the dark wood seemed to make the cream of the landing angrier, almost bruised. Shadows deepened. Her mouth drew a hushed, heavy voice.

"How?" she croaked. "How could you do this? Hasn't he been through enough? I mean, you give a gift, a second chance, and then this is what, the price? And how could you let that poor boy suffer? It was different when I got sick. A life for a life. That was fair. But how—"

"Mum?" Eric's voice reached through the door to her. Now was the time then, whether she was ready or not. "Mum, is that you?"

Her hands were shaking. She had to stop shaking. "Yes, love. Can I come in a minute?"

"Er," he coughed, "yeah."

Clenching and unclenching her fists, she shuffled into Eric's room. The landing light flooded around her, forcing Eric to put his hands over his eyes. She could see the sweat on his skin, the way it clung in the valleys of his thin limbs.

"I've been having some proper awful nightmares, Mum," he said, pulling the bed quilt tight around his waist. "A-about this room, right, where people are doing all these things, like eating—"

"Love," she interrupted him. "Eric. I need to tell you something and you need to listen."

The silence seemed to hiss like hot coals. "W-w-what is it?"

"I've had a phone call. We were listed as his emergency number, you know? So they.... They...." Her voice cut out. She cleared her throat and chased away a tear that had made a dash for it down her cheek. "The police. They told me whose body it is that they found."

She watched Eric glance at the mobile phone sat there by his bed.

"It's Tim, Eric."

"No," he shook his head.

"Tim's the one what was murdered. I'm sorry, Eric, *I'm so sorry*."

CHAPTER FOUR
UNTIL DEATH US DO PART

IT WAS TWENTY to one, the funeral car was due any minute, and Jhardine couldn't find her other sodding earring.

"Where the flipping hell is it?" She groped under the bed until she inhaled a ball of her own hair and decided to give it up as a bad job. Still coughing, she climbed to her feet and replaced her orphaned sapphire earring in her jewellery box, mourning all the while that Aunt Madeline's legacy had now been cut in half. She perched on the edge of the bed and smoothed out her midnight-blue skirt. It'd been her favourite dress to go out on the town in. Felt a bit proud, she had, that she could still get it on. Then came the realisation that in the past decade she'd worn it to more funerals than clubs, and that put the kibosh on that.

She checked her watch again, then looked to the wall that divided her bedroom from Eric's. The paper was peeling, and the small roses squiggled on it all looked sad and wilting.

Oh, Eric.

She slipped her foot from her shoe so she could massage her heel. *Feels like I've done a damned marathon,* she moaned to herself. *Only been wearing them for a ruddy hour.* She wanted to shake Eric. She wanted him to *react,* but after that first night when he'd shattered and she'd had to sit and hold him, it was like living with a bad-tempered chimp—hair everywhere and the distinct impression they weren't speaking the same language. Lord knows, Eric had always had trouble expressing his feelings, but this was something else. Jhardine didn't even know how to begin to fix it. If it could be fixed at all, that is.

"Please, let everything go smooth today," she called out to God, rubbing the gold cross on her necklace. "I know this is a test, that it has to be a test, but—" A honk of a car horn. "Well, you're all knowing, you get the picture," she said, walking over to the window and not even caring that she was sassing the Almighty.

She and Eric had both agreed—well, he'd not objected—that taking a hearse with the coffin in the back felt wrong, after all they weren't Tim's blood even if they were his family. Instead, they'd settled on renting a black car to take them down to the church where the coffin would be waiting for them. Respectful, she'd decided. Tasteful, even. Except the car that Jhardine was looking at now wasn't a hearse. It was a cream wedding car, red lace on the bonnet and streamers down the back. There are fuck-ups and then there are *fuck-ups.*

"Oh, heck," Jhardine breathed. She glared up at a water stain on the ceiling that sometimes doubled for the Lord. "It's this kind of thing. This is what I'm talking about."

Just then, her bedroom door slid open and there stood Eric.

"You all right love?" she said, trying to sound as conversational as possible. He was wearing his Jobcentre suit, the only difference being a charity-shop-bought black tie Jhardine had found between a Neil Diamond tour t-shirt and a coat with a giant label saying "Real Fake Fur". Eric looked back at her with that awful vacant stare. "Have you, er, seen the—"

"Yes." His voice was glass. His hands were clenched but shaking.

"Right, well, I can call them and I'm sure they'll send the right car—"

"If you're going to force me to go to this thing, let's just go."

She ignored the obvious bitterness. "But it should be perfect, shouldn't it? For Tim's send-off, I mean. It should be—"

"He doesn't care. He's dead."

A deep, deep breath. "Okay, love, whatever you want." She took up her hammerhead of a purse and, checking her cigarettes and lighter were inside, because *bloody hell* she was going to need those today, she followed Eric out of the house.

Outside the sky was marked with a detonation of grey cut through with just a knife edge of gold. Pulling her skirt down at the back just one more time, she and Eric did a slow walk down the drive. Sarah was there at the end of her path, cigarette lit and coils of smoke spreading all lazy-like off her lips.

"I hope everything goes all right today," she said.

Eric looked at her as though he'd never seen her before in his life.

"Thanks, "Jhardine smiled, putting her hands around Eric's shoulders and directing him toward the car.

The bald driver got out as they approached, ran round and opened the rear passenger-side. His smile faded. In his Liverpudlian mangle he joked, "Who's died? This is supposed to be your son's wedding day, isn't it?"

"NOT A BAD turn-out at least," Jhardine said as she and Eric walked down the aisle of St Anthony's church. She counted about two dozen people who had gathered to mark Tim's passing, and even that modest number was a relief. When they'd pulled up outside to see only a few cars lining the street she'd been worried. What with Tim's mum refusing to come back from Portugal and Tim's dad, well, who knew where, it was already a bit dicey but, everything considered, this group of mourners would do—even if they were an unsightly lot.

"We shouldn't have had it in church," Eric told no one in particular. "Tim didn't believe in owt."

"It was good of the vicar to offer on such short notice," she said, firm as she dared. Then a memory flashed in front of her eyes, of Tim at the table across from her one evening just over a year ago, and what they'd told each other during their night of honesty. "Anyway, you're wrong. He told me once, he didn't know if there was a God. Said he was a, what's it, agnostic, couldn't say either way. He said he suspected there was *something*, though."

Eric looked like he was about to ridicule the notion, his mouth open, his eyes narrowed—but then a change washed through him. "Yeah, he did say something like that, actually," Eric said in a turgid hush. "W-why did I forget that?"

"You...." Jhardine gave a great big sigh. "You're a lot like me, love, but thankfully only in the small ways." He looked at her nonplussed. "I've always had a knack for seeing what isn't there. That's what you say about all my God stuff, isn't it? But you, though, you see everything exactly as it is. You do, all the time, crystal clear. *Except* when it came to him."

Eric blinked. His mouth hung open. She could see his cheeks warming. "That's not...it's not...."

"Let's not talk about it now, eh?" she said, patting his arm.

"I saw him exactly as he was. I *did*," Eric insisted, staring at her as if to push that notion deep, like squelching a wax seal onto her soft tissue.

As they waited in the queue to get to the front row of pews, it dawned on Jhardine that the vicar had even gone to the trouble of roping in the flower lady, Ina. There were a few nice arrangements by the altar and lovely white carnations in golden urns to dress the windows, but some of Ina's other choices were a bit more *questionable*, Jhardine thought. Dry red rose petals littered the floor and they crunched underfoot as Eric and Jhardine shuffled towards Tim's black casket, which in turn lay wreathed in browning lilies. Annoyingly, with all eyes on them as they walked down the aisle like Jhardine was about to give her son away, the service *did* resemble a dower wedding. Perhaps she owed that car driver an apology. And a new ear. Her hand was still stinging.

"Jhardine!" Even outside of CC's kitchen, Ruth looked a little menopausal, her wide-brimmed black hat sagging under the heat of her latest hot flush. Still, it was nice that she came.

"Hi Ruth, hi Stan," Jhardine said, nodding at her friend and then the tall husk of husband at Ruth's side.

"Hello," he said, then switched his large eyes to looking at Eric. "Sorry about what's happened," he said. "Any more on who did it?"

"Stanley," Ruth croaked, slapping his arm and tutting.

"What? A fair question isn't it?"

"No, nothing," Jhardine said, cutting through their bickering as a means of damage control. She needn't have worried though. Eric was as blank as a nun's bedroom wall. "I've, er, talked to the police," she said by way of keeping the conservation short and to the point. "And they've been round to see Eric too, but nothing so far."

"Well, I'm not surprised this happened," Stanley said, folding his arms.

"What?" Eric growled.

Oh, chuffing hell.

"Well, I remember when you two were at school. That boy made my life hell. Can't care-take when there's a lad what's intent on breaking every rule in the book, can you? Mind you, they're all like that these days. Glad I left."

"No," Eric said. "Tim wasn't like that."

"Oh, yes he was." Stanley laughed.

"Stanley, that is enough," Ruth said, her voice loud enough to bounce off the church walls. People stared. Stanley's eyes looked like they were about to pop right out of his head. "I am so sorry," Ruth said. "He's been in a weird mood for weeks now."

"Oh, just saying the truth," Stanley heckled from behind his wife. "Don't know why that's such a bad thing round here."

That earned a glare from Eric that was of the hot, itchy-fist variety. "Can you believe the flipping nerve of some people," Jhardine said, pushing Eric away and down the aisle. "He was always a nasty piece. And look at poor Ruth. She's mortified. I hope his piles rupture, I really do."

As they slid onto the front row of pews Eric's eyes lingered on the coffin, the great black length of it, so dark, and it didn't seem to reflect any light. "Tim wasn't like that," Eric said in a warm quiet, his eyes still fixed. "He was always really kind and he, er, he didn't want to do wrong by anyone."

"He was always good to you, Eric, weren't he?" She rubbed at his hand and with gentle care pulled him down so they could take their seats. "Let's just concentrate on the nice times for today, aye?" She wanted to hold him, to hug him until the light in him would come back on, but even sitting there on the pew next to her, he was too far away for that.

"Thank you all for coming," the vicar began once everyone had taken their seats. His funeral pall reflected the candle shine to give him a lovely and soft spotlight that complimented his gentle voice. "You all know why we're here today. For Tim." The priest let that settle like confectioner's sugar clouding, drifting down. "So let us bow our heads now for our first prayer."

It was the resurrection and the life speech. She kept her eyes on Eric. Specifically, on the tense set of his jaw. He wouldn't stand for too much of this. She'd asked the vicar to keep the scripture to the bare minimum, but even so. Mercifully, the priest was quickly back into more secular territory. "He was a good lad, well liked around Willingsley. True, he had a troubled home-life. That was no secret. But he made good on the opportunities that were given him by his friends," the priest said and looked Jhardine's way. Though his mouth remained pious, she thought she saw a warmth in his eyes. "Tim worked at Jasper's in town, grafting to be a skilled mechanic. I am told he was talented and hard working, and this comes as no surprise."

"He was the best mechanic there," Eric said, scratching at his collar. Red raw, the skin there.

"Tim was into his fitness, of course, and he'd managed to put his skills to good use: he'd been a member of the local rugby team for a number of years, and had even done a few fun-runs to raise money for the Heart Health Research Foundation, all in the name of his closest friend, Eric. Some of you might know Eric's story. Now's not the place for it of course, but what we can definitely say is that Tim leaves behind a devoted family, one that he chose, and one that loved him when—"

A rebounding bang cut the vicar off. The sound of a couple of dozen people turning in their seats filled the church.

Bouncing through St Anthony's stiff doors there came a middle-aged man with a scraggly beard, a drunk's beetroot-red face, and Tim's indigo eyes. "Sorry, sorry," the man blurted as he lurched toward the nearest vacant pew. "Carry on."

The vicar swallowed. His hands curled over the golden lectern, which happened to be a rather strangled looking eagle. "I think," the vicar started and then stopped. "You'll forgive me, but I feel moved to speak." Jhardine felt the hair on the back of her neck prickle. Everyone seemed to feel it. Impromptu remarks at a funeral? Surely not. But he was. He was doing it. "I don't often find that I am as troubled as I have been about this awful, awful event. So while I am here talking about all the good things in Tim's life, I can't very well ignore the senseless—godless—way in which he was killed. "

Eric leaned forward and put his head in his hands. "This is wrong. This is all wrong," he moaned.

"I say this not to proselytise," the vicar went on. "I know how painful today is, but I feel I have to say this because I believe it needs saying. We don't know the exact motives behind Tim's murder. Perhaps we never will. Yet I believe that we will find this is a symptom of a much greater cause: our failure to confront the evils around us."

A woman two rows down on the other side of the church clapped. "Yes!" she said, her huge beehive of a hat sliding to one side on her curiously small head.

"It's the little lies," the vicar said, and Jhardine felt he was looking right at her. "The small unkindnesses." His eyes ticked over to the rows behind. "Our inability to face up to our addictions. To confront reality." Jhardine's stomach tightened. "They create the gaps through which the more horrid darkness can creep. Evil is among us, and quite often it looks like a friend." A murmuring, like a charm of bees. "We must, all of us please, cultivate vigilance and prayerful attitudes in this time of real danger. We must reach out to God and ask that he embrace us. That he strip us of evil. That he lead us back to the right path."

"Amen," the crowd said as one.

"Now, let us pray."

"Pray?" Eric whispered, low but just loud enough to be heard by the people sitting around them. "No," Eric said, rising up. "What we *need* to do is find the person who killed Tim and make them pay!"

"Eric, now's not the time, love."

"Not the time? He's *dead*, Mum. There's never going to be a good time. There never will be—"

"Eric," the vicar called, holding out a hand. "Please believe me when I say I meant no offence. I know you and I differ on a few things. That you do not believe, but—"

"Sorry, everyone," Jhardine said, smiling as she put an arm around Eric. "He's just a bit upset and—"

"Don't do that," Eric said, low and angry and ducking out from her hold. "Don't apologise for me. I'm not five. I'm not—"

"You're saying things you don't mean, love."

"No! No I'm not! I'm saying.... I'm...." His cheeks were wet. His chin jutted forward. The shadows on the wall behind him seemed to dilate, growing wider and larger, and then every candle in the room went out. He looked away. He sat down, slow like with one false move his spine might crack. Then he waved a hand in surrender.

"Go on, Vicar," Jhardine nodded. More bees murmuring in the back, but the priest's voice soon rose above them.

"Heavenly Father, though we stray from your light, may we always come home to your embrace. May you take your child Tim into your arms and...."

Thankfully, the prayer was soon over. Eric's rigid silence, however, proved a little more lasting. "Love," Jhardine whispered. He flinched under her touch and would not meet her eye.

"Before we end today's service," the vicar was saying. "I wondered if anyone would like to say a few words in memory of Tim? Any stories of him you would like to share?"

Jhardine looked around. Everyone had been stricken with laryngitis, it seemed. "Go on," Jhardine urged Eric.

Eric scratched at his neck again. "Tim can't hear owt I'm saying, so what's the point?"

"It's not for him. It's for other people. For you. You need to say goodbye properly."

"Tim is dead." The hardness in Eric's eyes, the unwavering conviction. Sometimes he looked so much like his dad that it physically hurt to even look at him.

"No one at all?" the vicar prompted.

Jhardine had her hand up in the air before she really knew what she was doing. "I'd like to say something."

Nervous but resolute, Jhardine walked her way to the front of the church. The vicar gave up his place with a comforting hand running down her back. She adjusted the microphone a little while she looked out at the motley crew who'd turned up to mourn Tim Jeffries. There was the woman in the beehive hat. Her name would come, give it time. Then there was Lazy-Eye Kelvin from the ice-skating rink, who'd been lovely to Tim and let him go down for a few hours every night for free when Tim was young and needed somewhere to go. She didn't recognise the chap sat four rows from the back; near white hair and wearing a bow tie. They'd brought back bow ties, hadn't they? A bit uppity for her taste but the lad looked respectable all the same.

Then her gaze ticked over to the back row and settled on one face in particular. When she'd stood she'd not known what she would say. Not exactly. Now, though, looking at *him* and feeling the metalwork of her insides creak with anger, she had everything she needed.

"Tim, he was my Eric's best...." She looked at her son. Her little man. Broken. "Well, his *best*. He was there for Eric when Eric wasn't well. He didn't leave him, though he knew things were going to get worse. I can't tell you how much that meant—not just to Eric but to me, too. Anyway, I thought I'd share something that Eric doesn't know. You see, Tim came round the house a few weeks after we found out our Eric was, well, ill." She had to take a breath. "He came in for a cup of tea. I thought he wanted to talk about it all. Get his little head round it. That I'd have to comfort him, you know. And I really didn't have the strength." Eric's lips were trembling, she could see. This was going to hurt, but maybe it could help too. "Instead of me having to comfort him though, we talked—about a lot—and then he says to me, really adamant about it as well, 'No matter what happens. After, *you know*, I'll always see you're all right.' And that's the kind of lad Tim was. He had his problems, don't get me wrong, but he wanted to do right by you. He did. That's why I loved him through the good and the bad." She fixed her gaze on the back row of pews where Tim's dad sat glaring back at her. "That's why I would have been proud if he'd been my son."

She let the silence stretch, let it bubble and froth as it lapped at Tim's dad. *Yes, that's right, you. Feel it.* And he *was* feeling it. In fact, he gave her a hot scotch glare and then, head bobbing in that way drunks have of carrying on moving when they think they're perfectly composed, left his seat and stumbled for the door.

"Thank you, Jhardine, that was wonderful," the vicar said as he came to vacate her from the lectern.

She took her seat once more. The vicar announced there would be the interlude of Holy Communion now. She'd expected Eric to be less than thrilled about this. Instead, a few seconds in, people getting out of their seats and walking to the front to receive wafer and wine, Eric turned to her. Though his neck was meat raw and his eyes were pink, he smiled at her and closed his eyes. He took a long breath. She saw it. The change. He was coming back to her. "I'm sorry." It wasn't a smile, was it? That thing on Eric's lips. It wasn't smiling, no, so much as relief. "When this is through do you mind if I just, erm, stand with the coffin for a bit?"

"You can do whatever you like, love. We'll just be through in the hall when you want to come join us," Jhardine said.

After the priest called the service to an end, Jhardine left Eric in his seat and, with much of the rest of the congregation, made her way toward the side door that took them into the community hall. The vicar soon joined her. "It was a lovely service," she told him. "I know the no-songs thing was a bit odd, but Tim had particular musical tastes, and they wouldn't have been appropriate for the church." All that rap music, effing and jeffing all the time. Pussy this and grinding that. Scandalous.

"I've always hated funeral hymns, Jhardine. If I ever have to hear 'Amazing Grace' again I think I will amazingly lose my mind," he smiled. "No, I'm glad you liked it. And please, do call me David."

"Okay, *David*," she said. "And I'm sorry about Eric." She looked over the vicar's shoulder to the splinter of a man stood by Tim's casket. "He's been a bit all over the place. Either frozen up like, or raging."

"It's quite understandable. How are you though?" David asked, his eyebrows raised.

"I'm, you know," she said, smiling as the last of the mourners filed past. "Doing okay, really."

"Jhardine, I thought you didn't like to lie in church?"

She laughed. When she was caught out, she was caught out. "It wasn't a lie exactly. I mean, I am getting by," she said.

"But your health...we both know you're not meant to have any stress." At there mere mention of it she felt a wave of tiredness slap against her eyelids and make them heavy. But, no time for that now. "It's him I'm worried about," she said, looking at Eric. "He bottles things up."

THE VENEER OF the coffin was odd to touch. Intellectually, Eric knew it couldn't possibly be as cold as it felt, but so it was.

"The Reds lost again last night." Eric sighed. "Listen to me. You know, I only watched football for you, I bloody hate it." The empty church was peaceful. Kind, almost. Suddenly he could understand coming to this place to get away from the outside world; could fathom why this might feel like a sanctuary. The coffin though, it remained impassive and as much as ever a perfect sheet of nothing. "God, what am I doing? You're not here. Who am I talking to?" Eric fiddled with the knot of his tie, running his hand under his shirt collar, trying to alleviate the horrible friction there.

What did Mum wash this in? Napalm?

He walked around the casket, pushing back the lilies strewn over it so that he could look at Tim's name on the golden plaque. He tugged at his collar again "You didn't deserve...." He screwed up his eyelids. "You've left me again, haven't you? You've left me. And I don't...." A few more breaths to try steady himself. "You weren't supposed to die, mate. We were going to do things, weren't we? I was going to meet someone, and you'd have hoodwinked some poor, unsuspecting girl to be your wife. Sunday barbecues and endless, mind-numbing football matches and...families...and pointless, pointless but good lives. And always, always us." Tears again. *Oh fucking hell, Eric, you're embarrassing yourself.* "And I really, really do need that board money back, you know?" he laughed. All the things that seemed to matter before, they were just nothing now. "What were you doing, Tim? They're saying...all sorts."

Little by little, day by day, more facts had seeped into the news reports about, as the nightly news dubbed it, "The Murder that Has Gripped Willingsley". The body—Tim's body—had been dismembered, they said. Worse than that, there were teeth marks on some of the bones, in some of the flesh. Human jaws had made those marks. It was probable, the police said, that Tim had been tortured over the space of a full night and day; that he'd been gnawed at until his heart was finally cut out. And there was something else, something in Tim's bloodstream that the police wouldn't elaborate on. A *substance.*

Growing, building, filling him up, these thoughts. He couldn't breathe. He couldn't even think. And he was angry. So angry. "You—"

"Eric?" His mum stood at the door to the community hall, a mug of tea in hand. "Why don't you come through now, love. People want to talk to you."

"Eric, I'm so sorry about Tim." He'd not seen Mel since they'd left school, and now she was hugging him. *Hugging* him. "He was a good guy, wasn't he?"

"I—"

"I mean," she went on, tucking her buckwheat hair behind her lugs. "He was just so sweet and kind. I can't believe it happened to him. You must be devastated."

"I'm—"

"I mean, I am personally devastated. You think you're safe, you know. And then this happens. Thank goodness I moved to Aberystwyth for university or else I'd be living here. *Me. Here.*"

A gap. Oh, so now was the time he could get a word in. Best make it good.

"I heard the tide down there can drag you out to sea. They'd probably never find your bloated corpse." Her hooded eyes misted with fear. "Excuse me, I think Mum wants a word. It was nice seeing you."

Mel only managed what sounded like "Meep."

He'd clocked his mum coming out of the kitchen with her arms full of trays, an opportunity to get away from folk and earn some grace.

"Let me help, yeah?" he said.

"Aw, cheers, chick."

She gave him the two largest platters, this as penance for his earlier misdeeds.

Balancing the trays of tuna sandwiches on the end of the long buffet table, Eric looked beyond the milling groups of people to Tim's portrait propped up on a pair of stepladders in the middle of the white stone hall.

It was Tim in his rugby shirt, smiling and about to laugh. Taken last year, Eric guessed, before Tim had packed on that few more inches of muscle. He looked so ripe with life, but not overstuffed. That thought gave Eric pause. *When did I ever think he looked too big?*

Eric studied the picture as people behind him chattered and joked, chewing their albeit lovely cud and saying the most inane things.

"He kept himself to himself."

"He liked all kinds of music, didn't he?"

"A really nice guy. Just so *nice*."

The crescents of Tim's lower eyelids. The wide bridge of his proud nose. The dark cleft of Tim's chin. They were all there in the picture but none of them was him. The parts did not make the man. Not even close. Eric wanted to reach out and pull the picture down because it was almost worse than not seeing Tim at all; to see him static, stolen from time. To see him dead.

"It's my son's funeral. I've got every right!" said a voice cutting through the chatter. Tim's dad, yet again showcasing his talent for a boozy entrance, staggered into the room. As he meandered over to Tim's portrait he managed to fell a coat stand, make a three-year-old boy cry, and upturn a rather disappointing tray of custard tarts—so it wasn't all bad.

"I'm sorry, we tried," said flower lady Ina to the room in general, her weaselly nose twitching. "But he has a point. It is his son's day."

At first, sheer disbelief had frozen Eric. Then came the thaw.

"No, Eric!" said his mum, Black Forest gateau in hand and too far away to intercept.

"You have a pair, coming here like this today!"

Tim's dad turned. Everyone did, except for the vicar who was over by the lavender shortcake. To be fair, it was good shortcake.

"I'm here," Tim's dad slurred, "to say goodbye to my son."

"Your son? Your son! You have no right to call him that after you abandoned him."

"Oh, aye, I'm sure that's what he told you," Tim's dad shouted, moving his drink-hand much too quickly and watering the floor with rum and cordial. "He was just lucky Miranda didn't want to take it further, the little bastard, gah—"

Eric caught the drunk by his cheap shirt and, in a surge of strength, held him up against the wall. Eric pulled an arm back, ready to strike.

"Hit me if you want," Tim's dad said. "But it won't change the facts."

Eric's fist tightened.

"Eric, no!" He felt his mum pulling at his arm. The vicar's hands were tugging at his shoulder. Rage had made him strong, and he *hated* Tim's dad with everything in him that could feel.

"What do you mean?" Eric spat. "Facts? What are you talking about?"

Tim's dad smiled. And then his cruelty reached new heights: the light in the room seemed to move, the shadows giving way to a sudden glare, and the drunk's eyes sparkled in a way that was all Tim. Bloodshot and yellowed as they were, but still so almost-Tim that it felt like Eric had been punched, and Eric's hands fell away.

"Help me," Tim's dad mewed as the vicar pulled the man out of Eric's reach. "He's a frigging nutter!" the man spat with venom.

"Well," said the priest, "in that case I think you'd best get some fresh air."

Eric was lost to static as hands settled around his shoulders and marched him toward the slender kitchen.

"Are you okay?" his mum asked once they were in the safety of the white tiled room, door firmly closed. She ran Eric a cup of water and pushed it into his hands. "Eric?"

"I don't know," he said. "Mum, I don't.... I'm just so *angry*."

"Come here." His mum folded him into a hug. "Here, it's all right. It's all right."

DYLAN JEFFRIES WAS a terrible father to Tim, a terrible husband to Miranda, Tim's mum, and an all round terrible human being. You wouldn't catch him saying the contrary. In fact, after some fifty or so years of living, he'd found he rather enjoyed being terrible. It made things interesting.

"Get out of my bloody way," he yelled at a group of teenagers as he turned down Summerfield Road. He'd gone the wrong way coming out of St Anthony's and had walked all the way around the outskirts of town to try to find a damned street just to get back toward the city's centre. He'd never liked Willingsley anyway. He'd only moved because Miranda had insisted.

The fault this time though was with that Mayfair lad, of course. Getting Dylan thrown out of his own son's funeral! Oh, he'd never liked that kid. If he knew anywhere near the amount he thought he knew about Tim, Eric'd think twice before mouthing off! One day, Dylan thought, he'd take great pleasure in telling that jumped up little shit exactly what the boy he mooned over was *really* capable of.

Ah, Salvation and Holy Grace: Dylan found himself outside the Richardson's Arms, its ageing white frontage beckoning him inside. Well, he'd just had to attend his own son's funeral so he thought he'd earned himself the right to a little snifter. He rubbed at his nose, jangled the change in his pocket and, anticipating the warm cling of alcohol already massaging his insides, waited to be served. Eventually, Dennis the barman approached.

"Give me a double whiskey," Dylan said.

Dennis folded his red, cracked hands around the stout pumps and spoke low: "I'm sorry; I heard it were Tim's funeral. Jhardine invited me, but I can't stand to lose the trade. As you can see, we ain't got much on at the minute."

Dylan took a gander around. Just a few blokes at that infernal pub quiz machine, but that was all.

"Give us a free drink and we'll say no more about it," Dylan said, gruff but as friendly as he could pretend.

Dennis's bald plate of a head shined under the bar's spotlights. "You know I can't, Dylan mate."

"My son is dead and you're saying I can't even have a drink?"

"You get violent when you've had something to drink. With your own son, no less."

"Well, he's not here, now. Or did you miss that part?"

Dennis stepped back from the pumps and gave a sad shake of his head. "No, I'm sorry, I can't do it."

"I come here to give you good business, and—"

"As much as you spend I have to lay out in clean-up. Smashed glasses, smashed chairs, and that's just from you falling down drunk. I'm not going to force the point, Dylan mate. If you want an orange juice or a tonic water, fine. Otherwise, you can't be in here. Lads?" Dennis said.

From over by the quiz machine the cavalry came. One was Jim Briley, often seen but rarely spoken to. The others were some of Willingsley's choice clowns, men Dylan didn't care to recognise and wouldn't piss on if they were on fire.

"Best be off, aye, mate?" Jim said, his shell-suit-wrapped thighs rubbing together so much Dylan wondered if Jim was single-handedly powering the north of England with his own static electricity.

"Fine! Fuck you all. I hope you all rot in this hell hole," he said as he lurched out the door.

Out on the street he felt the urge to spit. Blood again. That blinding pain cut through his stomach. *Ignore it.* He'd be back at his hotel soon enough anyway where he could delve into the mini-bar for a bit of pain relief and forget everything.

Off down the road he went, mind to a snicket he'd seen once a long time ago when they'd first moved to the crap-heap that was Willingsley. "When we," he corrected, muttering as he sidestepped through the metal gate that led to a thin track which in turn cut behind the supermarket and down through the town by skirting and interjecting the roads. "When we were happy," he puffed. "Were I ever happy?" Oh this, this was why he needed a drink. The thoughts. The thoughts that came when he didn't have a drink!

The bushes on Dylan's either side were clingy, and he had to keep his arms out in front so as to avoid getting torn up by thorns. The ground beneath his feet didn't help. It was soft and sucking and seemed to want to keep him. Nothing had been right, not really, not since that night twenty-some years ago when he'd met Miranda at a festival in Hebden Bridge. With a quill of a smile, she'd offered him a drink. "On me," she'd smiled. But the joke weren't. It was on him.

And now his good-for-nothing son was dead. He'd hated that boy in the rare way only a parent can, looking at their child and seeing them wasting their life. It hurt like nothing else. It hurt so much he began to cry. Not for Tim, but for himself. Right there, on the street, crying. "Fucking hell," he sobbed.

Look what they've reduced you to!

Dylan crossed a thin road, rejoining the snicket a few yards further down. A long stretch, this, and it saw him walking a good five minutes before he realised, *oh sodding hell*, that he wasn't sure it did take him onto Dazeem Street and the main road after all. He searched around but with the fencing so high there was no hope of finding a landmark, the dark sky saying even the moon had abandoned him.

"Bollocks," he shouted at the air. "Bollocks!" again. If only other people could hurt the way he did. If only they felt the boiling anger inside, like there was something cooking beneath his skin that wanted to get out and rip through this despicable town.

"You left me," said a voice.

Dylan turned. There was a silhouette a few feet away. It had to be someone huge, and they were coming closer.

"What?" Dylan spat. "I ain't never met you, mate. Wrong face." Dylan blinked, and when he opened his eyes, the silhouette was gone. "Tricky, tricky, tricky," he said to himself after a moment, a little amused that his brain was trying to pull a fast one on him.

"You left me," the voice came again, and this time it brought something sharp.

It was a pain through Dylan's stomach again, but it wasn't like the other hurt though. It didn't ease after a few agonising seconds. No, this pain just went on and on. Dylan looked down and staggered. There was a broken pint glass sticking out of his stomach.

"You left me," the silhouette stepped in front of him, so huge it blocked out the light of the streetlamps. "You deserve to suffer." The first blow snapped Dylan's left leg clean through, the second filled his head with shards of glass. Then a face, a terrible, distorted but familiar face emerged from the gloom.

"And now you die alone like I died alone," Tim said, as he bent his warped head and slipped his knife-like fingers under Dylan's skin—and began to peel.

CHAPTER FIVE
A ROOM WITH A VIEW

ERIC BUMBLED HIS way into the kitchen. "Isn't there a law against waking up this early?"

"Yeah, well, I thought I'd have to drag you out of bed with you getting in so late." Jhardine pushed a mug of black tea into Eric's hands and set down two thick slices of toast topped with what she could scrape from the jar of strawberry jam. The mould she was passing off as mulberry.

"Yeah, sorry. Didn't wake you up, did I?"

"No, I was reading my book anyway. It's dead filthy. I'm only finishing it because everyone at prayer group is." Three sugars to granulate her cup of tea or four? Everything tasted so bitter these days. "Anyway, I'm not sleeping that well." Eric bit into his toast. A blob of jam hurtled toward his orange work sweatshirt. She was on it in a second, wiping at it with a dishcloth. "Would you look at that, Eric! This is why I don't buy you new clothes."

"Leave off," Eric said, trying to shrug her away but to no effect. "You're all right, aren't you?" he said, a portion more tender.

"Course I'm all right," she said, still rubbing. "Just not been settling, you know? What with the funeral and then what happened with Tim's dad. Oh, I don't even like thinking about it." Ripped apart, the news said. And glass. So much glass. Well, it was a bloody killing spree, wasn't it? And Eric. He had that look in his eyes again. Not darker so much as definite. A hardness that hadn't been there before.

"Anyway, that's better," she said with one last wipe of his shirt. Once the damp cleared it'd be good as, well, as it was ever going to get. "Anyway, I've got the morning off. Tania's opening up." Jhardine gave a lion's yawn. "I'll see you out and then have a few more hours sleep. You coming round to the café for tea?"

"Aye, can do. I'll be off out again later on though." He glanced at the clock on the cooker and then set about stuffing the remaining slice of toast into his already full mouth.

"Off out again? Oh you aren't hitting the drink are you?"

"No, I'm not drinking," he said in the patronising tone that, when he was younger, would have earned him a clipped ear. Jhardine wondered whether there was a minimum or maximum age for when you could lawfully punch someone in the kidney. "I'm just driving round," Eric went on. "I know it's money down the wazoo but it's helping; seeing places me and Tim used to go together, you know?"

She didn't consider that wasted money at all. "Okay. Well, just drive safe, yeah?"

He clicked his heels together and offered a salute. At last, a hint that Eric was still inside the shell that was walking around and calling itself her son.

"'Ere, it's nippy out today so take this to work with you." She fished out Eric's woollen hat from behind the radiator in the hall and pulled it down over his head. He groaned, adjusted it, but didn't take it off. "You excited for your first proper paid day at work?"

"Oh, yeah, like a ball ache."

"Eric!"

"What?" He feigned innocence. "But at least I'll be earning some money, eh?"

"Aye." She caught his gaze and held it. "Eric, I—"

"I'm trying Mum. I am."

"I know darling."

She reached out to hug him but he pulled away. "I better get going." Eric checked his back pocket to make sure he had all the bumph the Jobcentre had sent him. "See you this afternoon."

"Yeah, see you!" he said, pulling the front door closed.

Jhardine sagged against the kitchen table. Bless Eric, but he was wearing her out. There, clinging to the table-top, she nibbled on a bit of toast she'd overdone. It was as black as the suit of spades, but it tasted sweet. Well, if this was the worst the new tablets could reek, she supposed she could cope. If only they could get rid of the damned headaches.

When Jhardine could muster the energy, she padded into the living room and stretched herself out on the sofa.

I'll just have five minutes, and then I'll get dressed.

"SHIT. BUGGERY. BUMFLUFF!" Jhardine cursed as she slid into the taxi." Just five minutes? Try five hours! She was late. Oh boy, was she late.

"Where to, love?" asked the driver, looking over the bridge of his round glasses while he popped a mint into his mouth. *Who was he trying to impress?* It was a good question though. Rolling in at work now would only make it look like she was late. She could pretend she'd taken a half-day—she was owed a truck-load of holidays, so they'd be all square there. "The church please," she decided. "St Anthony's."

She ran her hands through her hair, found a bit of tissue and threw it out the window.

"It's getting cold fast," the driver said. "Don't you think it's getting cold fast?"

"Hadn't thought about it really, love." Her gaze caught on the taxi firm's logo emblazoned there on the dashboard.

"Here, where do you lot at Jagdeep's get your sandwiches and that from?"

"What you mean?"

"You're not going to Denver's for your meals are you?"

"Well, yeah."

"You don't want to go on there. It was on the television. Filthy. They found bits of horse in everything. You want to go to that CC's in town. Her what runs it: magnificent. You ask for it and they'll do it for you. I happen to have a card for them, here."

By the time the taxi pulled up outside St Anthony's, Jhardine'd had the driver call in to base and she'd bartered over a daily lunch order for the entire firm. *Let Barry complain about that!*

"Cheers," she said, getting out the taxi.

"Er, yeah," the driver replied, looking like he'd been bum-rushed. Which, in a manner of speaking, he had.

"Hello, Jhardine," called the vicar from over by the foyer. "I didn't think we'd be seeing you this morning."

"No, well, it's a wonder you're seeing me at all, Vicar, to be honest. Dead to the world, I was."

"Is everything all right, Jhardine?" His concerned face again.

"I'm fine, yeah. Just these new tablets what I'm on. Playing havoc with my body clock, they are. Anyway, I know I'm late for morning prayers but would you mind if I bob in and have a quick ten minutes if no one's in there?"

"Of course not," the vicar smiled. "I have some free time so I'll join you."

"Oh, you don't have to do that, David," she said, and felt a kind of giddy thrill at using his name. It had just slipped out. "I don't want to take up your valuable time."

"Value for value, I think you're worth it." He held open the heavy door into the church. She slid by, their chests grazing. She felt like a teenager, reckless and patchy, a bit breathless, actually—but then solemn. This was a church after all. She bowed her head. "Hear not the words of my mouth, but the words of the heart," she prayed. "Let them guide the hand and release me from this mortal snare."

"What a lovely prayer, Jhardine," the vicar commented when she was through. He put a gentle hand on her back as he guided her up the aisle.

"Thank you. I learnt it years ago now, from the back of one of Eric's dad's books. He was a big reader, like Eric. Well, when Eric can be bothered."

"Is Eric a lot like Michael?"

The air went out of her lungs. The question was like pressing a thorn into her eye. "Yes," she said, putting down her grubby silver bag and doffing her coat. "Sometimes Eric'll do or say something and it will remind me."

"Through a glass, darkly."

"I wish it were darkly," she laughed, for the first time hearing how hollow that Bible quote could sound. "But Michael's always close. Always bright. I feel him. Feel him...." She looked around at the church walls. The pillars. The rafters. "Feel him near." She shook her head. *You old fool. He's gone. As good as dead.* "Can we, erm, start praying now, Vicar?"

"Yes, yes, of course we can. After you."

Jhardine knelt before the altar. After looking up at the empty cross a while, she closed her eyes and bowed her head. The creak of the vicar's knees, and then his shoulder nudged hers as he too crouched to pray. Before long, she felt the vicar swaying back and forth, the scratching of his shoulder on hers drawing her into that same motion. She heard David launch into a purr of prayer, and though Jhardine didn't really know the words she found herself mumbling along, repeating the sounds that she caught against the noise of her own breathing.

Sometimes, when they were alone together, Jhardine imagined what it would be like to touch the priest. Not sexually, of course not. Never! But just a touch. To his shoulder. To his cheek. *To his lips.*

"Jhardine?"

"What?" He was staring at her. *Oh God, how long have I been daydreaming?*

"I asked if you would like to receive Communion?"

"Oh, sorry, er, yes."

She'd had a quiet word about the wine, and David had promised to investigate. When he administered the Blood on this occasion it was in a different goblet: a chunky silver affair where the stem had been twisted into a thick rope, and the womb of the cup had a lovely, faded green about it. "I brought this from home," he commented when he saw her looking. "I think it was the metal of the other one that was making the wine taste awful."

Nope. From the first sip Jhardine could tell it still tasted like old dishwater. She coughed, her lips pulling away from her teeth as though they wanted no part in what was transpiring. Yet, a strange thing happened: Jhardine found herself taking yet another sip. Then the clench of an overwhelming thirst took her. She gripped the goblet tight to keep the vicar from taking it away and, before she knew it, had guzzled the lot.

"I am so sorry," she said, wiping her face. There were spatters of wine on the blue carpet around her knees. "It must be the pills."

"Please, think nothing of it. Oh, you've got a little...." He reached down and pressed the pad of his forefinger to the underside of her chin. When he lifted that hand, a carnelian drop clung to his finger end. This did something to Jhardine's internals, like that time when she'd leaned over the juddering washer to try to steady it and felt a particular kind of a revelation.

I have to stop reading that mucky book.

THANK GOD FOR Tania. The lavender-coloured floor was spotless and the smell of the good, simple food CC's had earned a reputation for already wafted strong in the air. It was a grand way to come through the door and start your working morning.

Jhardine did a quick check on which of their regulars were in. At table one sat next-door neighbour Jim, who gave a nod of acknowledgement and a report-this-to-the-wife smile; the lollipop lady from Coleridge Primary, Maude something-or-other, over at table four was chomping like a hamster through a wedge of cheese on toast; and the scarf-loving Niall sat at table eight in the corner by the window.

"Morning, Jhardine," Tania called from behind the counter, her unruly slug of a brow riding high as she smiled.

"Morning."

Though Tania had swarthy flesh and gorgeous sable eyes, she was short. Aggravatingly so. A tad overweight, too. But you could never say she was unattractive. She radiated beauty like a carnivorous plant.

"Y'all right, love?" Tania asked as Jhardine pulled back the squeaky-hinged leaf in the counter and walked through.

"Aye, not bad."

"How's Eric?"

"He's...." Jhardine broke off. Approaching the counter was Lance, the local tattoo artist. He had no idea he was handsome but, with his two foot of jasmine hair and a firm square jaw, he belonged to the Beautiful People, even if he did have all those blasphemous tattoos. And, she had to admit, maybe because of them, too.

"And you get something for yourself too," he told Tania as he placed his order, and she giggled through an octave. It was well known that the two wanted to jump each other, but Tania was a girl who liked to take things slow. Glacial, in fact.

"Oh I'm sorry, Lance," Tania grimaced as she opened the till and found it lacking. "We don't have change for a twenty. I can nip to the Post Office if you don't mind waiting?"

"Don't worry about it," Lance said, his thick moustache accentuating his flirty smile. "Number of times you've treated me to free buns on Fridays." Tania went a lovely shade of rosé. Lance, seemingly in full knowledge of the romantic havoc he had reeked, picked up his apple turnover and coffee and went to sit down at the table near the door across from Niall.

"When are you next off out?" Jhardine asked Tania.

"Two weeks on Friday when I get paid." Then, conspiratorial like: "It might be *the* night."

"Really?" *Thank the Lord!* "Aw, I'm dead chuffed for you. Right, I'll make sure there's something extra special on that wage-slip for you, love, and you do whatever it is you have to do to get Lance's tight pants off."

"Jhardine!"

"Well, would you look at those thighs." And they both did. For quite a while. Tania produced a bag of cheese and chive crisps from her pocket and started munching. The looking went on a while longer.

"Was heaving earlier, Jhardine."

"His thighs?"

"No, the café."

"Was it?"

"Aye," she answered in her slow and even voice. "I was glad Ruth showed up a bit early or I wouldn't have had enough hands."

"Well, I'm glad you did handle it. That'll be something to shove in Barry's face. Speaking of, he not in?"

"No, he's at the scrappers." Tania rolled her eyes, the azure and turquoise bangles on her arms clinking as she again dipped into her bag of crisps.

"Better them than us. Right, I'm going to go help Ruth in the kitchen for a bit, get ahead on our dinner orders. I'll come out when it starts to pick up. That okay?"

"Sounds like a plan, Jhardine."

She left Tania taking an order for a pizza surprise—the surprise was that it was margherita—and walked through the narrow corridor, turning left into the kitchen. Ruth stood at the stove frying tomatoes. On her exposed right shoulder she had a HRT patch, a nicotine patch and a plaster to cover a bruise. Or maybe she'd taken up injecting heroin just to take the edge off. Still, three patches usually meant a good day.

"Hello, love, you all right?"

"Aye, not too bad, Jhardine," Ruth said, checking her white sheaf of hair was still lacquered into place.

"You need anything chopped?" Jhardine asked as she set about washing her hands.

"Would you do me some onions, love? Plays havoc with my arthritis, chopping."

Jhardine donned her apron and dove into work. Conversation ambled in and out.

"You watch that programme last night, Jhardine?"

Well, give us a chance, Ruth! "Which one?"

"That one about being a doodad?"

Again, a bit of a wide field, love.

"Gay?"

"No."

"Transgender?"

"No, nowt to do with that."

"Vegetarian."

"Oh hell, no. What's the word."

"Well, you've lost me, Ruth, you really—"

"German," Ruth tutted at herself. "It was about being a German. Very eye-opening. We could do with a bit of that discipline round here."

"Could we?"

"Oh, aye. That'd sort a lot of stuff out. Oh, and then there was that lovely lesbian doing the gymnastics commentary. I could listen to her for hours. And then, there was a programme on about competitive dog grooming. The things people will shave into their dog's coats. A naked woman, Jhardine. Boobs, the lot. And on a beagle. Though, to be fair, it did take some skill."

"I bet it did."

Orders stopped up their chat for a while, but once the dinner rush had eased they found time to grab a quick tea-break.

"Being honest," Jhardine said, julienning a batch of potatoes for crispy fries. "I'm just glad this job is getting Eric out of the house and making him have to talk to other people."

"Don't he have any other friends?" Ruth popped a mushroom stalk into her mouth as she sponge-cleaned another batch of crimini.

"Not really. Well, it's not like how it was when I was a girl. They all talk on the bloody computer and on their phones. I have to say, I'm not averse to a bit of instant messaging myself, but the other day he pinged my phone to put him the kettle on, and he was only bloody upstairs!" she said, using a paper towel to take off the extra wet from the potatoes. "He doesn't go out and see anyone, so Lord only knows where he's going at nights."

"Happen he's finally got a boyfriend."

"Oh, no, our Eric's hopeless. Unless some bloke falls on him pantless and lubed-up, I doubt it's ever going to happen."

The serving hatch swung open and Tania poked her head through.

"Eric's here."

"What? Already?" Jhardine checked her watch. Half-two. Later than she'd thought but not nearly late enough for him to have done a full day's work. "Oh, I hope he hasn't been fired."

"No, I haven't," she heard him grumble. Heaven only knew where he got such good hearing from.

Jhardine walked out into the café, then stopped. Jesus, it was hot. She mopped her brow with her apron. Happen Ruth's menopause was catching? She forgot about the temperature when she saw Eric sat at the counter wearing a fluorescent pink high-visibility vest. *Mock later, get gossip now.*

"All right?" she said, trying to keep a straight face.

Eric played with the salt and pepper shakers on the counter. "I suppose."

"You go on your break, Tania," Jhardine said, picking up a dishcloth and giving the counter a wipe. When Tania was out of earshot she turned her attention back to Eric. "You suppose? Why do you suppose?"

"I wasn't actually doing anything. I just had to read from this book about health and safety. Apparently, before I go out with them I have to pass some kind of test."

"And that took all morning? I knew you were slow, Eric, but—"

"No, it did not take all morning. It took about half an hour but I think they expected it to be a full day's work. Reckon they think I'm simple or sommat."

"You? No!" Jhardine feigned shock.

Eric glared. "After that they had me making cups of tea for everyone. At least when I was on my trial I was doing paperwork. And at one point I thought the boss had stopped breathing. He falls asleep sometimes, and.... But, luckily, Grant was there. Told me you just have to mention a bacon sandwich and—"

"Here, where do they get their sandwiches from?"

"Mum!"

"Sorry, sorry." Jhardine dove into her pocket. "I'll just give you a few cards to leave lying around and we'll say no more about it."

"Me being there was a waste of time," Eric whined, ignoring the cards. She'd put them in his work trousers when he got changed tonight. *A mother has her ways.* "A complete waste."

Well, this was good, Jhardine soothed herself. Eric was moaning. A return to normal then. "You're being paid, aren't you?"

"Yeah, but I've not got a contract yet."

"Money's money. And you're bright and hard-working. They're not going to want to let you go." He shrugged as though to imply they might just be *that* stupid. "When are you next on, then?" she said, working the dishcloth harder.

"They said I'm doing Thursday and Friday. But just mornings until they figure out what my 'role' is. I don't know when I'm going out on collection yet. I asked to do some more filing and that, which is productive at least. I dunno though, they might just have me being Peter's nursemaid."

He took out a pen from his jeans and started scribbling on a napkin. Drawing again. Another good sign. "Well, give it a chance. It might end up being a really good job." Eric kept his quiet. "And no one's saying you have to stay there forever," she consoled. "You can always look around a few months down the line once you've got some money in the bank. Oh and, look at it this way, at least you won't have to go down to the Jobcentre anymore, will you?"

A begrudging flicker at the corners of his mouth. "I suppose not."

Ruth, a bandanna of sweat decorating her brow, popped her head through the orders hatch and chimed, "Crisis, Jhardine. We've run out of baps."

Crisis indeed.

"Oh, cripes. Here, Eric, go down to the bakery and get Dominic to give us, oh how many? Three dozen baps? No, four. We can always freeze what we don't use and have them for toast or something."

"Jeez, what did your last slave die of?"

"Being beaten to death for their cheek, now on with you." She pushed a handful of banknotes into Eric's hand and hurried him out the door.

"Did we not get our full delivery of bread this morning, Tania?"

"Well, to tell you the truth, Jhardine, I was eating a cheese pasty at the time so I had my hands a bit full."

"Happen Barry's trying to ration us," she wondered aloud. "I'll have to get on the phone and sort this out." As she put her mobile to her ear, her legs went slack. She fell against the counter but managed to stay upright.

"You all right?" Ruth asked, spying her from inside the kitchen.

"Cramp," Jhardine lied, swallowing down a few sharp breaths. She straightened up through sheer force of will. Then, phone to her ear, head high, she summoned a smile.

ERIC LACED TIM'S spare key in the lock. *Come on, you knob, just do it!*

The turning was the thing though. Since Tim's death it had frozen him. He'd come here night after night, trying to enter this rude museum, but he couldn't manage it. Now though, with that rotten day of mind-numbing work behind him, he'd thought it might just be possible, if only for the want of something exciting to do. The landlord had even called that day and said to come and clear the flat out or the lot would go. Extra incentive. So Eric twisted the key in the lock. Twisted. Twisted. When the click came it sounded like a shotgun blast. It felt like he'd been hit in the chest. Summoning his courage he pushed open Tim's front door anyway—only for it to jam.

"What the hell?" Eric pushed the door. It didn't budge. Then he put his weight against it and it gave a few inches. He looked down to see the corner of a white envelope peeking out. He shoved at the door again, then again. "Come on, you bugger."

Eric found room enough to squeeze through the gap and into the hall. An impressive pile of letters had united to form a blockade behind the door and spilling on down the hall. *Crap,* Eric thought. *I forgot about telling people.* He took out a carrier bag from his pocket and set about gathering the letters up. *Bill, bill, final demand. Final demand. Final.* The bold print and red flare of warning notices stung his eyes. Every letter he added to the bag served to inflate the ache he felt.

Eric decided he should take the carrier bag down to this car. Didn't want to forget it, did he? Besides, he was gagging for a drink.

The petrol station at the bottom of the road provided him with a bottle of overpriced water and the resolve to never shop there again. He sipped the bottle dry and paced up and down the street outside Tim's block of flats, listening to the car radio of a man out polishing his dick-extension of a sports vehicle.

"Isn't she a beauty?" the man asked, flashing a gold tooth.

"A bird's shat all the way down this side," Eric informed him. The man looked like he might cry.

Looking up at the flat, Eric put the voice out of his mind. No more stalling. No more pissing about. It was time.

There in Tim's hallway, warmed by the light that filtered down through the orange curtains in the kitchen, Eric let the silence fill him. He strained to hear Tim's laughter, to summon up the sound that had always been quick and full in this place.

A shadow flicked over the kitchen floor. Then again.

"Hello?" Eric called. No reply.

Again, the clot of a shadow.

Eric, one foot slow to put itself in front of the other, inched down the carpeted hallway into the kitchen. The room was empty, of course, and hurtfully still. He let his back rest on the doorjamb as, bright in his head, there came the memory of Friday nights when he and Tim had sat at the cheap pine table in the middle of the room laughing and picking their way through Tim's bad cooking or a half-warm takeaway.

"What do you think of her?" he would ask, showing Eric a picture of a woman, usually scantily clad.

Eric would laugh.

The fridge in the corner gave a gurgle. Eric remembered watching Tim wrestle the thing up two flights of stairs, plugging it in and it doing nothing but give off a strange moo. And when they'd lain together on the kitchen floor that summer day to enjoy the cool tiles against their bare skin. Their eyes had met. Words dropped away. Tim's barrel of a chest rose. Eric reached out a hand and grazed Tim's forearm, and Tim's flesh goose-pimpled. His eyes clouded. His lips turned full and dusky. Then someone knocked on the door and the moment had never elaborated on itself.

You abandoned me. It was that voice again. *You weren't there when I needed you.* It had been happening ever since the funeral, that creeping, awful hiss in his ear. But it wasn't real. It was just a figment. An errant sense of guilt.

Eric turned his back on the kitchen, his forehead hunched almost as much as his shoulders. With a hand that was half a fist, he pushed open the living room door. The room was as untidy as it had ever been. The overstuffed aubergine sofa on which Eric and Tim had lazed Saturday after Saturday, enjoying films and playing computer games, it sat as it always had. The pictures of them and some of Tim's rugby mates, back before Eric got better when they had all visited Eric at the hospital and Tim convinced them to do a much-needed striptease for the good of Eric's health, they still sat framed on the cheese-block of a coffee table. And the mottled mint-green rug on which Tim was prone to spilling tea, present and correct. But something was wrong. The television they'd watched, the games console on which they'd played, and even the much coveted collection of films—all were gone.

Vigour biting up his legs, Eric made his way back into the kitchen. Lost in his reverie he'd overlooked the finer details before, but now he noticed the microwave was missing, as was the digital radio that had always sat on top of the fridge.

The flat felt like a bad copy of the one he'd known when Tim was alive. A sense of violation prickled his skin. Down the hall and into the bathroom: the medicine cabinet hung open. Its lower shelf had been cleared but not the upper ones where Tim's dental floss and spare bars of soap still sat. What had been on that bottom shelf? Tim's electric razor, maybe? He couldn't remember but a grimy electrical socket made it a likely candidate. If so, the shaver was nowhere to be seen. Everything else seemed accounted for, though. Then again, there wasn't much that could be subtracted from the bathroom to begin with. He turned. A glint in the corner of the room by the door drew his eye. Just to the side of the small, round bin was a glass vial the length of Eric's thumb. It was empty or, as holding it up to the light revealed, almost. A few flakes of a black powder sat at the bottom. Eric unscrewed the top off the little bottle and took a sniff. A faint chemical smell rushed to meet him, and then something else. Something almost familiar. Before he could mull it though, an aura of colours flashed through Eric's field of vision and he yelped.

A migraine. Terrific.

Eric opened the small metal bin. It had been emptied, but the same scent preserved by the bottle was detectable there too. Metal. Heat. And *blood.* Eric reeled back, only now aware of the anxiety in his gut. He backed out of the bathroom, now seeing what he had missed before. The white tiles were too clinical, too contrived. It was like the place had been scrubbed within an inch of its molecular life.

Eric lingered in the hallway, trying to quieten his growing sense of unease. There was just one more room to try, and that was Tim's bedroom. He rushed at it before he could lose heart. The door sighed as it opened, rubbing against the plush green carpet.

The geriatric television on Tim's chest of drawers by the far wall was still there, his snaking phone charger still plugged into the nearby socket. Even Tim's bed, unmade and with one pillow teetering on the edge of the mattress, seemed as it always had. But this room was a bad copy as well. Only a vague outline remained in the chest of drawers' accumulation of dust where Tim's laptop used to rest. He only noticed that in passing, though, as he made a beeline for the pine side-table that they'd salvaged from a skip down the road a few months ago. He searched the top drawer for what he hoped would be there. A can of deodorant, condoms, an old fitness magazine, but not the gold chain Eric had bought for Tim's twenty-second birthday last year. The police had specifically said that the body was found with no jewellery or personal effects, so Eric had hoped that it would be here. His last gift. A keepsake.

You left me.

Eric sat down on Tim's squeaking bed. The police had been to Tim's flat. He knew that. He could understand the laptop being gone as they'd probably want to check it for any clues. But why, though, take his TV? His films? And the microwave? It didn't make any sense. It couldn't be the landlord either as he'd wanted the place cleared and would have pulled everything out rather than being selective, surely?

Eric suddenly felt so tired—and sad. It felt like the emptiness in the flat was crushing him. He nestled down in the rise of the untidy quilt, hugging a pillow. No trace of Tim's scent remained, only a vague musk that was not his living spice at all. The stillness in the flat grew. The grief in Eric clawed. He'd wanted some closure, but this wasn't even close. This was....

He coughed. He coughed again. A fierce, hot pain encircled Eric's neck. He couldn't breathe. The pulsing of the black growth in his chest became a hammering, the feeling stronger than he'd ever known it, and colours strobed through his left eye's vision. It created an autumn storm of hues that glowed to neon brilliance. When the rush cleared, he wasn't looking at Tim's bedroom at all.

"WELL, I'VE TOLD you, I'm going," she said as she walked down the stairs into the subway, careful not to get her apple-green trainers dirty. She was having a shit day, adding to a shit year. But soon it would change.

"Grace, Grace, I'm going to have to call you back. I'm going through the subway and, Grace! I'm calling you back! The reception's shit. Yeah, yeah, ten minutes. But you won't change my mind. All Right, bye."

Call ended, the light of her phone dimmed until it went out and she was left with only the jaundice of the subway's lights to guide her. Pulling a few strands of her deep red hair from her lips, she looked down the tunnel's length. Walking down here always gave her a strange feeling in her stomach, like she was expecting something bad to happen, and tonight was no different. But it was quick, and a quick getaway was exactly what she needed.

Splash.

She stopped, turned. The dripping from the subway's ceiling made the pools of water at her feet dance and ripple. Was it getting that bad that she was hallucinating now? Mind you, with the things she'd seen who could blame her? She pulled her coat tighter and tottered on.

Come next Tuesday she'd have enough money and then she could get away. She could leave this place behind, and all the things *he'd* been making her do. She should never have got involved with it. She should never have started selling it.

"Fucking Mineral," she spat.

Splash.

She turned. A footstep. That sounded like a footstep. There was no one in the tunnel though. But there was something. A certain...mist. Her gaze ticked down. The pools of water, they were trembling. Not trembling. *Boiling.* And now they were turning black.

"You left me," a voice over her shoulder said in a cold rumble. She turned. Needle teeth like shining mercury. "You left me."

Most people would have screamed, but Sally Lazarus wasn't most people. "I don't want any trouble. Just let me go, and I won't tell anyone about it. I won't."

"You abandoned me when I needed you." Its eyes stared down at her, white arrowhead tips in black. Its body was so large, so thick, that she couldn't hope to get by. It reached out a hand. Those fingers were thin and serrated, like saw blades. "Get away from me or so help me!" she roared, and it rang with truth. She could do it. She *had* done it before. But then the creature's giant hands wrapped her arms, and its strength was so absolute that she couldn't even breathe. She was going to struggle, but then she saw something in the monster that made her go slack. "I know you," she said, looking straight into its eyes. It wasn't just any monster. It was someone she had helped to kill. "I'm so sorry," Sally Lazarus said, bowing her head. And that was when she decided it was time to die. "Just do it."

ERIC HIT THE floor hard, tangling in the bed quilt. He fought to get to his feet as his shadow ran across the walls, round and around as though it were marking the Earth's rotation. There, in the dizzying noise of the moment, he had a choice to make. Did he go to her, that woman he saw in the subway, or did he stay and write off what he'd seen as just some delusion caused by stress? He'd not seen her die. There was a chance. Still a chance. But this was mad. Absolutely insane. It couldn't be real. Yet there he was, bouncing off the door frame and ricocheting into the hall. *I don't care if she's not there. I want to be wrong. I want her to be a figment. I want her to be alive. Please, just let me be crazy!*

He crashed out of the flat, slamming the door as he went, and pelted down the stairwell, leaping stairs four at a time and barely keeping his balance. He shook as he tried to get his car key in the door's lock, then in and seatbelt on, and too much time had already passed. He turned the key. Nothing. He turned it again. Twice more his car refused to start.

"Please, please, you bastard! Please!"

A wave of shadow, no clue as to who had cast it, and the car chuntered. "Yes." He slapped the wheel. "Do it. Do it." The symphony of a working motor broke over him. He yanked his way through the gears and, ignoring the squeal of protest the car gave, he pulled out. The man who was still washing his car barely had time to shut the car door as Eric hurtled down the road. He skidded to take the corner and almost lost control. He mounted the pavement, pulled on the steering-wheel hard and managed a U-turn.

Eric drove as fast as he dared, speeding toward one set of traffic lights and narrowly making it through on amber. He ran another set, not caring it was on red.

Life doesn't work like this. I can't have seen those things. It's fucking impossible.

By the time he reached Hainsworth Estate the sun had burned through the horizon, the remaining light in the sky like dilute orange in a dirty glass. He abandoned the car outside his house with the engine still running, and staggered down the street. One by one the streetlights above licked into life, near to far, lighting a trail to the subway. The buzz of the streetlights and the complaint of his car's engine were all that broke the lassitude.

It's too quiet.

He walked toward the maw of the tunnel, the cold of the subway reaching out to chill him the closer he came. The lights were dim in the subway, still on but somehow muted. Eric took a tentative step down the stairs, his back close to the damp wall as he tried to descend unseen. His foot fell impossibly loud. The next step. The next. *Hush, hush, hush.* Another step. Another. He could see something on the ground now. Legs. Eight steps down and Eric had his answer.

The lights at the Summerfield end of the subway were all out. This served to spotlight the woman. She was lying face down on the floor, her denim jacket torn, her arms splayed. Like a doll, he thought. One a child had thrown away.

As he walked closer it seemed like the floor cantered down toward the body, and he felt as though he might slip and be dragged into her stillness, like her death had an inescapable pull. And he knew she was dead. It was all over her. It had a taste, and it was awful sweet. Then a sound.

Eric's chest tightened. His head reeled. A blast of cold and the dead girl reached out and grabbed Eric's leg. He shrieked, kicking out at her as he lurched away. The corpse writhed with laughter until, as though her ankles were on an impossible hinge, she swung to standing.

"Hello," she waved and then hit him in the chest with the flat of her hand, knocking him off his feet and sending him rolling over the ground. "Your friend really did a number on this body," she said, and with a crack she corrected the wrong angle of her head and neck. She must have heard him whimper because she chuckled. "Oh, don't be frightened, Eric. Not yet, anyway. The fun's only just starting."

"H-h-how do you know my name?"

"I'm connected. I have friends in low places. I listen to the dark. Do you?" she said, but he barely heard her over the sound of an animal growling, and it sounded close. "I reckon you do. I reckon you hear the shadows whisper—"

You left me.

"W-what are you talking about? I...." Eric shook his head. "You died."

"She died. Your friend Tim took care of that."

"Tim?" The black growth in Eric's chest lurched.

"Whose eyes did you think you were looking through, eh? Yes, Tim. He's an umbra now, like me. You see, this girl's body? Just dressing-up clothes. But he freed me. I mean, he broke me. But free, none the less. And look at me," she smiled, striking a pose. The growling grew louder.

"Tim's dead. You're dead. I saw you—"

Sally laughed, slapping her thighs. "You don't know any of it, do you? What's to come?" Her smile faded. Then she began crying. "No, please don't. I don't want to hurt anyone. Not again. Please! He's just a boy! Don't make me—" The growling became a bark that ratcheted out of her throat. Then she straightened, running fingers through her bloody hair. "The brain's still firing. Still synapses of her left. She doesn't want you harmed, Eric. Isn't that sweet?" She glanced at her trainers. They were covered in thick, black blood. "Oh, no, these were her sister's. I suppose I'll have to eat her now and spare her the sadness."

"*Tim,*" Eric whined. He still couldn't see properly, and in his mouth there was the sharp tang of blood—and the pain in his head! It was so much. Which made sense, really, because he was mad. Off his face, off the rocker, gone doolally, *insane*. "You said about Tim!" he shouted, desperate. "I saw you through him. What does that mean?"

"It really wouldn't be to my advantage to tell you, Eric," she cooed. "Don't you think the better question is, where is he now?"

"What?"

"Tim. Your Timothy. The thing he's become."

"W-w-where is he, then?"

She chuckled. "I don't know...I was a bit dead at the time. And, I think you know, he's a bit of a ditch-'em sort, isn't he?"

You abandoned me. The voice came again, so quickly and so loud in his ear that it made Eric flinch.

"But maybe we can make him show himself. Umbras like blood, Eric." She threw her arm in his direction—only for it hit something solid. It was a naked man, wider than two average people stood shoulder to shoulder. His skin was a strange slick of grey, green and blue. And it smelled. It smelled of mould and rot. Then it turned and Eric saw it wasn't just a man. It was Tim, but its face was mottled and wrong and its eyes were black with crosses of white. Its teeth were needles, long and silver. But it *was* Tim. And then it wasn't. Just black smoke sinking into the ground.

Sally laughed. "I see." She crouched in front of him. "There's a war coming, Eric. And you're at the heart of it." He backed up against the subway wall, trying to put as much distance between them as he could. "But I want you to know something. Something that's very important. You're not special. You're not chosen. None of us are. Sally thought she was until she realised the truth: she was cursed. And so are you. You were both just in the wrong place at the wrong time." She straightened. "Now, I'm not allowed to kill you or *he* will be angry with me. Still, we can have a little fun, can't we? And sometimes accidents happen, right? Here's hoping. Now, would you like to see a trick?"

Eric's head rolled. The waters in the puddles around them were black and boiling, and the fumes were making it hard to concentrate.

She slapped him. "Eric! Do you want to see a trick?"

"Go on then," he said, his voice a croak, so disoriented now that the strangeness of the question didn't even register.

"That's a good sport," Sally said. And then she turned on her heel and screamed.

Something began to poke through the woman's tangle of wet hair. At first it seemed like a blunt, black wedge, but as the thing widened, lengthened and cleaved open, Eric realised it was a wet snout and a set of salivating jaws. The jaws snapped and clacked, revealing rows of shark-like teeth. Bones crunched, blood sprayed, then chasing the snout through that tight membrane came a head that, with sudden sharp hate, bore poached eyes set too far apart and yet still monstrously human. Two long, jagged ears that curved up to gilded points sprang free next, then shoulder joints heaved from the unnatural quim, stretching it wide. A taut and glistening body of dark hair followed behind, and the creature's now uneven weight—unbalanced between woman and beast—brought it to the floor, snapping and yowling as its front legs unfolded and scratched at the ground. The beast glowered at Eric as, last to breach, there came its back legs and a long, pointed tail. It looked at him with a hate he could almost taste and then, for no reason he could discern, the hound demurred, bringing its colossal head down toward the ground to let Eric see its little secret. Embedded along its back were all the features of the woman called Sally, her peaceful face and peach skin perfectly set, her eyes closed and her lips curled in joy. Even her arms were folded over her chest, as though arranged for her final sleep.

"Sally would like to have a little fun with you Eric," came a scorching voice.

The hound sprang back to its feet and roared.

"No," Eric yelled. "No. Help!"

The growth in his chest pulsed and his legs found their muscles again. Fear propelled him falling and scuttling on all fours across the slick ground, then up the cold stairs. He reached the sixth step up when—a tall figure loomed above him. Human, a long coat billowing in the wind, and hair that seemed to glow under the moonlight.

"Behind you," came the man's lilting voice, but too late.

A colossal paw ripped through Eric's back, pulverising his spine and tearing his organs. The momentum of the strike sent Eric crashing against the subway wall, rebounding to fall as a limp heap over the bottom two stairs.

Eric felt no pain. In fact, he couldn't feel anything at all except for the beating of the growth in his chest and the awful despair he felt watching the hound pace at the bottom of the stairs. Movement in the corner of his vision drew him. Thick canvas boots descended the stairs, unhurried by Eric's injuries and unfazed by the monster.

As the man in the long coat drew closer, the huge canine bellowed in a voice that was a mix of human and animal rage. "Not you! You weren't supposed to be here."

"I got done early, so I did." The man popped something into his mouth, and then he turned his legs out so that his posture tightened. "Let's be having you then."

The beast struck forward and the man spun a kick that met the hound square in the jaw, sending it crashing into the wall. The force of its impact cracked the tiles and loosened some of the deeper stone. The hound shook as it picked itself up, its jaw lolling and maybe broken. It roared so loud it rattled even Eric's dull ears, and then it charged.

But the man didn't move. The beast neared, its jaws wide, victory in its eyes, and still he remained still. Then, in a movement too quick for Eric to see properly, the man threw out his hand and clamped it over the creature's muzzle, flipped up onto its back and, carrying through with that momentum, slammed the beast down into the ground. Eric measured a slowing heartbeat of stillness, then a flash like the pop of a light bulb. Apparently satisfied, the man relinquished his hold and jumped away.

The beast stumbled up, shook its head and pawed at its muzzle. An earthshaking roar, and the monster broke into a run for the stairs out of the subway. The man was smiling though. "Won't help you now," he called. And he was right. The beast was two steps from the top when a violet light throbbed and the hound exploded into fine motes of tissue, making a bloody hail to waft through the air. When the storm cleared, Eric saw the girl named Sally lying where the hound had stood. On her oddly unmarked skin there was no hint of the violence that had ended her. A little fall of red rain dappling the stone around her was the only clue.

The man wasted no time though and walked up the stairs to the body. He touched his fingers to the corpse's lips, producing a brief tangle of violet light. "Happen the night wasn't a complete loss, then."

A wretched howl of pain escaped Eric. The man looked down at him. He had violet eyes, and after a moment of taking in Eric's face, they seemed to glow. No sympathy. No move to help. Just: "I remember you."

A sudden fanfare of thought cut through Eric's agony, and the beating growth in his chest quickened even more.

STEVEN B. WILLIAMS

I remember too.

CHAPTER SIX
THE LONG STRETCH OF SHADOW

HOURS WENT GLOAMING into nothing, and still Eric was alone.

His entire body ached, like it was protesting a lack of juice, and the coughing fits came with unnerving frequency. He was rattling toward what would be a sudden stop and then, too late, he realised what was left of his eyesight had begun to dim.

"M...."

How many minutes hurtled by he couldn't say. Everything was gone, including Eric. And then a sound stirred him from this cauldron of nothingness. Someone was in the room with him. Tim and his mum had come back at last, he thought, and in thinking he realised that he was still alive. For now. Yes, *now*. So, with his last spark of strength Eric set fire to his body and pried open his eyes to give to his mum and his best friend his very last moments of waking life, the final gift in the world that he had to offer.

"Mum?"

Even to Eric's stupefied eyes, though, it took only a glance through the sudden dark in the room to know that the person standing by the door wasn't his mother. It wasn't Tim. In fact, no one Eric knew had scorching eyes like those.

"Well, aren't you a rare little bird?" the man said, his voice thick like Bonfire Night treacle that had waited all year to be poured. "I ain't heard anything like you for a long, long while."

The stranger crossed the room, bringing with him the wild smell of rose water and lavender. He took hold of Eric's hand with cool but gentle fingers.

"Eric Mayfair, aye?" The stranger folded his lips into his mouth as though shy of their delicate amaranth. "Looks like you're about to fall off the wheel, so to speak. The long goodbye almost through." He let go of Eric's hand. "You lucky sod. Would that I could." The man harrumphed into a chair next to Eric, peering up at him through his long fringe of spiderweb hair. "Why you on your own, aye, Little Bird? Seems like there should be folk with you?"

The first strains of a knelling. The unmistakable peace was starting to take root inside. Not long now.

"You know there's nothing, right? It's just gone. You're just gone. All this *living*," said like a dirty word, "for nothing."

Eric couldn't help the whimper that escaped his lips, the tear that rolled from his eye.

This caught the man's attention.

"Hey, hey, I, er, I'm fair sorry, so I am," he said, leaning forward and washing a big hand over his pale face. "Look at you. You're so young. What life could you have had, eh? What little life at all?" He got to his feet and began pacing the room. "It's not fair. Why do I get to live while she," he turned, looking down at Eric, "while *you*...die. Were it in my power, Little Bird, I'd trade places with you in a heartbeat. I'd—"

Eric felt it, then. The thud.

The stranger was at his side in an instant. A grip on Eric's hand, painful, anchoring. The man's eyes were now searing pokers. "What are you doing?" he growled. He locked his hands around Eric's face. "What *are* you?"

Thump.

The man lurched back, a hand at his chest. "What are you doing to me?" he cried.

Thump.

A soft light took up, washing over the man's hands. The violet tone gave a lovely taint to the air. Eric, though, was so tired he could barely even care anymore. He was drifting. Drifting.

Thump.

But as the seconds stretched Eric began to detect a certain tether. That sound, that heartbeat, it was somehow keeping him close, on the right side of life. He didn't know how, but that sound—that sound was doing it.

For his part, the stranger was still. He stared down at Eric, his eyes fixed on just one spot. Then he brought his hands, still with a gentle light meandering over them, to hover above the ugly scar on Eric's chest, tracing in the air the mark of a half-dozen operations. At last, the stranger dared to touch.

The lights above them flickered into life. An aberrant warmth radiated out from where the man's fingers grazed Eric's skin. Those fingers stiffened. The violet light pulsed. The stranger tried to pull his hand away, but a certain gravity seemed to have taken hold. He clenched his jaw and tried harder. Still, the pull. Then at last, with one almighty tug, the man staggered away.

Eric's breathing came quick and fast. It was like someone had warmed his blood into flowing again. His mind simmered. Yet, even as Eric felt it, he could also feel it ebbing.

"I'd never thought to try. I mean this heart is my prison. But could it...?" The man squinted at Eric from across the room, as though trying to read some small detail that was, it would seem, easy to miss. "Could it?"

Still seeming leery of his disloyal hand, the man crossed the room once more and, after hesitating just a few seconds longer, let his fingers creep over Eric's chest. The lights in the room came on again. The windows rattled as though slammed with rain. That pulse of violet began to build. What was smoke threatened to become a fire until, with an almighty effort, the man took back his hand. He gave a giddy, high laugh. The laughter escalated as he moved around the room, leaving comet trails of light in his wake. "I knew there had to be more. That there had to be something. And this is it. This is me!"

It hardly mattered though. To Eric the world was starting to white out, like snowflakes falling into his eyes and freezing there. The diversion had been nice, a pleasant, sensual jaunt, but now it was all ending. Farewell, life. So long.

"I'll wager that this is going to hurt, Little Bird," said the man who was now standing over Eric once more. "But you'll be glad it did, I guarantee."

The man stabbed his fingers at the scar on Eric's chest, applying a vicious pressure. Eric screamed. His sternum began to creak as the man pushed through skin and what little muscle Eric had left; flares of violet fire burned up and down the man's arm and poured into the bore hole in Eric's chest, the overflow spilling out in cool liquid eddies. Blood gushed, tissue ripped, the night was thunder.

Eric gasped and choked on the pain. He gripped the man's arm and drew him closer until the two of them were looking one another square in the eye. Eric tried to plead with him to make it stop but all that would rush from his lips was dry air.

"Don't worry, Little Bird," the man said through a cluster of sweat, his large chin squaring up for the fight. "This will work. It will."

Eric felt the man's fingertip inch deeper, oh deeper still, until it grazed the useless meat that was Eric's heart. Eric's back arched. His body thronged. Shadows exploded across the walls and the night became a monochrome of violet light and black. The fire in the man's eyes flickered like candle shine as he rocked back and forth above Eric; the shadows in the room began to move, to strobe, running together to form a vortex; the machines around Eric all sparked to a clamour; the windows rattled; the light bulbs in their fittings above glowed to saturation until a blinding flash and then, one after the other, they burst in a series of cold pops!

The current cut out and Eric fell back on the bed, wet and barely conscious. The hand that had penetrated him was gone, leaving an unkind slop in its wake. Eric floated in the aftershock as minutes became sets, and then a voice from somewhere in the room rasped, "It's been a privilege and an honour, Little Bird. You don't know," the man gave a hacking cough, "how you've changed my life."

The door to Eric's room opened a crack, then closed. Eric was alone again, and the room was still, and all was quiet except for one little noise. It took Eric almost an hour to realise that his dying had yet to arrive, and then yet more time to fathom the odd feeling in his chest.

The thud of a strong, working heart.

"WASTE NOT, WANT not," the man with the violet eyes said as, one by one, he snapped the fingers off the dead girl's hand. He wrapped those fleshy twigs in a rapidly clouding white handkerchief, and when he had a neat little red parcel he popped it into his coat.

"What are you doing?" Eric coughed as he put a hand to the wall to try to get leverage enough to stand. He slipped, skidding his forearm against the step. The tiles behind him were briny with blood. His blood. Rubbing at his forearm, he repeated, "Are you deaf? I said, what are you doing?"

The man turned his head. He stood, his barely-there eyebrows knitting like needles. "You're talking to me, aren't you?"

"Who else?" Eric used the climb of the stairs to help him get some equilibrium, not quite standing but close to vertical.

"That's a turn, so it is. That must mean...." The man was suddenly above Eric, his hands tearing open Eric's shirt. A bit forward, but then Eric did have a taste for the aggressive. "There it is," the man said of the black thing and its snaking wires that were embedded in Eric's chest.

It was Eric's turn for incredulity. "You see it?"

"Oh, yes. But it's something you shouldn't have. Something I should cut out of your chest right now."

"No, no. P-p-please, don't kill me, I don't—"

"I do not kill!" The man's eyes blazed with violet shine.

Eric, his lips careful and a hand up to show he meant no harm, said in the most calm tone he could muster while his shirt was flapping so *rudely*, "The wolf thing."

"Oh, the hound?" The man laughed. The tension on his face smoothed itself out into a pleasant grin. "Well, it'd been dead a good half hour before I got to it, so it had." His hand went to his left breast pocket. From it he took out four little black sweets and popped them into his mouth. "I was tracking her," he said around the mouthful. "And a dozen others. There's something wrong in this place. It's murder following them. Ha! Murder, do you get it?"

Eric stared back at him.

"Right, okay, maybe not funny. Sorry about the back, by the way. Weren't much I could do by that juncture. I fixed it and your shirt too though. Full service, me."

Eric wasn't really listening. He couldn't process much. He'd just seen monsters and there was a dead body lying not even five feet away. And now this man was talking. He was *talking*.

Eric cleared his throat. "Are you actually, properly real? I mean, not something in my head?"

"Of course I'm real. What kind of a thing is that to ask a man what just saved your life?" he barked, but he still looked a tad amused. "You remember the first time we met, do you?" The man peered at him from below his long fringe.

"In the hospital. But I forgot."

"You would have done. Folk aren't meant to remember people like us. Well, until you become people like us." He smiled. "Your heart. Your strange, broken little heart. I'd not heard a song like that in an age. Almost like it was calling to me." His face slumped into a grim set. "Now who trained you?"

Eric rubbed at his temples, all the while trying not to look at the dead body. Then he said, more to himself than the stranger in front of him, "Nothing makes sense anymore. The world's wrong. Everything's wrong."

"I said, who trained you?"

"What? Trained? I don't—"

"A shadow heart." The man pointed to the thing embedded in Eric's chest. "Which shadow former was it? Was it Waxling?"

"Who?"

"Or was it Ember?" The man rubbed his chin. "I wonder if she still likes those goggles I made her? Tangent. Sorry. You. Shadow heart. How?"

"You aren't making any sense. What's a shadow thing? What's a waxling?"

"I don't like people playing games with me, Little Bird." The man's violet eyes seemed brighter. Hotter. Small suns of an unnatural hue.

"I don't know what you're talking about."

"You don't just *get* a shadow heart. You are given one. So someone intends to induct you into the fold."

"This is, well, it's gibberish, isn't it? You're talking absolute rubbish."

"You're not working for the Sisters, they'd have told me. So you must be working for the Cult. Tell me and I'll go easy on you. Who was it?"

"I said I don't know!" Eric's shadow raced out, slamming into the man's feet and pushing him back five or six paces. The shadow disbanded just as quick as it had formed, and Eric felt the loss like air forced out of his lungs. He slumped, but the man was laughing.

His eyes were full of understanding now. "You were telling the truth weren't you?" The man gave Eric a roving look, like Eric had just whipped out something a man should lust over. "I've never heard of a heart that can bend actual shadow. Happen it's old, so old that's where the namesake comes from." He took to pacing, his silver hair swirling in a breeze Eric couldn't feel. "But who would give a kid a shadow heart like that and then run off?"

"I'm not a kid. I'm twenty-one."

"Blurgh. Nearly everyone's a kid to me." He held out a hand and pointed. "And where are you getting your shades from? That's a question. Important question, actually. I—" His foot splashed in a puddle. "Oh, warm. Warm. These puddles are warm." He crouched and dipped in a finger. He put the finger in his mouth and sucked. "Interesting." The man looked up at Eric, his gaze curling over Eric's own.

"You've," Eric interrupted. There was something wrong with how the man looked. His pristine face was no longer, well, pristine. "Sorry, You've got some, er, blood. I reckon you're bleeding."

The man's eyes, slow but unmistakable, they widened. A finger to test the damp on his thin top lip. It returned a thick coating of red. "Bugger." The man's legs folded and he fell forward onto his hands and knees.

Eric trumpeted a laugh. "Wait, after all you've just done, yeah, you can't stand the sight of your own blood? Are you kidding me?"

"No, no, no." The man clutched at his sides. Sharp breaths and a peculiar creaking filled the air.

"What's wrong with—"

"Ahhhh!" The man's arms shot out. Snap. His wrists bent the wrong way. Crunch. His elbows swung round. Thwack!

"Holy shit."

Rigidity went slack, and the man flopped onto his side.

"This is...this is...yeah. This is insane. This is bloody crazy. I can't—" *You abandoned me.* "Oh, not you too. Not you. I do not need you now!"

"Here, Little Bird. You done yet?"

"No, thanks, I think I've got a good month of freaking out in me yet. A year, even!"

"Well, that's dandy, so it is, but you need to listen. Do you live near here?"

"What?"

"Ahhh!" The man's legs jerked. His knees blew inward. His arms whipped around.

"Are you one of those monsters. Are you becoming a wolf like her?"

His jaw cracked out of place, then back in, and his fingers all twisted with terrible snapping sounds until, at last, all of him came to rest.

"No," he panted. "There's always a price to our powers. I healed you and now I have to pay. Tell me, Eric Mayfair: do you live near here?"

"What? Oh, yeah. Just up the road."

"Do you have a spare room?"

"No."

"A garage?"

"No. B-b-but I have a shed." To Eric's ears it sounded like the lamest response ever uttered by a member of the human species. The joy on the man's face said it was golden though.

"Smashing. Take me to it."

"What?"

"Take me to your bloody shed!"

That was easier said than done. Dragging the man up the gravestone like stairs was surprisingly difficult. "Mate, you're heavy for someone so thin."

"A lot of me is vertical," the man hacked. Eric had no clue what that was supposed to mean but he kept hauling anyway, all the while trying not to look at the dead girl on the steps. He did falter however when they reached the top of the stairs and a stout, ash-grey fox trotted up to them and down into the subway.

"Piper," the man nodded its way. The fox, of course, didn't acknowledge him. "Suit yourself." Then to his ankles he said, "Oh, will you bloody work!"

Clumps of the man's silver hair were falling out, and the scalp underneath looked like a rotting head of cauliflower. "What's happening to you?"

"Bad hair day, isn't it?" the man said with unconvincing lightness. "You need to hurry. I can't keep myself together much longer."

Weirdly, Eric felt good. He felt strong. So strong in fact that he hitched the man up into his arms. "Oh, hello," the man replied to this, a sharp laugh buckling from his slack mouth.

Eric walked with a careful grace toward his house. He'd just reached the garden gate when a shriek from down in the subway tore the air.

"Someone's found her," Eric said, looking back to the swell of the subway's mouth and the embankment above. Another sound, closer this time, and next-door-neighbour Sarah's front door swung open.

Oh, shit.

"I'm going to see now. Keep Chanterelle inside." She clacked a few paces down the garden path, the cigarette in her hand becoming a little lamp in the dark. Sarah turned, stopped. She was looking at Eric. He tried to find words, excuses, some kind of explanation as to why he had what seemed to be a rapidly decaying man in his arms. "I...." Another shout and the sound of someone crying tore the air. Sarah's gaze seemed to slide away from Eric then, like butter on a hot potato, and she turned back toward the subway.

"She can't see you. Can't hear you." The man in his arms wheezed. "The shed. Quick."

Eric took him at his word and stumbled down the cracked path, kicking open the gate, then around to his concrete back-garden. He propped the man against the wall while he fiddled to get the always unlocked padlock out of its latch.

"You holding on there, mate?" Eric asked. "Mate?"

The man spewed a thick stream of blood, further soiling his already fatally marred waistcoat.

"Fuck. I mean...fuck!" Eric backed away. "I should get you an ambulance. I—"

"Just open the door," the man said, spitting his mouth clean. "Now!"

Eric obliged and, with that same creaking sound Eric had heard in the subway, the man lurched into the clutter of the shed.

"Are you—"

The shed door wrenched itself from Eric's grasp and slammed shut. Dead silence then, until the banshee cry of an approaching ambulance worried the night.

Eric wasn't sure what he was supposed to do next. He felt like he'd crossed a bridge into a dark, strange land where people came back to life and men went to pieces in little wooden sheds.

This can't be real. It can't be.

Yet, at the same time, the beating of the black thing in his chest seemed intent on driving home the point: if it wasn't real, Eric would be dead.

THE RUMBLING OF the kettle jolted Eric awake. *Wait, why am I in the kitchen? And note to self: never sleep with your head on a windowsill again, Jesus.*

"The shed!" Eric accidentally banged his face against the window trying to get a look outside. "Oh, shit...." His insides knotted. The shed door stood open and his mum's backside was poking out from around the door. She stepped back from the dilapidated hut and slammed the door shut, then marched up to the house and thundered inside, passing Eric without even acknowledging him. Cupboard to the left of the cooker opened, she took out a cup and banged it down on the counter. The twang of the metal tea barrel came next, then a slur of water.

He felt torn between making sure his mum didn't chuck boiling water his way and watching for signs of life from the shed. Well, she wasn't acting like the man was dead. At least that was something.

"I know what you're going to say—"

"I come downstairs to find the door wide open and mud all over my carpet!"

Okay, I didn't know you were going to say that.

"Look! Muddy footprints all the way down the hall." Eric took a gander and indeed, the carpet had been sullied. "And I asked you, didn't I? Are you off out drinking? That's what I said. And you said no. You lied to me. And you drove home, didn't you? That's flipping not on, Eric."

"No, I only had one," Eric spluttered, trying to keep up with a lie he hadn't meant to tell. "I was still safe to drive."

"I'm going to ask you just once, Eric. Do I need to be worried? Tell me truthfully."

"No. I swear. I was tired when I got in and...."

"Yes? I'm waiting."

"There...." He didn't like to lie. It didn't mean he wasn't good at it. "There was an ambulance down at the bottom of the road, so I went back out to see if I could see anything. I honestly thought I'd closed the door. I'm sorry." That, at least, was true. *I went out to the car, and I turned it off. Then I used my keys to get in. I closed the door and locked it. I'm sure I did.* And he didn't have a clue how his shoes could have got that muddy. He'd been careful. "It won't happen again," he said.

"You're damn right it won't." She sipped her tea. "Ambulance, eh?"

"Yeah. There was a lot of people down there. I didn't see what went off though."

"Oh, I hope it's nothing bad." Jhardine shivered. "What is the world coming to? Violence. Animal mutilation. Sons ruining your flipping carpets."

"I'll get the, er, carpet shampoo thing out and clean it up later, all right?"

"Fine. It's not in the shed, I've just checked, so you'll have to go up in the attic," she coughed, taking out the frying pan from the wonky cupboard by the side of the cooker. "You want some fried bread before I go to church?"

"Aye, can do."

She peered into the bread-bin. Its crummy innards were a disappointment. "I don't believe this. Now I've got no sodding bread. Where the hell does it all keep going?" She looked over at him. "Eric?"

"Don't ask me, I've not been in."

"No, I mean, will you go to the shop for me?"

"I'm sorting the carpet out, remember?"

Pouting, she closed the bread-bin door. "All right then. If you can hold on for your breakfast, I'll nip off to the supermarket now and do a quick shop."

"Won't you need me to drive?"

"No, Sarah said she was off down when I saw her yesterday. I'll get a lift in the taxi with her."

Eric totted it up in his head. When his mum went shopping it was usually, time to gossip factored in, about an hour and half round trip.

Jhardine grabbed her leopard-print purse off the kitchen counter, gave the change she had in there a quick rifle through, the notes the same, and then, still in her fuzzy slippers, headed for the front door. "Right, see you in a few."

"All right, see you!" Eric called after her, leaning over to watch her go out the door. When the door shut, Eric jumped off his perch and raced out into the backyard. Squinting against the morning's glare, he pulled open the shed door.

The man with the violet eyes had his shirt halfway over his head, the pale white of his little paunch hanging over the rim of his tailored trousers.

"Ah, there you are! You know, I was practically starkers when your mother came in."

"She didn't...." Eric needed a second to work through that image. "She didn't see you, did she?"

"Well, seeing as how she's not told you about a dangerously handsome stranger in her shed, I'm guessing not."

There was a rogue's smile on the man's face as he tucked his shirt into his trousers and stepped out, one foot in a canvas boot and the other still bare. The smell of creosote and blood came with him, and Eric noticed the deep carmine stains on the shed floor. Smears on the walls, too. The man hopped on one foot while putting on his other boot, obscuring Eric's view. His clothes, and in particular the waistcoat he was buttoning up, they were all somehow spotless now.

"You...." It felt intimate to talk about this. Eric didn't know why. "You were in a bit of a bad way. You know, when I put you in here. Do you remember?"

"I could hardly forget. Mind you, when your ma came in I was bent over, arse up in the air. That would have been a bad sight for her, too, I'm sure. Take the small mercies where you can, Alistair, that's what I tell myself. I'm Alistair by the way. Had I mentioned that?" He shrugged and went on gabbing: "Are you going to make me a cup of tea then, or do I have to die of thirst?"

A LOOK AROUND Little Bird's depressingly small bedroom told Alistair a few things. For one, Eric seemed like an ordinary lad of twenty-one, except that he was bright, and formidably so if the books he was reading were anything to go by. Two, he was boring. *Sorry to say it but it is what it is.* The room he called his bedroom, the space in which he supposedly dreamed his lofty dreams, struck so dull with its uninspired grey tones and a carpet that was more bare than thread, that Alistair thought about hanging himself from the light cord just to liven things up. *Too much?* he mused as he scratched his grainy throat. *Oh, now, what's this?*

He spied a picture—drawn, not a photograph—stuck to the wall above the shambles of Eric's desk. Little Bird with another lad, a strapping young thing. Physically older-looking but with enough youth to the eyes to say they were about the same age. The lad was looking out into the world, and he had a big, broad smile on his face. Little Bird, though, was looking only at his friend. The drawing was good. Exceptional, even. And possibly a lie.

"Tea," Eric said, kicking open the bedroom door. Alistair, with no time to replace the picture, had to lay it naked on the desk. If Eric saw, he didn't say.

"Much obliged." Alistair took the brew and had himself a sip. He winced. Something bitter in there. What was worse, it tasted familiar.

"Mum's just phoned to tell me the gossip." Eric crossed the room and sat himself down at the top of the bed.

"What gossip would that be? The dead woman or the dashing hero that swooped in to save her son?"

"Sally," Eric corrected, his rich brown eyes firm. "Her name was Sally. Even if she was a monster, she was human once."

"I know. I do," Alistair said. Eric was still peering at him with a vague disgust. "What?"

"You killed her—and yeah, she was a monster then," he said, putting up his hand to ward off protestations. "But then you took her fingers."

If this was meant to make Alistair apologetic, it failed. "I'd have had more if I'd not had to look after the likes of you," Alistair moaned. "Opportunity for a full fresh umbra carcass doesn't come around that often, you know."

Eric looked nonplussed. Or, happen that was his usual look. Either way, it seemed he wanted an explanation. "Her. What she was. Take a living thing—doesn't have to be a person—poison it with shades thick as night and heavy as time's burden, and with a little misfortune you get yourself an umbra. That girl was what's known as a hound. It's a wildling umbra, meaning it can be a handful and, unlike your run-of-the-mill drones, it's intelligent and it's infectious. Had I not healed you—and assuming you'd survived the attack—you'd probably have ended up one yourself. A hound, I mean."

Eric stared at Alistair. He stared, and stared. "What?"

Alistair didn't understand it. He couldn't have put it any plainer. "You seem a bit slow."

"Slow? Oh charming, that," Eric harrumphed. "It's just what you're saying is ridiculous. And none of that even explains why you took her fingers."

"Ah, that's where you're wrong, see: umbras—the monsters—are made up of shades. It's in them, like blood and marrow. It's all the hate and hurt boiled down into a pure filthy stew. And it just so happens that shadow formers like me, we can use those shades to crank our hearts, and that in turn gives us our powers. As you might have guessed, my power is to heal. Oh, and my devastating good looks, of course."

"Of course." Eric wafted his hands.

"But, see, you have to get those shades out of the umbra's flesh so shadow formers can use it. Can't have it straight from the source because it's poison. Ergo, collecting bits of umbra bodies to refine them later."

"Well," Eric nodded. "That is proper disgusting."

Alistair shrugged. "It's what we do." After a moment of smiling at Eric, the lad seemed to get it.

"Wait, you said...." He looked away and then back at Alistair like he couldn't quite believe what he was hearing. "You think I'm a shadow thing?"

"A shadow former, and yes, you are, there's no *think* about it." Alistair began unbuttoning the top of his own waistcoat and shirt.

"Aye, er, awkward. You're good looking an' all, but I'm not interested."

"Trust me, you are." Alistair revealed the black stone and coral-like branches of a shadow heart a few inches deep in his own chest.

"Oh," Eric said. "You've, okay, you've got one too?"

Alistair coughed. "Well, mine's bigger but yes, a shadow heart," he nodded.

"You said all shadow f...formers? Formers. Right? They have powers. Does that mean...?" When Alistair didn't correct the idea, Eric laid down on his bed, hands over his eyes. "This is mental. Actually mental. And what is Mum going to say?"

Was Little Bird aware that he had a fairly attractive stomach? From what Alistair could see, at least, with the shirt riding up and the hair that led places. Places good men don't look.

"Now here's a question for you," he said, clearing his throat. "I know why I was out last night. I felt the pull of that there umbra like any shadow former would. But why were you there? And don't you pretend you just happened to be walking by and felt it too. I heard enough to know that there was some intent behind your visit."

Eric looked away. He rubbed at his left ear. "Somehow, I saw her. I mean, I was at Tim's flat and then I was there. She said that Tim's a thing now. A thing like her." Eric huffed. "But he's dead. I went to his funeral. The police found his body. Well, parts. But then I saw him and he was there. I mean, he looked rough, but...."

"An umbra," Alistair said. "This is going to be hard for you. I'm sorry but the thing is, what you need to understand, once a person is dead they're gone. Finished. Over."

"That's not hard for me. That's a fact."

"Right, okay, maybe so. But the thing that they were, that body, it can be warped into something new. It might look like him and for all the world it might sigh and sing like him, but it isn't and it never can be him."

"But I think, I mean I'm not sure but I think I was looking through his—its—eyes when it happened. When he killed that Sally. And I think I'm...you know, I think I'm hearing him. Like, he's in my head. The voice is there all the time." Eric looked to latch on to something. "Isn't there even a chance that there's still something of Tim in there? That Sally, for a minute, she seemed to come back—"

"No, umbras don't work like that."

"Why?" And it wasn't obstinate, wasn't a refusal to believe. It was a question because, it seemed, Eric wanted to understand. *Oh, yes, he's definitely clever.*

Alistair sat on Eric's bed. He considered how to be gentle with this. Inspiration was found in the spots of blood up Eric's shirt. They were already fading, Alistair's presence enough to make good from ill, but they were just the needed prompt. "You were the first person I ever healed, you know that? Until a year ago, until you, I didn't know I could. Until then, I thought this heart just made me the perfect fighting machine. I heal fast. I can't die."

Eric took a moment to process this. "You can't? How can you not die? Everybody dies."

"Nope. Can't do it. The Panacea Heart, this thing in my chest, it regenerates. When it does, I regenerate with it. But I'll grant you this: I'm a little different every time. I have all the thoughts and memories of who I am, oh yes, because the heart remembers and so I remember. But it's never quite perfect. Sometimes I like liquorice more than mint. Sometimes spicy rather than sweet."

"Sometimes coffee more than tea?"

"No, never that. Tea all the way." Alistair smiled. "And I've noticed it too, when I've healed people of things, you know, like brain injuries, things like that. I can see it. The damaged neurons blinking out. The pathways that I have to retread. But I can't ever get it quite perfect. What I'm trying to say is, these are processes that are faithful. They are designed to copy." This time Alistair was the one to search. He looked for Eric's gaze and held it. "Umbras aren't even that. When it gets inside a body it's there to warp. Its very purpose is to steal flesh and live in it, to grow, to accumulate power and poison and become even more wretched and ever more perfect in its ugliness. There's no good left in them. The brain will fight. The brain will sing and it will roar and it will echo the stories that went before it. But it's being changed, it's being taken over until there's nothing left. Not a thing."

Eric nodded, and then he asked in a small, sad voice, "Why is he doing this to me then?" Eric looked out of his misted-up windows, seeming to search. He had a nice nose. A little upturned at the end. It had finesse. "The umbra? I mean if he wanted to get me he could just come through the window and do it now. Kill me. Or at work or, you know, anywhere."

"I reckon what happened last night was an introduction. He, or the person controlling the umbra, because we can't rule that out, he wants you to be afraid. That he can call out to you at any time. Umbras do that. They play with people. They feed on fear and anguish, especially from folk who were important to the body they now control."

Eric looked leery of it. "Why me? I mean why bother? If there's one theme in my life it's that I'm nowt special. That Sally woman told me as much."

"Well, I wouldn't sell yourself too short there, Little Bird, but happen it's not necessarily about you. The heart in your chest is valuable. I mean, I take it your friend was killed?"

Eric nodded.

"It might be that the cur who killed him is a shadow former, or at least someone who knows enough to make umbras and, possibly, to desire a shadow heart. And yours, well, like I said: I've never even heard of a heart that actually bends shadows, but it could be useful."

"First time that's ever properly happened, that," Eric replied, tracing a wrinkle in his bed sheets. "The throwing shadows about thing, I mean."

"Not the first time you've seen or done something strange though?"

"No," Eric confessed through tight lips. "It's usually piddling stuff, you know? Like hearing things even though I'm really far away, or seeing stuff in the distance I shouldn't be seeing. Lately though...."

"That's because your shadow heart, they, erm, exercise themselves, especially at first when you're new to your powers and you've not got a handle on your thoughts. Think of it like you testing how supple a new leather glove is."

That thought seemed to startle Eric. "You mean it's alive, then? A living thing."

"It is."

"And...people are after it?"

"Maybe. And with you using your powers, that brings them closer. That lights you up. But," Alistair's mind leapt to a thing that had been bothering him, "it must mean you're getting a few shades from somewhere. Which reminds me," Alistair said, holding up his mug. "This cup of tea: you make it with water from the tap?"

"Yeah, why?"

"I just need to check something." Alistair dove a hand in his pocket to pull out his hip flask. "Never leave home without it in case I need a nip or two of courage, you know?"

"Not really," Eric said, watching Alistair drink down the flask's contents.

"Gah!" *Good job my liver can heal itself, so it is.* Alistair poured the remainder of his tea into the flask. "Careful, careful," he said as he struggled to not wet Eric's bed. "Where was I? I suppose, oh, I suppose I should tell you about the Sisters. I—"

"I need you to leave," Eric said.

"What?"

"I'm sorry," Eric said, getting off the bed and opening his bedroom door. "But, you have to go."

"But I thought you wanted answers? I thought you'd want to know about your powers—"

"And I do. I would. Normally. I mean, we're talking about super powers and what bloke in their right mind wouldn't want that. But you just said a gobful and I won't pretend I understood even half of it, but I think I have the most important bit straight, though." Eric tapped his knuckles against the door. "These powers, these heart things, they're not...safe."

"You can't deny what you are, Eric. That heart chose you."

"Not *chosen*. That's what she said. That woman. Sally. Not chosen but cursed. Because as long as I have this," Eric pointed at his chest, "and as long as I'm near you, I'm a target, aren't I?" *Well, bugger me royally.* Alistair couldn't deny that. "And by extension, so are the people around me. My mum, for starters."

"Yes," Alistair said. "I just assumed...."

"Academically, I want to know. Course I do. How could I not? But...." Eric closed his eyes. "All my life my ma has protected me. Done everything for me. Until last year, she had to give everything up. I owe her. I owe her so much. So for once in my life, I'm not going to be selfish. I'm going to...I have to say no."

Alistair rose to his full height, examining Eric as close as he could without seeming to be doing anything at all. *Ah, there's metal there.* A little smile threatened to break. "Good for you, Little Bird."

"I'm sorry," Eric said. "It's not that I'm not grateful. I am. Truly, properly grateful."

"I get it. You don't have to explain yourself, so you don't. If I still had anyone I loved, I reckon I'd want to keep as far away from this as possible." Alistair held out a hand. "I believe this is what folk do here. To say goodbye."

"Maybe another time. A less dangerous time, yeah?" Eric said, giving the hand a shake.

"There's no such thing. But, if you ever do need me—"

"I won't. I'm not—"

"Please, just this one thing and then I'll go." A while to consider, then Eric nodded. "The hearts, they can call out to each other. It's something that's hardwired, doesn't require training. If you're in danger, if you need someone, concentrate on wanting to call out to me. Chances are, I'll hear you and I'll come running. Do you understand?"

"Yes, yeah," Eric said. "Listen, thank you. Really, thank you."

"No worries. So, what are you going to do, then, about the umbra. About seeing—"

"Ignore it. I have to, don't I?"

"In my experience, they don't, I mean, it won't stop."

"Then," Eric straightened again, becoming as hard as he needed to be. "You'd better sort it soon, hadn't you? I mean, that's what you do, isn't it? Kill these things?"

It stuck in Alistair's ears, that. He tried not to look bothered by it. "Yes. Best get on then, hadn't I?"

He was halfway out the door when Eric piped up: "The heart. How do I get it out of my chest?"

Alistair walked the hall and turned down the stairs. "You can't. They bond for life." Another few steps. "Your life. Not theirs." Then Alistair moved out of sight, as he had been to mortal eyes for so many centuries now.

CHAPTER SEVEN
WHEN THE WORLD FALLS

ERIC'S EYES HURT from staring at the television for so long. He couldn't resist it, though. Every ten or fifteen minutes the news would flash up pictures of the dead girl Sally and waffle on about what scant information they had on her: a woman with no fixed address, no criminal record, just one sister who was mysteriously unreachable. Their theorising was stupid and confusing. But then they started showing old university photos of her. Eric found himself tracing the lines of Sally's pixie features. He remembered the howl of the hound as it had unfolded from her body, and the moment when the woman she had been made a desperate plea to stop the monster she had become hurting Eric.

Alistair's wrong. There was part of her left.

Time wore on. His mum went out again. Church or something. He'd waved but only realised she'd gone in hindsight. The news cycle of picture, talking, picture, talking, continued and he circled with it, his thoughts coiling tighter and tighter around him like barbed wire. A bit later and he nearly shat himself while cleaning the carpet—which wouldn't have been conducive *at all*. The postman had taken to really slinging mail through their letter box and when those letters dropped with a thud, Eric heard it as the footstep of a giant dog. Of Sally.

Then back in front of the TV. Eric bit at his fingernails. He ran his fingers over his left ear. He rubbed at his neck. He'd drawn the curtains to get a better look at the pictures on the screen, but now he threw them wide. The light slid behind his eyes and made them tear. He paced up and down. Anxiety was making him tick, his lips quiver, his limbs shake. He touched his chest and felt this thing in him give a more solid beat. That was it. That was what he could do.

He went to the kitchen, trawled for the cleanest, flat-edged knife in the draw, and then raced upstairs. He locked the bathroom door and stood in front of the mirror. Eric threw off his shirt. Knife in his hand, he brought the blade up over his chest, letting it wobble inches away from the heart. Alistair had said the heart couldn't be gotten rid of. The knife in Eric's hand was saying different. Cut it out, bag it up, throw it away. Then all this shit would stop. Life could get back to some kind of normalcy. This was going to hurt, but it would be worth it.

He brought the knife down, ready to make the first cut, but when the metal tip of the blade pressed the rise of the heart the world flashed red. "Fuck!" A shot of pain ran up his arm and his fingers unclenched, making Eric drop the knife, which clattered as it hit the floor. Breathing heavy, Eric worked his fingers until the pain began to ease and with it the world slowly returned to normal colour. The shadow heart beat angrily, and there was a growing heat around his chest.

"You're going to have to do better than that," Eric told it. He stretched to pick up the knife again, only to be met by a wall of hurt that slammed his entire body, spasming up and down his spine until he too fell to the floor. Winded, he lay there a long while, the shadow heart not so much thudding as munching on his ribcage. He coughed. He looked at the knife again, there on the floor by his feet, and the shadow heart quickened some more, as though warning him.

Alistair had said it. "They bond for life. Your life. Not theirs." And now Eric understood. The heart might have chosen him, but it would kill him sooner than allow him to cut it out. There was no getting away from it now.

HAVING BEEN UNABLE to destroy the shadow heart in his chest, Eric still felt the ache to do *something* and take back some form of control. Looking through the letters he'd taken from Tim's flat was the best he could come up with so, he sighed, that would have to do. So, later that day, Eric peeked out around the garden path. A police cordon now roped off the bottom of the road, a van and police officers in attendance with a lot of folk milling around the subway's steps. They looked like albino flies on shit, and to Eric's mind the pong of trouble was in the air. Not wanting to muck about he darted round to the back of his car and fiddled with the boot lock until its stubborn mechanism gave way.

Using the cover of the car boot, he looked out down the road. There didn't seem to be much happening. Then he spotted a television camera being unloaded from a smaller van parked outside one of the houses near the subway and nearly had a stroke. *What if they want interviews? I left the car running for ages. Some of the neighbours must have heard.*

He took out the carrier bag from the boot and held it close to his chest. Better to get back inside and start working on some kind of story.

Boot closed and checked to make sure the lock hadn't broken again, he turned to go inside. "You all right, Eric?" next-door neighbour Jim said, scaring Eric into dropping the bag of letters. Jim had his hands round a four-pack of beer, which seemed to give an amused rattle. "Here, sorry to startle you."

"No worries," Eric said on his hands and knees as he stuffed every envelope he could find back into the bag.

"Listen, I wanted to have a word—"

"Can it wait, Jim, I've got, er, terrible diarrhoea." It was the first thing, the only thing, that came to mind.

"Oh, right." Jim's bushy eyebrows went high. "Well, I'll not keep you then."

"Cheers."

"THANKS, LOVE," JHARDINE said as she stepped off the juddering bus. Had it been another day, had she been her regular self, she might have chewed the driver out for nearly giving her whiplash as he came round the bend to turn down to Hainsworth and slammed all on when a fox ran out in the middle of the road. But not today. Not after that doctor's appointment.

Don't be alarmed? It was easy for them to bloody say.

Rain pattered down the street as she crossed the road for the crescent. It wasn't dark yet but the cloud cover was so thick that it might as well have been. The wind threw her a slap, and she had to pull her hair out of her eyes. The weird thing about the doctors and all that was that she'd actually felt fine; these past few days she'd had quite a bit of energy, and it felt like the pills were finally sorting stuff out. Well, except for the headaches. They were a bit much, but even they hadn't been *too* bad.

The police cars that had been down at the bottom of the road when she left were still there, she noticed. One poor officer was chasing a tangle of police tape as it rolled away. It sort of reminded Jhardine of her life at the moment, everything all knotted and always slightly getting out of hand.

"Excuse me!"

Jhardine stopped, turned, and had to fight to claw her own hair out of her eyes again. Coming down the garden path from Mrs Chandra's house was a woman in a moth-eaten blue jumper. She had jowls and eye bags that made her look like her face was running away from her skull.

"Wondered if I could have a word? It's about the murder down in the subway last night."

"Oh, right," Jhardine straightened. She'd expected the police to come knocking at some point. "Well, yeah, of course. What do you need to know love?"

"I, erm," the woman started, glancing down the street. "Do you actually live on here?"

"Yeah, just down there as it happens," Jhardine pointed.

"Oh, lovely. Would you mind if we did this, you know, inside? It's a bit sensitive, ain't it?" she said, with a sympathetic nodding.

"Yeah, course. Come on then."

"Lovely. Bruce!"

A man with a video camera balancing on his shoulder stood fiddling with the zipper on his trousers outside number twenty-nine. Gloria would cut his bollocks off if she knew he'd just taken a whaz on her prize geraniums—mind you, no one had a right to be *that* proud of what were essentially glorified weeds.

"You're not with the police then," Jhardine mewed.

Oh, chuff.

ERIC WAS TRYING to muster the courage to delve into the bag of Tim's letters, but every time he got his fingers around one of the envelopes he ended up dropping it. He tried to tell himself that it was the heart doing it, but he didn't really believe that.

The clatter of the front door, then chattering. It was his mum. The sound wasn't moving down into the house, though. That must mean she was talking to someone she didn't know.

Eric slid off his bed and opened the bedroom door so he could get a clearer read on the conversation.

"So you didn't see or hear anything?"

"Well, no. I mean, once I'm in bed I'm dead to the world, me."

"But you did know the other person who was killed? Er, Timothy Jeffries?"

With all the stealth of a two year old, Eric leaned over the banister and caught himself a glimpse of the inquisitor. She was a bit of a letdown, all truth be told. A woman in a blue wool cardigan and tight jeans. Dumpy, that was the word. Not a police officer, either, which meant she was probably, even worse, some sort of *journalist.* Either way, his mum had been collared and cornered. Now, Eric couldn't resist the slight pull of a smile. The thing about Jhardine Mayfair was, when under pressure, she came out snarling.

"I did know him, aye," she said, her voice cooling rapidly. "My son and him were mates. But I don't know owt about the police investigation. I reckon that's all I can tell you, love."

"Really? I wonder if," the woman said, sniffing up a glob of snot that threatened to dislodged from her sinuses, "you could tell me any more about the Jeffries boy having a drug problem?"

Even the back of his mum's head looked annoyed. "What?"

"The police report mentions," the woman said, scouring the wet pages on her yellow clipboard, "Ah, yeah, here, that there was a weird kind of drug found in Mr Jeffries' remains. They couldn't put their finger on what it was but sources have told us they're testing it to see if it might be a new kind of street drug that has, like, a muscle-building effect, which of course tallies with Tim's habitual gym use. I wondered if—"

"I don't know owt about that," Jhardine said, actually pushing the woman toward the door. "Now, I've really got to get on. That washing up won't do itself...."

"Really, because I would have thought if your son and him were so close that you might know," the woman said as she teetered at the threshold. One foot back in. "Is your son in? Could I talk to him?"

From a snarl to a belting roar: "Read my lips, love. We don't know anything."

"But—"

"I said we don't know anything. Now off with you. I've had enough for today."

"But, Mrs Mayfair—"

"It's Ms, and goodbye!" The door rattled against the woman's foot. She squealed, probably a bone bruised if not broken, then the door slammed and silence fell.

The quiet was prickly and cold and it seemed to grow and grow in the house. The feeling Eric had of things not being real shattered into more of itself. Jhardine turned in the hallway, a hand to the wall and another rubbing at her forehead.

"You might as well ask, Eric, I know you want to."

Eric sat down on the landing. She sat on the bottom step.

"W-was Tim on drugs?"

"Do we have to start there?"

"Yeah, yes we do. Drugs. Was he taking them?"

"Well, it depends, I suppose, on what you mean by drugs—"

"Please! Just answer the question. Was Tim on—"

Jhardine groaned. "Steroids. He was using steroids. Had been on and off for at least two years."

The cold Eric felt grew. "Why didn't you tell me?" Eric's voice was electron thin. Tim's voice, though, was a choir of robots: *I would have told you anything, if you'd only bothered to ask.* He'd lost so much, lately. And now this. It was hollowing him out. "Mum?"

"You know what, don't do this, Eric. I'm tired—"

"Mum!"

"Fine." He felt her eyes on him. The creak of the stairs. "I honestly thought he was sorting himself out." She'd reached the middle step but would come no further. "The first time he came to me for help it was after a, erm, fight with his parents. I never knew exactly what it was about, but he'd done sommat. You know, something that meant his mum didn't even want him near the house anymore. When I rang her she was just in hysterics."

"Whatever it was, she must have pushed him. She must have—"

"I think he hit her, Eric."

Eric's mouth hung open. "No," he said. "He w-wouldn't. He couldn't. I—"

"I think he did. I don't think he meant to, exactly," Jhardine said. "I suppose if you're decent you don't ever *mean* to but...he did. That's that. And anyway, it's about what happens after." A thick breath. "Tim was scared. He said he felt so angry all the time and it was getting harder to control. He was even worried that he was getting sick. He asked me for help, but he swore me to secrecy. So I took him to the doctors, didn't say owt to anyone. They, er, the doctors I mean, they found that his blood pressure was way too high. He'd been on 'em too long, or wasn't using them in any way that can make them safe. Or, less harmful. I don't know how they work, exactly. He had to spend a few nights in the hospital anyway. He was on a ward not far from where you were, actually."

"He was in the hospital with me? At the same time?" Eric croaked.

"He asked me not to say owt," she repeated.

"But I'm your son."

"And so was he," Jhardine said, tears and smiles. "In all the ways that mattered, so was he, Eric. And I think you forget that. I think you just think about what you lost." In turning his head, he could his mum there on the stairs. She tapped her fingers on the banister, trying to distract herself. "He was lucky though. Whatever he'd been taking didn't do too much damage and he got back on his feet. After that he swore to me that he'd quit and I think for a long while he did. Stuff at work picked up. He phoned his mum to apologise. I was there. It was awful. She didn't want to hear it, and who could blame her? But he was genuinely sorry. He wanted to do right by everyone. I think that's all he ever wanted. He just got in over his head. And then you got better suddenly and, I don't know, something changed. He changed."

"How do you mean?"

Quiet a long while, and then his mum rubbed her fingers over her gold cross necklace. "It was a little thing. A conversation we had the day before you came home. I was untidying your tip of a room so you'd feel settled when you got back, you know, and God I was so happy, and then he stopped me right as I was bringing in your bed sheets, and he said, 'I'll be strong enough for him now. I promise.' And he hugged me. I mean, really tight. I didn't understand it then, and I don't understand it now to be honest. I thought he was just being his dozy self, you know, but...." She shook her head and out came a little sob. "I wonder if someone sold him this drug saying it weren't like steroids or something. Maybe he thought he'd be safe? It only took about a month though and he was acting out again. I don't know if it makes everyone do that kind of thing, can't say that I've ever been that interested. But for him, it made him violent. He broke a lad's jaw after they got into a slanging match at some club. Heaven knows why no one pressed charges."

Eric took in a breath. He dragged in more and more air. He filled his lungs until they ached. He wanted to leave no room for hurt, but he could only hold his breath for so long. At least now he understood the unanswered phone calls, the missed meet-ups. "You were why he kept cancelling on me, then? Like, you made him do it?"

"You make it sound like I was ruining your life, Eric. I was trying to protect you from him."

"I didn't need protecting—"

"You didn't know what you needed. If you don't remember, when you came out of that hospital you were a mess." That was true, but still it stung. "Besides, I wasn't keeping him from you all the time. I said he could see you places where I could check, you know like at the pub. Or here where I could keep an eye on you both. Even his flat, so long as he answered the phone if I called. Just not places like that club he used to go to, that Lion Lion in town and that. And not the gym. I don't know why he said he wanted to meet you there that Monday. I wonder now if he'd done it because he was going to tell you everything. Or maybe if he wanted to prove to me that he could be trusted, or—"

"I'd lent him money," Eric said, feeling a shame that wasn't exactly his. "Your board money. He said he needed it for sommat. He was supposed to give me it back that day but...."

Eric's mum smiled, but it was watery and sad. "Well, if he wanted somewhere I'd never go, the gym would be it."

Eric yelped out a laugh. Then something else ignited. "That night, when I got better I mean, but before that when I thought I was—"

"Oh, Eric," his mum turned away.

"No, Mum, Mum, please. Did you tell him that he couldn't be in the room with me alone? He went, you know? That night after you left he stayed with me just a couple minutes and, and then, I think he left. And he didn't come back and—"

"No," she said, and Eric's insides knotted.

"You're sure?"

"Truthfully, I'm not sure of anything that happened that night, Eric, but as far as I know he was off the stuff and everything was right between us."

"Okay. Yeah, I just wondered, you know? It d-doesn't matter. It's not important," Eric said with a shrug and slight smile. "Do we, erm, need to tell the police? Some of this might help or—"

"I told them most of it already, love, and I reckon they already know more than what they're letting on." She reached out a hand to him, and he came down a few steps, allowing himself to be touched. "I'm sorry for not telling you. It was just, you were better and I didn't want anything to ruin that, and—"

"I understand," he said but, though he meant it, he wasn't quite sure he felt it.

"You shouldn't let this take away all your good memories of him, you know?" She pulled him into a hug.

"Aye, yeah. No one's perfect, right?" Eric said into her shoulder.

"Well, except for me," his mum chimed.

"Yeah."

She used her thumb to chase a tear from under Eric's eyes. "Are we okay, Eric? You don't hate me, do you?"

"No, no, course not. I know why you did it. But, please, don't—not again. Don't protect me. I'm not going to break at the slightest bit of bad news, you know?"

He hadn't expected that to shut her up. Then she ventured in a slow, slight voice, "You should know, then, that I'm back up to the hospital in the morning. Some tests they want to do or something so I have to see the specialist."

"That's good right? That they're taking it seriously this time?"

A pause. Then: "Aye, yeah, I expect so," she smiled, sudden and bright. "Here, you're right, let's have no more secrets, aye?" she said, rubbing his shoulders. She kissed him on his cheek. "I always want us being honest with each other."

"Yeah," Eric said, looking at the ghosts of their diverging shadows. "No more secrets."

ANOTHER FINAL DEMAND, and Eric was beginning to wonder whether Tim had ever paid any of his bills. He folded the letter and slipped it back into its mean white envelope, before tossing it onto the floor by his bed. He checked his bedside alarm. Half-three in the morning. *Shit, work's going to be fun in the morning.* He sat up and looked out the window. The streets were so calm, so peaceful. So suspicious.

It had stopped raining at about midnight, but now a thick body of mist hung in the air and wafted in lazy drifts around the red-brick houses, wagging fingers at him as if taunting him to come out, come out. The police abandoning the subway so soon, it was wrong. Why weren't they still combing the scene, looking for clues?

A sudden fear gripped him as a realisation twinkled: his blood should be all over that subway. They would be able trace him, surely? And what could he tell them then? Oh, that girl Sally became a great big hound thing and it busted open my back, but then this man with violet eyes, a man no one can really remember, came and slaughtered her and fixed me with his magic touch. Then he went to pieces in the shed. Oh yeah, that would go down well.

Certainly, he'd made a big song and dance about not putting his mum in danger and not pursuing these creatures, these umbra things, but the longer he sat there, the more his anxiety grew. He couldn't wait for the police to come knocking. He had to *do* something. He had to know if the scene down there was as bad as he remembered.

Eric put his ear to the wall. No hint of the relaxed dance music his mum liked to listen to when she couldn't sleep. Then a snort and the sound of her mattress springs complaining as she turned over on her bed. *Can't imagine why you can't hold on to a man.*

Assured he could make his great escape just fine, Eric pulled on a black jumper with a hood and some dark jeans so he could blend into the night, then wrestled onto his feet a nondescript pair of trainers from the bottom of the stairs.

Out in the misty wilds of the estate he stood, letting his dark eyes scan the scene. Blue and white police tape still cordoned off the subway, but no police officers could be seen and no vans or cars were there that weren't regularly parked up this time of night.

Swallowing down the acid dread in his throat, Eric approached the police tape around the subway's mouth and then ducked underneath, descending the stairs as quick as he could to make sure his courage didn't give out. The sound of dripping water jangled across his nerves. He heard echoes of the hound's wailing in his head. The gnashing of the monster's jaws.

The tunnel was empty. What was worse, the patch on the stairs where Sally had died was without a blood splatter or even a mark. Not just clean but obviously scoured. The entire subway, in fact, was crisp packet, beer bottle and condom free. Unnatural, that. Eric scanned the subway's tiled wall, searching for the ghosts of his own blood, but nothing. He remembered that the hound had crashed into the wall and broken the tiles, but they were smooth and glossy, good as new.

Everywhere was so clean, so neat. This wasn't the work of a forensics team. It was too quick. Too well done. Eric's anxiety reached new heights. He bit into his thumbnail and pulled. Sharp heat, and a rush of blood.

His shadow heart gave a thud, and a sense of being watched pricked up the back of his neck.

He turned his head to see a fox sat a little way down the tunnel. It was staring back at him, its ash-grey fur fluffed up and its eyes reflecting the glow of the subway's yellow lights with an added silver heat. It was the same fox as the night before, wasn't it? The one Alistair had said hello to. He was sure it was. *Sure.*

The fox got off its haunches and came slinking toward him, its tail brushing this way and that so that as it passed it managed a swipe at Eric's knee. "What are you up to?" he said. The fox soon reached the stairs and began to climb until it was six up, then it turned to look back at Eric—and began to yip.

"Shhh!" Eric brought his finger to his mouth to hush the creature, and then realised something was wrong. His thumb nail was still ripped, yes, but instead of being jagged and split, the slice was clean and the smear of blood that had welled there was gone. Actually, the wound seemed perfectly sanitised. "Did you...?"

The fox came down a stair and expressed an annoyed chunter.

"What? What do you want?" The fox moved up a step, circling on itself to look back at him. "You want me to follow? Has Alistair sent you to get me?" The fox gave a new yap and then skipped up the remaining stairs. "Oi! Lassie! Where you off?" He'd not wanted to get involved in all this, but maybe Alistair wanted to let Eric know something, like he'd caught Tim's killer. "Oh chuffing hell," Eric puffed as he jogged up the stairs. He reached the top in time to see the fox's tail curve around a nearby lamppost. With a great sigh, he gave chase. The running made his ankles complain—*Christ, I'm getting old*—but the cold, wet air felt sweet as it slid over his skin. Even so, he had himself a little grumble. "Bloody foxes at this chuffing hour. Alistair better have a good reason for this." But he didn't feel annoyed. Not really. The thought of seeing Alistair again, and despite everything he'd said just that morning, it made him pick up his pace. Half a mile down the road out of Hainsworth and the fog ahead rippled with light. His fox companion became a slip of black as a police van sped toward Eric with headlights on full. Eric lurched behind a nearby postbox, hands on the red metal and crouching low. The van drove on without stopping, sinking once again into the cotton white and black of the night. Eric squinted at the road ahead.

"Oi, fox," he whispered. "I can't see. Where are you?"

Two silver eyes bloomed just centimetres from Eric's face. He threw himself back. For its part, the fox sat there looking at Eric like it didn't have time to contemplate all the ways in which he was stupid and then, with a beckoning yip, it set off running again. "Here, here, wait up!" Eric called.

Twisting through the narrow, tightly packed lanes of Harris Street and Arthur's Road they went, and then faster through the damp backstreets of the older part of the city.

"Here, it's fucking Superman!" someone called after him as he raced over the smooth cobbles. He gave them the flash of a middle finger and kept running. A little faster, if truth be known. And grinning. Soon Eric lost all sense of where he was. He was running. Just running, and it was marvellous. He'd spent so much of his life lying in a bed hooked up to machines and held down by drugs and dodgy biology. Now, feeling his lungs fill with life, he knew it as the gift it was. It felt like flying. He could almost believe he could do this forever.

Oh, he thought. And maybe *this* was what Tim used to talk about when he was evangelising on lifting weights. *Feeling like you're free, like nothing can hold you down.* No sooner had the thought rubbed across Eric's thinking parts than the grey little fox disappeared into a curl of fog.

"Wait! Where are we?" Eric puffed as he lurched to a stop. He stumbled through the drizzle and murk, his legs feeling slack and dull from exertion. "I don't know where I am," Eric said. Until he did. Until he found a landmark that he had never wanted to see.

The police tape that cordoned off the lamppost to which Tim had been strung on Willingsley High Street had by this time become a faded banner trodden into the ground. The once vibrant flowers that had marked the scene, laid with such care and empathy, were now nothing more than sludgy brown garlands. The white lamplight above flickered as though agitated by the damp air. The rain began to pelt down once again.

"Alistair?" Eric croaked into the night. He felt like he was being watched, but no matter how hard he tried he couldn't see beyond the narrow curtain the heavy and heavier rain created. He turned. Was there a shadow moving in the fog?

The thud of Eric's shadow heart made him feel sick, and he staggered under its strange weight.

"Hello?"

You abandoned me.

"You're not real," Eric said, rubbing at his sore neck. "You're just a voice. You're—"

When I needed you the most, you weren't there.

"Shut up. Just shut up."

A noose of pain and, for one snatched moment, Eric thought he saw Tim in the mist. Tim as he had been, beautiful and true.

"Mate?"

Flickering then, another image that sent the mists rushing away in fear. A decayed and wretched Tim; a colossus with black lips, jagged needle teeth, and dead crosses for eyes. "You deserve to hurt," it said in a male bellow that was too icy and brittle.

"Y-y-you are just a dead thing. I'm not...." Eric was going to say he wasn't afraid, but given he was about three seconds away from pissing himself, that was a lie. "W-what do you want?"

"I want you to feel what I felt that night!"

The thing charged, its weight making the ground jump, its awful, jagged fingers reaching. Eric fell backward, hands up to guard his face. This was it. This was death. He waited, and he waited, but the blow never came. The patter of the rain hitting the street filled the night, like the footsteps of an army coming closer, closer. And one other noise, one single voice that slithered and sibilated louder than ever before.

You deserve what you get.

"No," Eric moaned, a hand over his face to hide. "No, please," he said. "I don't even know what's real anymore. I don't even know...."

The night was so tense that he felt like the air had become the skin of a balloon and one wrong-pointed vowel and everything might just explode. Eric's world was broken. Eric's mind was in pieces. The silence. The silence was thick. The silence hurt. Eric thumped at his temples. He spun on the spot, hearing growls and snarls that he was half sure weren't there. Then a fly landed on his cheek, and he almost turned inside out in fright.

"I didn't do this to you," he shouted, batting the fly away. "I didn't. So why are you doing this to me?"

Because.... It was such a faint voice now. *Because you shouldn't leave someone you love. That is the worst betrayal of all.*

CHAPTER EIGHT
THICKER THAN WATER

IT'LL BE SOMMAT *and nowt,* Jhardine told herself for the fifteenth time that morning. She poured enough milk on her cereal to make it more liquid than solid, then threw half of it down the sink. Couldn't bear to have bits in drinks. She hated bits!

The doctors were moving quick for a change. It'd only been a week since she'd gone up to the hospital for all those head scans. What a boring delight they were. Now she had to go in and see the so-called "specialist" again. When it came to doctors, speed was a bad sign, wasn't it? It meant they couldn't afford to wait. Jhardine harpooned that thought and left it dying on deck. *No,* she rallied. *It'll be another pointless round of test results. They're probably getting that Thompsette woman to tell me I've got hypochondria or something.*

"Morning," Eric said, his bare feet slapping against the kitchen floor. With his shirt off and scratching his hairy belly, he looked a little too much like his dad.

"Oh God, Eric, no one wants to see that first thing. My eyes!"

"Only what God gave me," Eric said, though he swiftly retreated into the hallway to take a shirt off the radiator.

Jhardine scraped her breakfast bowl clean over the bin and then rinsed the bowl under the tap. "Here, I might not be back until late today. I've got some stuff I've got to do, so you can fix your own tea, can't you?"

"Don't see why not," he said.

She noticed his red eyes and dark circles. "You know, I've been walking past your room on a night, when I'm off to the bathroom I mean. Three, four in the morning and you're still up. Click, click, click. You're on that computer, aren't you?"

"There's no law against that, is there?" he asked as he took out two slices of bread from the bread bin and slung them under the grill.

She threaded her arms into her coat. "No, there ain't but...." *Things you have to put up with as a parent!* "Listen, the other day on the telly there was a lad, about your age, suffering a terrible porn addiction—"

"Mum!"

"'Ere, I've seen some of that gay porn. I know how easy it'd be to get addicted to that stuff. Oh, the varieties you've got."

"Mum, I'm not addicted to porn—but I'm starting to think you might be."

"Well, what are you doing then?"

"Reading. Is it so hard to believe that something that managed to crawl out of your flipping womb is capable of having an interest outside of two men fisting each other?"

Jhardine made a mental note to look up "fisting". It sounded sporty. "Well, all right then. So long as you're not getting into owt unsavoury. Here, why aren't you at work yet?"

"I'm not on collection so they don't need me to come in as early. I'm working office hours."

"Oh, well, so long as they're paying you I wouldn't knock it."

"I'm not," he yawned.

"Right, I'm off. Ruth's picking me up. I'll see you tonight." She couldn't help a quick glance at the carpet. Oh, it had cleaned up fairly well, actually. As much as Eric might have thrown a wobbly, that fourth time going over it seemed to have done the trick.

"Right," she straightened up. "Have a good day at work, and don't get yourself into mischief!"

"As if."

"Oh, Ruth, thanks for doing this," Jhardine said to try to cut through the zero-temperature silence as they drove up Hitchens' Road.

"It's my pleasure, Jhardine," Ruth said, adjusting her white driving gloves as she gave the steering wheel a gentle turn. "I was running Stanley to a funeral, weren't I, Stan?"

Stan, who had refused to give up the front seat, gave an unimpressed wheeze.

"Dropping like flies round you, eh, Stan?" Jhardine said by way of trying to lighten the mood. Very obviously it was a joke. His morbid face turned her way and she knew he'd not taken it as such.

"Actually, it was a death in the family, if you must know."

"Cousin's aunt twice removed," Ruth added.

"I'm sorry to hear that," she said with as much sincerity as she could muster whilst trying not to punch someone in their square and somewhat chewed-looking face.

"Well, anyway," Ruth said, trying her best to smooth the tension and doing a royal arse job of it. "I was surprised that Barry let us both have time off, Jhardine."

"Yeah, well, he didn't have much choice. I've not had a holiday for months. Here, I never asked, why are you off up to the hospital anyhow? I hope nowt's wrong?"

"Oh no, you know me, Jhardine, fit as a tuba!"

"Fiddle," Stanley corrected.

"You what?"

"The saying. Fit as a *fiddle*, not tuba."

"Oh, is it? Well that doesn't really make sense, does it? They're right tiny, aren't they? Wouldn't take much doing playing one of them, but you'd have to be fit to hold up a tuba all that time and play it." She paused for breath. "Here, what was it you asked, Jhardine?"

"Why are you going up to the—"

"Hospital, oh yes. Well, it's not for me actually. Stanley's got piles, haven't you, Stanley?" Another unimpressed wheeze. "And I thought I'd go to the pharmacy at the hospital to get him some of that pile cream and maybe, oh, a spray if they have one. It's much better than the one in town, Jhardine. Here we are, Stan," she said, pulling the car over outside of Saint Anthony's.

A half dozen people were already crowding the church doors. They all had Stanley's grey box face, and that weird lanky quality that made him look a bit like a tent pole. As soon as the car stopped Stanley stepped out onto the pavement without even so much as a goodbye.

"Aren't you forgetting something?" Ruth said, tapping her cheek.

"It'd be like kissing a dog's ball bag. No thanks," he said, and he closed the door. Apparently unfazed by this slight, Ruth flicked the indicator and pulled out into the traffic.

Jhardine couldn't help it, she just had to ask: "Do you ever get tired of him, Ruth?"

"What? Who? Stanley? Oh, never. He's the love of my life."

Jhardine laughed. "But he's so...."

"Oh, you mean him being a complete arse about everything?"

"Well, er, yeah? I sort of thought you didn't notice?"

"Not notice, dear? How could I not notice? No, he's been that way ever since I met him, and the liver problems have only made it worse, but you learn to tune it out."

"Really?

"The money helps. And the affairs," she said, using a finger to test the set of her lipstick. "Until death do we part, that's what I said and I stick by it. Oh, while I remember, Jhardine, I am going on a cruise. I've got it all booked already. Don't worry, it's during the café's quiet months."

"YOU SHOULD HAVE been here an hour ago," the teenager manning the hospital's rather jumped-up sounding Yellow Desk said. She had contact lenses in that made her gaze vaguely purple and lizard-like. Unnerving, it was.

"No, right, the letter here, see, says half past nine."

"I've got half eight on the system."

"Well, I can't be held responsible for the fact that you lot can't get your records straight, can I?"

"There's no need to take that tone with me."

"Clearly there is," Ruth chimed in.

"Look, I'm going to ring Doctor Thompsette now, so just keep your wig on—"

"Now, listen here," said Ruth.

The receptionist held up her hand as she spoke into the telephone: "Yes, I have your late arrival here."

"'Ere, I wasn't late. Don't you dare tell her I was," Jhardine said, about ready to flatten the mardy little madam. "I'm always on time, me. I make a point of it."

"Yeah, okay, okay." She put down the phone. "Doctor Thompsette's only opening is later this morning."

"I guess I'll have to take that, then, won't I?"

"I guess you will." The woman shrugged. "Now, you can take a seat over there. Someone will call you when the doctor is ready."

"Yeah, thanks," she said, "for nowt."

An hour and three quarters and Jhardine was sweating. Why the heck was the place so warm? And how the hell were you meant to avoid getting sick when they make you sit in a waiting room with all the ill people? The least they could do is separate you off, folk who could give you something with folk who just had whatever the blazes it was she had.

"Jhardine, I'm just going to go get a breath of fresh air," said Ruth, peeling herself off the seat with an audible rip. Under the heat, Ruth's lipstick was bleeding down into the parched cracks around her mouth. "I'm gonna pass out if not."

"No, you're right, love. It's a joke," Jhardine said loud enough for the cocky receptionist to hear.

"I'll see if I can find us a drinks machine too."

"See if they do a box of wine," Jhardine said as she fanned herself with the TV magazine she'd found under her chair.

A few minutes of desperately trying to cool down, and a woman sat down opposite with a push chair containing a red faced and scaly baby.

"Ringworm?"

"Don't know," said the woman. More a girl really. Pretty, Jhardine thought.

"I bet it's ringworm. Our Eric was only at nursery a few days and he came home riddled with it. Let me tell you, that took some getting rid of. Which doctor you seeing?"

"I don't know. It was a bloke what saw us last time."

"Oh, that's no good, love. Not for kids. Right big hands. You want one of the female doctors. Besides, you can never get antibiotics out of the men. They think you should grin and bear it. I've been stocking up, me. Got a medicine cabinet crammed to the rafters."

"I think I'll be fine," the girl said, tucking her lanky, formless brown hair—more of a mop, really—behind her ear.

"Suit yourself." Jhardine turned away from the tramp. Baby was ugly as sin as well.

"Jhardine Mayfair?" a nurse in an eggshell-blue uniform called from a door across the corridor.

Jhardine snatched up her handbag and, glaring not so much daggers as broadswords at the receptionist, walked her way down the bright corridor. "Make yourself useful and tell my friend that I've gone, will you?" she shot at Lizard Eyes on her way past.

IT WAS YEARS since Jhardine had been down to Dawlish Park. Well before Eric's dad had left, she reckoned. It wasn't bad, though. Despite the fact it was getting late in the year, the green lawns still looked plush, and the trees above still had their leaves, now all wonderful and golden. Of the seasons, she enjoyed autumn the best. She liked that, just before the inevitable fall, a leaf would show its most beautiful colours.

Oh God, Jhardine, an autumn leaf analogy. Bloody kill yourself now.

She sat down on a bench near the glassy looking lake. Canada geese in their brown and black best honked along the water as they went about their geesely business. She wondered what a group of geese was called. A gannet? A gaggle? Something like that. Oh, and did the genus matter? It seemed very important that she know things like this.

After a while of listening to the geese squabbling, Jhardine unpacked the fish and slightly too brown chips she'd ordered from the Fish Dish over on Broadside at the other end of the park. She picked at the chips at first but, diet be damned, she found she was more hungry than she'd thought and started stuffing the buggers in her mouth. Back into the white plastic carrier bag she then went, retrieving herself a can of cola. She'd stopped drinking cola because apparently fizzy drinks give you cancer. *Well, what doesn't these days?* She sighed to herself and sipped. The bubbles rushed to the back of her throat, the syrupy taste not exactly pleasant but at least refreshing. Another chip as a woman ran by jogging like her life depended on it.

"You won't catch me being one of them types," she'd told Michael all those years ago when they'd sat on that same bench and seen someone jogging.

"D-d-do you not think you should do some exercise?" he'd asked, taking off his glasses so he could polish them on his sleeve. She was fairly sure he didn't need glasses. Had the eyes of a hawk when he wanted to. She liked the affectation though, and the thick rims suited him. They gave him a Ginsberg quality she liked. That's right. Once upon a time she'd been a reader too, but then Eric came along and....

"Are you trying to say I'm fat?"

"N-n-no. I just meant that it's good for you."

"Afraid of me putting on weight?"

"I would love you no matter what you looked like, Jhardine," he said, and for the first time in such a long while, he didn't stutter. "Besides, I know you like your figure."

"Well, it's what God gave me," she'd answered as they picked pieces of bread from the bag between them and threw the crusts out onto the pond. The mallards soon began to fight over this gluten nightmare of a meal, their jade and jet colours flashing.

Where was Michael now? Her memories, like a photograph left to the sly tyranny of sunlight, they'd faded so that she remembered him in slights and snatches. The only thing she could really see was that question. Where was he now? And she wasn't sure whether she was asking about Michael or about...God. Both of them, really, had disappeared from her life. When Eric had got better last year she'd felt that at last her prayers had been answered; that she had finally found the connection with the Lord that had always been promised. But now? Nothing. Not a jot. Why didn't God come now to take her illness away? Why didn't he spare her dad the pain of his own body turning against him—a pain she would now have to endure. Why did He take Tim, Eric's first love? And none of that claptrap about how people need to suffer to have their own way in things. Free will nonsense. That was a cop-out of the crappest order. She never let Eric suffer if she could help it. As a parent, you don't. It just didn't make any kind of sense and that was precisely why she'd made the bargain in the first place. The bargain. She'd almost forgotten. So that was it, then? *God's collecting.*

Jhardine chewed on another mouthful of chips, watching a lady on the other side of the lake walking her dog. The geese hissed at the pup, which barked in return. The woman shouted. Finally, the geese waddled off into the water and the dog squeezed out a celebratory chorus as the honking birds sailed away.

Why do some birds like water? Do dogs have different barks for different moods? For that matter, how did we end up calling them Man's Best Friend?

Another chip. But they were getting cold fast. It was nippier, now, actually. The sky looked like it wanted to rain, but none was forecast. Happen they got it wrong. Or happen the sky had.

Why does the sky turn dark when it wants to rain? Why is the sky ever blue at all?

What would Eric do without her? Surely, he'd be fine. He was a bright lad, but too clever for his own good, as her mum would say. He needed to learn to keep his gob shut sometimes, and other times to speak up. It seemed like Eric had got Michael's shyness and her gabbiness in equal measure and the two were always fighting. Her thoughts circled back.

Should I try to find Michael?

She'd tried before of course, ringing round his work and his friends, but they all had no idea where he'd gone. It was like he'd just vanished. Maybe it was worth trying again though, if only for Eric's sake, because if anything did happen, she'd want him to have someone he could turn to.

Jhardine walked the short distance to the bin, thinking to dump the rest of her chips. The park didn't like folks littering, and at every bend along the paths there stood signs promising hefty fines for those who did. Yet there was still a lot of food in her hands that, she thought, shouldn't go to waste. Jhardine walked over to the bushes and slung her bag of chips underneath. A gammy looking pigeon bending a few branches in the tree above cooed at her in appreciation.

Her good deed done for the day, Jhardine walked down toward the water, losing herself in the clarity of its surface. It would be winter soon. The snow would come. So would the ice.

If ice is water what is frozen, why does it float?

All her life Jhardine had taken what came at her and hadn't asked any questions. Oh, she wasn't like Eric. He wanted a light on, full whack, no detail left unexplored. Jhardine was a coper, though, and coping means you don't really ask questions, doesn't it? You grope around in the twilight and get on with whatever is thrown at you. You get stuff solved, you get it done, then on to the next. You fix things. You heal hurts. You weather storms. You last until...you last until you don't.

She folded her arms and her fake leather jacket squeaked just a little. She smiled and at the same time realised she was crying.

Oh, bloody hell.

It wasn't a death sentence. No one had said she was dying. She could fight this. Well, the doctors could fight it and she just had to be the battleground. That's what Doctor Thompsette had said. She could deal with it. It was going to be bloody awful for a little while, but she could get through it.

Jhardine watched the geese bobbing on the water.

How do their feathers keep out the wet? What makes them float?

The geese on the water honked in chorus, their voices magnified in a lovely twist of sound. On their own the sounds had been discordant and grating. Together, they were powerful, even a bit frightening. To her the message was clear.

Jhardine was going to need help, wasn't she?

"YOU LOOK SHATTERED," she commented, putting a plate of chips and beans on the coffee table in front of Eric.

"Cheers, mum. Just what you want to hear, that," he said, knife and fork navigating his plate by the light of the television. She stood there just looking at him. Eventually, he noticed. "I know it's hard to believe I'm this good looking, and most of the time I'd welcome the gawping, I really would, but when it's my own mum—that's a bit sick, isn't it?"

"Aw, give over, you, I'm just remembering when I used to do this when you were a little boy."

"Stare at me for hours?" Eric licked his knife. "People get arrested for less."

"No. Well, yes," she said, sitting down on the chair arm. "I used to love doing you your meals. Oh, and your little packed lunches for school."

"To your credit, I was the best fed kid at that school." Eric employed one of his smirks. "N-no wonder I ended up with a heart condition. I was the only five year old eating a bowl of profiteroles."

"Well, all the parents kept saying how thin you were, like I was starving you or something." Jhardine sighed. "You never have put any weight on. You get that from your dad. Me, I only need to look at a tiramisù and I...." Now she was the one being stared at. "What?"

Eric turned his attention back to the TV. "It's just, you don't...." He chewed on another mouthful. "I think that's the first time you've ever said that to me. About Dad."

"Oh," Jhardine folded her hands in her lap. "I suppose it would be, yeah."

"I, er...." Knife and fork down, he burped and said, "Don't, like, get mad at me but I sort of...liked it."

"Yeah, I...." Jhardine kept her eyes fixed on the TV. "You look like him a bit too. Your eyes are mine, that gorgeous brown. But you've got his eyebrows. Great stripes that they are and one always wandering up your head. Him all over, that."

"We must go to the same waxing place," Eric smiled, wiggling his eyebrows to make her laugh. "Do I," Eric started, then changed course. "I know this is hard for you, so if you don't want to—"

"Ask me quick, love. Because for some reason I can talk about this tonight and I don't know how long that'll last. I...."

"Okay, well, I...I know he left you. And that, in my book, makes him a tosser."

"Good, because he was."

"Yeah. Yes. But, you loved him once, didn't you? Was he worth it?"

"I...." Jhardine tried. She really did. "You have his smile."

"Right." She could hear his disappointment.

"It's a kind smile, Eric. One a person could fall in love with." She hoped that answered as much of his question as she could. "Right, so, I should get on anyway."

"Mum," Eric said.

"No, please, no more—"

"No, I just wanted to say thanks for the tea. And you know, I hope you know that, that you're going to be making me my tea forever, right? You'll never be rid of me."

"I hope so," she said, soft and to herself. A hand to her chest.

"Oh, how did you get on with the doctors?" he said, tucking into his chips again.

"I, erm...." She folded her lips over her teeth.

"What is it?" The fear. Not in his eyes, no. In the way he was holding his fork tight, his knuckles blanching.

"I just," she bumbled. "They're doctors. You know what they're like. I've got to, erm, go back on Friday. More tests, more talking."

"Ah, right. Seems like they're being, you know, thorough this time?"

"Aye, yeah, it's good. It is." Just a few days more. Work out how to tell him properly. In the meantime, she had something to take care of. "I'm just going to make a phone call, love. I'll do it in the kitchen."

"All right," he said, yawning. "Here, Mum."

"Oh God, what now?"

"I'm going out to a club. I'll be back in a couple of hours, that all right?"

Could it be Ruth was right and he had a special someone? Oh, she hoped so. That would take a weight off her mind, that. "Yeah, course. Didn't expect you to be stopping in tonight anyway love. Have a good time, won't you?"

"Yeah," he said, though he really did look tired. Mind you, he'd been coming in at all hours lately.

Jhardine picked up the phone handset off the sideboard and walked through into the kitchen, tapping out the number as she went. "All right, Sanj? It's me."

"I know it's you, Jhardine. I've got your name in my phone, haven't I?"

"All right, keep your flipping bra on," she bit back.

"Well, it's half-nine at night. What you ringing for at this time?" And now Jhardine remembered why they didn't talk that often. "Here, you better not have hung up on me—"

"Sandra, I need to talk to you."

"Well, given you rang me I'd hope so."

"Just shut up, yeah. This is...." She reached in and closed the living room door, shutting Eric inside. Then the kitchen door. "This is serious."

"Is it...Mum? Has she fallen?" Then a little softer: "Did you push her?"

"No, I've not pushed her."

"I wouldn't blame you if you did."

"Sanj—"

"Serious. I've often thought about giving her a little nudge next time she's at the top of some stairs—"

"Sanj!"

The phone-line filled with all the unvoiced things Jhardine wanted to say. How could she even start to explain?

"Jhardine, what is it?"

She couldn't. Not over the phone. "I need to see you."

"What? Now? Jhardine, I'm in my jim-jams."

"Soon, Sandra." It was then that Jhardine noticed her hand was trembling. A full on tremor, and it wasn't out of fear or nerves. It was this thing in her head *making* it happen. "As...as soon as you can."

HE'D HAD MIND to dress up, a black shirt and his best jeans and, even though it wasn't his usual getup, Eric felt like he'd made a reasonable effort. Walking across the car park to the front entrance of Lion Lion, though, it emerged he'd made a critical mistake: dear Lord, compared to all the tangerine men and women in line he was dangerously pale.

"Have you got a fag, love?" said one woman in the queue in front of him. She wasn't so much orange as an odd greyish brown, like she'd been covered in gravy. She'd also shaved off her eyebrows and then drawn them back on. It made her look like her face was throwing boomerangs. Permanent surprise. He tried not to smile.

"No, I don't smoke."

"All right. I don't need a lecture," she huffed, one of her fake eyelashes coming unglued and fluttering to the floor. She turned back to her friends who all were sucking on electronic cigarettes.

"Have one of these, Lauren," said one of the other girls, handing over what to Eric always looked suspiciously like a mini vaginal probe.

"You know they explode sometimes. Could take your face off," Eric tried, smiling. They glared back. *This. This right here is why you don't have any friends,* Eric admonished himself. He shrank back, resigning himself to waiting in line alone.

You're not here to have fun anyway, Eric reminded himself. *You're here to find out about Tim.*

The conversation with his mum the other day had given him the idea. Tim had spent a lot of time down at Lion Lion through the years, so maybe someone at the club could give Eric a clue about what was going on in Tim's thick head the last few months of his life, that kind of thing. Mind you, getting here had been a public-transport nightmare. He'd been forced to take the bus because his car had finally given up the clingy ghost and refused to start. Nice to know where his first full pay packet was going—not.

The main entrance to the club was a neon lion, the doorway its open and snarling mouth. A bit on the nose, true, but the effect was eye-catching, and at the door there stood two bouncers, a man and a woman who both had a certain tractor-like build. They were checking IDs and rifling through handbags. And so when Eric reached the front:

"ID please," the woman with the close-cropped black hair asked. Eric handed over his provisional driver's license. She studied the picture, then his face. She studied the picture some more. *Take your time, love, but if we stand here much longer the ravages of time mean I won't look owt like that picture.* "All right," she said, handing it back and then grabbing at his hand. An inky stamp descended and Eric was branded with a miniature snarling lion. "In you go."

Descending via the maw of the beast and what Eric remembered about the place was soon confirmed: the deeper into the pit of a nightclub he went, the more his feet stuck to the floor. It was like someone had spread a thick layer of cooking oil all over everything. Eric's displeasure was only added to by the creeping music thudding through the speakers which caused fractals of colour to spiral through his vision. Warm jades, browns. A migraine? An impending epileptic fit? And people. So *many* people.

Eric shuffled his way through the crowds. He tried to stick to the perimeter of the lower dance floor so as to avoid the thickest groups. Even so, the air was warm and smelled like stale alcohol and vomit. Then a denim-shirt-clad man tipped a tray of drinks down Eric's back and Eric knew he was going to have one bastard of a night. "Mate, I am so...." The man said to a chorus of laughter from his nearby friends. "Here, let me wipe that—"

"No, you're reet," said Eric, holding up a hand. "Just leave it." Eric unbuttoned his shirt and peeled it off. Fortunately, he was wearing a black t-shirt underneath which, thankfully, hadn't got too wet.

"Here, Bernese, I didn't know there was going to be strippers."

"You're kidding, aren't you? He'd have to pay me before I'd let him take owt else off."

Eric, wounded beyond words by this, retreated to loitering behind pillars that held up the upper floor, finding those fixed spots where the music was broken behind the gold leaf and apple green of the supports and where he was safely out of sight from the bacchanalia. He wanted a taste of the people. He wanted to know why they came to places like this. Why Tim might have come—because, quite frankly, it baffled Eric. They were wenches and wankers, the lot. Preening for a poke. That couldn't have been Tim though. He wasn't that interested. And if he was, he could pick up a lass easy. They never lasted, of course. No one ever did, except for Eric.

"All right, mate, what can I get you?" said the bartender. Eric hadn't realised he was so close to the bar. He was about to refuse a drink when he realised the man, whose hair was shaved round the sides with a mass of spiralling brown hair on top, looked like a pineapple. Though not particularly thirsty, Eric took pity.

"Er, an orange juice please."

"What with?" the bartender said, taking out what apparently passed for a clean glass.

"Just orange on its own, cheers."

"Come on, feller. Live a little," the man said.

Eric was already having a crappy night. This wasn't helping. "All right then, I will."

"Yeah, good for you. What can I get you?"

"You can get me orange juice and ice."

Suddenly, the lights went down and the blacklights came on. The bartender's pink shirt, the uniform Lion Lion insisted on, glowed menacingly. His teeth were now gleaming white fangs. "Suit yourself," the bartender growled. Eric decided that while pissing off the guy might not have been the best way to prime him for information dredging, dredge was what he was going to do. "Here, here, do you recognise this guy? He used to come here a lot."

Eric showed the bartender a picture of Tim he kept on his mobile phone.

"I don't know. Were he as adventurous as you are?" the bartender said, not even glancing at the screen. "That'll be four eighty."

"For an orange juice? You're having a laugh, ain't you?"

"For the attitude," the guy said. He held out his hand, waiting. Eric fished in his jeans for the money. Night-light bloody robbery, this.

"There. Have it."

"It's customary to leave a tip." The man's eyebrow came up to a heady point.

Instead of giving a sarcastic *tip*, Eric tossed a few coins onto the bar, hearing the satisfying clatter as they rolled and tumbled onto the floor so the bartender would have to get down on his hands and knees to pick them up. *Probably wasn't the first time he'd been on his hands and knees for money anyway,* Eric thought. He returned to the dance floor, this time determined to extract some information from the natives.

"Hi, excuse me?"

"Not interested, mate." The woman with the high heels and shoulder pads apparently wasn't buying what she imagined Eric was selling. *Always nice to get turned down when you aren't even trying. Really good for the self-esteem, that.* Eric bobbed off, trying to dance so as to fit in and look casual, not at all bothered about the snub. He caught sight of himself in the long mirror on the far wall and vowed to never again lapse into what could only be described as Mum Dancing.

Eric searched for a more approachable woman. For a brief moment he realised this must be what sex offenders do when they are searching for a victim. It filled him with a kind of disquiet he had, until then, only guessed at. He was further dispirited when he saw one woman stood alone at a small table at the side of the room and the word *perfect* flashed through his head.

He approached her, checking for leering boyfriends or potential signs she had a can of mace.

"Hi, excuse me, I w-w-wondered if you'd seen this guy around here?" Eric rushed, fearing an impending kick to the groin. "His name is—well, was—Tim?"

"Sorry, what?"

"Tim," Eric said, trying to find the picture on his phone again.

"I'm Geri," the young woman replied.

"Er, hi, I...." *Wait, does she think I'm hitting on her?* "My friend, his name was Tim."

"You're both called that?" she yelled over the music. "How mental is that? That's like, written in the stars, isn't it?"

He was developing a facial twitch, he could feel it. One last time, then.

"He used to come here. Do you maybe recognise him?" He offered her the picture.

"What?"

"Have you seen him?"

"No, but I'd like to. He's well fit. Once the acne clears a bit." Eric took back the phone. *What acne?* Ah. Oh. But he'd never noticed. How weird was that? "Do you have his number?" the woman asked.

"No, I...." Eric was thrown now. It was like the picture, which was about seven months old, was brand new.

"I mean, he looks beefy. A bit too much for my taste, but I still—"

"He's just big. that's all, he's...." Eric stared some more.

"And the nose is a bit off, isn't it? But the jaw's good. And he has a good smile. What's his cock like?"

"What?"

"His cock?" said the oddly sexually confident woman in the modest dress. "It's personal taste of course, but I don't go out with any bloke unless I know his meat's under seven inches. I don't want to feel like someone's laying siege to my lady parts, thanks. If I wanted that I'd pay a professional. No, I want a bloke—"

"Look, sorry, I've got to, erm, go," Eric said, almost sprinting away.

"Wait, you were asking me...."

He took the stairs to the upper level two at a time and, in a quiet corner, had a small nervous breakdown. There was confidence and then there was *confidence.* After he'd managed to recover somewhat, he started scrolling through the pictures of Tim he had on his phone. There bathed in the awful green lights of the club, a cold sweat washed his skin. The woman was right. Tim's nose *was* a bit wonky. And had the redness in Tim's skin always been there? The fact that his hairline had retreated by about an inch? Was that new? And what about the dark circles under his eyes, like smears of lovely soot. Eric searched the photo album. That day at the beach. That hot night in Tim's flat when they'd almost.... The time Eric's car broke down on the motorway. They'd done a lot in those months since Eric's release from hospital, and per Tim's insistence Eric had taken plenty of pictures. He'd looked through them many times, too, but it turned out he'd never really seen them because, while Tim's imperfections weren't always obvious, they were still there. Why was it, then, Eric had never noticed before?

"So I think I'm going to have to ask for an extension on my course," said a young lad with a patchy beard to his friend who had the droopy lobes of someone who had started stretching his ears and then thought better of it.

"Excuse m...." Eric found himself saying before he'd even thought about it. Suddenly he didn't want to keep doing this. He wanted to go home and study Tim's pictures, to run over every single memory and dissect it, because the person he was looking at in these photos seemed wrong. "Excuse me," Eric repeated, absently, then tore himself away from looking at his phone. "S-sorry, have you got a second?"

"Yeah, sure. You okay?" He had a pleasant, round face and a pleasing, gliding voice that while a little too high for Eric's ear was quite soothing all the same.

"Yeah, yeah, I am, I just wondered if you'd seen this lad round?"

The young man stared. His eyes widened. "Here, ain't he the one who got killed? Found his body in town?"

Eric tried not to flinch. "Yeah. Yes, he is."

"Are you with the police? Cos I'm legal. Honest. I have my—"

"No, not the police."

"Oh, right, good." Then his eyes narrowed. "Then why do you have pictures of him on your phone?"

"Because I'm trying to...." Eric searched for the right words. "He was my friend, and I heard he came here quite a lot. I just wanted to try talking to people who talked to him."

"Right," the young lad nodded. "Well, sorry, I didn't. Know him, I mean."

Great big flipping moonface waste of my time you are! "Oh, right. No problem. Yeah."

"Yeah."

"Sorry to have bothered you."

Moonface became part of the crowd once again, leaving Eric to stand alone with his rapidly warming orange juice and pictures of his dead friend. A friend he didn't even recognise anymore.

TWELVE MORE STRANGERS, then another dozen, and then five more, at which point Eric realised he was talking to someone from the first group, and none of them had a clue who Tim was or why they should care.

"All right, yeah, sorry to bother you. Sorry."

Looking out across the sea of heads that bobbed on the dance floor, Eric felt lost. He ran his hand over the gold railing that marked the bar's perimeter, wondering if Tim had ever done the same, like if Eric closed his eyes tight and concentrated hard enough, he might be able to feel Tim there. But of course he couldn't. Finally he put down his empty glass. It was useless. He wasn't going to get any information in the lion's belly tonight.

Eric plodded down the stairs to the lower dance floor and tried to fold himself against the wall as a swathe of young men who looked vaguely familiar filtered by. They were the local football team, he realised. "Then I told her, if she's not going to put out, there's no point."

"What did she do?"

"She ended up giving me crabs."

Nope, Eric wasn't sorry to be leaving this place one bit.

"Here, mate," a light male voice called out as Eric was about to start the climb out of this hell. It was Moonface from earlier, though he was redder of complexion now and obviously a shade or two more tipsy. He leaned in at Eric's ear and shouted. "My girlfriend, my—"

Just then, a woman in a pink Lion Lion shirt waded out of the crowd and clipped her hand into Moonface's. "This is my girlfriend."

Proud of that, aren't you?

"This is Deborah and she, erm...." He searched, trying to find the track of his thoughts. "Oh, I told her, right, about how you're looking for people who knew your friend and she says she did. You said you did, didn't you, Debs?"

"Hi," Deborah held up her hand and gave an apologetic sorry-about-the-drunk smile.

"You knew Tim?"

"Yes. Well, sort of. I used to serve him a lot when he came in on Thursdays and Fridays. They're my days for managing the bar staff. God, it's loud in here," she said, laughing. "Let's go out to the car park. Shaun, darling, can you go get me a drink? I'll be back soon."

Eric's ears buzzed with anticipation as, in the cold car park air, they leaned against the wall next to each other. She was a beauty, this Deborah. Her neck was long, but her shoulders wide. Her hourglass hips the same. She had the presence of being expertly cut from lonely stone, but it was how she looked away as she said, "He died, didn't he?" that truly allowed Eric to like her just a little bit.

"Y-yeah. Yeah, he did."

"I'm sorry. He must have been a good friend to you for you to come down here and do all this. I mean, you don't look like the type to want to be in nightclubs and all that."

"I'm not. Neither was he, really. Or that's what I thought," Eric said.

"Right," she smiled again. "I guess I should tell you what I know then. So, erm, like I said I used to serve him. He wasn't a regular like but he wasn't easy to miss, you know?"

"Sure, yeah."

"Well, anyway, he stopped coming in for a while. I don't know why. Then, just over a year ago, he was back and he was drinking really heavily. Like, I mean, he needed gills, he was putting the drink away so fast. I asked him what the matter was and he said, erm, that his brother or a friend, I don't remember exactly but, that they were really sick and he thought they were dying and that he couldn't handle it. He said that a lot."

I can't handle it.

"He kept saying he was a terrible person because he wasn't strong enough to say...."

"Say what?"

"I don't know," she said, an apologetic tilt to her head. "I never got it out of him."

"Oh," Eric said, trying not to let the ambiance of his hurt show.

She stroked her ponytail of plum-coloured hair that was hanging down over her right shoulder. If she knew Eric felt wounded, she didn't let on. "Well, erm, he came in fairly regular after that. We didn't get much chance to talk. That was sort of on purpose. Tim could be a bit, how do I say this?"

Eric could feel the edge near. They were tipping over into new territory. "Just say it. Honestly, it's okay."

"Well, he was a bit grabby, sometimes."

"What?"

"Like I'd walk past him and he'd put his arm around my waist and pull me over. Look, I'm not saying he'd have ever gone any further than that, but it made me uncomfortable, you know?"

Eric had never seen Tim do that to anyone. Not ever.

"You're sure you're talking about Tim Jeffries? This guy?" Eric showed her the picture on his mobile phone. She nodded and looked appropriately sad, though he noticed that her lips were pursed as though she was having to put up with a bad taste in her mouth.

"The thing is, eventually he stopped and I mean, he even apologised once for it. He said he'd been going through some stuff but he was better now. He seemed genuine enough, and he laid off the booze, so I made my peace with it, you know? But the thing was he was meeting this other woman here. Erm, oh God, I'm getting this all muddled," she laughed. "Okay, so I heard that the police were saying that there were drugs involved, you know?"

"Yeah?"

"Well, the thing is, and I'm not saying this as a fact, but the woman that Tim was meeting was on our watch list. We have this, like, thing where if we suspect someone might be dealing we get members of staff to keep an eye on them at all times. Like in the bathrooms where obviously we can't have cameras, and in the corners of the building where security can't see."

The music still thudding away inside the club seemed to make the ground lurch beneath Eric's feet.

"She was on our list. Thing was, we didn't think she was selling, like, normal drugs. There's this thing going round. I don't know if you've heard of it. It's called Mineral. It's—"

"A weird kind of steroid," Eric finished for her, feeling the crush as the two bits of information collided into one solid truth.

"Right well, it's not just that. It's like this stuff that you get off the Internet and it's for all sorts of like fitness stuff. Like if you want to get slimmer, there's a kind for that. And if you wanna bulk up, there's a formula for that too. And there's a type what makes you not have to sleep for days. That's what we were getting a lot of in the club. We caught her once, and she had this stuff on her. She said you can't do nowt because it's just a supplement, like. And she didn't have enough for us to take it to the police. She said that the vial she had was just her own, you know."

Eric straightened. "She was blonde, weren't she?" he said, his brain making the leap before his mind was even aware of it. "Thin like. Big eyes. Called herself Sally."

"Yes, yeah, how did you know?"

Eric swallowed. "Because I'm not lucky enough for it to just be a coincidence."

SANDRA SAWED AWAY at a gristly bit of fried bacon. "I don't know why we had to meet at this God-forsaken greasy spoon." She glanced round at the yellowed walls and cheap sets of tables and chairs with the air of a woman who wanted nothing better than to dowse the motorway-side diner in bleach, the other somewhat gnarled patrons included.

"We're here because I don't want folk knowing my business, that's why."

"But it's so late, Jaz. I'm probably going to have to stay with Mum."

"Well, just don't leave no fingerprints when you suffocate her and you'll be fine," Jhardine said, shaking out a sugar packet into her tea. *I'm sure these things are getting smaller, thank you, Nanny State.*

"So why am I here? I'm assuming you've not dragged me all the way up from Sheffield and then away from yours just so we can enjoy the ambience of this dive."

Jhardine used her cup of tea to stop up her own gob and ensure she didn't say something they'd both regret.

"No," she said, putting the cup down after a *long* drink. "I asked you up here, Sanj, because, well...." Deep breath. "You know how when we were kids we did that thing where we cut our hands and swore on our blood to always be there for each other."

"No," Sandra said. "I remember you coming at me with a butter knife and trying."

"Well, same difference isn't it?" Jhardine waved it away. "And I hope I have been there for you, you know. Like when you were going through that bad patch with your work and, even though you know I had all that to sort out with Eric, I was still there for you—"

"Yes, bloody Saint Jhardine strikes again."

"No, that's not what I...." Well, it sort of was what she meant, but people aren't really supposed to know you're emotionally blackmailing them, are they? Jhardine decided on trying a different approach. "You know we've always got on, Sanj."

"What house did you grow up in?"

"No, but I mean really."

Sandra shrugged. They'd never had a serious falling out, not like Sarah next door and her brother. They never spoke. Something to do with a three-legged horse, she didn't like to pry. "I suppose we've managed to be there for each other, haven't we?" Sandra smiled. She stuck a bit of fried tomato in her mouth and seemed unaware of the juice dripping down her chin. Jhardine reached forward and wiped it up with a napkin.

"Just like when we were kids. Used to be more food on you than in you."

"I always felt a bit bad, Jaz."

"How'd you mean?"

"I mean, there you are, seven years old and having to cook and that."

"I liked looking after you. God knows Mum and Dad weren't about to do it. Remember that time they phoned from bloody Portugal?"

Sandra laughed. "Useless, weren't they? Mind you, I think we had more fun that way." Her carefully tweezed eyebrows rose. "Remember Ricky Keller?"

"Oh my God." As sisters they'd made a pact to share everything. Ricky Keller, now a touring DJ, had been on that list. A few times. "But didn't he have—"

"He had gingivitis. He couldn't help the bad breath—"

"Oh, it were like someone had opened a sewer."

"Don't, I'm gagging just thinking about it!"

They laughed. Jhardine picked a tear out of her eye. For some reason, she thought this was the moment. "Sandra, I've, er, I've got a lump."

Sandra had half a hash brown in her gob. "You what?"

"I have a lump. You know, a tumour?"

"Jhardine...."

"The good news is, it's in my brain and you know that doesn't get used right often." Sandra was already starting to tear up. "Oh, don't make a big fuss about it Sandra."

"A big fuss? It's a tumour!"

"Well, it isn't spreading, they don't think, so I reckon I'll be okay," she said, reaching for Sandra's hand. "Only thing is, they can't take it out right now because of where it is. They're going to try to, I don't know, zap it or something. I've not been told everything yet. But they can make it shrink."

"Slow down. Just.... Wait, when did you find out?"

"Just recent."

"Does Mum know?"

"Course not. She's probably the one what gave me it. Always sodding running round after her. I never get any help...." She picked up her cup of tea and took a sip. "No. I figured that if I drop dead she'd find out then. Otherwise, I'm going to keep it from her for as long as possible."

Fortunately, Sandra was mindful of their mum's eccentricities and didn't press it further. "What about Eric?"

"Well, I'll have to tell him at some point but until everything is, you know, definite, like what treatment I'm having and when it starts, I don't want to say owt. You know what he's like, always asking bloody questions. Until I've got answers myself I don't want to be bothered with it."

"Make sure you tell him soon, Jaz," Sandra said, her voice warm and low. "You need support at a time like this."

"Well, that's sort of why I phoned you. I have a favour to ask, Sandra, and I thought I'd be better doing it in person."

"Say it, Jhardine. Anything you want." She pulled back her straight hair from her face, letting her pretty eyes catch all of the light. It was as if she'd planned to be the martyr tonight.

"You remember what happened to Dad?" Sandra's eyes misted again. "Yeah," Jhardine added but no more needed saying on that front, clearly. "Well, they reckon the treatments are a lot better nowadays but, even so, I don't want Eric having to look after me when I'm, you know, going through it. At my worst I mean. So I wondered if you'd come up here for a bit and, you know, help out?"

Sandra pushed her plate away and began tapping the end of her fingernail on the table. "I don't know, Jhardine," she said. "I'm really busy at the moment. I'm taking a new course. Media studies." Sandra was one of those people who collected degrees she never intended to use. It had always been a source of aggravation for Jhardine, who'd had to give up any dreams of going back to university when Eric got sick. She bit her tongue. Actually bit it.

"I'm not asking for a carer," Jhardine said as upbeat as she could. "I mean, from what I gather there are going to be some bad days but on the whole I could be okay, touch wood." She knocked on the table. "And I still plan on going to work and all that when I can. All I'm saying is that it would be nice to have a bit more support and not to have to worry about, sort of, well, being strong for Eric. Basically, I need someone who can manage him while I'm trying to manage myself."

"Jhardine, I just think me being there might be a problem—"

"No, you'd be no trouble at all. I'll just turf our Eric out onto the sofa downstairs and you can have his bed. I'll have to delouse it, mind, but—"

"No, I meant...." Sandra straightened. She'd made up her mind then. "It's just not going to be convenient, Jhardine, and I don't think it would be good for either of us. We might get on, but that's because we give each other plenty of space. I—"

"Yeah." Jhardine stood. "Forget it," she said, zipping up her coat.

"No, Jhardine, please don't be upset, I—"

"I'm not upset. It's just I should have known better than to ask you for help."

"What's that supposed to mean?"

"I'm the one...staring death in the face and somehow you managed to make it about you and your crappy media course!"

"I'll have you know it's an exclusive and rigourous examination of turn of the century—"

"If I die," Jhardine whispered, "don't bother coming to the funeral. And if I don't die, don't bother coming round on birthdays and Christmas. I don't want to see you or hear from you again."

She put her handbag under her arm and, turning away despite Sandra's breathless pleas, she walked out of the service station with her lip wobbling but her head held high.

ERIC HAD WALKED for miles, letting the night's sounds rush over him. The crowing of the traffic, the beady eyes of the birds that seemed to be on every streetlamp on every corner. The long tail of the town's sodium lights stretched behind him. Most nights he liked to look at that, but not tonight. Tonight it left him feeling sick.

Eric realised how cold he was. He'd left his shirt in the club and his t-shirt wasn't keeping out the frigid air. He didn't want to keep on walking anymore, either. As luck would have it, a bus stop up ahead stuck out with its happy cream L.E.D lights, and a glance at the bus stop's sign told him it would drop him off at the top of Hainsworth, just a five-minute walk away from home. He scraped up the money from his pocket and found he had just enough silver and copper to get by.

Eric took a seat in the domed red shelter two spaces away from the only other occupant: a middle-aged woman in a mass of reddish black shawls. She had eyes that were acid yellow, lips that were a dark purple, and black skin that shone bright compared to the dull of the fabric she was dressed in. For some reason, the sight of her quickened the thing in his chest, but he ignored that. He put his head in his hands, wanting nothing more than to be at home, in bed. To not be thinking. How he hated *thinking* all the damned time.

After a few minutes, the woman spoke up: "Do you happen to know what time it is?"

Eric looked up at her, as though needing to read the question off her lips. Then he went into his pocket and pulled out his phone. "Erm, it's quarter past twelve. It should be here any minute."

"Oh, I see." The woman folded her arms but in so doing exposed her right hand. It was a calm steel. A hand made of metal. She began tapping her metal thumb and forefinger together. She caught him looking. "A terrible accident," she said, smiling.

He nodded, not wanting to pry.

"I know why I'm out here at this hour, but why are you?" she asked in a crotchety accent he couldn't quite place.

"I was out. You know, a club?"

"It can't have been a very good club if you're leaving this early."

Eric leaned back and folded his arms. "I wasn't exactly there for fun."

"I see." She withdrew a packet of chewing gum from beneath the petals of her shawl. "Would you like some?"

The orange juice from the club had left a chalky taste in his mouth. "Yeah, cheers." He let the woman slip him first one, then two red tablets. Peppermint, he realised as he chewed. And another taste he couldn't quite discern. Tangy. Metallic.

"If you weren't there for fun, then what were you there for?" she said. "If you don't mind me asking, of course."

Eric didn't want to get into the story. Instead, he thought of ways he could give an abstract. "I suppose I was looking to find something. Something I've lost."

"Oh." The metal hand creaked. The sound scattered strange smells through Eric's senses. Petrol. Rose water. Blood.

"You know, when I lose something," the woman began, "I'm always careful to make sure that I'm looking for what there is to find, and not what I would like there to be."

He was about to reel off a rather witty remark, something along the lines of her talking out of a particular lower orifice, when what she'd said didn't so much as click as piss in his face.

I've been looking for the person I thought Tim was. But tonight shows it, doesn't it? I didn't know him at all. At least, not who he was when he wasn't with me.

As he was thinking this, the single-decker bus slurred its way to a halt just a little way after the bus shelter's door. Eric got to his feet, then he held back, remembering his manners. "You first," he croaked. He got no reply, and turned to look. The woman wasn't on the seats. He scanned about. There was no sign of her either up or down the road. Eric was alone except for a lazy bluebottle buzzing against the plastic window of the shelter.

"You getting on or what, mate?" came the annoyed bus driver's voice.

CHAPTER NINE
EVENING DRINKS

YOU DESERVE—

"Yeah, yeah." Eric slipped on a pair of jeans and pulled on his work jumper. Winter seemed to be coming in quick this year. Just opening the window to let some fresh air into his room was enough to make Eric's testicles ascend so far they might never come back down. *Great. It'll be Christmas soon. Christmas...without Tim.*

Picking up his rucksack, and with one final longing glance at his bed and the missed night's sleep he couldn't make up now he was among the gainfully employed, he shuffled out onto the landing.

"Mum?" Eric knocked on her bedroom door. No reply. "Mum." Again, nothing. He pushed open the door. The unmade bed was vacant. The bathroom? The door was open, the room empty. Then the sound of a car going past outside echoed through the house far louder than it should. He bounced down the stairs to find his mum stood in the open doorway. She was still wearing her dark green nightgown, and was looking out on the estate with a kind of stillness that was unnerving.

"Mum? You all right?"

"Ah!" She started when he touched her shoulder. "Oh dear God, you nearly killed me then," she laughed.

"Sorry. You been out?" Eric pointed at her muddy trainers that were dangerously close to the hall carpet.

"No, I...." She looked confused. "I...yeah. Yeah. I couldn't sleep so I came downstairs and then I stood here because, well, I suppose I must have needed fresh air. Yeah, that was it." She shook her head, her frazzled curls wobbling back and forth, and hugged herself. "I'm bloody freezing."

"Come on, I'll put you on a cup of tea and make you something to eat."

"I don't really have time, the church—"

"You'll have to make time, won't you?" he said, steering her toward the kitchen. "Now, sit yourself down, Madame, and let the staff cater to you."

He'd earned himself a laugh. "Sorry I'm being so weird love, it's the not sleeping right that's doing it."

"Aye. But then you've always been a bit weird, Mum."

"Oi, you!"

Tea and toast cooked up, he watched her eat.

"Car's buggered, but I could get a taxi back and pick you up tonight if you wanted?"

"No, ta, love, but Ruth's offered. She's going to take me down to the café just so I can collect a few things. I've decided to take a couple of days to myself, even though we can't really afford it."

"We can. I'm working now, remember?"

That seemed to cheer her. But only for a moment. "I've got a hippo's arse of a headache," she groused.

"Sometimes you're so ladylike Mum, I don't know if I can stand it."

SHE'S GETTING WORSE.

It was the sound in every footstep, the blare in every car horn, the greeting of familiar faces as Eric walked his way through town.

She's getting worse.

That fact chased him all the way to the industrial estate and through the peevishly slow metal gate into the Radley firm's yard.

"Aye up, Eric," Grant nodded his way as the group of lads he was chatting to parted to let Eric join their circle.

"All right?"

"Aye, good. Jamie's just telling us about his nights out."

Jamie, a big lad with greasy black hair and a bit of a squint, gave Eric a friendly nod. "So, we were just walking out of this bar and this lass fell into the road and, honest to God, a taxi crawling up the street ran over her head."

"Bullshit!" Grant announced.

"No, I swear on my life, right, and then she gets up and she's absolutely fine except for the dirty great big tyre mark over the side of her face. She says she needs a drink. She did Jell-O-shots for the rest of the night."

"Well, that's typical of lasses round here, at least," Grant blew out cigarette smoke. Eric hadn't even seen him take a drag. "What do you think, Eric? They're all slags, aren't they?"

"No more than the men," Eric replied, which earned him a round of laughter. Grant, however, looked a tad suspicious.

"You got yourself a girlfriend, Eric?"

"Can't say I do, or that I'd want one."

"Why? You a bender, Eric?"

So quiet you could have heard a mouse fart. "When you've got a face like mine you take it where you can."

Grant laughed around his cigarette. The group of lads, given this most gracious of cues, tinkled with laughter too. "You're all right, you are, Eric. Know how to take a joke, don't you?"

"Among other things," Eric nodded, earning himself another bout of strained laughter. *Yes, all laugh at the funny homosexual. That's right.*

"Listen, Peter's going to tell you you're off out with us today," Grant said, putting an arm round Eric's shoulders. "I've wangled it so you're with me. I've got us a special job."

"Special?"

"Aye, but don't say anything to Peter. The old coot doesn't know. If you fancy earning a few more bob on the side though, you keep it schtum, yeah?"

"Ah, Eric!" Peter waddled up, his face the colour of a rotting strawberry. "You're early. I like that. Right, has Grant told you?"

"Yeah, boss, I did."

"Good. Right, Eric, I need you to go see Kathy in the office to sign a few forms, you know, to say you won't sue us if you fall through a floor or something."

"A floor?"

"Hopefully just a precaution. And then I'll take you through the procedure."

The procedure wasn't nearly as grand as the title implied. The firm emptied repossessed houses and anything that was valuable was then sorted out back at the depot with an eye for selling whatever they could. "And here's stuff what you should look out for."

I was recently told I have preternatural powers and my best friend is now marauding round town, apparently killing folk. But today I'm going to be clearing up some poor family's abandoned tat. Eric stifled a sigh and listened as best he could.

THE VAN RIDE through to the city was ball-achingly bumpy thanks to Eric, as the fledgling member of the group, being consigned to sit in the back of the van on a makeshift and unpadded wooden seat. Annoying to say the least. The journey also gave the boys, Grant, Jamie and the driver

Morris, who wasn't nearly as jaunty as his name suggested, a chance to talk—which, in Eric's opinion, was never a good thing.

"You live near here?" Grant asked, taking out a toothpick and digging at the gaps between his oddly white teeth.

"Hainsworth Estate," Eric rattled as the van rocked over another sleeping policeman.

"I'm out on Grange Head, near the football field."

"Do you play?" asked Morris of Eric, and then started honking his horn at the traffic.

"No," Eric said. "I used to when I was little, but I had to give it up when I was ill. Keep fit now like."

"Yeah," Grant said in a husky drear. "Peter told us about you."

"Is it true?" Jamie's moist eyes narrowed as he turned to peer at Eric. "That you were going to die?"

After over twelve months worth of practice Eric had come to realise exactly what people wanted to hear. "Well, I was sick, and I did get better when they didn't expect that I would. But my heart problems weren't nearly as bad as they reckoned in the papers."

"I knew it," Jamie tutted.

Grant cracked his brawny hands. "Almost there now, lads."

A few minutes later and the van pined to a halt. Eric peered out of the window.

"I thought you only did abandoned homes?" he said.

"This was my idea. I have a mate whose dad works on the council. They've been wanting to empty this place for months," Grant replied, rummaging in his pocket until he found a rusted metal hoop on which dangled four large keys.

"And Pete—"

"Don't sweat about Pete, yeah? There's loads of stuff in there what's mint. Look, we're just going in and having a look around, take out some odd bits of furniture what could have been in anywhere and, if it's worth it, we'll tell Pete all about it. No harm." With those last words he smiled, but his eyes remained fixed on Eric like two knives hovering just meters from Eric's face. "So, let's crack on," Grant added at last, and the lads piled out of the van leaving Eric stuck in the back. In the silence he listened as the van's internal workings muttered and groaned. Finally, Grant yanked the back door open. "Look alive, Eric."

Eric stepped out onto Manning Street, letting his eyes adjust to the grey temper of the sky. Heath Library stared down at them, its unloved windows all mostly smashed, its rash of a garden turned to brambles that had flowered with crisp packets and old water bottles. The library's aged doors weren't in much better condition, either. So many people had carved their names, or left behind graffiti dicks, that it was hard to see the grandeur the library once held.

Grant reached forward and inserted a thick key into the lock. It took a good shove, but the doors eventually opened with the slow pine of a dying animal.

Oh.

After the atrium of the reception and through the gated inner door, the main room of the building was illuminated by high windows that extended the room's length, and in that dusty light Eric could see tables and chairs on which were stacked spires and keeps and little villages of books. Rows and rows of shelving on the sides and at the rear of the room were similarly packed, but heartbreak and horror: many of the library's books lay strewn across the floor, their pages spread and bent so they looked like mangled beetles. Grant crunched the books into the ground as he walked about the place with hungry eyes.

"Not bad, not bad at all."

"Wonder what's up them stairs?" Morris coughed, pointing to one of two separate curving staircases at either side of the room that interrupted the run of shelves.

"It's a mezzanine," Eric said. "They used to have the computer bays and media catalogue up there. I—" The sound of birds moving in the rafters made Eric jump.

"We've got ourselves a flincher," Jamie guffawed. Eric gave him a condescending glare, but he didn't seem to notice.

"Right, lads," Grant clapped his hands. "Let's pack some of this furniture in the van. We'll see what computer stuff there is. Then we'll work out a price and see if it's worth bothering about." Grant handed Eric a chair. "Anywhere else in here likely to have owt?"

"They, er," Eric stumbled, "they had their offices down at the back. And there was a supply cupboard, I think."

"Good stuff. Let's get cracking."

Searching through just half of the back rooms took the rest of the morning. At some point Grant had noticed there was a fireplace in the roomy staff office that, with the ornate scrollwork and dark metal, looked like it might be worth something, and then became obsessed with getting it on an auction website as quickly as possible. He'd also ripped down two of the low hanging ceiling lights that he couldn't bear to leave up just in case someone else stole them.

"Tell Jamie," Grant said as he examined the coloured glass of a lamp shade, "I want him to have a look at the roof tiles. I reckon they're slate. We'll get a fortune for that."

I'm going to regret this, Eric thought. "I don't…." No sooner was it out of Eric's mouth than Grant's eyebrow turned crooked. Clearly, he could hear the dissent in Eric's voice. "No, I know that this isn't legal."

"I told you, I'm doing it for a friend on the council."

"Still, we could get in trouble for this. Big style."

"What are you saying?" Grant put down the light fitting on the carpeted floor. With a screwdriver still in hand, he advanced on Eric. The shadow heart in Eric's chest zinged with interest. "Listen, Eric, if you're going to be part of this team you need to learn to shut up and take what I say as gospel. And I say we're doing this."

"No, I—"

"Besides," he said, pointing the screwdriver and smiling, "you'll get a few grand from all this when we're done, so…."

"A few grand?"

Grant smiled. "Aye, at least. Maybe even more if you play your cards right. So you going to help me load this lot into the van then?" Grant pushed the heavy chandelier into Eric's hands. "Or should I send you back to the office?"

LAMBY SLAPPED THE bonnet of Eric's sorrowful looking car. "To be honest, Eric mate, I don't even think there's enough that's working on this thing to class it as a repair job."

"Aw, come on Lamby, please, mate. I can't afford a new car right now," Eric pleaded. Then, to sweeten the deal: "I'll take a look at your tax return if you give it a good go." The prospect of clawing back a few quid from the state was enough to make anyone round Yorkshire more amenable, but Lamby was a tough customer. He didn't cave easily. He stroked his beer belly like he was gestating something to be proud of and squinted at Eric's wreck of a car, his raisin-like face scrunching even more than usual.

"All right, but you better save me a fortune!"

"I will, I will!"

"Fine, you just hang round for an hour, I'll get her up on the blocks and see what I can do for nowt. I'm not promising anything, though."

"Cheers, mate!" Eric said, handing over the keys.

"Aye, you're right." Lamby, cigarette threatening to fall from his mouth, leaned over Eric's car and started prodding its insides.

Now was as good a time as any, Eric reckoned.

"Here, Lamby, you know Tim?"

"Aye," he said. "May he rest in peace." Lamby crossed himself. Eric hadn't even realised Lamby was religious so this was a bit of a revelation.

"I just wondered, erm, what was he like? To you, I mean. When he was here."

"Tim? He was a good laugh. And when I first took him on, you know, I was impressed. He was a hard worker, though I had to stop him from bloody doing free work. He couldn't say no to anyone with a pretty face." Lamby took out a torch from his pocket and shone the light on the car's workings. He leaned over, running his fingers over wires and bolts. "But toward the end things got a bit...sticky."

Eric knew enough now to have prepared himself for this cold hit. Even so, it felt like a splinter of bone had worked loose and was stabbing the back of his throat. "How's that?" he asked, head down, eyebrows hunkered. These defences never worked but his body did it anyway.

"Well, I'm sad to say I had to let the lad go. Like I told the police," Lamby said, beginning to tinker. "He was a good worker. Really was. But just lately he'd been so unreliable. I mean, he wouldn't even show up some days. I didn't want to have to do it. And I said to him, you know," Lamby looked up at Eric. "I said to him, when you've sorted yourself out, come back. There'll always be a job for you here. But it weren't to be, I suppose."

"No, I guess, guess not. D-did Tim have, erm, a locker here?"

"Yeah, he did. Actually I've been meaning to clean it out for a while but since he died, I don't know, I've not been able to stomach it."

"I can do it for you if you want?"

"Yeah, if you don't mind. They're just back there, and they're not locked because we all kept losing the bloody keys. But just be careful, yeah, there's car parts everywhere. That new girl I've hired is great but she's chuffing messy."

"No worries," Eric said as he slipped by Lamby and ventured down into the dark of the garage. The motor oil smell was pleasant, the black grease that seemed to cover the walls a joy. Eric had always had a liking for anything that vaguely whiffed of petrol. It was a bit of a fetish, truth be told, but he didn't have time for that now.

He reached the row of blue lockers by the stairs to the office only to realise that Lamby hadn't told him which locker was Tim's. Eric's first few attempts at guessing resulted in a whole lot of nothing as well his stumbling on Lamby's hidden stash of chocolate bars and porn magazines. Women of colour with large breasts were apparently Lamby's choice selections, though Eric was pleased to see he only kept soft-core porn at work. A little decorum goes a long way.

As it turned out, Tim's locker was the final one on the middle row. It had been dented so, even though it wasn't locked, it was harder to open than the rest. It took a good few tugs before it gave and, in rattling the locker door open, a piece of paper dropped to the floor. Eric bent to pick it up. A closer inspection revealed it wasn't just paper, but a picture of Eric and Tim. In fact, it was the original picture from which Eric had drawn the one at home above his desk. Looking at it now though, there were a few differences to what Eric had depicted. Where Eric had drawn smooth skin, Tim's cheeks were pitted; where in Eric's drawing Tim's eyes were full of light, there in the picture his eyes were glassy and unfocused. And their postures were wrong, too. Eric had drawn Tim looking directly out at the person taking the picture while Eric was looking only at Tim. Yet, in the real photo Eric wasn't even looking at Tim. No, he was looking past him—at what, Eric couldn't remember. And in the true picture Tim wasn't smiling. In fact, he didn't look happy at all.

Eric ran a finger over the image before pocketing it with a deep breath and no small hit of pain. Trying to resist that bitterness, he turned his attention to what else was in the locker. A pair of Tim's jeans. They'd be huge on Eric but he decided to take them anyway. Next was a half-empty bottle of energy drink, something that wasn't a surprise as Tim had hardly ever turned up anywhere without one. Can thrown in the bin, Eric rummaged further. A crisp packet, a pound coin, a ten-pence piece and then, right at the back of the locker, Eric found a white box about fifteen centimetres long and wide enough so that Eric couldn't quite fit his hand all the way around it. Opening it he found there was a vial inside, like the one Eric had taken from Tim's bathroom, but this one was still half full of a syrupy black liquid. Eric strained to remove the bottle's top, and eventually it came away with a begrudging pop. He sniffed.

The smell made Eric's shadow heart throb. His eyesight misted with colour, and the music from the speakers around the room became iron violin strings wrapping his chest and cutting into his flesh. Eric choked as he put the top back on the bottle. Taking deep breaths, Eric steadied himself against the wall. Slowly. his vision cleared and his senses stopped their over-boil. He turned the box over in his hands wondering, though not really convinced, if it had a manufacturing mark or some clue as to its origin. In the left corner of the box, in small, square lettering that Eric had missed before, sat a single word.

Mineral.

Making sure the lid was on tight, Eric slid the vial into his coat pocket. He was about to close the door when he noticed a small piece of dark blue card in the corner of the locker that he'd missed before but now it seemed to shine with an odd neon outline. He picked the card up. There, in silver ink, was written a simple message:

Green View Bridge
9:00 pm

Eric's hand curled around the card. "Let's have you then, Tim," he whispered.

GREEN VIEW BRIDGE had the look of a medical suture gone slack and rotten, its crumbling brown and black stone sagging over the old railway line. The local council had sought to preserve the bridge with thick metal supports until funds could be raised for a proper repair job. In the daylight there was no hiding the fact that it looked ugly, like barbed wire snaring a dying bird, yet at nighttime the cage gave off a docile shine that, from a distance, looked like a heavenly split in the sky or a rift into another world. But the bridge, oh, this bridge, it had emotional weight. It had gold. Oil wells. Poetry. It was where Eric'd had his first kiss with Tim. Not their only kiss, but there was something special about that night.

Remembering this but not feeling particularly happy or comforted by it, Eric put his elbows on the black stone of the bridge and looked out across the uneven land. The hills were like bodies sleeping side by side, but they'd grown cold and turned away from each other. He tried to cheer himself up by stirring the ash of other memories.

There. The grassy dip and then the rise before a steeper slope down to Coleridge Primary School. Eric and Tim had flouted school rules and come far out while they played catch with a round, hard squash ball they'd found. Tim had accidentally clobbered Eric with it when he'd lost a few games too many—the day before school photos, too.

You deserve what you get, said the hissing, nasty voice in his head.

There. At the other side of the bridge by the long expanse of fields, a dead tree. After one long and boring summer day at school, Tim had found a wasps' nest there in the hollow. He'd wanted to stick lit cigarettes into it and see the insects rise into the air as one angry noise. Eric had stopped him, though for that he'd earned Tim's dangerous silence for nearly a week.

"You don't tell me what to do," Tim had spat in Eric's face when they finally spoke again.

It was one of only three times they'd ever had a falling out, and to make up for it Eric had let Tim have his pick of Eric's manga comics. They'd had their second kiss not long after.

You left me.

And there. The electric pylon. The place where Eric'd asked his mum and Tim to spread his ashes when life killed him.

"You planning on having us join you quick, are you?" Tim had asked.

When I needed you, you were gone.

Eric uncurled the little blue card he had kept all night in his cold hand. Sure, this spot on the bridge was as good a place to kill as to kiss. The schoolkids would be long gone by nine at night, and the industrial park to which the track under the bridge led, well it would be deserted, its clanging steel voices resting until the tease of sunrise.

So, was it here that it was done? Was this grass underfoot stained by Tim's blood? Eric looked but he couldn't see it. Did the air move with Tim's screams? He imagined that the echo of death might not fade so quickly, that such an horrific event might reverberate in this place. Yet, though he strained, he could find no hint of it in the night.

Eric's shoulders felt heavy. He was tired. So tired. He let the blue card drop to the ground, and soon after he followed it. He pulled his black jacket tighter as he looked up at the dark sky. What would it feel like to die here? Then, *Oh, you're a fucking cheery sod, you,* he thought. *Fill your boots with it then. Get it out of your system. Have done with this. Move on.*

After a while, Eric took out the vial he'd found at the garage and held it up to the sky. He looked at the drug, the black liquid and how it could eclipse the stars. Why did Tim use it? And what *exactly* did it do for him? Reason said it probably worked like other muscle-building drugs, but not exactly the same. Eric liked to think Tim was at least smart enough not to make the same mistake twice. After a while Eric found his thumb was playing with the cap on the bottle. Testing the drug would be one way to find out exactly what it did. Stupid, but efficient. He sat up and unscrewed the top. Uncapped, the smell of the liquid raced through his senses once again.

Thud. It made his shadow heart beat faster. How could it do that? He knew something, a faint scrap of a thing dancing on the wind just outside his reach, but it wouldn't settle. He knew he knew, but what it was he couldn't drag into the light. Something about this substance, this poison that had been Tim's drug of choice. And something to do with the dark art of shadow forming. He knew it, and yet....

"Bah!" he complained.

Thud.

A bolt of colour shot through Eric's vision. Fumes erupted from the bottle, and the sudden gush of odour rushed to the back of his throat. Through a hacking cough Eric placed the cap back on the bottle. It felt warmer, and when he held it up in the light the liquid seemed to be pulsing, surging up the bottle's length and then retracting.

"You abandoned me," said a throaty voice somewhere in the dark. Eric couldn't see anyone, but that voice was familiar—and close. "You just left me."

Eric pocketed the vial and scrambled to his feet. Searching, searching, gaze roving over the track down past the school, then the other side out to the industrial park, but there was no one there.

"I would have been everything to you, but you couldn't see me for who I was."

Eric backed up over the balding ground, turning, straining his eyes to try to find where the monster stood.

"You're n-not him," Eric said, rubbing at his neck which had begun to hurt fiercely. "You're just a figment. You're a bad copy—"

"And you were always a bad friend. Never good enough!"

Pale, almost blue arms, slid up from the ground and brawny hands latched on to Eric's ankles. Eric fell forward, landing half on his side. Pain shot through his ribs, but he had presence of mind to kick and struggle—he needn't have bothered though. The hands that had grabbed him were already gone. Eric, shaking with adrenaline, stumbled as he regained his feet and broke into a desperate run.

The moonlight made the grass of the fields look like knives. He slowed. A blaze of light, like someone was cooking his eyeball with a cigarette lighter, then tears rushed down his cheeks. When he brought his hand up to wipe them away he discovered they weren't the clear saltwater they should be, but were black like tar.

"Everything that we were, you have destroyed."

The voice set off fireworks of taste. Blood. Bile. Death. It was behind him. He knew that now. His hearing was somehow sharper, and he could hear it panting. It made his eyesight pulse, and now he could see himself through its ruined eyes and how it was reaching for him with hands like needles. It was going to kill him, to slice him through. "No!" he screamed.. "Alistair! Alistair! Please! Someone!"

In great long strides, sucking in air, Eric slashed through the high grass, pumping his legs as fast as they would let him. He didn't have to look behind him. He could somehow feel the weight of the monster, like it was bending gravity so that for every few steps he struck forward, it managed to drag him back one more, and still Eric ran, screaming "Alistair!" and the grass whipped at his legs and the cold air bit at his wet face. Far from his right but coming closer, something large loomed. "Alistair?" But no, it was the monster. To his other side, another moving scab of black. The monster again, and no sign of Alistair.

How do you fight something that's everywhere? Eric screamed in his own head, running faster, faster still. One thing was for certain: he was on his own. Maybe he wasn't calling out properly, or maybe Alistair was too far out of earshot—or heart-shot or whatever—but he wasn't coming. And the monsters were closing, and he was far off from the boundary of the field that would take him to the road. Too far. His lungs crackled with the effort, and his muscles resounded with the echo of their own hurt. And the shadows were close. In dizzying moments he caught glimpses through their eyes, all of them rushing closer. All about to strike.

"No!" A palpitation of the thing in his chest, the so-called shadow heart, and, as though the inner workings of his muscles had just been oiled with loving oxygen, he began to sprint like never before. Fast, faster, so fast he feared he couldn't stop, but the shadows were falling behind him. Even the ghostly Tim couldn't keep up. And Eric could see the boundary wall now and the dense trees there. All he'd have to do is veer sharp to the left, take the path out of the field and up the track. It wasn't that far, and running was easy now. Running was brilliant!

His foot snagged and Eric lurched forward. With his hands out he managed to claw at the ground to keep from falling, but he'd lost seconds and momentum. Excruciating pain shook his legs.

"Fuck!" he screamed as his thighs cramped. He couldn't breathe. He hobbled over, trying to find some burst of energy again but there was nothing left. Whatever power had let him run, it was gone now. Then in the haze of his hurt, Eric realised that he should be dead. The monster that looked like Tim, it should have caught him by now.

Then why not?

He dared to look up. Tim's silhouette formed a blot at the edge of the field, its huge shoulders going up and down as its chest expanded with every breath.

"What do you want from me?" Eric yelled. The thing remained unmoved. "Please, just tell me what you want me to do. Let me help you!"

No hissing reply came this time. Instead, the monster's shape blurred and it sank in on itself until, in an unsettlingly neat way, it was gone. The minutes stretched. A passing breeze made the grass whisper. Eric scanned the dark field. Alone. No more monsters, nothing. He had survived. Eric turned, and the Tim monster screamed in Eric's face, a raking arm descending, fingers like blades whistling through the air as it passed through him.

Soon, it promised in a faint voice that only sounded in Eric's ear as the monster turned to smoke once more.

In the heavy silence after, Eric eventually realised he was shaking. He reached up a hand. The monster might be gone but the black streaks of Eric's tears were still there. He began to wipe at them, fingers slapping at his skin until he felt his fingernails bite. Then Eric's stomach turned and he threw up, hard and long. When it was over he remained crouched, hands threaded in the cool grass. His dry, acrid mouth worked to spit out what was left of the awful bile. Eric made his own vow then, this for his own safety as much as anyone else's. *Soon.*

"WHAT IF HE'S been murdered?" Sarah said as she paced up and down her shabby living room.

"Come on love, don't worry yourself." Jhardine turned down another page in the clothing catalogue, wanting to come back for a second look at an argyle pattern green jumper. "He'll be fine. You know, he's probably just been out on the lash. He might even be down at the Richies now. Listen, I—"

"At the Richies?" Sarah started bawling again. If Jim was down the pub, he was probably with some woman he'd just met. Jhardine reached across the sofa and pulled Sarah into a hug.

"Look, you're better off knowing one way or another, aren't you? Can't keep on in this state, aye?"

"Yeah, you're right," Sarah sniffed.

"Good. Now, I have something I need to tell you, Saz."

"Oh, all right," Sarah said, wiping her face. This was it then. Another person that she had to let in on the Secret Lump. "Well, you know how—"

"Let's go down the Richies," Sarah said all at once, her eyes wide and wild.

"You what?"

"The Richies. I want Jim to see us down there having a good time, you know? That'll show him." The prospect had Sarah smiling like she'd just discovered the joys of online bingo.

"O-okay, sure," Jhardine said, deflating a bit.

Sarah was about to stand and get ready when she caught herself. "Oh, sorry, Jhardine, you were wanting to tell me something, weren't you?" she said, using a man-sized tissue to give her nose a sloppy blow.

So this was it. Ask Sarah's help or keep quiet. "Oh, it were nowt," Jhardine said finally. "Well, it can wait at least. We've got a pub to go to, haven't we? Now get up them stairs, put on sommat slutty and we'll bloody go down and scope it out, yeah?"

"Yeah, good idea. Come up with us, Jhardine. I've got a right nice zebra mini that will go great with your skin tone."

Twenty minutes later Sarah and Jhardine stood in front of the mirror in the sad rose of Sarah's bedroom, applying a quick bit of lippy.

"Never asked, did I, how Eric is?" Sarah said, slapping on some earthworm-coloured bronzer.

"Here, love, go easy, you don't want to look like you've caught something," Jhardine advised. A quick dab of a wet-wipe across Sarah's cheek, a thumb to smudge and everything was a bit more subtle. *Lovely.* "Our Eric. Oh, well, he's being a bit weird, to be honest."

"More than normal?"

"Well, you know how it is. He's been out all hours. Not coming home while four in the morning. I reckoned at first he might be seeing someone, you know, but I've been through his trouser pockets and he's not leaving owt in there. Can't find owt in his room either."

"That is strange," Sarah nodded. "Do I look all right in this top, Jhardine?"

"Aye, you do. Just your label's sticking out, turn round."

"Cheers," Sarah said, wobbling on her high heels. "But he's okay, though?"

"Well, he seems it. You can't really tell with Eric. It's the constant sarcasm. Means you can't get a read on him. I don't know where he gets it. David reckons it might be a defence mechanism."

"David?"

"Oh, the vicar." Jhardine tried not to blush. "What?"

"You and him on first-name terms now are you?" Sarah said with an impressed squeak.

"Here, stop that. He's a man of God."

"Aye, but he's still a man." She watched Jhardine trying to tame her hair into a ponytail. "No, leave it down. I always like it when it's down. It makes you look younger."

"Do you think?" Jhardine said, sucking in her cheeks.

"Aye. And try this eyeshadow. I got it from the catalogue for you anyway."

"Aw, thanks!"

"Don't thank me, thank Jim. It's his money what's paid for it. And he's paying for tonight's drinks too so don't hold back."

THE USUAL MISERABLE faces were waiting for them down at the Richardson's Arms, but no sign of Jim. Perhaps that was for the best though.

"I'm not sure about this anymore, Jhardine," Sarah said.

You and me both, Jhardine thought, rubbing at her head. She could feel another one of her headaches coming on. But this wasn't about her, was it? "Look, you sit there. I'll go talk to what's-his-face. Dennis! That's his name. What do you want to drink?"

Sarah dithered. "Well, er, I suppose an Irish cream."

"We'll make it a double."

Jhardine left Sarah in their little booth by the window and trotted over toward the bar. She'd not worn heels since the funeral and they were rubbing her to distraction. That was forgotten when she slapped eyes on Dennis. He was more handsome than she remembered. Another place, another time, a tub of emollient cream to help soothe his red skin, it could have been a date.

"Jhardine! Not seen you in a while, love."

"No, I've been busy, Den. You all right?"

"Aye, can't complain, you know. What can I do you for?"

"Well, I'll have an orange juice and a double Irish cream and, here, I want to know something about Jim."

"Jim? Which Jim?"

"Her Jim," Jhardine said, pointing to where Sarah was sitting. Unfortunately, Sarah had chosen that precise moment to start mining her ears and was almost knuckle deep. *Charming.*

"Jim Briley?"

"Yeah, you know him?"

"Of course I know Jim Briley, he's keeping me in business."

"Right, well have you seen him?"

"Er, he was in last night. Briefly, I mean."

"And...?" Jhardine waited.

"He said he had to go meet someone," Dennis said, handing a packet of pork scratchings to a girl who looked like she'd put on her makeup with a base coat of porridge.

"Any chance you know who he was going to meet?"

"Even if I did, Jhardine love, I couldn't tell tales on my best customer, could I?"

"It's for Sarah, Den. Look at her. She's an absolute wreck, poor thing." She was also going to lose her wedding ring in her lughole if she wasn't careful.

Dennis puffed out his cheeks and sighed. "Look, you've not heard it from me—"

"Well, I have heard it from you because you're the one who's telling me it."

"Right, but you know what I mean."

"Oh, fine," Jhardine said, rolling her eyes. *Happen that's where Eric gets it from.*

"Right, well, he's fairly friendly with that prozzy, Christina."

"She knows that—"

"I know she knows that, but I doubt she knows *how* friendly they are. I overheard something and, well, it sounded like they were talking...well, it all sounded pretty serious if you get my drift."

"No!"

"Shhh," Den winced. "Yes. That's the impression I got at least. They kept saying all this stuff about Blackpool. Going back to Blackpool."

"Sarah's going to rip his todger off, she really is."

"Oh God, I'd hate to have been party to that."

"Well you are, Den. We all are," Jhardine said somewhat wearily. "What time does he normally come in anyway?"

"No, you're not starting something in here."

"No, I mean so I can get Sarah out of the place before he does turn up."

Den sighed. "Right, well, about half past nine usually. So a couple of hours."

"Well, we'll just have them drinks then, Den, and a bag of crisps and we'll call that a day, love. But here, do you mind getting the money off Jim when he comes in. I'd like him to know Sarah was here."

"Oh, bloody hell," Den said, plonking down Sarah's order of Irish cream.

With both drinks in hand, Jhardine fought her way back through the clusters of chairs and tables to where Sarah sat.

"What did he say? Does he know owt?" Sarah was going on forty but, in that moment, her eyes said she was barely more than a loved-up teen.

"He just said he'd been in last night and that he'd said something about having an early job this morning."

"Oh." The glass paused on its way to Sarah's lips. "Do you reckon that means maybe he slept in the car? Sometimes he drives halfway down to the job and then parks up."

"I don't know, love," Jhardine said, wrestling with her bag of crisps. "Happen that's why he's not phoned. He's got a flat battery on his mobile maybe."

"Yeah, maybe." Jhardine certainly didn't believe that, and by the look of it Sarah didn't either. After a few more sips of her drink, ice tinkling in the glass like nagging little bells, she said, "I don't know why I haven't packed my bags yet, Jhardine. You know I've tried."

"But you're staying in it for Chanterelle, aren't you?"

"That's what I tell myself. But...." The sound of someone hitting big on the pub quiz machine blared. Jhardine looked over to find that, curiously, there was no one actually playing.

"It keeps doing that!" she heard Dennis say as he dashed over to catch the rattle of money spilling out onto the pub's carpet.

"I know this might sound pathetic, Jhardine, but part of the reason I stay is because it's easier, you know, than having to be on my own. Than starting again."

"I don't think that's pathetic," Jhardine said, sipping her orange juice. "Take it from someone who knows. Starting again ain't a picnic."

"Yeah," Sarah nodded. "Jaz, do you ever think of your Michael?" she asked, and then looked annoyed the words had escaped her mouth. "Sorry, if you don't want to talk about it, that's fine...."

"No, it's all right," Jhardine said, feeling a little lighter. "I've been thinking about him a lot lately."

Sarah nodded. "Were he good to you? Besides running out on you?"

"That's a big thing, that. You can't just put it to one side. Not easily at least."

"Aye, I know."

"And I was about to have Eric, and I didn't have any money of my own." Jhardine looked down into her lap where she had folded her hands. Her thumb and finger were searching for a wedding ring she'd thrown in the bin years ago. "He was kind. To a fault. He treated me like I was equal. He expected stuff of me. Like he knew how good I could be at my catering, at being a mum, at everything. And he loved me. Truly, actually loved me. I...actually I think I took that for granted for a lot of years."

"Aw." Sarah rubbed Jhardine's shoulder.

"Eric's a lot like him. Clever, you know? And he's got this thing. This hardness sometimes. It's not like he's unfeeling. But he can be so *certain*. Just like Michael." She took a sip of her drink. "That's what made it worse when Michael left—because it was so out of the blue. I thought that no matter what he'd be there for us and then he was just gone. We moved to Hainsworth because I couldn't stand living in that posh house up on Rhodesia, even if I could have afforded it. And no way was I taking a loan from my mother." Jhardine looked to the bottom of her glass. She'd supped the lot. "But every day I look at Eric and, well, there's Michael."

Sarah held Jhardine's hand, kissing it to her lips. "Do you, I mean, in the years since, have you ever been able to figure out why?"

"He left? Sometimes I think I must do. Buried in my head somewhere there must have been a sign, or something he said that would have told me what was going on if, you know, I'd paid attention. But looking back: it's no use. I can't see any of it, Sarah. We were just in love. He kept himself to himself, like our Eric, but we were. We were in love. And then, I suppose, we weren't. Or he wasn't." Jhardine rubbed at her forehead. She felt cold and misplaced, like she wasn't supposed to be in the pub and talking about this. She stood up. "I'm just off to the toilet, get us another drink, will you?"

"Yeah, sure."

Jhardine walked a few yards and then her legs went on the wobble. She felt dizzy. *That* kind of dizzy. She blundered her way closer to the bar, hoping to find something to catch her before her fall.

"You all right, love?"

"Yeah, just a bit...a bit...."

Her legs buckled. She was falling, falling, but in such slow, calm motion. Fractals of colour, and a strange disposition of the air, and there were arms around her, lowering her to the ground. He looked into her eyes with a face that was as adoring as ever. "Softly now, softly, my love," Michael said. "I'm here. I'm always—"

"Jhardine!"

Jhardine didn't feel scared. She didn't feel worried. There, lying on the pub's beer-soaked carpet, she began to laugh.

ERIC STARED AT the vial of black liquid sitting on the coffee table.

Soon. That's what the thing that looked like Tim, the umbra, had said. And Eric agreed. It had to be soon. His mum was out, so he was on his own. This was as good a time as he was likely to get. Before he could even think about it any more he leaned forward and took up the vial. He raised it to his lips.

"And we can now go live to the police station where a spokesperson for DCI Milligan is about to give a press statement." His eyes ticked to the television in the corner of the room. He lowered the vial a little as a spokesperson in a cobalt glaze of a jacket took up her position at a makeshift podium outside the police station. She had a doughy sympathy to her face but such thin lips and suspicious eyebrows that it made Eric doubt her warmness. As she stepped up to the microphone she cleared her throat, a sound that rebounded through the sound system with an additional squeal.

"Thank you for coming out," she said to the gathered reporters. "I won't dawdle. I'm here today to talk to you all about our investigation into the murders of Timothy Jeffries and Sally Lazarus. I regret that tonight we can add one more name to that list. It appears that Tim Jeffries' father, Dylan Jeffries, may also have been murdered by the same person who committed these earlier violent crimes."

Eric felt that settle. Of course he'd known that Dylan had been killed but there was nothing then to say that the deaths were connected. Now though, the police seemed to think they had some similarities. *Couldn't have happened to a nicer bloke,* he said to himself.

"I can confirm for you that, even though there are marked differences between the murders, the violence with which they were carried out means we are treating the incidents as linked. There have also been a few other deaths in the area that we are currently investigating for that same reason. While this has opened several avenues for our investigation, I cannot as yet say we have any suspects."

A ripple of chatter danced through the crowd. A camera flash, then a woman off-screen shouted, "What if there's more? What if more people get killed?"

Doughy ignored the question. "As we have said, we suspect that a new street drug called Mineral is tied to two of these murders. This drug, this Mineral, is billed as a health supplement. Based on some of the video advertisements we have seen online and interviews with known users, people are being led to believe it is an all-natural substance." Her face took on a hot, cross quality. "It certainly isn't a natural substance. It is usually taken orally, and it has certain androgenic effects. I also need to stress that in higher concentrations, such as in products that have been dubbed Mineral X, the drug behaves in a way that is...*unusual.*" She paused, as though feeling the weight of what she was about to say and needing a few seconds before she could shoulder its burden. "You will appreciate we do not want to risk scare-mongering, but we believe that even one instance of exposure to Mineral and in particular Mineral X, could be very dangerous. We've had reports of heart attacks, muscle spasms, bleeding, hallucinations and loss of consciousness. We do not know if the person or people dealing this drug are themselves linked to the murders or whether the murderer has merely taken advantage of the psychotropic effects of the drug, but we would caution anyone who has bought Mineral or Mineral X to cease using it at once and to stay clear of suppliers."

"What are you doing about the sale of this drug?" asked a journalist.

"This isn't a question and answer session," the spokesperson said sternly. "But, as you know, we've closed down several gyms in the area as a temporary measure to try to disrupt the spread of Mineral—and we'd like to thank those gym owners who have been very cooperative. We are also in communication with other constabularies, tracing the possible source of the drug from outside our borders. We are urging anyone out there who may know something to come forward, because it is only through the public's help will we be able to bring this killer to justice and stop the spread of this dangerous substance. I repeat, if you even think you may know something about these incidents, or know someone who is dealing Mineral, it is imperative you come forward."

"What about the rumour that you've lost the bodies? Any truth to that?"

Doughy stared down into the crowd. She didn't look surprised by this question, or even alarmed, just very, very tired. "Thank you very much for your time everyone, that is all we can say today." She stepped back from the podium and a group of officers surrounded her, shielding her from the tide of questions, flickering lights and scrambling journalists. Together, like one insect working its way across the ground, the group of police made its way back inside the glass and sandstone station building and out of sight.

"Georgia Thale there, speaking on behalf of Willingsley Police Force. Now, in an hour we have a special interview with a woman who, in exchange for anonymity, has agreed to talk to us about her use of the drug Mineral which, she says, has transformed her life."

Eric sat there, stunned. He'd been ready to do it, to drink the stuff. And he thought he'd had good reason. Ever since the night he'd spoken to Deborah outside Lion Lion, Eric had been unable to shake the feeling that he knew more than he was putting together. Finally, at four in the morning, and during a smidgen of furious masturbation to try to relieve enough tension to get at least a couple of hours sleep, it had hit him. Well, not *it* but what he had been missing: it was Alistair. When the man with the violet eyes had been in Eric's bedroom he'd poured what was left of his tea into a hip flask. He'd said something about shades. It didn't make much sense at the time, but he'd been quite clear: that Eric must have had access to shades because they were what powered Eric's shadow heart, and it was certainly alive and working. Alistair's taking the tea seemed to suggest he thought that it might be in the water, but Eric had drunk nearly a gallon and all that had happened was that he'd ended up pissing like a racehorse. Then it occurred to him: the other night, when the Tim umbra reared its ugly head, the vial of Mineral had started to boil. The only other time something similar had happened was back in the subway the night Sally Lazarus had come back to life as a wolf-woman, and the puddles on the floor had all started to fume. Eric suspected Mineral was made out of shades. That explained why Eric felt so weird every time he uncorked the bottle and got a whiff of its contents, because it was exciting his shadow heart. How he was regularly coming in contact with it, well, Eric didn't know, but the bare fact of it seemed to tally: Mineral was made of shades.

So Eric had devised himself a little plan. He wanted to drink the shades, to try to use his powers to find the umbra, to look through its eyes again, and hopefully see the person who was killing folk and making them into monsters because, he figured, if he could stop the killer then maybe it would stop the Tim umbra—or at the very least stop any more monsters being made. He'd let Alistair do the rest.

As plans went, it wasn't foolproof. For one, there was no guarantee that the man or woman who made the umbra was still in contact with it, but at the very least it might give Eric some kind of clue as to what he should do next. Now, though, there was more than just one spanner in the works. It turned out Mineral was dangerous. That's what the police spokesperson had said. That it could cause hallucinations, and bleeding and heart attacks. He stared at the vial, unsure of himself. It was one thing to try the drug when he didn't know what might happen, but quite another to think about sampling it now that he did know the possible risks.

"Eric!" A bang on the front door. "Eric!"

"Oh, what now?" Eric turned down the television. "Yeah, I'm coming."

"Eric!"

"I'm coming! Jesus." Door open and Eric found Sarah on the doorstep and his mum leaning precariously against the hedge. His mum's face was slack, her makeup smeared like a Rorschach test. "What happened? Mum?"

"I don't know," Sarah said as she dragged Eric's mum inside. "We were in the pub, she had a drink, and then she just had a turn."

"Eric," Jhardine mumbled. "I'm all right, Eric."

"Maybe we should call the hospital?"

"No, I don't want it. I won't," his mum slurred.

"Eric?" Sarah pressed.

"Right, okay." Eric slipped his arm under his mum's, taking most of the strain off Sarah's shoulders. "We're going to get you upstairs and into bed, Mum. Then I'm going to call the doctor."

"No."

"Well, it's either that or the hospital, ain't it?"

"Flipping 'eck," she slavered as Sarah and Eric set to the task of trying to fit three people up the stairway. "Ring Doctor Thompsette. If you say it's for me, she'll come."

"It's a Saturday, Jaz, I don't think she will...."

His mum laughed. "Oh, she will." Then, as an afterthought. "Number... the number...it's in my mobile."

By the time the doctor arrived, a woman with pinched looking eyes and red, rosacea-crossed cheeks, Eric's mum had propped herself up in bed and she and Sarah were chattering away like nothing had happened.

"Oh, it's him," she said, pointing at Eric. "He's a bloody drama queen. I'd asked for an orange on its own but maybe I'd ended up with some spirits. It probably mixed with the pills you lot have put me on."

"Yes, perhaps so," said the doctor in a thin voice, but she didn't sound convinced. "Your blood pressure is a little high but it's within tolerance." The woman removed the blue cuff around his mum's biceps.

"Yeah, apart from now I can't use my arm."

"Here, I know," Sarah piped up. "When I had Chanterelle they kept doing that to me. Seemed like, never mind deliver the baby, they were trying to amputate themselves a few limbs!"

"Well, the NHS is quite strapped for cash," Doctor Thompsette quipped. Silence settled over the room. Nobody could quite believe it. Even she looked a bit taken aback by what her mouth had managed to accomplish. Then Eric's mum broke out into a raucous laugh and Sarah began cackling.

It wasn't that bloody funny, thought Eric. Had they all forgotten his mum had just collapsed?

"That was a good one, that," Sarah said, wiping a tear from her eye. "Anyway, I'm gonna go down and make a cup of tea. You want one?"

"Aye, that's just what I need," Jhardine said.

"Doctor?"

"No thank you, I must be going."

Sarah squeezed past Eric, "See, love. Nowt to worry about," and, quite subtle-like, pushed Eric a few inches over the threshold before closing the bedroom door, shutting herself and Eric out of the room. "Let's let them have a talk while I get that tea." Then Sarah jangled her way down the stairs, still smiling, still trying to convince him everything was fine. Unsurprisingly, the cold clamp in Eric's gut refused to budge. He pressed his ear to the door, doctor-patient confidentiality be damned.

"You have to make a decision, Jhardine. You know that."

"I've made arrangements. I just need about a week. Just to get stuff sorted with work, you know?"

"Time is a factor—"

"I know that. Sandra, my sister, she let me down. I just need to find someone who can help with the day-to-day stuff when I'm, you know, indisposed—"

"Do you want a tea, Eric?"

"Ah!" Eric jumped.

"Eric? Tea?" Sarah repeated, her voice sharp and carrying up the stairs with a slap. Eric, face screwed up, managed a polite "Er, no, no thanks," while secretly cursing Sarah and all her forefathers.

"Suit yourself," she replied, and he heard her clack her way back into the kitchen.

Eric paced up and down the hallway, trying to figure out what he'd heard. There was something wrong with his mum. Of course, he'd known that before, but this sounded far worse than she'd been letting on. Possibly even....

Just as he was teetering on the edge of a full-blown panic, the door opened and the doctor came out. She looked a touch more sallow than before, he thought.

"Is she okay?" Eric rushed.

"Your mother needs plenty of rest."

"Well, what's wrong with her? Do you know?"

Doctor Thompsette glanced at the door as though Jhardine's face was there, ready to judge. "That's for your mother to tell you." She seemed like she would walk off then, but stopped. The doctor reached out and put a very unsure hand on Eric's shoulder. She squeezed it lightly. "I'm given to understand you're a fairly bright lad, Eric," she said, and returned her hand to her side. Everything was very *deliberate.*

"Th-that's what people keep telling me."

"Well, all right then. I'll put it like this: your Mum doesn't appear to be in any immediate danger." Eric felt the tightness in his gut ease a little. "But," Doctor Thompsette said, "if she were to have a repeat incident, I would not hesitate to get her to the hospital. Quickly."

He got his ears around that. He heard the salt in her words. "Are you saying—"

"I've said everything you need to hear. Now, I should be going," she said, and before he could ask her anything else, Doctor Thompsette had turned down the stairs, and was walking out. People kept doing that. Why didn't anyone ever finish what they were saying before they started walking away?

A few minutes later, and after quite a bit of dithering, Eric pushed open the door to his mum's room. She was staring down toward the foot of the bed, her eyebrows together. It seemed like she hadn't heard him come in, and then she turned and looked at him. A smile. "Oh, Eric. Aw, cheers, love," she said as he gave her the mug of tea in his hand.

"Thank Sarah. She's just gone back round to hers. Jim pulled up, so I reckon there's going to be some trouble, you know?"

"Ah right, I might ring her up and ask later," his mum said, taking a sip of her drink. She made a sour face and put the cup down. "I bet the milk's gone off again. I'm not buying it from Singh's anymore. It's always lousy."

"Mum?" Eric said, sitting on the bed. "What's up?"

"What do you mean, what's up? I've just told you, the milk's off."

"No, I mean, what did the doctor say?"

"I'm bloody useless, that's what. Haven't been taking my tablets right, have I?"

He looked down at the floor. Heat flushed his cheeks. "You're lying, mum. I know you are."

He should have known better than to try to badger it out of her, though. She snuggled down into her blankets, still smiling like nothing had happened. "Here, I'm tired. Close them curtains, love, and leave me alone for twenty minutes. I need a nap."

Eric didn't close the curtains. Instead, he got up, got himself out of the room and slammed the door. There, on the landing, anger mixed with fear and he found himself fair stewing in a resentment he couldn't quite place. She was getting worse and she was keeping it from him. Lying to him. If the doctor—someone from the hospital, no less—was making home visits at the beckon of a phone call, something was seriously wrong. He had to help, but what could he do? He knew nothing about medicine. Healing just wasn't in his blood. He was too sour for that. Too full of himself. Too...healing.

That turn of phrase distracted him from his own self loathing. "Oh, how could I be such a dick head?"

"Here, I heard that," his mum shouted through the door.

"Oh, go to sleep, you bloody witch," Eric shouted back, but a smile met the corners of his mouth. "I'm, er, just going to get a bath."

"Good, cos I can smell you from in here!"

ERIC RAN THE bath water until it was elbow deep. The room was thick with steam and he opened the window to let some of it escape. Then he picked up the vial of Mineral and rested it at the side of the sink. A few more minutes of indecision, and then he unscrewed the lid. He'd made up his mind.

"Let it be true," he mumbled. "Please, let it be true." This was the most reckless thing he had ever done. He knew that the universe did not reward people based on their good intentions, their courage, or their pigheaded brainlessness, yet still he hoped. So, he downed the black water.

It tasted exactly how he imagined petrol might, burning all the way down. He tried to stop himself from gagging by running the cold water and filling his cupped hands so he could take a drink, but his hands were shaking so much he was just throwing water about. He settled for necking the water from the tap, banging his teeth against the tap's nozzle in the process. The bathroom seemed to spin. He stepped over toward the bath and in the haze decided that the bath that had just been a cover story might be a good idea after all. With lazy, dull hands he slowly got undressed and, feeling punch drunk, crouched to slip into the water. The heat made his skin tingle. The water was too hot, but he wouldn't get out. The pain was good. It drove out everything else. It made Eric's thinking very simple.

In that broiling quiet, he felt his shadow heart beat.

Thud.

Now it wasn't just patches of coloured lights that danced through Eric's vision. The room was aglow in strange phosphorescence, and his ears heard music in the dripping tap and the faint hum of the light fitting. So many more sounds than before. And he could taste the wet air. The water, too, he could feel it like silk, but also like stone. He could parse it differently.

Thud.

It felt like he had hot copper coils in his stomach, anode and cathode, and they were beginning to make the acid in him bubble. He put it out of mind. He shut down his senses. Alistair had kept eating, hadn't he? Those tablets or sweets, or whatever they were. Eric suspected Alistair needed to keep topping up his supply. If that was true, these things called shades burned up fast. He'd only have a little while to make this work.

If I can make this work.

Alistair had said, hadn't he, that shadow formers could call to one another. Eric'd tried it before, but back on the bridge he might not have had the juice to make it work, or maybe hadn't had the right frame of mind. Rather than search for the monster, Eric decided to use this one chance to dial up some help.

Thud.

"Alistair."

Thud.

"Alistair."

Thud.

You left me!

Tim's voice came so loud in Eric's ear that he hissed against it.

"No. Not you. This is for Mum."

You left me!

"For Mum!"

And for once, the fear in Eric worked in his favour and eclipsed the sound of the Tim umbra's voice until it was just a nagging buzz.

"Alistair."

He clenched his fists.

"Alistair."

He screwed up his eyes. The water around him was getting hotter, he was sure.

"Alistair!"

Thud!

It took Eric a few seconds to realise the sound hadn't come from the shadow heart in his chest. No, it was an external sound that had vaulted over the backdrop of wailing sirens that filled the air outside. Eric opened his eyes. The man with violet eyes stepped down from the window sill onto the toilet and then to the floor. He wore a simple cotton shirt, high-waisted grey trousers held up by tan braces, and thigh-high tan boots with a curved toe.

"You came," Eric said, standing.

"And you're very, very naked," Alistair laughed. Eric would have been bashful about the fact he had his knob out, but his body was already working on a diversion. His muscles began to spasm and heave, and he was having trouble staying upright. Something was terribly wrong, and he was about to scream when Alistair's hand clamped over his mouth.

"What have you done?" the man said, his eyes shining bright. Something red, thick and foul smelling poured out of Eric's mouth and through Alistair's fingers.

Alistair dragged Eric from the tub and, there on the cool bathroom floor, the man clamped his hands around Eric's face, bringing him in close. Eye to eye, Eric could see violet storms raging inside Alistair, and something else. It was like watching the shadow of a cloud run over the Earth. Then he felt the tingle of electricity, like that first time back in the hospital when Alistair had rewired Eric, and slowly the pain in Eric's stomach began to ease.

"There," the man said. "I've purged the worst of it. Had to leave a few of the shades behind though or your heart would go into shock. Now, as lovely as this sight is, let's get you covered up." One hand holding Eric, Alistair reached for the orange towel that was hung over the top of the glass shower panel and, with tentative hands, wrapped the towel around Eric. "Where in the Verse did you get those shades?"

Alistair helped Eric to sit on the edge of the bath, and Eric put his head in his hands, trying to wall himself off from the still bright pain in his guts and the ringing in his ears. "Keep it down. My mum will hear."

"You've not answered my question," Alistair said. "And no, she won't. Other folk don't hear me unless I want them to, remember?"

"Whatever," Eric said. "Erm, Tim was taking some stuff before he died—"

"Your friend?" There was emphasis on that word. *Friend.*

"Yeah. You called them shades, right? What powers this thing. This shadow heart." Eric touched his chest. He felt the heart prickle. His senses flared. "I found a vial of this stuff, they're calling it Mineral. It was in his things at his work. I reckon he got it off this bird, that girl what changed into a monster. Sally."

"Well, that's a distinct possibility. I tracked down her sister and Sally had a few empty vials in what was left of her things, and one under her bed that wasn't quite drained. Laced with shades."

"And deadly, right? I mean, I've just vomited up my stomach lining," Eric said, looking to the dark red mess on the floor. "Speaking of, do you mind?" Eric asked.

"Oh, sure." Alistair waved a hand over the considerable red and black mix of fluids. The air flashed hot. The stains began to fade.

"Cheers." Eric sighed. "What I don't get, right, is how did Tim do it for so long? Take that stuff I mean, if this is what it does to you?"

"Well, for you it's different. It makes you sick because you're a shadow former and your shadow heart and those foul shades do not get along one bit. See, in people without shadow hearts, shades start changing them. If you want to get yourself a strong umbra you feed them plenty of shades, especially the tainted kind. Some people are more resilient than others, though, so happen Tim could stand it a good while longer than most. Course, that means he's made a stronger umbra." Alistair shook his head. "What you did was reckless, Little Bird. Foolish. It was—"

"It had to be done." Eric said, standing but holding his still aching stomach. "Because I need your help."

"You didn't need those rotten shades. You could have reached out—"

"I tried before. I did. The umbra was going to hack me up the other night and I called out to you, but you didn't come."

"I...never heard you." Alistair looked frustrated at this news. "Even with minimal shades, you should be able to get through. Unless something's interfering. Draining your powers, or blocking you." Alistair mused on that a few seconds more before remembering they were in the middle of a conversation. "Anyway, needing my help, aye? What's changed? I thought you didn't want anything to do with me and my kind?"

"That was before," Eric said, like it was an apology. "It's my mum. She's ill. Like she's really, really sick."

Alistair's eyes searched. "You want me, oh, to heal her?"

Eric nodded. "I know this probably breaks your rules or something, and I know what I said but I—"

"No, I'll do it. Of course I will," Alistair said, pulling his hair back from his face. "You've already lost someone, you shouldn't have to lose her too. Besides, I was—"

Alistair's head snapped around and he stared out the window.

An ache took up in Eric's chest. It made him pant. "What is that?" he asked.

"That, Little Bird, is a powerful umbra. Without enough shades you won't have felt it much before but now you're on the juice, well, it'll come in clear."

"Oh." Eric wiped at his tongue. All of a sudden his saliva was running bitter. "Shit." He spat into the sink.

"What is it?"

"Oil. I can taste motor oil. What the bloody hell is wrong with me?" Eric blinked, screwing his eyes up, trying to clear his vision.

"Others who have powers that can extend their senses sometimes get flashes of umbras and where they are. Happen you're doing the same? Anything else?"

"No, I...."

"Eric, this is important. Try for me."

"I don't know how, I—"

"Just concentrate. See what information it is you're getting and just, whatever it is, just go with it."

"A-all right. Okay."

Eric fought for some focus.

You left me!

He tried to push the voice out of his mind, but it was too late. His concentration was cracked. The sirens outside weren't helping. "I can't. That bloody ambulance is putting me off."

"Ambulance?"

"Yeah. Listen, there it is again."

Alistair went to the window.

"What?"

"Well that's the thing," Alistair said. "There's no ambulance outside."

"What? No it's right...." At the window, looking out onto the streets, there was no sign of an ambulance. And still the sirens wailed as though they were parked outside the bathroom door, blasting sound at him. "So, what, you're saying...?"

Alistair had his hand out of the window, jimmying it about as he tried to work out the flow of the land. "It tracks. The pull is coming from near the hospital." When Alistair looked at Eric again, his eyes were burning. "You could be useful. Really useful. Now, do you want to come, see another monster?"

"What? But what about my mum?"

"I'll see to her, I will, but I have to take care of this. My sworn duty as a Servant to the Sisters as set out in my oath of blah, blah, blah. Basically, I've got a job to do. You want to come with?"

"I can't. My mum's—"

Alistair hopped up onto the windowsill. "Suit yourself. I have to go hunt."

"No, wait!"

"I've got to go—"

"I'll meet you there. At the hospital, I mean." He couldn't let Alistair get away again, not with his mum still ill. "I'll get dressed and sort things out here. Like, twenty minutes." Eric said, trying to pull on his underwear without dropping the towel.

"See you shortly, then."

"No, wait I—"

Alistair leaned back and fell out the window.

"Al!"

But, by the time Eric got to the window, Alistair was gone. "How does he keep doing that?"

CHAPTER TEN
CRASH

Given the shouting coming through the walls, and the sounds of plates, cutlery and possibly a small child being thrown, Sarah wouldn't be coming back round anytime soon. That left just one person Eric could call.

Mum's going to kill me.

She was busy emptying a tin of curry into a saucepan when Eric walked into the kitchen, shuffling his feet because it helped him feel more awake and grounded. The sound also helped him make his way through the jumble of lights and flashes his eyes were still seeing. He played with his car keys nervously before remembering that he no longer had his car—still at the garage, wasn't it? *And to top it all off, I'm going to have to walk!*

"You sure you're all right cooking?" he asked, stealing an apple from the bowl and crunching. The sudden rush of intense tastes made him nearly cry out.

"What?" his mum yawned, not noticing. "Oh God, yeah, I'm fine."

"I can do it for you before I go out."

"Will you stop fussing? You're making me feel worse."

"I can't help it. You collapsed."

"I *do* know. I was there." She stirred the sauce. "I don't want you making a big deal out of this. Like I said, I'd not been taking my pills properly and—"

She was lying. Again. "But it's going to be okay," Eric said out loud.

She looked at him. The smile on his face was probably a bit confounding. Eric figured it this way: The world might be filled with more arse-clenching horror than he'd ever imagined, monsters and people with weird powers and all that crap, but at the same time there was a power that could help his mum. She could be healed. For now, that was reason enough to smile.

"I know," she smiled. "I've prayed on it, Eric. He'll make it all good. You'll see."

A cold slap, that. He could see his own smile on her face and everything felt dangerously mystical. It made him sober up to it. A hand to his chest. He'd study the hearts. The substances. The drug Mineral. The lot. He'd find the logic. The sense. *This isn't faith. This is reason. This is...reason enough.*

A knock on the door.

"Who the bugger is that?"

"I'll get it, you stay there," Eric said, pulling the kitchen door closed behind him as he jogged down the hall.

"Eric," the vicar grinned when Eric opened the door. "How are you?"

"Not bad. Thanks for coming. If I didn't have to go out I wouldn't, but—"

"Don't even think of it. I'm happy to come round. I've not seen your mum in almost a week. I was starting to have withdrawal," the vicar chortled, running a hand down his check shirt. He was wearing jeans and loafers too. This was the first time Eric had seen the vicar outside of his religious garb. He looked almost average. Nearly fanciable. *Oh Lord.*

"David! I mean, Vicar," Eric's mum said from the kitchen doorway. "What are you doing here?"

"I've, er, got to go out, Mum, so I've asked the vicar to come round and keep you company."

"Eric!" she glared and pointed a threatening wooden spatula. "There's absolutely no need." She straightened out her clothes and ran a none-too-subtle hand through her hair. "I'm mortified he's bothered you, David, I really am. What happened earlier was nowt."

"Not at all, Jhardine. As soon as Eric mentioned the curry I practically invited myself," he lied.

"Oh, well, go through and help yourself, I've made enough to feed the five thousand." She led the holy man through into the kitchen, then wheeled about and slapped Eric with the spatula.

"Careful, that bloody hurt," Eric said, rubbing at his arm.

"Yeah, well I'm gonna have you."

"Save some room for dessert," Eric said, wiggling his eyebrows.

"Oh, you little—"

"I'll be back later on. Don't wait up!"

CAR AFTER CAR. Face after face. But it was here somewhere in the hospital grounds, Alistair could feel it. "Where in the Verse are you, you complete pain in my arse?"

Problem was, there were too many people around. Of course, there was a time when that wouldn't have been a problem. That woman with the buggy and the little pink kid—he'd have sacrificed them in a heartbeat. That college student with the ridiculous quiff but lovely, if slightly scrotum-like, satchel. Gladly. That wino hanging off the metal bench at the far side of the car park and the friend, a boxy-headed streak of a man who, Alistair knew at just a glance, had a terminal cancer of the lower regions—bam, dead and gone. A quick wreath of violet flame, a blanket covering of it to send out across the grounds, that would have forced the umbra to out itself. Course, it would have killed a few of the locals, no doubt about that, but no matter how many people it tore through it'd be worth it to kill one more umbra.

"Never let affection for the living distract you," Alistair repeated, hearing what the clerics had drilled into him—literally through his skull—with their ashen lips leaving their trails like iron filings over his skin. For a long time he'd followed their words, had done so with knee-aching, hand-wringing faithfulness. Until a year ago. Until *him*.

"Al!" A pale Eric, still clutching his stomach, waved from the road as he hopped over the wall and into the car park.

"Ah, so you found yourself a mum-minder, eh?"

A flicker of annoyance crossed Eric's face. "Aye, a willing sacrifice."

"You what?"

"It's nowt." Eric shrugged.

"Well, you've not missed anything." Alistair leaned on the railing that separated the car park from the road.

"Why, did it get away?"

"Oh, no, it's still here." Alistair scanned the milling people, the folk walking through the sliding glass doors in and out of the hospital, and the dribbles of people going between the car park and the hospital itself. "I just can't get a lock on it. Tracking ain't my forte. And I don't have no other shadow former to join forces with. Who would have thought I'd miss being part of a team? By the Ashen, what have I come to?"

Eric had on a questioning look. That or he had some wind brewing. "Come again?" he said.

Alistair instructed his tongue to be damned careful on this. He'd tell Eric everything eventually, but in Alistair's considerable experience this stuff was better drip-fed. "Shadow hearts, see, they have their own strengths and weaknesses," he said. "True, there are some that are far more powerful than the rest, but even then they tend to divide into groups. Short of it is—"

"Wait, what are the groups?" That. That sparkle in Eric's eye. Oh yes, he was definitely thirsty for it.

"All right," Alistair sighed. *Nothing wrong with giving him the CliffsNotes, I suppose.* "Weapon hearts. They're what the name suggests. Powerful, not too subtle. They're your fire starters, your lightning throwers, all that gaudy nonsense. They usually offer sympathetic effects to the host too, like strength, speed, resilience. There are a few what are exceptional though. Blood. Breath. Steel. Very good. Then there are Augurs. They can read the world like it's a book. Read people. Plants. Other hearts. They don't usually have offensive powers like Weapons but they can give their hosts a whole range of other powers what support their abilities. Some of our best hand-to-hand fighters come from the Augur group because they can see what's coming before it happens, you know?"

"Right, so they can, like, predict things? See things."

Oh, you clever boy, Alistair thought. *Let's throw you a bit of a curve ball like you threw me, shall we?* "Then there's the Alchemy lot, and they're where the real power is. Changing what was one thing to another. Technically, though my heart behaves like a Weapon in the way I use it, it's Alchemy. Others can change flesh to metal, inanimate to animate."

Something flashed. A little green light in Eric's hand. Alistair noticed it then: Eric was clutching his mobile phone. Alistair had watched enough bad television to know that Eric was recording this conversation. He pointed at the phone. "It won't work. My voice won't record on your tech. Sorry."

Eric blanched. "I didn't, I mean, it was just so that I didn't miss anything important. And also...."

"Also what?"

Eric slipped the phone back into his jeans. "No one else but me sees you. I just wanted to be able to play, just, like, a snippet of your voice to someone. Just to prove that—"

"I'm not imaginary?"

Eric laughed. "Kind of. Sort of. I have a history of...well...that were a long time ago. It was just for my peace of mind, really."

Alistair nodded. Oh, he knew how that felt. All the people that weren't brought up in the world of shadow forming must have gone through the same. And it would only get worse come the Fading. "I don't blame you, but we aren't meant to be seen or heard by types that aren't like us. Non shadow formers don't even see the monsters until it's too late, which is why on this here street, should the umbra attack, not a one of these people will be safe." An elderly lady with her cane tapping against the ground walked between them. Alistair touched at his chest. *If only I was better. If only I could dare to be better.* "The last group of hearts," he went on, clearing his throat. "It's the Warp hearts. They're dangerous. Real dangerous. The Alchemy hearts make relatively small changes, even if they're complex. Fire to ice. A son to a daughter. But Warps can bend reality, time, whole swathes of people. There are only a few true Warp hearts, Storm, Empathy, Terra, and the Sisters have collected all that they can to stop them getting into the wrong hands."

"Why not just use them on the umbras, then? The Warps I mean," Eric said, still rubbing his stomach. "End this once and for all."

"Because those hearts are often uncontrollable. The power. It poisons the bearers. It destroys them and everything around them. The Sisters would only ever allow the use of a Warp if every other attack had failed—and even then, they might not want to risk it."

"They're that bad? You make them sound worse than umbras."

"Some shadow formers are. I mean, just because we get these hearts, it doesn't mean we'll do good. That's another reason to work in a team. We all keep an eye on each other, just in case any of us start to turn...."

Eric blinked through that. "So...you're saying that the hearts have their own strengths, and their own weaknesses. You can't track like an Au—augur?" Alistair nodded. "So you work in groups."

"The system's fairly efficient. Well, when everyone wants to be there, at least." Alistair started another full walk of the pavement, gaze prowling over every person that went by, reading the shadows in every car and behind every tree. "I'm advantaged in that I can heal myself and also burn the umbras. But until they show themselves I can't see them," and Alistair gave a great sigh.

"B-b-but I can," Eric offered. "I felt it from across town, didn't I? Give me some shades and I can help you."

"Oh, a world and a day of no."

"What? Why won't you use me?" Eric rushed to backtrack on that. "Okay, maybe that came out wrong but—"

"It puts you in danger. This umbra's young but it'll still feel you the minute you start probing around. Probably already did when you sensed it from across town, in fact. That's likely what made it put on its flesh disguise."

"I don't need to do it for long, though, do I? If I could sense it from across town then I should just be able to dip in and out and find it for you now."

"I'm guessing your power doesn't work like that, Little Bird, or you'd be able to feel it just on the vapour of shades you still have in you. Not your fault, that. Augurs rarely work that way. You stand back from the painting and, eventually, you find the red mark that shouldn't be there, but up close there's so much going on you lose it unless you've been trained. Turning up your powers now could put you in real danger."

"But if we don't catch it today it'll hurt more people, won't it?" Eric rolled his lips together. "And you can't let that happen."

Clever, annoying little bugger, Alistair thought. "Fine," he said. "You want the power, Little Bird, you can have it." Hand in his coat pocket and a royally pissed off, fat breath. "If you end up dead it's not my fault, so it isn't."

"Got it," Eric smiled.

"Wipe that grin off your mug. This is going to bring you a world of pain." From his pocket Alistair produced a black lozenge of liquorice. "This. It's what shades that have been properly treated look like. I mean, most formers have a preference. Some like 'em in sweets. Some in their drink. Others in, er, raw meat, but never that muck you had. Like drinking toilet water. Never, ever, do that again. You hear me?"

"Loud and clear, boss," Eric said, hand out to take the shade sweet.

Alistair pulled back. "You get half." He nipped the sweet in two and offered Eric the slither. Eric sighed. That didn't sweeten Alistair any. "That should give you just enough mileage for a quick scan, no more. Hopefully, it'll be weak enough that the umbra won't feel it. And neither will you, though I wouldn't count on that."

Eric took the sweet and, wasting no time at all, started to chew.

"You'll feel your shadow heart quicken," Alistair said, giving the street a quick scan before returning his gaze to Eric. He stopped. "Eric?" The lad's eyes had rolled up into his head. "Eric?"

"I can.... I can...feel...."

"All right, um." Alistair tried to wrap his mind around it. What had the clerics told him? "If you imagine slowing your breathing to get your, you know, nerves under control, it's sort of the same for the shadow heart. Tell it to slow. Command it. Measure it out." Alistair let his fingers hover over Eric's chest. The lad wouldn't know it was taboo to touch. But no, Alistair couldn't do that. It would make him no better than the clerics. "I find holding the shadow heart with my hand makes the connection more real. Concrete, you know?"

Eric, eyelids now shut tight, put his hand to his chest and, holding it there, began to mutter. Counting, Alistair realised. Counting out his breaths. A car went by. Eric flinched, blinking, hissing.

"What is—"

"Don't shout!" Eric yelled, slapping his hands over his ears. "Crap, I can't, I can't, this was a mistake."

"Oh, now you get it."

Eric began to shake. Another car and he whirled on the spot, his eyelids fluttering, his body jerking. "Everything's so loud and bright, but I've got my eyes closed. How can it be bright?"

"Little Bird?" Alistair grabbed hold of Eric, took his chin, angled his face and eye to eye, chest to chest, they stared. "Concentrate on me. Nothing but me."

Eric was still vibrating, his breath coming quick. A cold sweat slicked his skin. "I can't...."

"Yes, you can," Alistair said in his softest voice. "Can you feel your shades?"

"They're burning. It feels like dying again. Why does it feel like dying?"

"Never mind that," Alistair said. He glanced around. Nothing advancing. No hint of the umbra. Maybe it wasn't experienced enough to know what it was feeling yet? That would be a rare stroke of luck. "Just concentrate on me, Little Bird. Turn your senses onto me. What do you get?"

"I...."

"Come on, anything."

"Sweet. I...." Eric's eyes found a focus. "You taste sweet like lavender and rose water. But there's something...." Eric winced. "Something else. Something almost...bad."

Alistair flinched. He'd hoped that Eric wouldn't see that far, that deep, but it seemed the lad had some good feelers. Still, it would serve their purpose. "What about it? Eric?"

"I don't know."

"Yes, you do. The heart knows so you know. What is it?"

"No, I don't want to—"

"Eric!"

"You're lighting up!" he said, his eyes wide but his voice low and mournful. "A funeral pyre. You're maggots. You're bones. You're—"

"Always dying," Alistair finished for him. "I am. That's my curse. Always but never quite. Now look past it. Feel deeper. Can you hear my shadow heart? Can you?"

"Yeah. Yes. Reds. And greens. I see them. And they're coming from you. And the dark, like splinters of black. I think they're shades because they, oh God, they smell the same as that stuff. That Mineral stuff."

It shot panic through Alistair, that. *He's far too strong too fast. He can see too deep, too early. He can see me.* "Right, good," he hummed. "The umbra won't be exactly the same," he said, turning Eric on the spot to look out across the hospital car park. "But remember it's made of shades. It's dripping with them. It will mask itself but the whiff will be there. You just have to get a hint."

Eric moaned. "Shit, my head." Tears escaped his eyes. "I'm cracking open. I'm everywhere. I can't—"

"Come on Eric, or all this has been for nothing," Alistair said. "Just look."

"No, please, I...can't. It's just a jumble, it's—"

"Concentrate, because you can do this, Eric. I promise you."

"I can't. I...." Eric's head ticked to the side. "Wait w-what's that?" he said, but Alistair barely caught it.

"Come on Eric. Come on—"

"It's here!" Eric shouted, and Alistair heard the sound, the rushing of a fist, but it was too late.

"THEY ALWAYS SAY you should want to get ahead. Well it looks like I just did, get a head that is." Tim's dad pulled his fist out of the back of Alistair's ruined skull, letting the dead man slump to the ground. The corpse landed by Eric, squirting blood over Eric's trousers. Alistair's eyes were vacant and a thick red began to taint his silver hair.

"A waste really. I'd have liked a taste of his grey matter. Oh wait, there's some," the umbra said as he licked his fist.

It looked just like Tim's dad, even down to the twitchy, hamster-like nose.

"Dylan," Eric panted, trying to reign himself in. The world was spinning and Alistair was dead. And Eric cared. He cared a lot.

"Mr Jeffries to you, thank you very much," the creature laughed.

The umbra had been watching them from the bench in the corner of the car park. As soon as Eric caught a hint of its awful power it moved too quick. He couldn't warn Alistair in time, and now Al was dead.

"Do you like?" the umbra asked, splaying its gory hand as though seeking opinion on a new suit. It was then that Eric saw the resemblance wasn't totally exact. The fingers were slightly pointed. In fact, all the man's angles, from the cut of his brow to the angles of his hips, were all slightly too pronounced.

"Oh, yeah. Dylan was one of my favourite people, weren't he?" Eric spat.

Tim's dad laughed, its lips moving too far back from its jaws and so giving an unnatural crescent to the dead man's face. "You always were a jumped-up little shit. I'll enjoy—"

"Oh, if you're gonna kill me, don't talk about it, just do it," Eric said. "I didn't like you when you were alive, so imagine how I feel about listening to you waffle on now."

"Don't worry, Eric, I *am* going to rip you limb from limb. The question is, what should I do after that?" It flexed its spindly fingers. "Dylan always wondered what she'd taste like. That religious nut you call your mother—"

You left me.

"Shut up."

"I suppose I could kill her in front of you. Would you like that, Eric?"

"You won't touch her!" Eric's shadow heart gave a violent pulse. His shadow surged out across the ground and then rose up like a wave, smacking into the umbra. The creature went flying through the air, rolling across the ground and out of sight.

Eric spared a glance down at Alistair's dead body. "I'm sorry." He turned and pelted through the car park between the rows of cars, ducking down and padding as quick as he could to the next row, then the next. *Alistair said he always comes back,* Eric reassured himself. *I'm not abandoning him. I'm being smart. I can't leave the monster here with all these people, so I need to buy some time.*

"Come out, come out wherever you are," a voice far too close said.

Eric peered out from between two large four-by-fours. No sign of the Dylan umbra. He ran the gap between the cars, then looked back the way he had come. Still no trace. Then he saw it: shoes, torn through with pointed toes made of what looked like little glass crystals, two cars over and walking away.

"Let me put it another way, Eric. Come out, or I'll start picking off people in that hospital one by one."

Eric slumped against the tyre at his back. *Damn.*

"I think I'll start with the children's ward, and then work my way—"

"Oi!" Eric stood.

The Dylan umbra was in front of him in a flash. The umbra slammed Eric into the car at his back and pinned him there, splayed on the bonnet. The skin on its fingers split, glass points sliding out and through Eric's shirt, cutting into his shoulder. "I see it now. What you really are. What your purpose is. But...." It searched his face and then drew in close. Its eyes were flat and the colour seemed to be draining away. "I don't think you know, though, do you?" The thing's breath smelled foul, like stale beer. "Want to see a trick of mine?" it asked.

"Not particularly," Eric managed to wheeze.

"Oh, go on. It'll make you fall head over heels." The creature hoisted Eric off his feet and threw him. Eric crashed against the side of a nearby van, rolling over himself and down onto the mercifully softer grass at the other side.

Eric lay stunned and breathless as the laughing umbra came to stand over him. Its eyes were now clear sheets of glass, and the face in which they sat looked even more angular and wrong.

"You gonna make another bad pun?" Eric coughed, tasting blood.

"Oh, Eric, Eric, Eric, I always knew I'd be the one to kill you," the creature said and kicked him. Something inside Eric snapped.

"You are not him," Eric gasped as he tried to sit up and scurry away. One of his ribs was broken, another bruised. And he couldn't put much weight on his left ankle. But alive. *I'm alive. Until this wanker finishes me off, that is.* "You're not him. You're just a bad copy."

"A lot like Tim, then? A bad copy of a bad original?"

"You don't know anything about Tim," Eric shouted. "You're just finding that stuff in that head there. The memories. Alistair explained—"

"Tim's dad's memories, yes," the creature smiled. Its teeth were clear and jagged shards. "Such a lot of memories. And a great deal of it hate." The monster seemed to swell. To grow bigger. "Delicious." It rounded on Eric. "So, let me tell you something about Tim."

"Go to Hell."

"I don't like being interrupted, boy." The umbra stepped on Eric's forearm and then, with one swift hand, snapped that limb. An elemental scream rocked through Eric. The shadows around him became knives, but the monster pulled back too quick to be cut.

"Tim did that to his mother on that night she kicked him out," the umbra said. "Well, it wasn't quite as clean as I made it. He hit her in the chest, actually, and she fell and broke her arm. But the effect was pretty much the same. What do you think about your boy now, Eric?"

"He took after his father really well, then, didn't he?" Eric hissed, and then, quite unexpectedly, found himself laughing. "It won't work, you know," he said.

"What? You don't believe me?" The monster snarled. "You're pathetic. I should—"

"Oh, no, I *do* believe you," Eric said. Even if he couldn't stand, he'd look the monster in the eye. "I worked it out a good while back, actually. Didn't want to admit it but what's true is true. So if you were planning on taunting me, this bit of theatre where you tell me exactly what kind of man Tim was: just fucking save us both the trouble and snap my neck now, yeah, because you're not going to break me. Not like that. I know who he was and even though I might not like it...." Eric shut his eyes. "I love him anyway."

The creature snarled. "Love? Love him, do you? Ha! How about this, then? This little fact about Tim." Again, that too wide smile. "It's all your fault."

"I'm not to blame," Eric laughed.

"Really? Think about it. You're the only one whose opinion ever mattered to him," the monster said. "When he was alive, he would tell me that it didn't matter what I said. That nothing mattered. We could do nothing for him, me and his mum. But you. He listened to you. And he hurt the most when he thought that he let you down."

"Let me down?" This was unexpected, and it stung. It ripped and twisted. "Shut up. You don't know what you're talking about."

"I know what his dad thought. And I can see how that struck home." The monster put a glass talon under Eric's chin and lifted Eric's head so that they were staring at one another. "Why do you think that Tim's dad hated you so much? You hollowed his son out. That night he caught you two at the flat, liquor on the floor, the smell of bodies in the air—"

"We didn't do anything. He didn't feel like that about me—"

"Even if his dad believed that, bodies rutting? That's nothing. Tim loved you, sex be damned." The creature laughed. "You think you're the victim in this, Eric. But you weren't. You were Tim's enemy because how could anyone ever meet your disdainful high standards, eh? The night you didn't die is the night his life ended!"

The monster laughed, and the sound, so hollow in the night, was too much. Eric hawked and spat. The glob of spittle ran down the creature's face. Then that fluid clouded, turned black, and began to burn. The creature gave a shout of surprise and tried to wipe away the smouldering wet.

"You little gnat!" A kick to Eric's face, and Eric reeled there on the floor, nose broken and bloody. "You killed him," the creature said, grinning some more, and finally its jaw split too far and shards of glass spread through the cracks. "You're the cause. You're why what's left of Tim in this life, well, why it killed me!" The creature drew back its arm. "Think about that as I end you."

Eric looked up as the monster raised its fist, a snarl of hate written in its features. Eric straightened his back, raised his chin. If he was dying, he was going with dignity.

"Die!"

A ribbon of violet fire shot from the ground, making the creature reel back.

"My sentiments exactly," someone called from above. Someone standing on a lamppost, as it happened.

Eric, in the blur of hurt and the dregs of consciousness, gave a bloody smile. "Alistair."

The Dylan umbra screamed. "I killed you!"

"Aw, no one's staying dead anymore, sweetheart, haven't you heard? But I'll see if I can make yours stick." A volley of violet flame sent the creature running for cover. In the next, Alistair landed at Eric's side. "Where are you hurt?"

"My arm," Eric groaned. Then he noticed Alistair was wearing different clothes. A business suit, complete with cufflinks. "Did you go home and *change*?"

"No, this was a happy accident. I did like those thigh-high boots though," Alistair said a little sadly. Then his eyes flared, and Eric felt the electric current of Alistair's care making his right arm whole again. A touch and Eric's nose snapped back into place, the pain already dulling. "I need to conserve my shades so I can't fix the rest of you yet. Unless you're desperate?"

"No," Eric lied. "I'm fine now." The pain in his ribs was almost as bad as the broken arm had been, but he would have to manage.

"Good, and as for you," Alistair said, pulling Eric to his feet and spinning them both away as a lance of glass sped past, gouging a chunk from a nearby tree. "I think it's time we danced, so it is." Alistair shoved Eric a good distance out of harm's way and then took to circling the Dylan umbra.

"That's fine by me," it said, holding up its left arm that was now just one long sword. "The runt there was getting boring anyway."

"I see you've fashioned yourself a weapon."

"Oh, I'm sorry. It does throw off the balance, doesn't it?" the creature taunted.

"Not even close," Alistair said, squaring his shoulders. His left hand slid down to his hip. Violet shine, and then he lifted his arm with slow, deliberate motion. His right hand, his right hip, all the same, until his hands met at the top of the arc and from his shoulder blades two grisly bone spears emerged. The monster attempted to dart forward, sword out, but a thump of Alistair's foot and a wall of flame shot up again, forcing the creature to spin away. Alistair pulled the spears free of his own flesh with a grunt, and then spun them around in elegant, air-singing arcs. He laid the bloody weapons one over his shoulder and the other ready in his hand.

"Interesting," said the umbra, for the first time sounding scared.

"It's adapting. Working around this heart's limitations. Right, Little Bird?" Alistair said.

"Er, yeah," Eric said, pretending he understood the lesson he was being taught. All he could think, though, was what the umbra had said.

I'm the reason Tim's dead. The reason he took Mineral. He wanted to be good enough for me.

"I reckon those spears will make nice toothpicks after I've made you my meal," the umbra replied, its blank eyes catching the glare of the streetlights above with hot menace. Then the monster shrieked and struck forward. Alistair jabbed at it with a spear but with an elegant turn the creature deflected and kept moving, its glass sword high and lethal. Alistair sprang back, landing on a nearby car roof and cartwheeled down, sending a spear whistling through the air. It sliced into the umbra's side, taking a chunk of shattered glass with it, and then embedded in a car tyre. The umbra's scream melded with the hissing of the punctured tyre to create a horrible, snake-like sound.

"It's why we win. It's why we always win," Alistair said. "The shadow hearts can adapt. My heart can heal. Overclock it and I can fashion some nifty little weapons. But umbras can't. You do not adapt. You can only infect and pervert. You are legion but you are born to be dispensable. To die."

"Dispensable, you say," the umbra glared, holding its wounded side. It licked its chops. "But I think today I'd rather live." The creature gave a terrible shriek, like nails clawing through stone, and in a bone-cracking beat, its remaining human features blew out with a wave of force that knocked Eric and Alistair to the ground.

By the time Eric could fix the moment again, get his brain around it, Alistair was pelting after a blur running out of the car park, shouting, "You little git!"

"Al! Wait up!" Eric shouted, trying to give chase, but the pain in his ribs was excruciating. A slow walk was all he could manage. When, eventually, he caught up with Alistair the man was stood at the side of Hitchens' Road, looking up and down the street. They were near the roundabout down from the hospital, and the baleen plates of Jody Woods loomed in the distance, dark and imposing.

As though to break that apart, the streetlights began to blink on, one, two, three.

"I can't find it, Eric. Being glass and all, it's got a good bit of camouflage," Alistair said, turning on the spot, searching.

"It's still close, though, isn't it?" Eric asked, touching his heart.

"Why you say that?"

"I can feel it. Sort of. Like air pressure. Something, I don't know, nagging at me."

Alistair's eyes fixed Eric. "Here," he said, holding out his hand. There rested a sticky black shade sweet. Looking at it, Eric had the distinct impression it might be one Alistair had recently regurgitated. "I wouldn't ask if there was another way, it's just—"

"I get it. You need to track this thing." Eric held the sweet in his fingers. Burning these shades and turning his powers on: earlier it had felt like his head was going to burst with all the things he could see, hear and feel. He wasn't keen on repeating the experience, but what choice did they have?

"If you don't want to I can—"

"No, it's fine. This is the fastest way. It's the only way." Eric lifted the sweet to his lips and swallowed the thing down. Eric was reassured by the fact that, as soon as he felt the shades reaching his shadow heart, the pain in his ribs began to lessen to a dull ache. They wouldn't heal like under Alistair's power, but Eric would take whatever pain relief he could get. Steadying himself, he was preparing to turn his power on when Alistair shouted: "Wait! It's there."

Eric followed where Al was pointing. The monster stood in the middle of the road, between the rows of traffic. Given its now completely translucent body it would have been indistinguishable from its surroundings except for the car headlights shining through it and the light bouncing around the various planes of its insides, making the creature flare and glow. It looked oddly beautiful now, and somehow even more deadly for it.

"End of the line, umbra," Alistair yelled, holding out his hand. A seed of the violet fire began to gather.

"The cars," Eric reminded him.

"I know what I'm doing, don't worry." Then, to the umbra, "It's over!"

The beast walked a few paces closer. "Let's see, shall we?" It turned its sword arm and the light that filled its body shot forth in a jagged ray. It struck Alistair square in the chest, sending him skidding into the ground.

"Al!"

"Never mind me," Alistair said, kicking out to regain his feet. His chest was smoking from where he was struck, and a deep gouge was slowly closing in his skin. "The umbra? Where is it?"

"I don't know. I can't see it," Eric said. He couldn't take his eyes off the smoking wound in Alistair's chest. "I thought you said umbras didn't change? Didn't adapt?"

"I didn't say their power couldn't grow," Alistair grumbled. "Though whoever made this thing gave it a leg up. Given time enough, it might even reach fomorian level."

"What does that mean?"

"Short answer, bad answer, concise though: Your entire city becomes an umbra."

"Is that...." Eric could barely process what that meant. "Shit."
"Exactly. Now where in the Verse is it?"
A minivan barrelled down the road, its headlights on full. "There!" Eric pointed, seeing a strobe of light, but it was too late. An impossibly bright flash erupted in the middle of the road. An ear-needling screech of tyres came next, then bang after bang, collision after collision.
"I'll see you soon, Eric," came a salty voice at Eric's ear as, still blinded, Eric stumbled over the pavement. "I can't wait until you see the murderer you really are."
A withering screech tore through the air, then finally the blazing light dimmed. Eric blinked away the novas in his vision to see that the umbra was gone, and in its place was carnage.

"Do you want more rice?"
"I'd love some, thank you."
Jhardine reached over the table and deposited a ladle's worth of rice on the vicar's still quite full plate. The priest, with a pleasing finesse, threaded his fork under the mound, sifted out a delicate nugget of chicken and ran it through the thick curry sauce. He had such lovely table manners, Jhardine thought. *I could watch him for hours.*
"I was just thinking," he said, wiping his mouth with the flannel Jhardine was passing off as a serviette. "Do you have a favourite hymn, Jhardine? We've fallen into a bit of a rut at our Sunday services and I'd like to try something different."
"The Prayer of Saint Francis," she said without hesitation. "I do love that. Not the Latin one though. The proper one. The English. It's lovely, that. Always warms my heart."
"Oh, yes, I like that too. I'll put that down for next Sunday."
The gentle scrape of their forks and the sound of the washer working through its last spin cycle filled the silences, but they were pregnant. Ready to pop in fact. There's no getting around it, Jhardine thought. This feels like a date.
Jhardine sipped her water. "David, I've, er, been wondering, did you always know you wanted to be a priest? Like, did you want to be part of the Church when you were little?"
"Yes. Yes I did." Then, the wobble of his eyes said he was studying. "Actually, that's not quite true. My parents wanted it for me first, and so from

a very young age they secured me some private lessons to develop my knowledge of scripture and my skills at reading Latin and a smidgen of Greek. I'm very grateful to them for that. I don't know what I would do today without having had those early opportunities."

"Really. I bet that was pricey," Jhardine said and then blushed. She'd turned into her mother: always thinking about things in terms of how much shrapnel it cost. "Why did they want you to be a priest?"

"Ah, well, they wanted me to serve people. My father always used to tell me, 'A life must matter, David. Your life will matter.'"

"That sounds a bit...."

"It was, *a bit*. But the captain—he was in the Air Force—he could be that way. But actually, despite my studying and my endless praying, I didn't actually hear God's voice for many years. I was in my thirties before it happened."

"No! Really? But you're so *good*."

"Well, that's nice of you to say," and he seemed genuinely pleased to hear it. "The Bible tells us, though, that the good are tested, aren't they, Jhardine? You and Eric know that. But yes, God withheld his voice from me for a number of years. It was disappointing for my father. And you didn't want to disappoint the captain. No, sir."

Jhardine sank into her chair. "Do you mean he...?"

"Yes. More than once. Until I was too old, that is, by which point he simply stopped talking to me. He died not long after I...but I never got to tell him I'd heard the Call."

"Oh, David...." She put her hand over his.

"It's fine. I've put it behind me."

The washer's spin cycle cut out. Jhardine rushed to fill the noiselessness. "Celibacy!" She hadn't meant to blurt it out, but anything to change the subject. "I mean, I know you don't have to be celibate but you seem to have gone that way. Is it hard?"

"Well, I do hope that's not a loaded question." He raised an eyebrow, making his forehead wrinkle. She nearly choked on a store-bought papadum. He laughed. "For some of my fellows, fidelity is difficult. I know Reverend Coaley before me, he in particular had trouble in that area."

"No! Really?" Oh, this would just stick in her mum's craw something delicious. She'd loved Reverend Coaley, and she'd missed her chance. Hilarious.

"Yes, it's why he left so abruptly."

"You mean he was...?" Jhardine couldn't help her mouth gaping. "With who?"

"I wasn't told," the vicar laughed. "But yes. Some do struggle. I personally haven't." He looked up from his plate. "I've just never found the right person. One doesn't come across many opportunities in my line of work, and God bless me, but I am rather picky, too." The vicar smiled as he sipped his water. "Eric," the vicar started. "He said something on the phone about you having one of your turns?"

The way he said it, so light and casual, it almost stopped her feeling annoyed. Almost. "It were nothing. He shouldn't have bothered you. I was down the pub and, well, it's stuffy in there, isn't it? And I think I accidentally ended up with a vodka and orange and I got a bit dizzy and fell over. That's all it was really. I—"

"Jhardine."

She chased a clump of rice across her plate. Her cheeks burned. *Too much chilli in this curry, that's what that is.* It made her thoughts warm. Made them too hot to keep to herself. "The tablets, you see. It's the tablets. They're not working. None of them."

The vicar put his hands around his glass of cucumber water. She could see his fingers turning whiter, whiter. Why was he gripping so hard? "Well, not now. They'll give you some others and you'll be fine."

Jhardine put down her fork. "I should wash up."

"No, Jhardine." He caught her arm. "What is it?"

She looked at the washer. At the floor. Anywhere but at him.

"Jhardine, are you crying? Oh, don't...."

STRETCHING OUT IN either direction sat long trains of now stationary cars. Most had come to a halt without serious damage or injury to their respective drivers except, that is, the cars where the two lines met. Stood about a meter apart, crumpled and broken, both cars were on fire. The door of one car was open and people were already tending to the female driver. She was elderly and had so much loose skin around her neck that Eric could literally see her wobbling with fright. She was scared but alive. The driver in the other car, however, hadn't fared so well. It was as if something heavy had rolled right over the top of the car, which as Eric remembered the minivan he'd seen just seconds before the crash, was precisely what might have happened. A faint shadow behind the car's crushed windscreen drew Eric's attention, just as a nearby man began to shriek, "Oh *Gawd*, he's dead!"

"Eric!" Alistair called from over by the embankment. "We can't help folk who are already gone, but there's people here we can save. Come on."

With a last glance at the stain of a man in the destroyed car, Eric jogged through the snaking line of traffic to meet Alistair halfway down the embankment. Though a gentler slope than Eric had imagined, he soon saw that the minivan had indeed cut a long path across the road and run deep into the field below, finally coming to rest against a row of sturdy trees that, though a few had bent, had largely managed to withstand the blow.

"So there are s-survivors?" Eric asked.

"They're all hanging on," Alistair said with the hint of relief. "But we're going to need some cover if we want to help them."

A cotton darkness collected around Alistair's palms as though Alistair were leeching ink from the air itself. Then, he crouched and put a hand to the floor and began to inscribe diagonal marks that looked like a series of crosshatches. When he took back his hands the clods of dark stayed fixed to the ground, and the shapes he had formed seemed to emit an odd heat that made the air above them waver and bend. Alistair put his fingers to his mouth, sucking.

"We need to hurry," he said around his fingers, then he set off running down the gouged hill and disappeared around the side of the wreck. "Eric!" he called after an unsettling moment of quiet.

Eric struck forward, crossing the horizontal line of the symbols—or, at least, he tried. The air resisted him like the repellent force of two matching poles on a magnet. He tried again, and the same force gripped him. Then his shadow heart gave an annoyed beat and, after a second or so of resistance, the symbols' grip on him loosened, the air flowed over him like silk and Eric stumbled through, but this made him slip and he ran and fell until he reached the bottom of the hill.

Looking up from the muddy ground, it was easy to think of the minibus as a huge upturned hog. The wreck's front end was crumpled like a snout and the metal of its body squealed laboriously. Eric coughed against the fumes pouring out of the wreck as he turned the corner to find Alistair waist deep through what had once been a window. There came a faint throng of electricity in the air, like the static of an excited party balloon, and then Alistair pulled back. Blood and sweat slicked his hands and face.

"I've done the driver," Alistair said, wiping his hands on his charcoal linen trousers. Then he wrenched open the door, tossing it to one side like it was nothing more than a block of printing paper. He hauled out the driver, a sealion of a man with a generous bruise still darkening one side of his face. Alistair deposited the guy a good fifteen yards from the wreckage and then walked his way back toward the van. "Eric?"

Eric couldn't stop staring at an arm that dangled from the wreckage a few yards down the minivan's length. It had deep lacerations, and Eric could see a glare of white bone beneath stringy tendons.

After a moment of silence, Eric's gaze ticked to Alistair. He seemed annoyed. "See if you can make yourself useful," Alistair said. "Go check that the lock I put on the hill is holding."

Eric, a numb slave to his need to get away from *that* arm, nodded. "Okay." He clawed his way back around the minivan until he had a clear view of the embankment.

A crowd of eight people had gathered there, one of them uncommonly short. Going by what they were wearing, none of them belonged to the ambulance or police. None were making a move to help either, as though it hadn't even occurred to them that there might be survivors.

"I think it's working," Eric said.

"You what?"

"The lock. It's stopping them coming down."

"Good! Come back here, then, I need your help."

"N-no, I think I should stay here."

"Eric, I—"

"I...." Eric swallowed down a glut of rising bile. "I can't, Al. I can't see stuff like this."

"They'll die, Eric." The voice was flat, hard and unapologetic. "If you don't help me, they'll die."

Eric bit down on his lip. "Shit," he said as he put one hand to the metal carcass of the van and, slow but moving, retraced his steps.

"Al?" There was no sign of the other man. Eric tiptoed over the ruined ground. He scanned the stillness of trees surrounding the crash site. "Alistair?" A hand gripped the back of Eric's neck. He shrieked, and his arse felt like it might never unclench.

"Don't move the guy in the middle," Alistair chuckled from inside the minivan. "The chair in front has twisted and there's metal through his stomach. I'll need to take care of it without shifting him or things will get really messy." The hand released him, and Alistair retreated into the carcass of the van.

Eric realised his fingers were at his earlobe again, trying to trace out some comfort. He stilled that hand and let it fall to his side.

The next moment Alistair emerged from the window at the head of the wreck, wheezing a "Come on, you bugger" as he pulled to safety the first of the passengers. The man was enormous, his shoulders nearly twice as broad as Eric's. "It would have to be a sodding rugby team."

Alistair dragged the unconscious man a few feet across the ground and then crouched over him, placing his hands on either side of the poor bugger's sliced-up face. The air turned hot.

"The others," Alistair panted as the violet storm in his eyes shone.

Eric dithered.

"Eric...."

"Okay, yeah."

Eric made his way down to the farthest window, skirting the dangling arm with a wide detour. He clawed the inside of the van, feeling glass bite his palms but ignoring it, and hoisted himself up and inside.

"Crap!" He slipped on a long streak of blood, sliding and crashing into what was now the far wall.

"You all right?" Alistair called from outside.

"Er, yeah." Sore but nothing broken, Eric gripped the scratchy fabric of one of the twisted seats and pulled himself to standing. His foot knocked something, sending it rolling away. It was a familiar looking vial.

"Mineral," Eric croaked.

"You say something?"

"Yeah. I think one of them's been on the drug that's made out of shades. That Mineral stuff."

"Great. Like we don't have enough problems. Just keep going, Little Bird. I'll see if I can take care of it."

"Okay, y-yeah," Eric said, clambering his way down the inside of the wreck. A groaning leaked through the squeaking death knell of the van's frame. He tried to pick out where the noise was coming from, and then something touched his leg.

Credit where due, Eric didn't scream, void his bowels or anything of that variety. Instead, he rounded to see a man suspended by the seatbelt that had tangled under his shoulder and around his chest.

"Help me."

"Don't worry, mate," Eric said as he worked to find the button on the seat belt clip. "How's your neck. Does any of that hurt?"

"No, no, I don't think so."

"Okay, I'm going to get you down. You're going to be fine, yeah. Stay with me?"

Eric positioned himself underneath the man, then pressed the button and released the seatbelt's grip. Eric staggered under the rugby player's tonnage as he untangled the man and then, with hip-grindingly slow steps, shuffled for the nearest window. Once outside, Eric reached back in and grabbed the man by his ankles and, using the lip of the window as leverage, he pulled.

"Fuck!" The man's eyes shot open.

"W-w-what's wrong?"

"His leg's broken, that's all," Alistair called, yanking another man out further down the wreck. "You need to get him out, though. He's got a blood clot making its way to his brain. Ignore the noise."

Noise? This was someone screaming in agony! And then Eric remembered the first time he'd met Alistair, how callous he'd been that night in the hospital. Maybe this was how he kept his distance and how he was able to be around so much death and keep people on the living side.

Eric gritted his teeth against the screaming and red fury in the man's face, and he pulled and pulled until he could get his hands under the man's lower back and, encircling the man's thick, heavily muscled waist, draw the rest of him through the window. Every pull and tug made the man yell. Eric had hoped he'd be able to block it out but he felt every single cry of pain like a punch. Mercifully, the man soon lost consciousness and so didn't feel the jarring drop as Eric pulled him down onto the ground. There, Eric hooked his hands under the man's armpits and dragged him across the ground to where Alistair stood.

"Put him down there," Alistair said, voice crunching in his throat. "Now the others. We need to be quick."

Eric, shaking from the effort of just one rescue, gave Alistair a baleful stare.

"Never said it would be easy," Alistair retorted, setting his hands on Eric's rescue. "Sorry, Little Bird."

And so Eric crossed the distance and slid his way back down into the wreckage. This entry was more graceful than his last, but only by degrees. By now the air was thick with the smell of petrol and blood, and Eric had to fight not to gag. He climbed his way through the minivan, his hands now hurting something fierce from gripping and pulling. That was forgotten, though, when he came across a man nestled between two uprooted chairs. The man's foot was twisted to a wrong angle and on his face there was a deep cut that ran from his temple to his jaw.

"Right, bud, you'll be on the mend soon," Eric said as he wrestled the man up to standing. Seven and a half long minutes later, and shaking with the effort, Eric dropped the lad at Alistair's feet. Then he stumbled and fell, panting on the ground.

Alistair came to stand over the man. He spared a second to concentrate, and then proclaimed, "He's going to be okay on his own so long as he gets to a hospital soon."

"But, that cut on his face."

"The others are dying and I don't have much juice left in me and no more shades to draw on. Besides, it'll leave a fetching scar." Alistair staggered, almost falling himself until Eric caught him and the two served to prop each other up. "Thanks."

"You need to rest."

"No, not if we're going to save all we can. I need to get back to—" Then, a strange, awful sucking sound cut him off.

Eric swung around. The man Eric had just dragged out from the wreckage was twitching, fitting.

"Al!"

A black ooze leaked from the man's nose. His gaze locked onto Eric's. He was crying.

"He's the one who was taking shades. And he's close to turning," Alistair wheezed. "I was wrong. One of them died."

Somehow, Eric knew what Alistair would do now. "Al, no, don't—"

A spike of bone shot from Alistair's palm, sliding straight into the man's forehead and through his skull. The man went limp.

"You, you could have healed him!"

"No. No, I couldn't," Alistair coughed. "If I can get to them before the process starts, yeah. But once it's in motion I don't have the power to stop it. I wish I could. See, he was dead the minute he drank from that last vial. He'd taken too much. Sooner or later, it was going to turn him."

Eric stared at the dead man. For all the world, that could have been Tim. "Shit," Eric said, hearing that obnoxious plug break in his throat that meant he was crying without being aware of it. He wiped off his face.

"Well, that's all the others out," Alistair said, his tone softer than before. "I'll need your help with the last."

"I don't want to do this anymore," Eric said.

"Us with hearts," Alistair said, "we don't get to choose."

Mournfully, Eric followed Alistair back to the minivan. A plume of white smoke hissed from the vehicle's front and the squealing of the structure grew louder still. "Help me up," Alistair said. Eric lifted the waif of a man and Alistair slid through a window and into the wreck. Eric, with what little strength he had left, hauled himself up and followed. Together they worked their way through the broken shafts of metal, the empty beer cans and soiled rugby kits, until they came to the back of the wreck where just one man remained.

In his late thirties, bulk of a sportsman well cultivated, the man had taken the worst of the impact and it showed. One of his eyes dangled from its socket on a long, frayed thread, and his was the arm dangling out the window, slowly blackening. But none of that could compare to the metal spike through the man's stomach.

"How? How is he still going?" Eric said in disbelief.

"You'd be surprised," Alistair said, bitter and low, "how easy it is to die, and how stubborn some people can be about it. Now, this is going to get worse before it gets better, so it is."

"I can't watch. I can't—"

"This is it, Little Bird. This is the price of these powers. We are the ones that deal with this. We don't get to choose."

"I can't. Monsters is one thing, but this is—" He took himself a sidelong glance at the wound. There was a sucking sound and the man gave an awful gurgling cry. "Oh, shit."

"Eric," Alistair said again.

"No, no, I can't."

"He needs you. Hold his hand. You care, Eric, I know you do. We couldn't save that man outside, but help this one."

Eric let that bubble and build. Finally, he crouched to take the man's hand. He didn't look—couldn't look—but all the same, he held the man's hand tight and said, "Come on, mate, yeah. Come on."

For his part, Alistair hooked his fingers around the metal shaft and then placed his other hand on the man's broad chest.

"Ready?"

"Not even a little bit."

"Here goes!" Alistair shouted as he pulled, and the sound of wet suction assaulted Eric's ears. The metal came free in a spray of red, and then a clatter as Alistair dropped the spike to the floor and let it roll away. Eric watched as blood gushed out of the hole in the man's midsection, and then realised that it was timed to the pumping beat of the man's own slowing heart.

"Now, let's see what we can do," Alistair said as he clamped a hand over the wound. The electric field of before crackled into life, but it was weaker now and no sooner had it arrived than it faded away. Alistair sagged. A choking cough seized him, and inch-long wounds split open over his cheeks and neck. "I can't," he wheezed. He looked up at Eric and his eyes were dull and fish like. "I'm too weak. I was never meant for this. I don't know how to do more."

"But, you have to! He's going to die."

"I can't. I just...."

Eric seized Alistair's wrists and locked their hands over the wound. The man's blood gushed between their fingers. Eric swallowed his fear, his disgust, his epic desire to run. "If there's sommat in me, something powerful, then use it."

"What?" Alistair winced. "No, I—"

"Can't we do that? Can't we share powers?"

"Yes, but you're talking about cyphering and it's dangerous unless you're trained. It could kill you, and—"

"Help him, Al. I have those shades you gave me before the crash, remember? You can use them."

"No."

Alistair tried to pull back but Eric kept his wrists in hand. And then Eric gambled on a hunch. "For all the people you haven't helped."

"Don't."

"For all the people you ignored."

"Shut up."

"For all the people you *killed*."

Alistair bared his teeth and howled, "I am not a killer!" He slammed a hand to Eric's chest, to the black heart, and a ripping current surged through Eric. He screamed, and for a moment he was back in the hospital, that first time when Alistair had slowly penetrated his chest, digging into him to plant a spark, to make a heart beat again. The power grew until it reached a point where it seemed it could go either way. Two hearts beating, one rhythm, and where Alistair was weak, Eric was strong.

"Come on, Al! Use it. Use all of me if you have to. Just do it."

"Be careful. What you. Wish for!" Alistair growled. The power grew. The surge in the current made Eric's skin prickle. His nerves twisted and throbbed.

"Come on," Alistair said, screwing his eyes tight. "Heal. Heal!"

"Ahhh!" Pain ripped through Eric's insides but, just as he thought to pull away, he saw the crash victim's blood retracing its slide, threading back into open wounds that were slowly closing themselves; the man's dislocated eye went winding back up into its socket, and the gushing of blood under Eric and Alistair's hands slowed until it stopped. At last, the man's chest hitched as he began to breathe properly again, and lively colour slowly returned to his face.

Alistair broke away then, and the electricity faded. Eric let exhaustion claim him too, and he fell to the floor. Together they watched the hole in the man's stomach close to become the blackest of bruises on his bare skin.

"That was...mint!" Eric laughed, feeling the buzz of power still fluttering. "He's fine, yeah, Al?"

"He'll survive," Alistair croaked. With a staggered cough Alistair shifted to face Eric. The impression of Alistair's teeth showed through his dried, flaking lips as he added, "But I need to get out of here. The dark is coming for me."

"We're here," said Little Bird, his voice reaching through the gloom to rouse Alistair. "Though why here? Wouldn't you be better at the hospital?"

"Put me down," Alistair commanded, ignoring Eric's questions. After a few minutes he pried open his eyes to find he was laid out on the ground beneath a towering, moss-speckled tree in the woods near to the hospital. The pattern of light draining from the sky could be seen through the canopy, and it was enchanting.

"What's that on your shirt?"

As Eric's question tripped the gates in Alistair's head, Alistair wobbled his head down so that his eyes could get a look. There, on the rise of his stomach, there was a thumbnail's worth of blood. Not much now, but it was growing.

"Be a dear and take off my shirt," Alistair said with an apologetic lilt. "I'm afraid I can't do it, my arms are dislocating." Then Alistair's arms popped out of their sockets with a sound like the burst of a pickle jar opening.

"No, I...."

"You have to," Alistair wheezed. "You have to understand that these powers have a price. And this is mine."

Eric, a hand to his earlobe, shifted from foot to foot. "All right," he said, bending over Alistair and unbuttoning Alistair's shirt with a slow, deliberate care.

"You having a good time now, Jingoro?" Alistair laughed.

"What's that?" Eric asked, catching the smile and mixing it with a bit of his own desperate anxiety. The night was coming. Alistair was cold. He hated the cold. "Is that a word from where you come from?"

"A war cry. A funeral rite."

Eric seemed puzzled. "I've been meaning to ask you, how come we speak the same language? We're from different worlds, but we understand each other just fine. Surely that's, like, a massive coincidence unless—"

"The hearts understand each other, we just hear what they translate," Alistair smiled. "You're a smart lad, Eric. That there's a question most forget to...to ask. I know I did. I—"

The pain squeezed his breath away. The circle of red over Alistair's stomach grew, its radius increasing by each creeping second until it was larger than an average man's palm.

"There's, there's something coming through your stomach, like a, a bone or something," Eric mewed as he peeled away Alistair's shirt. "What do I do? How can I help you?"

Alistair's stomach broke open in a spray of blood, splattering the ground, Eric's clothes and Eric's hair.

"I'm sorry," Alistair tried to say, but it came out as a wet gargle. He thought that Eric would leave him then. After all, pieces of Alistair's insides were dripping down Eric's face, and even in the most uncouth of circles that was frowned on, but Eric just stood there, mouth open. Dripping.

A bird in the canopy above shrieked. Then a whole flock of them up and flew. They let loose a rain of black feathers that came eddying down to the ground around them, a sluice that was in no way natural.

Eric, shaking, came to sit by Alistair. He covered Alistair's exposed guts with his own jacket and pulled Alistair closer, threading his hand beneath Alistair's head to cradle him. "You can go now. It's all right," he said, and then: "I won't leave you."

CHAPTER ELEVEN
BLOOD AND SHERBET

I'M SITTING IN *this freezing bloody wood with a dead man. And, sadly, this is probably the closest I've ever come to a proper date.*

A sound. Somewhere in the line of trees, something moved. A cold wash of fear pulsed through Eric. Had the umbra come back? What about the Tim creature? That was still out there somewhere, too.

How could I love you? its sly, insidious voice whispered in Eric's ear. *You were broken. You were wrong.*

He looked back at Alistair. What was it that was taking so long? Before, Alistair had come back in just minutes, but not this time. It was nearly morning now and Alistair showed no signs of reviving. Eric wondered if it was connected to how hard Alistair had run himself. Did it mean that the more people he healed, the longer his putting himself back together would take?

A snapping sound. This time he'd definitely heard something. Eric searched the trees. His sensitive ears could hear a strange, low humming. Or was it moaning? Then another sound, like air being let out of a tight canister. Eric glanced about, feeling cool insect legs of fear pattering up his spine. The sound. Where was the sound coming from? A crack from above. Eric looked up to see the canopy above was black—and murmuring.

Maybe I should move his body? Get him out of here? He reached arms under Alistair's body, about to stand and run, when he looked down, yelped and dropped the other man. The flesh on Alistair's bones was melting, running, dripping away. His eyelids were gone, his bald eyes leaking from their sockets, and his hands were now just wire frames. Soon, all that was left of Alistair was a skeleton and a business suit.

"Al?"

The ground at Eric's side exploded in a great bilge of earth. Another pale, skeletal hand clawed at the dirt. Eric scrambled away to take refuge behind a nearby tree. He peered out. A bald and mottled head was rising from the hole in the earth. Eric couldn't see the face but he had the distinct impression that it was probably rotten.

Run, you fool. But if he did that, Alistair might return to life only to have to face whatever the hell was crawling out of the ground.

"I..." Eric started, "I'm a shadow former," he called, for the first time trying the title on for size and rather liking the way it sounded. "And I will kill you if you don't do one, do you hear me?"

"Eric?" a strange, threadbare voice called. "Eric?"

Eric peered out from behind the tree again, and there the creature was, naked as the day is long, white hair growing back in tufts and a black heart over its chest pulsing with violet.

"Al?"

Alistair's throat gaped open but the wound was closing, closing and then gone. "Eric," he said, smiling, which was a rotten sight because his lips hadn't fully regrown yet.

"You-you-you crawled out of the ground!" Eric said, rushing to the man's side. "Is that normal?"

Alistair shuffled the short distance to what was left of his former body and took up the vacated trousers, then the shirt lying on the ground a few meters away where Eric had tossed it. He finished it off with Eric's jacket, and by the time he'd dressed himself he was more or less whole again.

"The heart," Alistair started, and then took to clearing his throat. "The heart," sounding too low. "The heart," a little squeaky. "The heart, ah!" he smiled. "It finds a corpse for me to take. Some are fresher than others."

"You should have told me. I bet people are dying in the hospital all the time. I could have took you up there."

"You'd have been in danger back there. The umbra, or umbras as the case is, they could have attacked. But not here. This is fox ground and it'd take something more powerful than an, albeit talented, youngling to violate this space, so it would."

Eric thought of the grey fox, Piper, that he'd met in the subway. "You don't mean normal foxes, do you?"

"No."

"Like that one we saw the other night?"

"Aye," Alistair looked Eric's jacket over. "I've ruined this," he said as he held up a sleeve and let the black slop that used to be his flesh drip away. "I hope it wasn't expensive."

"It's a knock-off," Eric said. "Pretty much everything I own is."

"Well, don't mind if I jazz the lot up, do you?" he asked.

"No, er, go for it."

Alistair did a turn, and in spinning the clothes he was wearing flared into a grey and crimson suit.

"Wow, that's handy," Eric said. "And could save me a few bob too. Any chance I could do that?"

"Who knows. Maybe, in time. Some powers overlap. And that shadow of yours is versatile. But," he sighed, "this is just a cheap trick, a ghost of a time long ago. Other than healing, it's about all I'm good for these days." Alistair sat down on the ground, slow and careful. "Ah, that's better," he said, leaning against the tree. "I'm going to need a few minutes. Pulling myself back together always takes it out of me, so it does."

Eric picked a spot across from Alistair and set to leaning. "Can I ask you something?"

"You can but I won't guarantee I'll answer."

Eric shrugged. "Fair enough. It's just, you seem to, well, not hate exactly but...."

"Yeah?"

"You don't seem to enjoy this life. So why do you keep doing the same stuff, like fighting monsters and all that? Why not run off and, I don't know, do something, anything, else?"

"I'm bound to do it. I...." Alistair laughed. "I sort of signed a contract with the Sisters. Not the paper kind, but still. And I get something in the end. Something only they can give me. That's if the end ever comes."

"What did you ask for?"

"You don't need to know that."

"Is it—"

"I said no."

Eric stared back at Alistair. "You can be a real wanker sometimes."

"Can I?"

"You keep trying to give me all these hard lessons, but then you get pissed off when I try to ask a few simple questions. I don't get you."

"Well, they're personal. Those things you're asking. And I'm trying to protect you. Not so long ago you were the one telling me to be on my way so you could protect your mother."

"That's different and you know it."

"I know you have your reasons, and I have mine."

"That's bullshit. Arrogant bullshit. Like, I'm feeble or something? Like, I'm a kid that you need to handle carefully?"

"Compared to me you are a kid."

"Arg! Do you hear yourself talk? I mean, seriously?" Eric put his hands on his head. "You can't protect me, not from this. Not now. Because I'm already a part of it. My best friend, the only person I ever...." Eric put a hand to his mouth as if to stuff those words back into their secret place. "He's dead. And I'm seeing him. I hear him calling all the time. And you say it's not him and, fine. But I need you to tell me what all this is because I am seriously close to going out of my mind."

"Did you eat your own toenails? I ate my own toenails once, you know, when it all got a bit much. Just pulled them clean off and ate them," Alistair said. Then he noticed Eric's sour face. "Well, you wanted to share."

Eric gave that a moment, thinking it through. "I sort of assumed this was all natural to you. The powers. The monsters."

"Well, it wasn't. I was just as thrown as you. More so. Took me a good few years to get my head round my situation. Granted, things were quite a bit different for me, but still."

Alistair seemed to study him then.

"What? What did I do now?"

"Nothing. Just, you're a fair spark, you know that, Little Bird? I just wonder...." There was a knowing sadness in his eyes. "How far you're willing to go."

"To go?"

"What would you trade to keep the ones you love safe?"

"For the right people I'd do anything," Eric said without hesitation. "Speaking of. My mum, you said you'd heal her."

Alistair's expression softened. "Aye, we'll sort that out today. I need to go back to camp first, get some more shades. For you as much as me."

"I thought you didn't want me using my powers?"

"Ideally I don't, but you burn through shades and starve your shadow heart and you'll get sick, like I told you. Now, time's ticking. I assume you brought your banger of a car?"

"Nah, the car's dead," he huffed.

"Well, go fetch me a ride then," Alistair said. "I'll not be walking far in this state."

"What?"

"You heard. I need a car."

Eric climbed to his feet. "Wanker," he growled as he traipsed off through the trees.

"YOU LIVE IN a quarry?" Eric said, looking past the high metal fence's rusted struts to see the abandoned wasteland inside.

"I live in lots of places." Alistair wrapped his oversized hands over the fence's metal bars. "Sometimes I live here." A dark blur clipped with violet and the struts that Alistair touched, their neighbours and their neighbours' neighbours, began to bend and twist away from one another, the metal whining until a gap opened in the fence just wide enough for them to slip through. Before following Alistair, Eric took a glance at the hire car he'd managed to cadge and made sure it would be safe sat at the side of the road. Its pristine and sexy green chrome was nice, sure, but it wasn't a patch on his old, faithful ride. *Peace be upon her.*

The quarry's bistre valleys were lacerated with wide puddles and discarded bits of scaffolding, and the quiet of the place was broken by the loose arm of a digger creaking in a swirling, uneasy breeze. Eric rubbed a hand over his ribs. They were still smarting, but close contact with Alistair the night before seemed to have mended the worst of the damage.

"Why here?" Eric asked. "I mean, it's a hole in the ground. Literally."

They skirted a mound of rocks and peat to find a wide stretch of flat ground. In its middle sat a small, shabby caravan and next to it a wide lake of dirty water.

"Well, it's secluded. And I need my space."

"Space? Really?" Eric pointed to the *very* modest caravan.

"Don't laugh. Murder, it was, getting that thing in here." Alistair squelched toward the caravan door.

"Actual murder, or the metaphorical kind? It's hard to tell these days."

"I'll grant you the place isn't much to look at, but it's what I call home," Alistair said. He touched the three metal locks on the caravan door and each unbolted.

"Is that another of your shadow heart's powers? Locking and unlocking stuff?"

"No," said Alistair. "Panacea mends things. This power, small as it is, is something from before I got the heart. The shades sustain it all the same. It's not much use in a fight, at least not in this form. And, would you mind taking off your shoes, please," he said as Eric climbed the three stairs to the small porch. "I don't want no mud on my carpet, I'm sure you understand."

Eric suppressed the urge to scream. *Everybody is flipping carpet mad!*

Doffing his shoes, he followed Alistair into the cramped little caravan, which was made even smaller by a largess of books piled high along the narrow caravan's interior walls. "You a big reader?"

"Practically illiterate," Alistair said, walking down into the caravan and turning on an old television with a wonky aerial that sat on top of a refrigerator. The clashing fuzz of two competing stations filled the caravan. "Come on, you bloody thing." Alistair gave the television a slap and fiddled with the rotary dials on its front. Eric took the opportunity for a more comprehensive look around.

Five plastic jars of boiled sweets flanked the refrigerator, one empty and the others at varying levels of fullness. Mint humbugs, lemon sherbets, midget gems, and even two tubs of rhubarb and custards that Eric swore to himself he'd dip into before the day was up. Mouth watering, Eric skipped his gaze to the upholstered seat under the far window. A crumpled blanket in one corner suggested this might also be where Alistair slept. But it was the worktop that ran down the left of the caravan that stood out the most. In stark contrast to the rest of the caravan, the worktop was immaculate and clear except for a few metal bean tins pushed against the wall that had scrawled labels on for tea, sugar, and coffee, and one other far more impressive object: a sword, far longer than Eric's arm and made of twisted lengths of bone. A rich black fabric bound the sword's falu hilt and a long, glossy plume rose from the handle's end.

"You can pick it up if you like."

"No," Eric said. "I'd be dangerous with it. It's beautiful though. Where's it from?"

"My wilder days," Alistair answered, a bit cryptically in Eric's opinion. Though, admittedly, there *was* something a bit wild about it, an aura of power, and he felt like he needed to give it room. He took a few steps back, only to knock over several stacks of books.

"Sorry," he rushed, bending to pick the books up and stacking them as neatly as he could. Eric stopped when one book's olive cover flared with golden and elaborate symbols.

"Now that's interesting." Alistair commented from across the room. "The cyphers respond to you."

"Is this a language?"

"Yes. It's the written form of the symbols and rituals shadow formers can use to pool their talents."

Eric looked down at the book in his hands and the swirling, glittering symbols there. Inside the book, darker symbols darted across the page like scurrying insects. Eric picked through the tomes at his feet. A few had titles he could read. "Cypher Arrays: The Skeins of Power". Another, "Shades, A Compendium on Creation", and another, "On Transelementation".

"I can read the covers but not what's inside."

"The hearts don't translate the cypher language well. That's intentional. Some things are best kept hidden, so they are. Having said that, they seem to know it. In fact, some researchers believe the cyphers are the language of the hearts, though I don't know anything about that. At any rate, over time the symbols become clearer. The more you study, the more the hearts seem willing to share. So if you want, you can take a couple of them books. I don't mind," Alistair said. Eric looked up at him to see he'd switched his clothes again. Oxford-blue trousers and a matching shirt with mint-cream ruffles at the neck. It was getting to be a bit off-putting, this constant need for a wardrobe change. "The other outfit didn't have enough ruffle, so it didn't," Alistair explained.

"You're...weird."

"Well, course. How else would you be? Now do you want the books? I've got a bag somewhere in here." Alistair searched through his kitchen draws until he found a carrier bag, then gathered up a few of the books and chucked them in. Yet, when his hands closed on a small blue book that looked like it was made of some kind of leather, he became careful, almost reverent. "This one, this is something I was given when I first started shadow forming. It sort of, well, even I could read it. The clerics what gave me it, they said it looks into you and it shows you what you need to see. If, for any reason, you're in a bind and you need some help, and you can't find me, I reckon this would be a good bet, yeah?"

Alistair didn't put the book in the bag, but instead held it out for Eric to take.

"What if there's things about you in this?" Eric said. "I mean, you said it looks into you, so?"

"I was hoping you'd do me the courtesy of waiting until I was ready to tell," Alistair said, no hint of anger but a cool, calm talk. "I mean, since you read me the riot act on my wanting to protect you. I thought we might come to some kind of understanding, right?"

Being treated like an adult was a new experience for Eric, and it took him by surprise. "Er, yeah," he said, taking the book.

"It might take a while to warm up to you, the book. So don't be worried if, you know, you open it and nothing makes sense."

With care, Eric folded back the cover. He flicked through the pages. Blank after blank.

"Oh, now you're making me look bad," Alistair said, a smile of apology on his face.

"Never mind," Eric groaned. "I'll keep trying it." And then, because he knew they'd crossed a distance in this little moment, he added. "Thank you."

They shared a moment, a small rosy feeling circling between them, and then Eric was reminded of his mum and he decided there wasn't time for that now. They had a mission. "We need to get on," he said as he rose to his feet. The world tilted.

"You're right." Alistair said, still picking through the books. "Do you want me to come round now? I can grab some shade sweets and—" Despite the distance between them, Alistair was at his side, catching him in a tight clutch. "Little Bird, you okay?"

"Yeah, yeah, I'm fine. Just dizzy, you know? I'll be reet."

"This is because you're low on shades. Come on." Alistair helped Eric over to the window seat. "Seems like all that fun yesterday's taken a bigger toll than I would have thought. It's stressed your shadow heart out." Alistair opened the door of the refrigerator and searched. It was filled with small tubs of boiled sweets in neat little rows. "Ah, mint imperials. They're good, right?"

"Aye, yeah."

"Oh, but I've not infused them," Alistair looked down at Eric. "But, I know, you can come with me. Come on," he said, pulling Eric out the door.

"What the bloody hell?" Eric complained.

"This here place. I didn't choose it at random," Alistair said, arm under Eric's as he led them round to the muddy lake. During their brief spell inside the sun had managed to dig its way through the cloud to add a lemon chiffon to the water. "I needed somewhere to help the cooking process."

"Now that's starting to sound a little bit, er, druggie, you know?" Eric slurred, still feeling dizzy. His chest hurt, like the burning emptiness a stomach gets when it's not been fed.

Alistair left Eric's side and walked to the water's edge—then stepped out onto its surface.

"How the?"

"Lock the water, see. Make it like ice," Alistair smiled. "I was pretty proud when I thought of how to do this. Now, normally when you want shades, you would work in a team with a shadow former what can refine shades properly. Me, I've had to get by and improvise, so I have. So, in this water is my shade store."

Eric felt shaky, and he could feel a headache brewing. Even so, his brain made the connection. "When you kill umbras you.... I mean with that girl, Sally, you took her fingers, didn't you?"

Alistair nodded, seeming pleased Eric was following along. "Every time I fight and kill an umbra I bring what I can salvage of it back here and I sling it into this pit. The body parts break down in a few days, decomposing into unrefined shades, which is that black mush you guzzled down from that Mineral stuff."

Eric groaned.

"Aye, I told you it was disgusting. Now, most folk need machines what can refine shades, if they don't have the power that is, but I have a method. It's not pretty, it doesn't give top quality shades, but it's as good as I can do and it gets me by."

Alistair knelt down on the water's surface, slipping off his shirt and throwing it to the side of the makeshift lake. A few breaths to prepare himself, and then he plunged his hands through whatever film it was keeping him above the water. He cupped his hands and raised a portion of the water up to his lips, guzzling the water down. He repeated the process two, three, four times. Every swig provoked Alistair's skin to break out in a net of silver lines, and they warmed up brighter and brighter until they turned into a haze of violet hues. They weren't just random lines though, Eric realised. They were long chains of symbols that all linked together so that they formed a net over Alistair's skin.

"Now," Alistair said, sniffing, closing his eyes. "This will look worse than it feels, I promise."

Alistair threw his head back and screamed. Black spikes erupted through his skin. He gurgled and hissed, pure violet burn leaking out of his closed eyelids.

"Al?"

"Don't worry," he panted. "This is just a trifle. Nothing, this." The spikes cleaved and, as one, began to caw. The flesh around every apparent beak began to bulge and stretch. Alistair roared as, one by one, the beaks and the birds who owned them tore through Alistair's body and, wings strung with gore, flew off into the sky, circling above and creating a bloody rain. Alistair, on his hands and knees, retched and writhed as, in no small spray of red, bird after bird burst from his back and his chest. The wounds closed in flashes of violet but the rhythm was quick, so fast in fact that it sounded and looked like Alistair was being shot with a rapid fire gun.

Eventually though, like the last kernels in a pan of popcorn, the rhythm eased until Alistair popped no more and he was left on the water's surface breathing heavy but apparently no worse for wear. The same couldn't be said for Eric however, who had slumped to the ground; he felt as ill as he was sure he looked.

"The birds, they're...?"

"They're the taint that I can't do anything about. I purge them using the fire. The shades are in me," Alistair said, crawling across the water's surface until he was at Eric's side. "Eric?"

"Yeah, yes?"

"How are you feeling? Can you hold on a while?"

Eric couldn't think. He couldn't feel. All there was, was the urge, the need for shades. He'd do anything for them. Anything. "No. No...I need...."

"I know, Little Bird. Then I...." They were eye to eye. They were close enough to touch. And so Alistair did. He reached up and laid a hand on Eric's cheek. Eric's skin tingled as he felt Alistair's hand slide down his chest. "Is this okay?" Eric nodded. "For what I took before, then," Alistair said as his hand landed on Eric's shadow heart. The sensation was abrupt, like being touched from every angle all at once. It wasn't exactly pleasant, but then a warmth began to pool and the world dropped away. Seconds piled on top of seconds, and Eric was lost in a wash of sensation. He could feel his shadow heart filling, feel his teeth grinding, feel his—

"Eric, Eric, you all right?"

Eric opened his eyes, heat flushing his cheeks. "Yeah. Yes. Yes I am."

Alistair laughed. "Good to hear."

They were still close, and Eric couldn't help but take in how attractive Alistair was. The overly large chin was endearing. The thin, barely there eyebrows gave his forehead an immaculate quality, and Alistair's silver-white hair made Eric think of starlight. Eric looked to Alistair's lips. They were good too.

You forgot me so fast.

Eric straightened up, retreating from Alistair's reach. "We should, erm, I mean, my mum. You said you'd help my mum."

"Yes." Alistair blinked. "Course. I...." His face crumpled up. "Did I, did I do something? Something wrong? You seem upset all of a sudden."

"No, I just...can we just go please? Sorry, I know I'm being rude and I'm not meaning to be and we were close, and last night you were dead, and Tim—"

"No. Yes. Sure."

A moment ago they were together, Alistair doing something to Eric that felt so intimate Eric didn't even have a word for it, and now Eric had ruined it. That at least required an explanation. "I'm—" But Alistair was walking away toward the caravan. The moment lay in tatters around Eric's feet, like his lumpy, misshapen shadow. "Couldn't have got the heart that stopped me being a knobhead, could I?" Eric sighed.

ERIC SAT STARING at the TV, so glassy-eyed a bomb could go off next to him and he'd probably not flinch. "Folk are dropping like flies round here, and then there's all these weird accidents, but look at you. Not a care in the world." Jhardine gave Eric a proper study. "Here, you look well grubby. I hope you took your shoes off when you came in—"

"I swear to God, mum, if I hear one more thing about carpets."

"Well, it's not you what's got to pay for it, is it?" she said, sitting on the chair arm. "What've you been doing to get so muddy, anyway?"

"Went to the park for a kick-about this morning and ended up getting tackled a lot."

"Oh, aye?" The innuendo was nearly too much for her to take. "I didn't think you knew anyone who liked football?"

"Well, I do now."

She narrowed her eyes. He was being cagey. And after he spent all last night out somewhere. She took out her mobile phone and started a text to Sarah, spreading the news around a bit. "You'll be pleased to know," she said, by way of covering up her gossiping, "that you'll have to ferry me up to the doctor's tomorrow in that snazzy new car because I've got an appointment. Got to be there for nine."

"You know what it's for?"

"Not exactly," she lied. "Just, you know, a blood pressure test and that kind of rubbish."

"Ah, right," Eric said, but she felt like he didn't believe her. Oh well, his prerogative. "How did things go with the vicar last night?"

"What do you mean, how did things go? How were they meant to go?" She didn't want him pushing this, not after what she'd told the vicar.

"I just mean, you two seem to get along. Wondered if you had a nice time."

"It were perfectly...*pleasant*, thank you."

"Pleasant, aye?" A twinkle of mischief took up in his eyes. "I don't know why you don't ask him out, mum, I know you want to."

"Eric, he's a man of the cloth."

"He's not taken a vow of celibacy though, which is probably good for all the kids round here because we know what happens when priests are celibate."

"Eric! Don't be saying stuff like that."

"It's a joke, mum."

"Well, it's a very serious matter for the Church."

"And I'm sure it's pretty serious for all those little boys and girls."

"Eric, what have I just said?"

"Oh God, fine. Well, you had a good night anyway?"

"Yes. We talked for a while. It was nice. I don't remember a lot of it, mind. I think I was a bit crackered after what happened yesterday at the pub. Who'd have known that fainting could be so tiring? Anyway, he told me that he's starting prayer group again so I'll be going to that. He's asked for some sandwiches from CC's which is a nice little order. That'll keep Barry happy for, well, a few minutes at least."

"That's good," Eric said, a genuine smile on his face. "Is work a bit better at the moment? You seem, I don't know, more settled with it."

"Well...." It was just as stressful as always, truth be told, but she didn't want to worry him. "We've got a bit more business coming in, so that takes the pressure off there." Not technically a lie, she just didn't know what she'd do if the doctors told her that she had to take more than a few weeks off.

"Here, what've we got in for tea?"

She put her phone back in her pocket. "That a hint, is it? Well, I've got some potato croquettes I made the other day that want eating up, so I'll do them with something. I'll go have a dig around in the freezer and see what I can come up with."

ERIC WAITED UNTIL he was sure his mum was in the kitchen and beyond earshot. He turned to Alistair who had been sat on the couch at his side the entire time, apparently unnoticed. "You sure you can do this without her knowing you're there?"

"Well, she didn't notice me when she was farting her way down the stairs earlier, so...."

"Yeah," Eric chuckled. "She does that sometimes. For some reason she thinks you can't hear."

"You will have to distract her though. Using my healing takes a lot out of me and there's a chance the glamour won't hold. The wall separating us isn't what it used to be."

"Right," Eric said. "Wait, how am I meant to distract her?"

"Be your usual charming self, I'm sure that'll work."

Eric wasn't sure why, but he felt like this wasn't the compliment it sounded. "You've got a lot cheekier lately."

"What can I say, you bring it out of me, so you do."

They were close again, and so was Tim.

You forgot me.

Eric couldn't help but flinch.

"Right." Alistair nodded. "I...I really got this wrong, didn't I?"

"No, Al, it's not—"

"Let's just do it."

Eric was wrong-footed by that. "Well, it's a bit s-s-soon, but—"

"I meant your mum."

"Er, no."

"*Healing her,*" Alistair said, rolling his eyes.

"Oh, yeah, yes." Eric nodded. "Healing her. Right."

As luck would have it Jhardine had adopted her usual position for raiding the fridge: arse up in the air. Perhaps Alistair could have tried healing her through her ample rear, but it seemed a bit rude when they'd not been properly introduced. At any rate, he silently positioned himself behind her and gave Eric a waft of his hand as the signal.

"Oh, um, Mum? You got a sec?"

Jhardine straightened up and looked Eric's way. Alistair took the opportunity and slipped his hands over her face, waiting for the power to rise as it always did.

"What, love?" Jhardine asked Eric, wearing Alistair's hands like a mask. A few seconds barged their way through the room, and still nothing happened.

"What's going on?" Eric felt a zing of nerves run through his chest.

"Well, I'm looking through the fridge for something to eat, aren't I? Are you all right, Eric? You're looking a bit peaky."

Alistair let his hands drop away and gave them a shake. Next, he grabbed her by the shoulders. She trembled.

Yes, Eric thought. *Here we go.*

"Oh, I just feel like someone walked over my grave." She gave another shudder. "Go upstairs and get me a cardigan, Eric. My nips are like bullets."

"Mum!"

"Well, I'm having to sort this freezer out—frost-free my arse—and I can't help biology, can I?" she went back to looking through the contents of the fridge.

"What the bloody hell was that?" Eric asked after he and Alistair had fled the room for the top of the stairs.

"Look," Alistair protested, "I know people who fail to perform say this a lot, but that really has never happened to me before."

"You mean, what, you don't have your power no more?"

"No, course I've still got my power. Look." Alistair noticed an ailing aspidistra sagging over the upstairs hall table. A touch of his hand, a second to concentrate, and the brittle plant turned vital and green again. "I can still do it," he said. "Seems, though, someone's got to your mum first."

"What do you mean?"

"Well, the short of it is," he took a breath. "I'm sorry, I *can't* heal her."

Eric's mum had gone to bed hours ago. Eric, on the other-hand, was wide awake.

He sat himself down on the living room floor next to Alistair, handing the other man a pot of tea. They had all the books Alistair had brought from the caravan spread out across the floor, but it was the blue book Eric brought to his chest. It could tell you anything you wanted to know,

Alistair had said. *A cure for Mum. Please.* He folded the book open. Still it was just blank pages, as it had been every time before when he'd tried.

"So you're sure there's nothing you can do?" he said to Alistair again.

"Not on my own, no. There are a few ways to remove a voiding—that's, er, what we call it when someone's been made immune to direct shadow forming—but they need very particular powers and cyphering, you know, connecting our hearts up, and I don't have the numbers let alone the skill. I do know someone who might have the resources, but...."

"But what? Get them here."

"No, listen, it's not that simple Eric."

"I'm making it that simple. My mum is sick. Like, really properly ill. I need—"

"You have to understand, Marishka won't do this for free."

"Marishka? Is she a shadow former?"

"She's the, well she's a lot of things. She's the highest of the Servants of the Sisters. She's the keeper of the Blood Weapon heart. She's the Lilithian bearer. She is...well, one of the most accomplished shadow formers to have ever lived."

"Then she sounds like just who we need. You should—"

"And she's ruthless," Alistair said, cutting over Eric. "She can help your mum. I'm sure of it. But there will be a price; there is always a price."

"I'll pay. Whatever it takes, I'll get the cash—"

"I don't mean money." Alistair seemed humoured by the very notion that this Marishka woman would ever need money. "If only."

"Then what? I'll get it. I'll do it. Anything." There was that look of hesitation on Alistair's face again. Eric straightened, defiant. With just a few qualifiers, he stood by that. "I'll do—"

"Whatever it takes. I heard you." Alistair washed a hand over his face. "I'd hoped to keep you apart from her for as long as possible. That heart of yours, she'll want a look at it." Alistair seemed to search a moment. "Maybe I've missed something in the Codex of Alchemists," he said, picking up a large grey tome.

Eric's hand moved to the blue book again. This question, oh, this one might be easier. He could just ask the book. He was sure it would tell him this. "You know that I could ask the book about her, right?"

Alistair peered at him. "I do. But I notice you aren't asking yet."

Eric took a deep breath. Why was he hesitating? Well, Alistair had shown some trust in him by giving him that book. It would be a shame to wreck that bond. "I need to help Mum," he said. "But if you're saying that this Marishka is bad news...." After a few heavy seconds, Eric put the book down between them. "If we don't find anything else, I'll do it and I won't even feel bad for it. I won't. But I get that you're looking out for me. And I want to...." He stopped. *Just say it,* he thought. *Just say it.* "Things, er, with me and Tim. They were complicated. There was a lot of, I don't know, bargaining. A lot of, I suppose you could call it manipulating, on both sides actually. And I never thought of it like that, but I guess it's true. It sort of made everything messy and, looking back now, kind of awful. Well, I don't want that to happen between us, you know?"

"Okay. Thank you," Alistair said with a slight incline of his head. He went back to searching the book in his lap.

They sat reading by the bruised light of the television, listening as regular programming gave way to late-night music shows. Time wore on. "This is nice," Alistair said after a little while. "I've not had this in a long time."

"What do you mean?"

"Well," Alistair said, scratching at his neck. "Being with someone. A friend, I mean," he added, a little hasty.

That stung Eric. Whatever he and Alistair were now, surely it wasn't just friends? He tried not to let it show as he asked, "You, er, said a long time. How long's long?" Out of the corner of his eye he saw Alistair flinch.

"Well, I've had folks who I was in the wars with. People I've fought beside. But if I'm honest, not since raising my daughter."

Eric stopped drinking. "Your daughter?" Oh Lord, he'd kissed a man who had kids. Was he a home wrecker now? Oh, that thought was bad wasn't it? And a bit sexy. Eric hesitated. *Okay, I aren't that nice, am I?* "J-just how old are you?" Eric said as light as he could.

Alistair grinned. "Let's say I've got a few years on you." He picked at the plate of biscuits Eric had brought in, breaking off half a chocolate digestive and popping it in his mouth. "Back home, I used to sit with my daughter and we'd watch the shadow screens together. She was only a little thing, barely two years out of the womb, but she loved it."

"That's nice. Where is she now? Did you have to leave her and her mother behind to come here?"

Alistair drank down a marble of tea. He shook his head. "Dust. They're dust now. Long gone."

"Oh, crap. Mate, I'm sorry."

"The fault's all mine." Alistair sat back against the sofa.

Eric made a grab for a different subject. "W-what is your world like? I mean, another planet. With life. That's...boom." Eric made the necessary head exploding gesture.

Alistair laughed, like he'd never seen that before, and maybe because he hadn't.

"Well, that's a good question. I've not seen it in a good long while. In fact, not since—" He made a choking sound and began to cough. "Oh, the binding's that strong I can't even get my gob around what happened. That's interesting."

"A binding?"

"Aye. Part of my oath under the Sisters. My planet was involved in some, let's see, unpleasantness—yeah, that will do—that they'd rather not let folk talk about. What it was like before though, maybe...." He searched, rubbing a biscuit crumb from the corner of his pleasantly dusky lip. "I can tell you, I think, my village was a poor one. And, where I lived, we got around on these big metal ramps and scaffolding between buildings because you could never touch the ground. That's where the dead lived, see. And they were hungry to claim you. Or at least that's what we were always told. In reality, I think—well, I know—there were lowly umbras down there but, back then, I didn't know anything about that. Only that we should stay away to stay safe." His eyes were shining now, made pretty with tears. "Anyway, I lived in a shelter not far off the floor, down close enough to fear for my daughter's life every night. That's how poor I was. And every night the black mist would come wafting at the windows. I'd close the shutters and, to distract Claera I'd make shadow puppets. I was naff at it, not like the professionals you know, but she loved to watch. It wasn't much of a life, I'll admit, and sometimes we had so little food I had to go hungry a week at a time. But, out of the box and looking back, I miss it now. Or, to be more exact, I miss...I miss what it could have been."

Eric considered. "I suppose you can't really understand until you've lived it but, for what it's worth, I'm sorry. Your daughter. That world. It doesn't sound like much fun."

"You're an old-headed lad, Eric Mayfair," Alistair said, laying a hand over Eric's. He saw Eric stiffen and pulled his hand back. "Sorry."

"No, I am." Eric pushed the blue book away from his feet. "I fucked up before, back at the caravan, I...." Eric felt his jaw tightening, trying to stop his words from coming out. There was more than one binding at work to-night. "Tim. I heard Tim before. When we touched I mean."

Alistair looked away. "I get it. I—"

"No. No that's just it." Eric let his hand rest on Alistair's knee. "I wasn't thinking of him. And I felt guilty because I wasn't, you know?"

Alistair sat forward, and his inquiry came through in light, gentle breaths. "Did he ever.... I mean, did he love you back?"

Eric felt his cheeks warm. He'd never spoken about this. Not with anyone. Not even Tim. "I didn't think so. But the umbra, the one who was wearing Tim's dad's face, it said Dylan always thought so." Eric rubbed a hand over his forehead. "It was such a mess. And I know that the umbra might have been lying but—"

"Why would it lie when the truth could hurt you just as bad?" Alistair said.

"Yeah. Exactly. I...." He wanted to say it. He wanted to tell Alistair about what he'd felt this past year. About Tim, about what had happened on the night Eric had been about to die. "I...." But he couldn't. "I'm sorry.... Can we change the subject, please?"

"Sure," Alistair said, straightening. "I was approaching my third decade when I died, but I don't age anymore. Hence why I look so devastatingly handsome."

Eric nodded. "Obviously."

Alistair shoved Eric. "A little less sarcasm, please."

"Sorry, sorry," Eric laughed. He'd not laughed in a good while. Not like this.

"I don't actually have to eat or drink," Alistair said, taking a sip of his tea. "Oh, that's a good brew. You know, I don't even need to sleep, but I do it all because, well, I'm a sentimental idiot, so I am. I like to pretend."

"I don't think that makes you an idiot."

"Thanks." Alistair huffed. "I'm not finding a damned thing in these books. I mean, I'm not a very good shadow former. I know enough to get by. Now, I'd say I'm out of my depth but that implies that I'd been able to swim properly in the first place."

"What if...." Eric knew he was risking a lot with this, but he'd much rather get Alistair on-side than exploit the blue book. "Look, I'm sorry to press this, mate, but what if the person that was sick was your daughter—"

"Eric," Alistair warned.

"But, just hear me out, what if it was? And someone told you they knew someone who could sort it? What then, Al?"

Alistair held up his hand. His eyes were dark, his jaw grim-set. "Point made," he said at last. "Get your coat."

"Yes, thank you!" Eric said, slapping Alistair on the shoulder. "I promise I'll behave myself. I'll do exactly what you tell me. You won't regret this."

"That remains to be seen." Alistair clambered to his feet. "I really could have done without seeing her tonight."

"I CANNOT IMPRESS this enough: don't talk to her. Don't even look at her unless she says something to you. And—are you listening?"

Eric glared. "Yes."

"Good. And, this is critical, don't let her touch you. Touching is bad. I know your culture is obsessed by it but just say no."

"All right, God. You'd think she was radioactive or something."

"Well, I've not seen her in a few months so she very well might be."

They walked the slim groove between buildings at the very edge of Willingsley as cars and waggons hummed by. Then the streets parted, revealing a regimental row of garages to one side and a steep, stone driveway on the other. Eric knew the off-white stone building to be Critchly's, the old wire-drawing mill. Closed for nearly twelve years now, the building itself was still in good nick. In fact, it was in *too* good a condition. The eyes of its windows shone bright in the streetlight glare, and none were smashed through. This was unheard of in Willingsley. Hell, you couldn't even put out a garden gnome without coming back to find it had been molested by a threatening hedgehog.

"Are you sure she's here?" Eric asked. "You said that shadow hearts sense other hearts, and I do. I can feel you. Like a pull in my chest, you know, but I don't sense her."

"That's the thing about Blood. She's exceptional." Alistair frowned. "And exceptions are often dangerous."

Alistair gave the rusted metal handle of the building's large shutter doors a rattle. The door wobbled but remained fixed.

"What kind of a name is Blood, anyway?"

"Formers refer to themselves by their shadow hearts. Marishka is the shadow former of the Blood Weapon heart, so Blood."

Eric looked up the building's façade, then around the grounds, trying to get a flavour of the place. He couldn't sense Blood, or Marishka, or whatever she was called, but there was *something* about this place that felt off, and the more he concentrated on it, the more the sensation grew. A sudden knocking broke his thoughts. He turned to see Alistair was tapping on the door, using his fingers to trace the door's design. "Why don't you just tear it open?" Eric asked. "You're plenty strong."

"Wouldn't work with this. Besides, did no one ever teach you manners?"

"Well, my mum tried but—"

Eric's words were cut off as Alistair gave a shout.

"What is it?" Eric peered over the other man's shoulder to see that around Alistair's hand was a creeping red sap. As Eric watched, the stain crawled into Alistair's fingers, turning his nails a dark incarnadine. Alistair's jaw went tight. He turned his head to face Eric, and his eyes were bloody, the pupils dilated and deep crimson.

"Don't come any closer."

"Al?"

"It's okay. It's just tasting me. It'll be...over...soon...." Alistair continued to spit and pant until, after several long minutes, the red ink pulled back from Alistair's fingers and sank back into the door as though it had never been there at all. Alistair took back his hand, shaking it to bring back some feeling. "A triple seal, eh? What you worried for, Marishka?" Alistair said to himself. Then, to Eric, "Right, so, what did I say?"

"Erm, er, don't let her touch me." Eric counted off on his fingers, "Don't speak to her, and don't even look at her, right?"

"Good. Now stay close." Alistair tried the door again and this time it slid on its squealing casters with hardly any effort at all.

Inside, the warehouse wasn't as dark as Eric had imagined. The pale light coming in through the door and windows created a long, narrow corridor of illumination over the stone floor.

"Why choose here?" Eric whispered. "I'd go for a hotel, you know?"

"Ideally, me too. But, like me, Marishka has very particular needs. And she always prefers places that are stone. It reminds her of home."

A notion occurred to Eric. "You're not from the same place, right?"

"My world was sealed off long before Marishka was even born, so it was."

"Which, actually, is an interesting question right. Do all the shadow formers look like us? I mean, as far as I can tell you're pretty much human? But are they all—"

"Hush now. What did I say?"

Eric folded his arms. "You are really robbing all the fun out of breaking and entering for me, you know that?"

They came to a blank white brick wall and a conventional fern-green door. Alistair made Eric stand a good few paces back from it before he opened the door, but nothing. No monsters ready to jump out at them, no biting shadow forming to try to taste them. The door didn't even so much as squeak. Again, another slight disappointment.

Regardless, inside the corridor Alistair and Eric had two directions to pick from: the left did a sharp turn straight down, or they could go to the right which was a long corridor with a number of doors on either side, before one final brown door at the end.

"Do we search the rooms?"

"No, she'll have put herself somewhere open and probably toward the back of this place, so I'm guessing the warehouse bit proper? We'll take the left."

"Why?"

"Because it's the one I picked," Alistair said as he led the way down the corridor with Eric trailing behind. The warehouse was so cold that Eric felt the chill creeping up through his trainers and into his feet. As they walked, Eric noticed that the yellow walls were turning a poisonous green.

"I don't get spooked easily, but I got to admit, I don't like this."

"That's a healthy attitude, so it is. Especially if...."

Eric's shadow heart twinged, and then the walls bloomed with poppy bursts of colour that, in turn, winked open to reveal glaring, beady eyes that followed Alistair and Eric's every move.

"She knows we're here, that's for sure," Alistair said, holding a hand out to bring Eric to a stop. The corridor had opened up into an atrium, and a few feet away was another wide shutter. Perhaps it was just Eric's imagination, but he thought he could detect a faint but persistent buzzing coming from behind that door. There was a kind of heaviness coming from that room, too. A depression, he thought.

"Yeah," Alistair nodded, seemingly thinking the same thing. "She wants you to carry that weight on your shoulders. To feel the burden of her power."

This time, Eric didn't have a sarcastic retort. There was a strong taste in his mouth. Blood.

Suddenly, the door in front of them peeled back without so much as a hand to help.

"It seems the wizard will see me now," Eric said, drawing level with Alistair.

"If I tell you to run," Alistair whispered.

"Yeah, don't you worry. You won't see me for dust."

"Good lad," Alistair said, and together they crossed the threshold.

The room before them was quite extraordinary. Across the ground, in a hundred different shades, bloomed huge foxgloves. Their stalks were as thick as Eric's wrists, and their flowers ranged in size from grapefruit to melon-size. The air was heavy with their perfume, and it made Eric feel dizzy. This wasn't the only thing to marvel at though. The reddish light that rushed from the candles dotted around the place caught on the walls, revealing they were heavily studded with what looked like jewels of jade greens, lustrous blacks, and mesmeric sapphires. Despite this beauty, Eric's gaze could not linger for long because, pulling at him like a needle through cloth, drawing his eye through the room, down, down to the other side, there was a massive throne. Deftly carved out of ornate metal to resemble the open jaws of a snake, it seemed to loom out of the dark, as did the woman perched on the throne's lower jaw who was connected to it by rows of long, bloody teeth that grew out of the back of the chair and plunged into her skin. His eyes caught on the woman's acid gold glare, then her purple, full lips. She was dressed in scarlet black veils, and was tapping her throne with a metal hand.

"It's you," Eric said before he could stop himself.

He could almost hear the growl in Alistair's throat. "What did I say?"

"But I know her," Eric replied as quietly as Alistair had spoken.

"What do you mean, you know her?" he said, without taking his gaze off the woman.

"He means," Marishka boomed, her voice slicing through the air. "That we have met before."

"I hadn't realised," Alistair replied, and this was about as meek as Eric had ever heard the man. It didn't suit him.

"Eric," she said, as though not having heard Alistair at all. "It is nice to see you again."

"Erm, same to you, I guess." Eric remembered how she'd appeared at the bus stop. A little eccentric, maybe, but by Willingsley's standards she'd been positively cordial. Now though, just looking at her made his skin prickle with unease. "I—"

"I can't help but notice you were admiring the Blood Throne," she said. "I suppose you're curious about it?"

Eric, remembering Alistair's warning, simply nodded.

"Every shadow heart demands a price for use of its powers. You might not know it. They can be subtle or, as Jingoro has found," she said looking at Alistair, "they can be severe." She tapped a metal finger against the curved scroll of the chair arm's end. "My heart taints my blood. It makes it poisonous. That in itself is a powerful weapon, but it could also kill me. Therefore I must submit to daily blood transfusions. For the heart's former hosts the prospect was a series of needles and lines, countless infections and wasted hours. So primitive. Then Ashlar Roween, the first of my heart's true hosts, commissioned this special chair to allow him to take in the sustenance of new blood without having to resort to, well, desperate measures."

"She means drinking." Alistair whispered. "The Blood heart—"

"You keep mumbling, Jingoro. Are you ill?"

Cold. That was the anger in his eyes. Hatefully cold. "I was saying, the Blood heart has a history of making its bearers into blood-drinking monsters."

"The Panacea heart isn't exactly friendly to its hosts either, is it?"

"Sorry, excuse me," Eric said, stepping closer. His leg nudged one of the foxgloves and a growling came from the large teal bulb. *Oh, what fresh hell is this?* "Erm, but it's about my mum."

"What are you doing?" Alistair hissed.

"Saying something about Mum before you piss her off any more than you already have."

"Fine," Alistair said. "Yes. His mum. She's sick and getting sicker. I went to heal her but someone got there first and voided her. You wouldn't happen to know anything?"

Blood remained impassive a while longer. All that Eric could hear was the gentle hum he'd experienced outside, and the strange, occasional pining of the foxgloves around him.

"Is it voiding through the loss of a shadow heart?" Marishka said at last.

"As far as I can fathom she's never had one," Alistair said.

"And what of Eric's shadow heart? Where did that come from?"

"I don't know," Alistair said, his voice small, careful. "Eric says, don't you, that he got it the night I healed him."

Tap, tap, went Blood's fingers against the throne. "I would like to get a closer look at your shadow heart if I could, Eric?"

Eric looked to Alistair. He nodded.

"Yes. All right."

With a soft whoosh the teeth of the Blood Throne uncurled from Marishka's skin, leaving red diamonds across her forehead and down her long exposed neck. No blood escaped her, though, and within seconds the wounds disappeared.

"She can do what you can do. Heal, I mean."

"Not quite," Marishka said, walking down the three steps from the throne and then through the flower grove. She trailed a hand over a couple of their buds. Those that she touched, one vermilion and the other chartreuse, began to throb with a gentle light. Within seconds they opened and from them slipped adult foxes. The foxes lay on the ground a moment looking stunned, then stood, shook themselves and slunk into the flower grove and out of sight. "Blood is the medium of my shadow forming. You can see, I hope, how it would be a great benefit to heal quickly and conserve that potent weapon."

"Sure," Eric nodded. He was watching her veils. They shifted in a way that wasn't like any cloth he'd ever seen; undulating when they should simply glide. That taste came to his mouth again. *They're made of blood,* Eric realised.

Marishka held out her gloved hand as if to invite Eric closer. He stepped forward, finding to his disquiet that proximity did nothing to soften her, especially her golden eyes which were too hot to meet. "Take off your shirt, please."

"Do I, erm, have to?"

"I would greatly appreciate it," she said in such a manner that Eric knew this wasn't really a request. He pulled his denim shirt up over his head and stood there bare-chested. Her eyes fixed on the heart.

"In-ter-es-ting."

"What is?"

"Finder is dead," she announced, as though this was the natural progression of their conversation.

Eric looked to Alistair for some kind of help, but Alistair's eyes were wide and fixed on Marishka. "What? When?" Al asked.

"Three weeks ago. A fomorian umbra proved too much for the party Merigru was with. They're springing up everywhere in the new territories."

"But why was she fighting anyway? Finder doesn't fight. It finds!"

"Finder does what we tell it to do, especially when we are short on weapons." Blood looked back at Eric. "You can put your shirt back on now. I've seen all I need."

"I think the war is already here, isn't it?" Alistair said.

"I couldn't comment."

"Someone's dosing people here and people are supping down gobfuls of poisonous shades. Tell me it's not arrived!"

"Alistair, you know better than to give me orders," she said, her voice light and almost amused.

"I'm sorry, I meant no disrespect."

"Of course not," Blood replied, but Alistair's act of contrition seemed to please her. "You might as well know that before Merigru was killed, I had her sweep this planet for shadow hearts."

"And?"

"She didn't find any evidence of seeded hearts. Not unusual, of course. They're notoriously difficult to sense. But she did find that some of the renegades are here."

"Wax?"

"Yes, and Metal, Clay and Stitch."

"They're quite a team."

"My foxes have not located the hosts, but the Stitch heart was found. It had all the signs of being abandoned."

Alistair slid a glance at Eric. A quick look back at Marishka and she nodded, giving him permission to speak. "Some of the hearts are notoriously difficult to control. Stitch is...a challenge. The shadow former might still be alive and, given how relatively rare voiders are, it might be that they were the one to void your mother."

"Finder couldn't say how they were operating," Marishka went on. "But at least one of the hearts has changed hosts. And I think you are right, Alistair. They probably abandoned Stitch, thinking it more trouble than it's worth and seeing the advantage of having a voider on their side as an even greater incentive."

"Could...." Eric tried hesitantly. "I mean, could the person who killed Tim be one of the shadow formers?"

"Tim?" Marishka repeated.

"Eric's friend was killed," Alistair said wearily. "The death was particularly violent. And now there's an umbra—"

"Well, it's possible," Blood said. "If so, I would hazard a guess that Wax is leading the charge. You know what that heart is like."

"I do." Alistair said. "But I can't go after them all and—"

"Hello?" Eric said when he could no longer take being meek and quiet. "I am still here, you know."

Blood gave a chuckle.

"I really wish you hadn't done that," Alistair groaned.

"No, I like him, Alistair," Blood said. "But he will have to be taught some manners. Kneel."

It was Eric's turn to laugh. "If I wasn't going to blow that nurse in the hospital when I thought I was dying, I am not gonna get on my knees for you, love. Sorry."

"Oh, I think you will. Now kneel."

Eric's knees struck the floor hard. His chin clapped to the top of his chest, like there was a lead weight pressing down on the back of his head, and his hands welded into his lap, upturned and servile.

"Was that necessary?" he heard Alistair crow.

"Very," Marishka replied. "He can consider it his first lesson. Never take sweets from a stranger."

It took Eric a few moments to figure it out, but it soon came back to him: That night after the club she had offered him chewing gum, hadn't she? Eric winced because, he realised, the news was even worse. If blood was the medium through which her power worked, that meant: "Wait, you fed me your own blood?"

"He's quite clever, Alistair. I approve."

"You're sick. You're worse than sick. You're a loon. A—"

His mouth slammed shut with an unceremonious clack.

"Ah, silence. How I have missed you," Blood sang.

"Marishka," Alistair growled.

"Oh, calm down. I only gave him a very mean dose. It'll have burned through in a few minutes. I'm actually doing it as a kindness. I want him to know that what I will ask of him next will be entirely his to decide. I will not influence him in the least."

"What are you planning?"

"He has a shadow heart, Jingoro. One I do not recognise but one that excites the Sisters. They believe that this world may hold other such hearts. And if Finder could not see them, well, that means they could be new. Undisclosed powers. That's an exciting prospect. And then there is the escalating war. We need fighters. Tacticians. To put it bluntly, we need him and, it seems, he might need us."

Alistair was silent for a time, and that gave Eric all he needed to know.

"I don't fight," Eric forced through his tight lips.

Blood peered into his eyes. "Oh, you're snapping out of it already? Interesting. Alistair, what are his powers?"

A beat, and then Alistair answered in an empty, almost defeated tone: "Senses. He can sniff stuff from miles away. It's like he can go to it somehow. He...." Alistair stopped.

"Go on," she urged. "What else?"

"Nothing. That's it. It's just a bit strange the way he does it. I don't fully understand, but you know that I've never really been all that good with how the hearts work," Alistair said. But that wasn't true, was it? Sensing things wasn't *all* he could do. Eric had been able to throw his shadow, knocking Alistair back a few paces, and he'd knocked the Dylan umbra clean off its feet. So why lie?

"The Sisters had hoped that if this world had been seeded it would yield more useful hearts," she said. "He sounds like a pure Augur though. Not without his uses if he is as strong as you seem to think, Alistair. If he were trained right, that is."

"Yeah," Alistair agreed. "He'd be good behind the scenes, helping those of us who fight. And with your permission, I could test him for you. Develop his skills a bit. That is, I'm assuming that you'll want him tested—"

"I do. And your assistance will be helpful no doubt. But I have a different plan for you, Eric."

"What's that?" he said, straining to lift his head. He managed enough height to watch Blood walk her way back to her throne and sit.

"You are seeking a cure for your mother, yes?"

"Er, yeah."

"That is something the Sisters can help you with."

"You have it? A cure?"

"I do not. But as the Lilithian Bearer," she held up her gloved hand, "and Voice of the Sisters, I can vow to you that if you pledge yourself to the Servants of the Sisters, *and* you are accepted, the cure can be found."

"Alistair?" Eric called. "Can they do that?"

"The Sisters are incredibly powerful. They can get around a voiding. But there's always a price. In this case...."

"They want you for their war," Marishka announced, and her black skin seemed to glow in the candlelight like she was made of hot coals.

It was an easy decision to make, though. Too easy, in fact. "Yes. I'll do it. Cure her now."

He heard Alistair sigh.

Blood gave a metallic laugh. "I'm afraid it's not quite that simple. First you will have to do something for us. Something that, as it happens, may prove convenient for you, too."

"What do you want?"

"The umbra. The one with whom you share a connection."

"Tim?"

"No, Marishka, it's too powerful. It might even be—"

"I am confident Eric can handle it—alone."

"No, he can't. You can't do this."

"By the Sisters I invoke."

"No, Marishka, please, be reasonable."

"You are not to interfere, Jingoro. If you do, the test is voided and you prevent Eric from accessing the cure. Do I make myself clear?"

The symbols across Alistair's skin, the ones Eric had seen at the caravan earlier that day, they all flared blood red. Alistair's eyes were burning, his chest rising and falling with a rapid pulse. "You can't do this, Marishka. You—"

"What exactly are you asking?" Eric said.

"No, do not agree to this," Alistair rumbled. "It is binding, Eric. Don't."

"I said, what are you asking?" he bellowed at Marishka.

"I want you and you alone to unmake it," she said.

"H-how? I don't have those kinds of powers."

"I think you do," Marishka said. "And if you don't, I suggest you find a way to outsmart it. After all, you are a clever boy, aren't you, Eric?" She leered at him, smiling. "Do you accept?"

Eric looked to Alistair, his eyes pleading. He really didn't want to go against Alistair's wishes, and he could feel the weight of Alistair's fear, the warmth of his care. But what other alternative was there? "I'm sorry, Al," he said at last.

Then Alistair smiled, small and sad. "It's okay, Little Bird."

"Your answer, Eric?" Marishka asked.

"It's yes. I'll do it. For the cure, I'll do it."

"Then so be it. Come here." When he was close enough she seized his wrist and, with the tip of a metal finger, began cutting into his skin. "You are honoured to have me be the one to induct you."

"Yeah. I feel special, don't I?" Eric said through gritted teeth. It didn't hurt that much, but he could feel something brewing. A power.

"You are very funny, Eric," she said, slicing deeper still. He didn't give her the satisfaction of crying out. "But your wit belongs to them now. Their will is in you. Their power commands. You are their instrument. By this oath, do you swear all that you are to their service?"

"I...yes," Eric said. "In return for making mum better. Yes."

"Then," Marishka said, "let it be done."

She held her hand up and clicked her fingers. The walls exploded into a frenzy of buzzing, and now he understood that sound. The jewels encrusting the walls weren't crystals at all but fat bluebottles each at least the size of a penny. They swarmed, filling the air so densely that all Eric could see was black cut through with occasional knife flashes of colour, and then they began landing on him and congregating around the cut on his wrist. One purple-backed thing with menacing red eyes worked its way under his skin. Then another. "No! Help me! No!" But no one did, and the flies scratched their way into him until the symbols on his arm flared and Eric screamed.

When Eric thought he was about to go mad with the pain, Marishka's even voice boomed: "When it's done, call out for me and I will come. Until then, my friends, I have business to attend." And with that, the flies left him and, rising into the air as one menacing cloud, rushed out through the windows. The Blood Throne was left empty. The foxgloves bobbed until still.

Eric was on his knees, holding his wrist. The cut was already healing over, turning silver, and the pain was just a memory now.

Alistair offered him a hand. "Let's get out of here, comrade."

"SHE'S A TREAT," Eric commented.

"Isn't she just?" Alistair replied, feeling the chill of Marishka's presence lingering like a cold sweat. "I didn't think she'd bring the chair. She must think she's going to be here a good while. That doesn't bode well. The foxgloves too. And a fair glade of them at that. She must be planning on birthing a full set."

"So can we stop dancing around it?" Eric said, rounding on Alistair. Finally, they were going to talk about their relationship. *About time,* Alistair thought. "I just got inducted into a war, didn't I?"

Alistair had forgotten about that. He leaned over the railing, watching the river rush by. "That you did."

"So...who's winning? Us or the umbras?"

"It depends how you define winning, though I will say that once they're on a planet it's a fair job getting them off."

"You mean, this world is...." Eric sucked in a breath. "We're doomed, aren't we? And I've just spent all that money on a hire car."

"'Doomed' is a strong word, so it is. But definitely in trouble if we can't stop the people what are creating umbras. Though the Tim umbra's still our top priority," Alistair said, rolling his head on his shoulders. "And then there's the Sisters."

"I didn't like to ask in front of Marishka but, are they like actual sisters or is this like some group of nuns or something?"

Alistair laughed. "No, the Sisters aren't people. They're beings who were once incredibly powerful, probably the most powerful things in existence. That's about as much as I know about their history. The clerics went on and on about them but to be quite honest I tuned most of it out. Can't listen to everything, can you?"

"You just said a bunch of things I have no way of getting," Eric said.

"Oh, sorry. I'll try to keep it simple then. So, to save the worlds from the growing umbra threat the Sisters made a deal with the shadow formers. The Sisters gave up a lot of their power to seal off the worlds the umbra infected, mine included. Every now and then, though, some umbras pop up or are created brand new, but for the most part the Sisters have been able to protect us. Yet...." Alistair rubbed at the spot on his chest where the shadow heart rested underneath his clothes. He concentrated on speaking his next words as delicately as he could. "They've become harder, the Sisters, and they're demanding more and more out of us. Like the bindings so we can't talk about certain things. Some of the hearts have refused to serve them. Some have even gone to serve the umbras we fight. And there are factions that say the Sisters can't be trusted."

"What do you think?"

Alistair didn't think. He didn't even approach that question. He was mindful that there were a fair few flies on the stonework of the river wall. "I think you need to make your own mind up on it, Little Bird. That there blue book I gave you, that might help. With the history, I mean." He gave Eric a pointed glance and said nothing more.

Together they walked along the river back toward town, the moon shining on the still, dark water. Crows barked in the trees around them. They were staying closer than usual, those birds he made when he purged shades. They'd taken a liking to Eric, it seemed.

"How the hell am I going to beat an umbra on my own?" Eric said after a long while.

"That's a good question. I happen to think Marishka knows something. Either about your powers or about that umbra. Well, that or she just wants you dead so she can take the heart."

"Reassuring, that. Just what a bloke wants to hear."

Silence lapped at them in the sound of the water beating softly against the overflow barrier.

"I can teach you some on how to fight. More on how to use your powers—"

"Remember when I was pissed off at you for not wanting to share with me? I take that back," Eric said.

"Just a testament to how wise I am, so it is." Alistair nudged Eric. "You know she's barred me from the fight. If we meet the thing together it means I might not be able to help."

"Then I better win, hadn't I?" Eric said, and there was that metal again. "I have to, for Mum."

"I need you to know, Eric, this umbra isn't behaving right. It's had plenty of opportunity to kill you and it hasn't. At first I thought that it was trying to hurt you some more, but...there's no pattern to the people it's killing or how it's attacking." Alistair clucked his tongue as he tried to slow his racing thoughts. "I'm sure Marishka knows. I'm absolutely sure, but she won't say. This is, it's one of her games, this. And any way you look at it, it's all about you. Everything."

"As it should be," Eric gave one of his wry smiles. "It's about time I got to be the main event," he said. "Not had enough of that in my life."

"Eric! Hello!"

A woman in a peacock nivi-folded saree waved at them from the verge that boarded on the cinema car park ahead. On her arm, in leather and a little bit of lace at the collar, was her heavily tattooed suitor. He had a large white slab of plaster over his neck hiding what Alistair guessed was a fresh tattoo.

"Tania and Lance," Eric said to Alistair, and then to the couple, "All right?"

"Aye. We was going to see a film, but we couldn't agree on owt, could we, Lance?"

"No, love."

"So we're going up to Lion Lion instead. You fancy joining us, Eric?"

"Aw, no, cheers, Tania. I've had a long day."

"Wouldn't really be your kind of thing anyway, I suppose," she said. "But after we've had some cheap drinks, Lance is taking me to a biker bar, aren't you Lance?"

"That I am. We welcome all sorts, though, Eric. And if anyone gave you trouble, well, they'd get that." Lance held up his tattooed fist. Alistair caught a hint of a smile on Eric's face.

"Out of the way! Coming through! Hello Eric!" A blonde woman more bone than flesh jogged and jangled her way past on the river track.

"All right, Dee," Eric said. "Here, wait a sec!"

She turned, still hopping from one foot to another. "Yes. What is it?" she said, breathless. Even by the moon's palsy light, this Dee woman looked pale. "I need to keep going. Don't want my heart-rate to drop and my body to leave its fat-burning zone."

"What fat?" Tania exclaimed. "There's nowt on you."

"Oh, well, that's kind of you to say."

"What it is, right," Eric started. "I just wanted to talk to you about the job."

"Oh, well, I've sent you a letter about that anyway. Some paperwork has gone missing—thank you, admin department—so I just need you to pop in at the centre and straighten out a few details for our records. I think I said for next Tuesday, but check the letter."

"All right, yeah, cheers."

"Right, right, okay, poppet. Must dash! Ta ra!"

Dee, with her stick of an arm waving a goodbye, set off running again.

"There was a time," Tania started, rummaging in her bag of toffee popcorn, "when I'd have killed for a figure like hers. Now I'm just like, bugger that, have a baked potato."

CHAPTER TWELVE
CLICK

On many an occasion over the past few weeks Eric had stood on the mezzanine over the library, watching as Grant and the rest of the lads methodically harvested the library's vital organs; as they trampled the books the library had once kept dear and treated them like dull cuts of paper and ink to be sold for a profit or scrapped. The absolute horror of it, and Eric was letting it happen. In fact, he was an integral part of the operation—given that he could, you know, read. For the first time in his small little life, Eric felt the true burden of shame.

"Eric? You right?" Grant said from the bottom of the stairs.

"Er, yeah," Eric said, placing a book he had loved as a child in the pile that he'd been forced to dub 'worthless'. "Yeah, I'm fine."

"Great, I've got another box of books from the cellar," Grant said, coming up the stairs and handing Eric the box. "See if there's owt valuable in there, will you?"

"Sure. I've got to go at four though. I've got that Jobcentre thing."

"Ah right, yeah, no problem," Grant nodded. "Well, I've been on at Peter. We'll get you that contract sorted by next week. You can tell her that, all right?" He touched Eric's shoulder. "And, here, you've been a great worker, yeah, mate. Done everything I asked."

"Yeah," Eric said. *And that's the problem.* Eric knew he had some faults, but one thing he'd always thought would be to his credit was that he couldn't be bought. Turned out that he was wrong on that front, though, wasn't he? "For Mum," he affirmed, when Grant was out of earshot and talking Jamie's ear off. "I'm doing this for Mum."

He opened the box Grant had given him and started sifting through the books, all the while counting the seconds to his afternoon appointment with Dee. She was his last hope.

Listening to someone throw up for a sustained five minutes didn't give you much confidence they could help improve your life, but it did give you a certain appreciation for the tenacity of the human gullet. And Dee's was definitely *impressive*. "I knew I shouldn't have had that dragon fruit for breakfast," Dee said as she walked out of the Jobcentre's disabled toilet, fanning herself with one of their binge-drinking brochures.

Eric shuffled behind Dee as she opened the door to her stuffy office.

Oh my frigging good God.

Propped up against the far wall of the little room was a battered dressmaker's doll, one arm missing and half its head crumbling away. Pinned to its torso were swatches of fabric in different blue tones. It made the thing look like a mermaid's rotting corpse.

"Bridesmaid's dresses," Dee said, a disgruntled look on her clammy face. "I can't decide, and the bridesmaids are no help. They keep complaining all the dresses are too tight and that I won't let them have them altered. Over my dead body, that's what I say. Now, sit yourself down, Eric."

Eric pulled out his usual chair, only to find a pile of catering brochures had already claimed his spot.

"I'm eating no more than nine hundred calories a day before the wedding," Dee explained, hoisting the brochures across the floor. "But after the wedding I am going to stuff myself solid."

"That's pretty much my standard diet," Eric said. "I just chuck the lot down my neck and try not to choke." He gave her what he hoped was a friendly smile.

"Anyway," Dee said, apparently ignoring Eric's wit. "I needed you to help me fill in some of the gaps we have in our data and then you can get on with your evening. If you want to take a seat, poppet, this will only take half an hour."

"Half an hour?"

"Ahuh, ahuh. I do like to be thorough. Oh, I'll just get the case load folder. Give me a second." She moved toward the filing cabinet, and then teetered. Given he'd seen his mum collapse enough times to recognise the glazed look folk get, he was prepared when Dee lurched forward to grab her desk.

"Here, are you all right?" he said, hands to her shoulders for support.

"Oh, yes. Ahuh. I'm just a bit lightheaded," she said, wafting her jacket. "It's this suit. Very warm."

"I think you need to eat something."

"No, no, absolutely not." He helped Dee settle back into her chair. She opened her eyelids wide as though trying to catch something to focus on. "Well, all right. Maybe just a smidge. Do you have anything?"

"Oh, erm, I don't...." Eric checked his pockets. Besides several till receipts, the only thing he had in his pockets was an old bag of mint imperials that Alistair had given him to tide him over for his shade supply. "Er, I've these."

"What are they?"

"Mints."

"Oh, they'll do. Give them here," she said, snatching them out of his hand. She popped one, then three in her mouth, slurping so hard her cheeks began to redden.

"Why you doing this to yourself, aye?" Eric said in as soft a voice as he had.

"I've got to be beautiful for the wedding," she said, crunching the mints and already readying their replacements. "My Trevor won't marry a blimp. He's said as much."

"Well, I've got to be honest with you, Dee, he sounds like a tosser."

"No, see, I was fat when I was younger and he doesn't want our kids to be. He can't exercise, you see, because he has a bad back. So, it's up to me. It's all perfectly reasonable."

"That's not reasonable. That's—"

"And, on my wedding day, everything will be perfect. I'll be perfect and he'll love me. For once in my life, someone will love me," she said, her voice sounding like a knife scraping the last dregs of a jam jar. "And then we'll have a wonderful life together."

Eric, clearly, had no idea what love was supposed to be. He thought about Tim. Then he thought about Alistair and how that felt different. "I don't think that's love, Dee. I think that's loneliness. And I know a bit about that."

She wasn't listening, though. She wilted to one side, opened the bottom draw of her desk and took out a bottle of water. A small gathering of tears brimmed in her eyes. *Oh, no, not crying,* he thought. As a distraction he considered knocking over the mannequin, fabric samples and all, but reasoned that might push the bride-to-be over the edge.

"Er, here," he said, rubbing a fingertip on her shoulder. "What's wrong?"

"Oh," she said, putting her hand over his. "Well, this might be the last time we ever see each other."

A bit dramatic, but at least a nice thought.

"You go to the same church as my mum," Eric reminded her, and himself. "So I might see you around."

"No, silly, I mean it's the last time I'll see you like this, as a jobseeker," she pointed at Eric, then turned that hand on herself, "and employment assistant." She opened her desk drawer again and took out a tissue, dabbing at her eyes. "Oh, Eric, you know, I'd have loved to have you at my wedding."

Well, Eric was genuinely touched. "Aw, thank you—"

"You'd have made a great waiter."

Impressed. That was the word. He was impressed by how devastated he felt. He snatched up the mint imperials and put them back in his coat pocket.

"I'm feeling a bit better now," she said. "Shall we redo your files?"

"Actually," Eric said, "the reason I came to see you—"

"Oh yes, yes, that's right you wanted to chat with me, didn't you?"

"I did, yeah."

"Ahuh, ahuh, ahuh." She checked her watch. "If you don't mind making it snappy, love, we really should be getting on."

Eric was glad his shadow forming powers didn't extend to making people explode or he would currently be picking bits of Dee out of his hair.

"Well, it's about my job at Radley's."

"Ahuh, what about it?" Dee asked, slipping another mint into her mouth Eric hadn't even realised she'd taken. A few wouldn't hurt, he reasoned, but how many was too many?

"Well...." He tried to think how to phrase his current predicament. "It's not that I'm not grateful for all the work you've been doing for me and all the time and effort you put in. And it's not that I'm not glad to be working either. I mean, properly, I am. But the thing is—"

"Eric, I have to say, I don't like the way this is going."

"Well, the thing is Dee, there's a guy called Grant what's my manager. And I think that he's—"

"I hope you're not thinking of quitting, Eric." Her voice rose like the sound of lard frying in a pan. "No benefits!" she said, and brought her hand down on her desk with the swoosh of Madame Guillotine. "If you quit you won't get a thing."

"But, it's this lad called Grant. I think he's making me do stuff that's illegal, I—"

"No! I do not want to hear your excuses."

"It's not—"

"I will not have you messing up my spreadsheets. Whatever the problem is, you'll have to sort it out yourself."

Eric let the room settle into quiet. Then he stood. "Your future husband is a cock, and he's just what you chuffing deserve." Eric spied the mannequin in the corner on which she had her dress patterns. "Oh, and by the way, you've got lousy taste."

"Get out," she said. "I work my arse off for you lot, I do so much, and this is the thanks I get! Get out!"

"Fucking gladly!" Eric slammed the door.

Outside the office, though, Eric hesitated. The aftershock of what he'd just done rippled through him and he knew that, if he wanted to get out of Radley's, he needed Dee on his side. Maybe if he said he was sorry she might listen to reason. He was about to go back in when from the other side there came a terrible and ugly shriek: "This is why no one likes you, you stupid, ugly cow!"

Eric's fingers slid off the door handle. Head down, Eric walked out of the Jobcentre feeling even shittier than when he'd gone in.

"I KNOW YOU were with her, Jim! Everyone saw you!"

Jhardine moved the glass further down the wall, straining to hear. Sarah and Jim were having the mother of all rows. She'd get Sarah's version tomorrow, but there was nothing like catching a live broadcast.

"And how many times do I have to tell you, nothing was going on. Christina is just a...friend."

Jhardine gasped. "Don't you dare believe that!"

"I don't believe you!"

"Now punch him, Sarah. Right in the face!"

"Did you hear that?" Jim said. "I could have sworn I heard someone say—"

Drats! Ratted out by my own big gob.

She put the glass down and sat herself on Eric's bed. With Eric out and nothing on television, Jhardine was bored. But this was a new low: so bored that she'd stooped to trying to listen through paper-thin walls to someone else's marital troubles. *That's sad,* she said to herself. *Really sad.*

She looked around Eric's pigsty of a room. Dirty clothes everywhere, a suspicious loo roll by his bed, and then her gaze caught on the now stained drawing of Tim, grinning like he had a mouth full of tile caulk. Eric had embellished to buggery in making Tim look prettier than he was in life, but the likeness was still there. Tim looked good at that weight, she thought. He wasn't too big. Just burly looking. Must have been before he started back on the steroids.

She stroked a finger over Eric's side of the picture. He'd done himself a disservice; he never drew himself as handsome as Jhardine thought he was. Always missed something in the eyes, she thought. Still, he had his father's talent. She cleared a small space so the picture would be safe and wouldn't end up getting thrown out with the other scraps of paper when Eric finally cleared his room. Then she went out into the hall where the cord dangling from the loft's hatch made her stop and consider. Michael had been on her mind a lot lately and she was feeling the itch. A harsh five minutes slid by before Jhardine gave in and tugged on the cord to open the loft hatch. Naturally, the ladder refused to unfold all the way, stopping at the mid point.

"Oh, chuff."

She yanked. It didn't budge. She tried again, but it held fast. A third time, and with all her strength so it felt like one of her eyes was about to pop with the strain, and then a sudden click and the metal ladders zoomed down, narrowly missing hitting her in the throat. "Sodding house is trying to kill me now," she grumbled as she climbed the ladder.

Jhardine balanced at the top of the stairs, groping for the light's pull switch. After catching a few squeal-inducing thick spiderwebs, she found the cord and, after a firm pull, the naked bulb hanging near the attic's centre beam flickered an uneasy yellow into a boiled-egg white. She'd told Eric the boxes in the attic were books and things she was storing for Eric's nan. That was a lie.

Pushing boxes out of her way as she went, Jhardine quested toward the back of the room. Sat on the far box from her was a jacket made of a heavy reddish leather. It was riddled with tiny pockets across its front and sides, each about the size and width of her thumb. When she bent to pick the coat up the leather was so cold to touch that it threatened to make her fingers ache. She let the coat drop to the floor, using her foot to kick it out of sight. Some days she loved that thing, others she hated it.

Next, Jhardine peeled off the brown tape from the middle box and let her hands sink beneath the water stained leaves. Her fingers settled on a familiar, cold shape and she withdrew Michael's cut-throat razor. She took it out and held it up in the light. She could almost hear Michael cursing as he cut himself during his morning shave. She smiled. Then, when that smile began to fade, she placed the razor back into the box and lifted the box to the floor at her side. The floorboards beneath gave a loud groan.

"Don't have any pictures of your dad, Eric. I don't know why you keep asking. I tore them up. And do you blame me?"

She'd told Eric that. Drummed it into him as a kid until he stopped asking. It was the middle box on the lower row that proved her a liar. She opened it and withdrew a small green envelope.

A creased picture of Jhardine and Michael slid out, the one at the canal with them holding hands and eating ice creams. She studied the picture for a good while, trying to conjure up that day in her memory. In the background, like stray dollops of ice-cream themselves, there sat two large geese. Michael hated birds. They always hissed at him. That day they'd honked off into the sky as soon as they clapped eyes on him.

She set the picture down on the top of the box and moved on to the next. It was Jhardine outside the tattoo parlour. Not Lance's. No, back when it was called Wolf's and it was owned by another feller with a strange Russian sounding name. The tattoo she'd ended up with was one of Michael's own design. They were meant to get matching ones but Michael passed out as soon as he saw the blood being scraped out of Jhardine's chest. Delicate thing, he was. She probably should have had the tattoo removed. She'd even booked some laser sessions, but for some reason she could never go through with it.

Jhardine let a bugle note of upset force its way from her throat. She put the photos back in the envelope and dropped the envelope into the box. Michael's blank notebook and its thick woven binding caught her eye. She could never bring herself to use that either and, oddly, never wanted to throw it away. She ran a hand over it.

"Ow." A paper cut.

Setting aside the now soon to be burned blank journal, she continued searching. There was one picture in a simple black frame that she had set apart from the rest. Poison, it was, and she knew Eric would hate her for keeping it from him. Yet, like the journal, she just couldn't throw it away.

"Make sure Eric hates him, Jhardine," Eric's nan had said. "Make sure he boils with it. It's the only way my girl. The only way."

She'd told Eric that Michael had walked out on them not long after she announced she was pregnant, and through deference to her no one had corrected that version of events, but it wasn't true. Michael had been there throughout the pregnancy. He'd held her hand at the birth in fact, even when the doctors had to barrel her down the hospital corridors and into surgery because of that dreaded word, that hated portent, *complications*. And then Eric was out and he was fine and bawling, and Michael said to Jhardine that he'd like to hold their boy. That was when the slice of time Jhardine was holding had been captured. Jhardine, still woozy from the pain-killers and one of her tits half falling out of her coral pink bathrobe, there with Michael who was holding Eric and kissing his little ear. They were happy. In that moment, now sealed off in dark space forever, they were a family.

"Why did you leave me?" Jhardine asked the picture. Then something impossible happened. She felt a gentle touch on her shoulder blade, and it slid up to her neck the way Michael had done so many times when they had been together. She felt his breath on her cheek, and then—

The sound of the front door closing made her jump.

"Jhardine?" It was Sarah.

"Just in the attic, Saz. I thought I heard a...bird or something." Jhardine looked about her. There was no one in the attic with her, obviously. "Just a second, I'm coming down."

She worked to put all the shards of a life she'd once had back in their respective caskets; pack the blank book away and fold her hurt along with it; place the coat back on top as though it was a shroud to cover all that had happened; put it all back as though it had never been moved. Let what's dead rest. Let what's living hurt. With one last look at the boxes of her secret relics she clicked the light off and started to descend the ladder, her mind already on what she had planned for tonight.

Sarah stood at the bottom of the hall stairs sporting lipstick on her teeth and puffy eyes. "Just wondered if I could stay round here tonight? I can't be near that scumbag!" Sarah said, shouting the last few words at the wall.

"Of course, love, but actually," Jhardine said, "I need to go up to the church tonight. A prayer meeting."

"Oh, Jaz, can't you skip it?"

"Not this one, no," Jhardine said, pulling on her jacket. "But I'd really love you to come, Sarah."

"I'M REALLY NOT sure about this, Jaz. I mean, I'm not very Jesusy, you know?" Sarah said as they walked through the foyer of the community hall.

"I know but," Jhardine said. "It's just important that you be here tonight."

"Why?"

"You'll see. Anyway, that's Ruth there," Jhardine said, pointing to the retired schoolteacher who was fanning herself with a *Lady's Lunchtime* magazine and arranging a tray of coconut-cream fairy cakes. "She's always got a flask of sommat strong in her handbag if you need a bit of a pick-me-up."

"Bless me, Father, for I'm about to sin," Sarah said, leaving Jhardine's side for waters more alcoholic.

"Hello, Jhardine," the vicar smiled as he went about taking chairs down from a stack by the long table of refreshments and food.

"David, thank you for this."

He nodded, his eyes bright with concern. "Well, I understand the need to tell as many people at once as possible. Tania's just in the back getting us an extra set of chairs and then we can begin. Strong like an ox, that girl."

"That she is," Jhardine agreed, pushing the chairs they had into a rough circle.

"Are you absolutely sure you want to do this, Jhardine? What with Eric not being here?"

"Said he's working late so...it will have to be in the morning. But I know, vicar, I know I have to tell him. Just, for some reason, he's the hardest one to break this to."

"Of course he is. He's your son. You're used to taking care of him." His hand lingered on her shoulder. There'd been a lot of that lately. Lingering. That was another thing she needed to sort. "Right," David said when Tania returned with the stack of chairs. "Are you ready?"

She nodded. This was not going to be pleasant.

"AND WE ALSO pray for Nazreen who has had a terrible time of late getting to," the vicar stumbled, reading the small bit of notepaper in his hand, "getting home through rush-hour traffic. I probably should vet these more carefully," he said. "A few moments then to pray for Nazreen." They'd barely bowed their heads when the vicar said, "And that's quite enough. Now, I'd like to open the floor and ask if any of us here would like to talk about things that are on our minds this evening." This was a very British, very Anglican, method of confessional: elective public shaming.

Ruth climbed to her feet. "I'd like to ask for a prayer for my Stanley. He's got a big day coming up. Test results to see if the liver rot is back. "

"Let us pray for Stanley and Ruth," the vicar said, somewhat begrudgingly.

"Maybe he can finally get a personality grafted while he's at it," Sarah whispered to Jhardine, and Jhardine had to fight hard not to giggle.

"Stop," she whispered.

"Any other, er, things on anyone else's mind?" the vicar asked, somewhat hesitantly.

"Well, the Madeira cake at last week's—"

"Anything of substance?" he barked in a tone that was as close to admonishing as Jhardine had ever heard him use.

"I would, if that's okay?" Jhardine said, standing.

"What?" Sarah asked, wide eyed. "You're not going to...?"

"If you're sure you want to, Jhardine?"

"Yes, it's okay, David," she said. "Right. Okay. Well, where to start? I mean, a lot of you know about my Eric and how, just over a year ago, he was at death's door. What some of you might not know," she continued, "is that around that time I started having these funny turns. Thing is, well, I'm...." Oh, it was such a small but big thing to say. Impossibly so. "There's a tumour."

Absolute silence. Absolute blankness. Then Sarah sat forward. "Jaz?"

"It's a brain tumour. They tell me—"

"They told you when I took you to the doctor's the other week, didn't they?" Ruth chimed in.

"Yes." Jhardine felt like a school girl marched in front of a headteacher and made to retell her lies and half-truths. "I didn't know as much then, so I was, you know, waiting—"

"Is it going to kill you?" Sarah asked, straight as a knitting needle.

"No. Well, hopefully not. There's, erm, well, they're going to try to shrink it."

"They can do wonders," Ruth said, waving a finger. "I've seen it myself. And you're young Jhardine, you can beat this."

Before Jhardine could say anything, Sarah croaked, "Yeah, it's different to when your dad had it. There's a lot more they can do now."

"Yes, of course. But...."

"But?" the vicar asked, his eyebrows taught. "Surely you're not thinking of foregoing the treatment?"

"No, of course not, well not exactly. I...." *I've been praying on it.* That was what Jhardine had told Eric, but what she'd not said was how she'd once had a reply on this most fundamental question. "Well, I did wonder, you know, about faith healing. What happened to Eric, you know, and you hear stories—"

"It's insane, Jhardine," Sarah said. "Sorry, but it is. I mean, I don't know what happened to Eric that night, but you can't rely on it happening again. Sorry, Vicar."

"No offence taken," said David. "And to a certain extent I have to agree. While I am a great believer in the power of faith, and I do think what happened to Eric was a miracle, we should not forget the God-given power of the good men and women around us. Today's medicine is capable of so much, Jhardine. Science is capable of so much. We cannot turn our backs on that. We have these abilities as part of our free agency. We are meant to help ourselves."

"I know, I know. I do. It's just...." Jhardine's mouth ran dry. "I've never... never told anyone but, the night Eric got better, well, I left him. I did. I had to get out of there. Just for a minute. Just for.... And I know it was an awful thing to do. I could have lost my son right then, and I wouldn't have been with him. But I needed to just get out of that room; I had to or I was going to break. And I couldn't do that. Not in front of him. Not...."

"Yes, you phoned me," the vicar said.

"That's right, I did." Jhardine took in a thick breath. They were at the heart of it now. Something she'd never even told Eric. "And you, David, you told me to pray...."

SHE RAN THE tap to wet her face. Though she looked to find herself in the wide set of mirrors, all she saw was a blurring mass of lines and shapes, as though she could no longer process things properly. Eric was going to die, probably tonight, and there was nothing she could do about it.

Slowly a thought coalesced, reaching through the smoke and all the sirens in her head. She took out her mobile phone and dialled.

"Hello, this is David Jackson," the voice at the other end said, and this alone was enough to bring her a measure of calm.

"Hello, Vicar, it's Jhardine." But after that, she was faced with a problem. If she had to say it, if she had to tell him what was coming, that Eric's expiration date had now been given the stone carved treatment, she knew her last defences would fall and she would crumble.

Fortunately, she didn't need to say a word. "I'll come straight over, Jhardine," David said, interpreting her silence like he always could.

"There might not be time. He's already... ."

"Pray, Jhardine. God is with you. Ask him to intervene and help the doctors save your son. Give him all that he needs. Have faith. I will be there soon."

With that, the vicar hung up. She looked around the bathroom, feeling lost and childlike. God, the place was a state. Mounds of tissue paper covered the floor, a broken bin sat in the corner with rubbish leaking out of it like organs spilling from an eviscerated body and, most strangely of all, there were indecipherable scribbles on the walls. One of the symbols even looked vaguely like something she recognised, she thought.

A sound.

"Hello?" she called out. When there was no answer she turned toward the mirror. She tried to forget it and searched her handbag for a tissue. She dabbed at her nose. The vicar would arrive and he'd know how to help. He would be able to—

Another bang.

The hand dryer to her left turned on and began blasting out frigid air.

"Who's there? This isn't bloody funny!" Jhardine marched up to the stalls and one by one knocked them open. There was only empty space in each.

A hissing.

She turned to see the taps in every single water basin were now on full, steam eddying thick and heavy. The water wasn't running clear though. It was black.

"Stop doing this, please!"

She looked up at the mirror and her own reflection. Her breath caught. Something was terribly wrong. Slow at first, easy to miss, but when she moved, the image was moving slightly out of time with her, breaking her lines. She turned her head this way and that, watching the reflection do the same but now faster than she was moving. "What is this?" She moved her hand, and the hand in the mirror raced through its trajectory, the reflection moving quicker and quicker until its features blurred; quicker, quicker still until it became a crackling black mark. Then it stopped dead, looking right at Jhardine. It smiled a smile that wasn't hers. It laughed, and she heard it. Actually *heard* it.

Jhardine ran to the nearest cubicle, slammed the door closed, locking it. Putting the toilet lid down, she huddled on the little seat. Seconds turned to minutes and she wanted to go outside. She wanted to go to Eric, but she dared not open that door because something was out there. Something that was not normal.

"Please, please, I have to go to my son!" She closed her eyes and she started to cry. "Eric." She rubbed the gold cross on her necklace. "Please."

"What would you do for him to be better?" her own voice said.

She shut her eyes tight and instead began to pray. "I need your help, God. Please don't let him die. Please, God, if you are there, do not steal my Eric away. I'll give anything!"

"Would you really?" her voice said, thick with honey and hope.

The thought popped into Jhardine's head as if from nothing, and yet it made such perfect sense, and it grew in her, becoming the only thought that mattered.

"Yes," she heard the voice that was hers say.

"Okay. Yes, of course, t-take me instead." It slipped off her lips but it was more than words. She could feel it twisting around her, tightening around her neck until it became a searing noose. She got down on her knees on the tiled floor and clasped her hands tighter, her thumbs rubbing the little cross until they burned. "Take my life instead," she choked. "That'd be easy for you. Please, please, please. My life for his. My life for his. My life for his."

"Your life for his. Your life for his. Your life for his!"

"BLOODY HELL, JHARDINE," Tania laughed.

"No," Sarah said. "It's a coincidence, Jaz. Or, not even that. You were under, right, a massive amount of stress that night. It must have brought on an attack or sommat. You said it yourself. You was hallucinating, seeing things, and then they found you having a fit on the bathroom floor. You have to fight this, Jaz. You have to."

"Well, I want to. Don't get me wrong. I don't want to die! But I just needed to be sure. You know, that it definitely wasn't a bargain or something. That my getting better wouldn't break the deal. With God I mean. My life for Eric's. That's what I said, and—"

"Of course not, Jhardine! Of course not," the vicar said, putting an arm around her. "I am certain. Absolutely certain. You must do all you can to live for as long as you can."

"I will, I...." Jhardine said, pulling out of the vicar's embrace. "I can't do this without all of you, though, because you're, well, you're like my family. Well, you *are* my family. I've tried my sister and she doesn't care enough. But I was stupid, see. You lot have always been there for me. I should have come to you."

"Course you should have," said Tania.

"And I know this is going to be hard," Jhardine went on, words spilling out of her now that she'd finally let herself speak. "It's going to be hard on Eric especially. I mean, he seems like he's a tough little thing but he feels stuff. He does. He takes it to heart. And he's going to think...he's going to think this is his fault. I know he is. For all the years that I had to look after him. So I need—"

"Yes. It's not even a flipping question." Sarah put her arms around Jhardine, pulling her tight. "You silly mare, I can't believe you've been thinking all these mad things all this time."

Tania and Ruth and the others in the church circle stood and came to enfold her.

"You'll get through this, you mark my words," Ruth said in her ear.

"You've got to keep your strength up, Jhardine, have the rest of this lemon cake, here," said Tania.

But, Jhardine noticed, not everyone came to her. Stanley stood at the back of the hall, rattling his car keys while he waited for Ruth. He caught her gaze and turned away. And Deirdre, who always had a face like a gone-off turnip anyway, was busy fiddling with her awful mint-green blouse.

Still, the folk who were hugging her far outweighed those who didn't. Now, if only she could get one of them to tell Eric the bad news, that would be terrific.

GRANT AND THE rest of the Radley crew had begged off hours ago, leaving Eric to sort through the latest haul of books they'd brought up from the cellar. Being alone was just fine with Eric, though. Now that he was stuck in this shitty job, the less time he had to spend talking to Grant the better. Besides, it meant he could do a bit of reading.

An aviation manual in a peeling blue hardback jacket had reminded Eric of the book Alistair had given him, and so Eric sat alone on the mezzanine of Heath Library, the blue book open in his lap just waiting for him to ask it a question. That was all he had to do, Alistair had said. But when there was so much to wonder at, so many things to think about, it wasn't quite that easy.

"You always make things bloody complicated, you," his mum always said. A smirk. Maybe she had a point. Maybe that was why he couldn't get it to work. He had to simplify.

Start at the beginning, then. But where was that? *Well, what are the shadow hearts?*

Much to Eric's surprise, a rush of those strange symbols crossed the page, and then gave way to paragraphs that Eric could read. "Halle-flipping-lujah!" he mumbled.

"The exact nature of the shadow heart is unknown," wrote Cadence Ember in her lengthy tome The Shadow Powers. *"That the shadow heart is organic is largely agreed upon. That it is capable of intelligence and self-determination—this is more controversial, but there is a good body of evidence to suggest decision-making and even a certain eloquence in the hearts' various communications. The problem of course is that shadow hearts cannot be engineered, so attempting to test them to any serious degree runs up against a host of problems, ethical dilemmas, and most Shadow Families will not—indeed, by Servant contract, cannot—allow their heirloom shadow hearts to be subjected to anything but the most rudimentary tests. There is one thing we can safely say however: that the shadow heart fulfils quite nicely the role of symbiont. Some of my colleagues would go further to argue the hearts are parasites, but I believe this...."*

Eric touched the shadow heart underneath the fabric of his grey shirt. He'd known it could affect him, after all it had resisted him that night when he'd tried to cut it out of his chest. But if the heart could affect his thinking, it seemed it only ran one way. Eric still couldn't control his powers to any useful degree. Since getting a supply of shade sweets he'd been trying on the sly, of course, just little things like extending and reeling in his senses, turning them up full and bright and cutting them off, but so far he'd had little success. Well, except for causing himself quite a few headaches. He seemed to be a savant at that. It raised the question though, how the hell was he supposed to face the Tim umbra if he couldn't even use his meagre shadow-forming powers? It was frustrating, and he knew that he wasn't the only one who felt that way.

Alistair was wary for him, too.

THE CRACKLE OF electricity as it ran between pylons was almost soothing. Alistair clung to a choice metal rung, looking out over Willingsley as it sprawled in the valley below. A fine drizzle cooled his face, but Alistair, all big cuffs and collar, was dressed rather well for it. He reached up and pulled up his hood, then checked the bone spear across his back had not degraded as they were wont to do.

The sun was setting, sky turning from a faded blue to black, and he could see the streetlights throughout Willingsley twinkling on region by region. He didn't want to be out at this hour. Had better things to do, like keeping an eye on Eric. But when Marishka gave you an order you had to obey.

"I'm concerned that there may be a group of scavenger umbras out in the hills," she'd told him when he'd reported in earlier that day. "I've been tracking reports of animal mutilations, dead carcases of livestock, that sort of thing. I want you to go out tonight and see what you can find."

And so, here he was.

Alistair scanned the rise and fall of the farmland around the pylon; tracking wasn't his thing, no sir, but even he would get the pull in his shadow heart if there was a concentration of active shades about—which usually meant an umbra or two. But so far, nothing. He'd come to the spot Marishka had told him about, a point where the animal deaths seemed to converge and which in turn usually indicated an umbra's nest. He couldn't see it, though, and that was unusual. Scavenger umbras were a subset of drones that, unlike their more regular counterparts, liked to work in large groups. They were often smaller in size and slightly weaker, their creation requiring the death of one victim be divided among many. That reduced their power significantly, yet what they lacked in sheer size and strength they made up for by their *annoying* numbers and a certain talent for being devious. As such, their numbers and the havoc they could create on their nesting sites should have made them easier to find. Unfortunately for Alistair, it appeared he was tracking the most anally retentive of all scavenger groups because it seemed like they had cleaned up after themselves as they went.

"An evening well spent," Alistair tutted to himself, swinging from one corner of the pylon to the other with a graceful leap.

He'd told Marishka he'd bring Eric out with him, this being a good training experience for when Little Bird finally confronted the umbra of his dead friend. Surprisingly, Marishka hadn't gone for it. "I envisage his training being a bit more direct," she'd said, no elaboration or anything.

Alistair's shadow heart pulsed.

"What a pretty little shadow former," came a gliding high voice from somewhere near the bottom of the pylon.

It's about time.

"Come on out!" he called. "I'd like to get this over with as soon as we can."

"Oh, you do not wish to play with us?" said the swirl of black at the pylon's base.

"Not much."

"We were cut from a suit-and-desk type. A man who lived to climb the corporate ladder. He never got to play." Ten figures rose into the air around Alistair. Their fur was a golden red, their faces a slate grey. They had the proportions and features of tamarin monkeys, except that each bore upon their backs a cross of dragonfly wings. "We very much want to play with you."

They raced forward with alarming speed, rushing Alistair. He jabbed at one with his spear, but their wings gave them a manoeuvrability that made Alistair's attacks go wide. He tried again and again until, with surprising strength, another of the mob wrenched the spear from Alistair's hands and, jabbering, flung it into the night.

"Not so fast, not so tricky, this one. Not like Her. She was a handful."

Alistair snagged one of the creatures as, with jaws wide, it surged for his throat. He pumped it full of the violet fire and watched it disintegrate with a grunt of satisfaction. Then another sank its teeth into the arm he was using to hold on to the metal fretwork, and Alistair knew he was in trouble.

"Venom, right?" he said, sliding down the pylon as his fingers slackened and he lost his grip completely.

"Oh, yes," said another of the umbras as Alistair laced his still working arm through a metal strut and regained his balance.

He had to find the alpha, the umbra that got just a little bit more shade juice than the rest. Kill it, and the rest would die too.

As if hearing his thoughts, the creatures bared their teeth, hissed, and descended on him as one.

"You owe me, Marishka," Alistair growled, swinging at one of the umbras as another swiped at his neck. *This is going to be a long night,* he grumbled to himself.

ERIC TOUCHED THE cypher marks on the back of his hand, tracing the etchings Marishka had made. A weapon in a war. A tool to be used. That's basically what she'd said he would be. Eric had never given much thought to wars, really, except in the abstract—they're for idiots, and unfortunately sometimes necessary. Now though, like it or not, he had been drafted. *Me, a fucking soldier. I shit myself when I have to phone someone I don't know,* he thought.

He let the blue book rest on the floor as, with the hours ticking on, he decided to sort through the few boxes he had left. Grant had been impressed that some of the books Eric had picked out of the last bunch made a profit on the Internet. Nothing so far with this lot, though. He shifted one box out of the way and opened the next. The rainbow glare of a few dog-eared comics shone back at him.

Eric picked one comic out of the box, holding it out in the light. It was a children's comic, a title that Tim had loved when they were kids. Eric liked to think that perhaps this was the particular issue that Tim had read over and over again, but that was highly improbable, he knew.

You deserve everything you get.

His hands were shaking as he let the comic book fall back into the box. He'd thought he'd known Tim so well, but now he wondered if he even knew him well enough to say what his childhood favourites were; comic books, sweets, footballers, any of it. That hurt something fierce and, as quick as the realisation came, Eric tried to distract himself.

Over to another box, he stripped back the tape holding it shut and unfolded the leaves expecting to find yet another set of barely legible textbooks or some coffee-stained novels that the library had taken out of circulation. Instead, a plume of livid flies erupted in his face.

"Holy shit!" He kicked the box away. The bloody flies poured from the box and began to spin around him with a menacing drone. Then came a laugh at Eric's side.

"Time is ticking, Eric. If you want that cure you better get started on killing the umbra. After all, it'd be a shame if someone got to it first." She stood by the stairs, her veils all pulled back to reveal a full but athletic figure wrapped in a deep incarnadine leather armour. Her bare right arm had blood stains up and down its length, a bit of worrying marbling under any circumstances, but knowing that she had control of the Blood Weapon heart, this sight put Eric on edge in quite a different way. All of Alistair's warnings rang in Eric's ears.

"You'd best let me get on with it, hadn't you?"

She smiled, rubbing the pink of her naked palm against the metal of her other hand. "I'd forgotten what good fun you are."

"Yeah, laugh riot me. Is that what you came here for? A bit of entertainment. Because I'm not a performing monkey."

"You could be if I willed it," Marishka said. "But no, I thought we'd have a chat, you and I. About your powers. I'm guessing you're curious about them." Her gaze fell on the blue book that, now, was crawling with flies. "I also feel that Alistair wasn't entirely," a flash of red across her arms, "forthcoming about your abilities."

Blood seeped from a cut just above her elbow and ran down her forearm to add itself to the blood collecting with a suspicious precision on her fingertips, pulling itself together there into perfect little red disks. He could feel the electricity of shadow forming in the air and his shadow heart quickened. He had a pocket full of shade sweets, but what could he do against her?

"So, what?" Eric said, hoping that she could hear just how bored he was with all these theatrics. "Are you going to make me try see something? You know, have a vision or something? I can do that, if you want."

"Really?"

"Wait, yeah, yeah, I'm getting, I'm getting something...." He looked down to her feet. "Your shoes are fucking ugly."

She smiled. "Fun, but it seems like you won't be cooperating tonight, yes?"

"Finally you're getting it. So why don't you push off back to your warehouse with all your bloody nasty flies, and leave me to my work, yeah?"

"Or, an alternative proposal," she said, holding up a metal finger. All humour drained from her face. "I will hunt you."

Eric flicked his gaze to the floor below the mezzanine. He could fall and survive, he was fairly sure, but it would hurt.

"You're not going to kill me. You've already—"

Snap.

"Ahhh!" His left leg gave out from underneath him and he fell. A searing pain collected just above his knee. He imagined that this was what it felt like to be shot. "Fucking hell!" he swore, red faced and rolling on the floor.

"I didn't say I would kill you. I said I would *hunt* you. And you'll find no wound," she said, looking down at him as he tried to fathom how his leg could hurt so much when there was no hole through his trousers, no obvious entry wound in his flesh.

"Why are you doing this?" he said, gritting his teeth against the pain.

"I told you. I want to see your powers, and even when the former is new, the shadow hearts can be drawn into fighting when they feel suitably threatened."

But she'd made a mistake. The pain had made his mind sharp. He couldn't beat her, course not, but he knew someone who might be able to. "Alistair. Al! Al!"

Marishka seemed bored. "He won't come. The flies you see. My perfect little sentinels. They have more than just one use and they can drown out your heart's tiny voice without much effort at all, I'm afraid."

"Then I'll shout louder," Eric said, concentrating. And, for one moment, Eric and his shadow heart were of one mind. He couldn't say how, but in his head he screamed Alistair's name, and he felt it leave him and radiate out. He felt it spreading unhindered by the walls of the library, spreading through the town, before, at last, finding Alistair's shadow heart somewhere on the outskirts of Willingsley. The smell of grass, the clang of metal, the bitter odour of wet animal hide.

"Ah," Eric heard Marishka say. He sat glaring at her, but triumphant.

"I did anticipate that you might have figured out how to contact one another. You have, after all, spent quite a bit of time together. That's why I arranged a, shall we say, little diversion for Alistair. Just a few umbras."

"You sent umbras after him?"

"No, I sent him *to* the umbras, quite different. But the long and short of it is, you are on your own."

Eric bit back his fear and concentrated on trying to stand. He wrapped his hands around the bars of the mezzanine's railing and managed to pull himself up to standing. He began edging away from her.

"Why don't you want to play, Eric?"

"Because I'm not twisted like you are, am I?"

"Is it that you don't have enough shades?"

"No."

"Come now, there's no need to be shy. Here, let me help." She snapped her fingers. Flies rained down on him. Guessing what she'd try, Eric clamped his mouth shut but it was no good. The flies vibrated as they scrambled up his nose, as they forced their way under his eyelids, burrowing into his ears, filling him until he screamed and they found opportunity to funnel down into his mouth.

He woke face down on the floor. Just a few seconds? Or had he been out longer? The room was spinning and, as he opened his eyes, he found that everything was changed. With his shadow heart full the library was a technicolour wash, its every sound too loud, and the textures of the place too bright and too muddled. He could taste the cool slide of the leather Marishka wore, could feel the wiry snatch of a hair as it clung to her left sleeve.

"Better?" Marishka asked, her voice all high strings and low organs. It sounded like a wasp buzzing even while sinking its sting deeper.

"Get bent," he said, a hand to the railing as he tried to pull himself to standing. But the pain in his thigh. The sodding pain. And the world kept tilting. Colours. Colours. And the noise. *Oh, shit!* The noise. Even his own breathing was hideously loud.

"Have it your way. Tick, tock, Eric." She held up her hand poised for another click. Just then, like little flicks of a brush across his skin, he felt one, two, three, four, five flies land on various parts of his body.

Eric threw himself into a limping run, pushing past her to the stairs. His vision was clouded by lights, the light of sound, he realised, and the noise of his own steps flashed before him, almost blinding. By the third step down he tripped, rolled and hit the bottom of his back hard against one step, his head on the railing. He came to a stop folded on himself at the bottom of the staircase. After a stunned moment he turned himself over with a groan, only to see a clump of flies land just centimetres from his resting fingers. A thud of his shadow heart caused him to lurch back.

Bang!

The floor in front of him exploded. He shielded his eyes and then dragged himself into a lolling run through the plume of smoke. Just meters. He could feel the cool air reaching its fingers under the library's big double doors. Just an arm's reach. He was going to make it. *Yes,* he thought. *Come on. Yes!*

He flung the doors open. Marishka was somehow stood there, hand raised and ready to click.

"Really, Eric?" she smiled, but her acid eyes burned cold.

Eric flung the doors shut in her face and staggered into a run.

Boom! A good chunk of the wall to his left, there, then gone, and he was knocked off his feet. Then came the slamming of the wooden doors as they hit the ground. Shielding his face from the plaster, coughing against the cloud of dust, Eric scrambled to his feet and limped down the corridor, twisting as another bang rang off the walls. Almost falling, he careened into a turn. He wasn't exactly sure where he was going, only the general direction. But then, those doors. He recognised them. Those gorgeous doors. Because there was another way out.

At the far end of the next corridor was a recess that led around to a small, tiled coatroom—and, if he was right, a door out to the car park behind the library. He ran for it, throwing open the coatroom door and, *yes!* The door to the car park. A modest door by any stretch, but to Eric's thinking it might as well have been gilded. He took a step toward it, and the walls began to bleed.

"There's no escape, Eric," Marishka's voice echoed in the room, but flat, like it was vibrating through very bad speakers. Eric soon realised why the sound was so distorted when flies began to pour into the recess through tiny holes in the broken false ceiling. They descended in clumps, finding his hands, his face, their buzzing like mocking laughter. He swiped at them, racing the short distance for the door but as one the flies congregated there, all settling their drone into one awful rhythm. "Eric, I'll give you a countdown to start running. Three. Two."

He pelted back into the library's main rooms, mind working on another way out, but he didn't know.

Nowhere else? Come on, there must be. Think!

Marishka stood at the far end of the room, her veils wafting out behind her and looking, he had to admit, regal.

"Did you think I'd make it easy for you?" she called. "Though, I suppose, it must be nice to see what a real shadow former can do."

You're a bit up yourself, aren't you? Another time, another place, he might have raised an eyebrow, let his face turn sour, and certainly would have given her a fair portion of sass. But not now. He straightened up, pushing away thoughts of the pain in his leg. *She gets off on her own power,* he realised. Now that was something he could use.

"Al," he breathed, laying out the bait.

"I told you, don't bother calling for him."

"No. I mean, he's," Eric cast around, using this time to try to fathom a new plan. He had books. Just books. And an empty library. A big library. Two floors. No, no there was another floor, wasn't there? And, if he remembered rightly, a window! "He says," Eric said, catching his breath. He'd need to run his bollocks off, but hopefully he could get some cover out of her. "Yeah, he's said you used to be good but, you know, not your fault, everyone goes off the boil a bit eventually. He said that he could take you, easy. Piece of piss." He positioned himself in the middle of the room to give himself a chance.

"Oh, he did, did he?" Hands out and her veils came to life. They wound up and flowed down her arms in spinning clouds of flies that divided up to settle themselves across the eight decorative pillars running the room's length. "Why don't I show you what a real shadow former can do? Ready?"

"Set," Eric said, watching her hand rise, her fingers find their friction and then, the click. "Go!"

The detonations went off in pairs, a cloud of smoke and rubble chasing him out of the room. The noise was deafening, which actually was a relief, but the rushing haze meant he lost his ability to navigate the library's corridors.

"Come on," he hissed. And then, "Ha!" as he found a cheap canvas wall print that he was sure, yes, absolutely sure, meant he was in the right place. He shoved his way through the doors into the mostly dark room. The lads from Radley's Clearance had stacked many of the tables, chairs and shelves against the walls, hiding much of the wood panelling. They'd also inadvertently obscured something else: another door, one that led down to the cellar. It'd been unlocked the other day and, with a twist of the round doorknob, Eric found it was still open to him. He slipped through unseen just as Marishka's silhouette threatened to invade the room. On the other side of that door, eyes shut, Eric didn't even dare to breathe. He listened, and his superlative hearing heard the creak of her leather boots, caught all too loudly the cooing of her voice. "I'll find you, Eric. You can't hide forever." Then footsteps. She was moving away.

When Eric opened his eyes he had expected to be in complete darkness, but no. With his shadow heart so full of such potent shades his eyes could pick out the faintest of light so everything in the room seemed covered in a pale silver dust. The shine that came under the door behind him was enough to illuminate in stark white the stone stairs down to a floor that gave way to a maze of shelves and boxes. Light that sneaked through the gaps in the wood floor above gave Eric enough illumination to then navigate deeper into the room. And then, of course, there was the window at the other side of the vast cellar, a small, thin thing that peeked just above the ground outside and gave him a tantalising view of the street and maybe, just maybe, if he could fit himself through, freedom.

He pushed his way into the room, shoving away boxes, tripping over discarded books the Radley lads had just abandoned, and oh, this poor library, but moving, always moving toward the window. He was getting close now. No sign of her, and he was getting close. Hope began to build.

I'm going to get out of this. I'm going to....

Eric froze. A meandering orange light with a red core crawled up a shelf just inches from his face. He looked closer, breath fluttering in his throat. In the middle of that aura was a fly. It buzzed, and its sound sent out a ripple of jagged light, like it had shattered the glass face of the room's stillness.

Found. She'd found him. He was sure. *Fuck!* But it didn't matter, he just had to get to the window. He ducked down behind some boxes and tried to navigate his way through the room, keeping away from the flies as they descended through the ceiling and began filling the space. Boxes and stonework exploded, small detonations throwing him this way, that. Auras of orange, all turning red. And more explosions. He was thrown to the floor, taking nearly an entire wooden shelf with him.

Stillness, then he heard the door to the cellar click shut.

"Eric," she said, her voice like a whiskey burn. He peered over a row of boxes that had fallen into a barricade. Though he couldn't see her features as she stood there on the stairs, to his juiced-up eyes Marishka was outlined in blade-flashes of red around a black core that was her shadow heart. "It seems Alistair was right," she said. "Your powers clearly put you among our augurs." She came down the stairs, looking out over the room, probing the boxes, the shelves. She couldn't see him, but then again she didn't need to. More orange lights filtered in through the ceiling and down the walls, and Eric was forced to scuttle away. Her gaze didn't follow. "And even so, I still think there is more to you. Why is that, Eric?"

"Because you need a hobby?" Eric skirted behind a tower of empty boxes, keeping his back against a line of shelves and inching away. He was close to the window. The trick would be to stay out of the light until he was positioned just underneath it and then—what? There was no way to put it through and climb out before she got to him. But maybe if he could distract her. "Seriously, take up knitting. Or, you know, origami?"

"Believe it or not, Eric, I don't want to harm you," she replied.

"You've got a funny way of showing it," Eric growled, rubbing at his aching thigh. He didn't notice that a fly landed on his foot until it was too late. A red flash across his sight. He kicked away. A click. He threw himself in the opposite direction. *Bang!* Wood and cardboard rained down on him as the metal squeal of Marishka's gloved hand descended. He turned, and those fingers were ready to click again. The flies raced to cover him, their red eyes glowing menacingly in the dark. And she stood there, smiling. This close up he could see her features illuminated by the soft blue pulse of her shadow heart. It made her look like she was constructed of polished steel.

"You anticipated my attack didn't you?" she said. "Even for augurs, that's quite remarkable."

"I-I," he tried. "I see lights. Whenever you use your power, there's a red glare. I couldn't see it upstairs because there was too much, I couldn't focus, but down here...." He closed his eyes, trying to block out the awful sensation of the flies crawling on him; of their always pressing mouths. "It gets brighter j-j-just before you trigger it."

She straightened. "It's a crude example of my power. But can you tell me how I do it?"

"Don't you know?"

"Remember the last time you were smart with me, Eric," Marishka said, holding up her hand again.

Glaring. Oh, glaring. "The f-flies. You can blow stuff up with them. But... I...."

"Think, Eric. You seem good at it and, as much as I'm interested in what that heart can do, I want to know what your mind can manage, too."

He thought. He thought and thought. And to her credit, Marishka allowed him all the time he needed. "Well, you're Blood so...." He stole a glance at the window. The golden light of outside was slowly being eclipsed by crawling flies. "If I had to guess, the flies drink your blood. Or, maybe you've made them from your blood. Then when you click your fingers which you've covered with your own blood, you can send the message to make them explode."

"Very good. Shadow forming isn't a blunt process you see. It requires finesse. It doesn't matter how powerful you are, if you haven't thought about your power, you are weak. Alistair—"

"Is better than you in every way," Eric said, hot and bold.

She seemed amused. "If you say so, Eric."

"I do," Eric said. He felt his mother's snarl turn his lips. *When backed into a corner, we Mayfairs have bite.* "So here's the thing. I can't volunteer you what you want. The heart in my chest doesn't listen to me. So whatever you're going to do, just get it over with!"

She laughed. "You expect that, don't you?" The question caught him off guard. She seemed pleased, for when she next spoke there was a hint of satisfaction in her voice. "I believe you have grown comfortable, Eric, at playing the victim."

"What? No," Eric blurted. His cheeks felt hot. "You don't know anything about me."

Her fist slammed into his jaw.

"I suggest you defend yourself, that is, if you can." Another punch hurtled through the air. Eric could see it coming, like a burning meteor, but his attempt to deflect was too slow. *Smack!* And again. And again.

"A victim, your entire life."

Punch after punch. A tooth broke loose in his mouth and he turned his head and spat it out to keep from choking.

"Poor little Eric. So, so weak."

He kicked out at her and got one blow to her chest that, while not doing any damage, at least pushed her back.

"Good," she laughed. "Yes. There's some fire in you after all." She cracked the knuckles of her bare hand. "Let's see just how much."

"No, just stay away! Get away!" Eric backed up across the ground, throwing boxes at her, paint cans, anything he could find, but she deflected each, knocking them aside with ease. And then his hand settled on a piece of metal piping on the floor, and he stood, holding it high and ready to swing.

Marishka's gaze fixed him. "Yes," she said. "Do it. You know you want to. I can see it in your face. You hate me. Hate is good. It gives you power. It keeps you strong."

Eric felt his mouth run dry. "No."

"You've done well, Eric, to keep it locked up all these years. Held down. But you hate with a passion, don't you? You are talented at it. So do it!"

"No, I won't."

"Do it!"

"No!"

"Then you leave me no choice: I command you by the power of the oath you swore, by the majesty of the Sisters, attack me!"

A searing pain went through his hand and he dropped the metal pipe. The cyphers Marishka had carved into his skin burned until one of them turned to smoke, fading off his flesh with a sound like the burn of a lit cigarette.

Thud.

You deserve this!

He looked up at Marishka. "Oh, no," he whispered, then a concussive force threw Eric and Marishka apart from each other. While Eric sprawled on the floor trying to figure out what was happening, Marishka was already on her feet with a ball of blood spinning in her hands.

"The friend Alistair mentioned, I presume?" she said to the Tim umbra that had risen between them. Its skin hung from its frame in long, sloppy trails, and every time it moved a putrescent smell filled the air. It turned to look at Eric, its now bulbous white crossed eyes fixing him, its jaws running slick with black slaver. Then Eric's superlative vision cut out. Everything turned black but for the faint light coming from the half obscured window above.

"You left me to die," the umbra bellowed in its usual, slippery gravel. "You betrayed me."

"I didn't," Eric whined, clawing his way up the wall. An explosion. The sound of fists hitting bodies. But nothing mattered to him, nothing but getting out of that cellar. The Tim monster's face loomed out of the dark at his side, gurning at him. "You abandoned me when I had no one."

"No, I didn't. I—"

The umbra ripped Eric from the wall, sending him to the ground again. It towered over Eric and was lifting up a huge cloven foot to crush him when a bloody arrow shot through its kneecap and a lance of blood slashed at its face. The umbra lumbered back, shrieking in a way Tim never had.

"I believe I was the one pulverising him, thank you!" Marishka said.

Eric sat up, his face already swelling where the monster had hit him, and his left arm twinging like it might be sprained or worse. But he didn't have time to listen to his hurts.

The window. Come on. Come on!

Up and onto his feet and he tried to climb, slipping, skinning his fingers, and climbing even still. A huge bang and he felt icy cold water gush from the ceiling and over his back. Fighting somewhere in the room, raging at each other, Marishka and the monster had managed to burst the water pipes, but Eric didn't care. One more pull and he came face to face with the small window. He used his hand to skim away the flies there, and at last he could see the golden light of the streetlamp and the road just a little way off.

The umbra screamed. Cracks ran up the wall by Eric's head. The floor began to rumble. The sound had so much force it threatened to make his ears bleed, and it went on and on, and on. Desperate, Eric hit his hand against the window over and over, punching at it until the glass gave way and fell out to the other side. Eric was about to hitch himself up and thread himself through when, at last, the scream died. The room fell to silence.

"Well, well, well."

He turned. There was a click and the room was lit by the red light of a firefly swarm. Marishka stood looking at him. There was blood on her face, down her arms, but it didn't seem like she could control it. "That caught me off guard. But it answers the question."

Eric slid down the wall until his feet met the damp floor. He couldn't run now. She'd never let him get away. He spat out blood, and then he took the bait. "What question?"

"I dare say you'll find out soon enough. But what I said stands." A whirring of flies at her feet seemed to lift her up off the ground even as she dissolved into the cloud. "You will have to be the one to kill that thing, but not just because I say so."

"Th-th-then why?"

"Because no one else can." The red-lit cloud throbbed over his head, then rushed out of the window and was gone.

"Well," Eric said after it, "I've got to give her one thing. She can bloody make an exit, that's for sure."

Time wore on, and Eric stood a while, shock making him shake and, though he'd never admit it later, blubber. Eventually, he had sense enough to slosh his way through the cellar and up the stairs. It took him an hour or so but he made it back to the main room of the library. The windows above had all blown out, and the mezzanine had fallen, crushing the tables and chairs beneath.

The book.

He shifted over the ground, aching every time he bent but he searched the rubble like a man possessed. There was so much *stuff*, though, and the dust that rose every time he moved something was sticking in his throat and making it hard to even breathe. It was useless. *I'll never find it, not in this lot!* And then a thought occurred; a tiny thing that made him laugh because even now his little brain was making connections, trying theories.

"Book," he croaked, touching his shadow heart. If it was in any way composed of shades that should mean his heart would sense it. *Please, just find it for me.* The pull was faint, but after a few steps off the trail, he found the place where it was strongest and began digging down. His hands were cut up and bleeding by the time he uncovered the blue cover. Quite remarkably though, when he pulled the book from the dust, it was dirty but undamaged.

"What the fuck happened here?" a voice from the doorway shouted. Eric stuffed the book up his shirt and secured it there as best he could. Then he turned to face Grant, whose eyes were wide and wild. "Well?"

THE CLOUD OF flies disgorged her onto the warehouse floor. Marishka reached out her gloved hand, took hold of the nearest clump of grass surrounding the fat foxgloves, and with weak hands she pulled. Inch by inch, foot by foot, she clawed her way through the warehouse to the raised throne. The foxes of the grove, most silhouettes, stood to attention. Their eyes shone, almost accusing, and by the throne sat two foxes larger than the rest. These foxes, resplendent with their black and jade eyes, bowed to her as she approached but, given that she was actually crawling on the floor, this felt like an exercise in sarcasm more than reverence.

"I didn't know I'd have to face something like that," she grumbled as she hoisted herself up onto the Blood Throne. "Otherwise I would have purified my blood before I left." She settled back into its arms, stole a breath, and then rapped her metal-clad fingers against the throne's side. The throne disgorged its teeth and they slipped through her blood armour with ease, sliding into her back and legs but, per her instruction, left her arms and head free. As soon as her blood started circulating she felt the awful hurt in her limbs begin to ease.

The male of the black fox twins at her feet turned to look at her.

"Yes," she panted, feeling sweat roll down her temple. How *undignified*. "I believe it's time for a different formula, Mojes. Arrange to have my Bane tools brought."

The fox bowed again, then turned and walked away. It took eight steps forward and then burst into black flames, a clean burn that left no trace that it had ever been there.

"Now, Dianna," Marishka said. "I have a task for you." The remaining black fox, always more wilful than her brother, showed little sign of acknowledging her, but Marishka knew the fox was listening. She was sworn to, after all.

Marishka clicked her fingers. A swarm of bees descended from above and landed in her lap. When they cleared, they left behind a thick mottled arm on a silver platter. When it became clear that the police would never be able to find evidence of the killer because of the shade substance interfering, Marishka had taken matters into her own hands—quite literally, as it happened.

The fox named Dianna turned, eyes on the limb.

"This belonged to Eric's friend Tim," Marishka said. Her gaze was on the arm. Her mouth was full of saliva. "The others were killed by, well, umbras and other things. But Tim's death was at human hands. The marks...." She traced the cuts up and down the skin, a complex weave of cyphers. "They suggest the killer attempted a ritual to extend their own life at the expense of the victim, but the cyphers are poorly drawn. This was an amateur at best. Until now there was no point tracking the killer. The creature was the thing. But now I know its secret it would be advantageous to find the murderer, if only to prevent similar attempts in the future. Of course, I cannot locate the...the...." That wasn't true. The Blood Weapon heart couldn't be used to find people, sure enough, but there was one way it could be used to trace the killer. If they'd bled on the limb, as her flies sensed and as the ritual would demand, the blood would still be in the cyphers. All she would have to do is....

Marishka's trembling hands raised the limb until it was just inches from her mouth. The cold of the dead thing teased her lips. Her shadow heart was racing. It wanted this. It *needed* this. Her veins ran black with shades.

The Blood Weapon heart has a history of making its bearers into blood-drinking monsters.

She turned her head away as Alistair's words echoed in her mind. Dianna cocked an ear. "You eat it." Marishka threw the dead arm onto the floor. "Enter the Hollow and devour the limb. I trust you will be able to locate the killer from there?" The fox looked away. "You will do this. I command you by—" The fox snapped at the air, then picked up the limb in its mouth. In a wreath of black light, like a hole in the world, the fox disappeared.

My control is not slipping, Marishka repeated to herself. *It is not slipping.*

"Bring me the Stitch heart," she said, but her foxes had all gone.

CHAPTER THIRTEEN
CONFESSIONS

ERIC'S LEGS WERE on fire. The bloody heater was right at thigh level, and while Grant and Peter might be pleasantly warm, he was about three minutes away from being grilled alive. He dared not move though. Things were, well, precarious.

"Ruined! The entire lot!" Grant repeated for the umpteenth time.

"Now hang on," Peter said, holding up a sweaty pink hand. "You're not claiming Eric burst the pipes and, and, blew out the walls are you?"

"No, but—"

"Then, let's hear the lad out."

Peter and Grant turned to look at him. "Well, I don't know exactly how it happened," Eric lied. "Like I told you before, I was working up on that mezzanine sorting through the books. I wondered if there were any more in the cellar what needed looking through, so I went down. That's when I saw the pipes had burst. I tried to stop it leaking myself, and I fell. That's when I got this." He pointed at his cut lip and the oval bruise across the side of his face that had come courtesy of the Tim umbra's massive hand. Alistair had fixed the worst, but the minor injuries were a necessary part of his alibi. "Something must have fallen and knocked me out. When I came to, I didn't really know where I was. I made my way upstairs and, er, I saw the place was ruined. Grant found me not long after."

"See, that checks out with what the fire people told us," Peter said, scratching at his man-cleavage.

"I leave you alone in there for five fucking minutes—"

"Well, you weren't exactly supposed to be there at all, were you? I mean, I did tell you, Grant. There's a reason that building got closed down. Wasn't safe, was it?"

"Yeah, but the stuff in it was mint!"

"Given how full the warehouse is, I reckon you've got enough."

Grant straightened up. His nostrils had flared so much Eric expected the prospectors for high-speed rail to be making an appearance. "So you're not going to fire him?"

Peter looked between Grant and Eric, then to his desk. "I," he started in a small, cat mewl of a voice.

"What?" Grant stared back. "Fire him now!" Peter was going red. Well, it was more mauve really, like holding your finger too tight and feeling it pulse. "I made this company what it is. Me!" Grant yelled. "How could you do this? How could you do it to me! You are a joke!" Grant, in one wrenching pull, overturned Peter's desk.

Peter didn't stand. He didn't flinch. He remained a solid lump in the middle of the room. "Do you think I don't know what you've been up to? Do you think I don't hear what you tell the lads when you think I'm not around?"

"Has *he* been telling you?" Grant's heaving shoulders, his sweating face. If Eric hadn't been madly anxious he would have been uncomfortably turned on.

"Him?" Peter said, glancing at Eric. "Of course not. He needs this job. He wouldn't rock the boat. I thought he might. I thought, maybe this one's got the balls, but no. I heard it from my sister, you soft-head!"

"Mum?" Grant bellowed. "I can't trust no one, can I!" Eric's head spun with that grammar conundrum. "You're all at it! You're all—" Grant's words were lost as he raged out of the office and into the yard.

After a time, Eric bent to pick up the desk and righted it. "I'm really sorry. I did want to say something—"

"It's done now," Pete said.

"Please, I really don't know what happened, I—"

Peter held up his hand.

Standing in there, listening to the cabin around them groaning as the wind outside battered its flimsy walls, Eric began to feel a new sense of unease. He knew there'd be some explaining to do, but he didn't think it would put his job on the line. Now, though, he was fairly sure that he was about a minute away from being fired—and the worst part was, Eric couldn't think of a good reason for Peter to keep him.

"I'm in a bit of a predicament now, aren't I?" Peter said. "See, I can't fire Grant. My sister would never let me hear the end of it, and you've seen what he's like. On the other hand, you're a good worker. I'd be sad to see you go. Now, if you've got something to say, this would be the time."

"I...." Eric thought hard. "You were bang right, yeah, about what you said. I should have told you about the job. And...."

"And what?"

Eric ran the truth back and forth in his head. "I was going to say Grant sort of intimidated me into not saying owt, but that's not what happened. I'm not scared of him."

"Then what?"

"You hit it. You did. I need the job to help out me and my mum. And he said he'd pay extra for helping him at the library. He did say that he'd tell you about it, properly like, that we weren't really doing anything wrong but if I'm honest, really honest...."

"So what you're telling me is, you knew you were doing wrong and you did it anyway?"

"I...." Eric rubbed at his ear. "Yes. I did. No excuses. I'm actually, properly sorry." Eric took a great big breath. "And I'm fired, aren't I?"

Peter folded his arms. "You seem like a nice lad, Eric. And I know things with your mum's health ain't brilliant right now." He coughed. "That's why I'll pay you until the end of the month your normal rate. And, as far as anyone knows, your contract just came to an end. It's what I'll tell the Jobcentre."

Eric could feel his legs shaking, a sense of queasy dread taking him. Even so, Peter's kindness still struck him the hardest. "I understand."

"It's the best I can do, lad, under the circumstances. And, to tell you the truth, you're probably better out of it. Away from Grant. He's a nasty piece when he takes a disliking to someone, you know?"

Eric nodded. "Yeah, okay. S-sorry," he said again and then laughed at how feeble that was. "I just, I wanted to say thanks for giving me the chance. And being so nice now. I properly...I wish.... Well, you know."

"So do I, lad. So do I."

Eric walked over to his makeshift desk, put on his coat and tucked his laptop under his arm.

"See you around, Boss," he said to Peter as he walked out into the cold.

"Off are you?" Grant called from over by the badly parked forklift truck, lips tight around a cigarette. He smiled the way only ash-draggers can.

"Yep," Eric said.

"And don't think you'll get another job in the trades," Grant smiled. "I know folk. They won't touch you with a barge pole."

"A lot like your love life, I suppose."

"What did you say?" Grant crossed the distance and shoved his forehead to Eric's, eyes wide and glaring. "Nobody—"

"Talks to you like that. Yeah, I get it. We all do, sweetheart," Eric said, feeling calm. "But you don't scare me."

Grant raised a fist. "How about now?"

Their voices had brought out a crowd. Morris, Jamie and all the lads.

"Do it. I'd love to have a reason to crack you in front of them," Eric said.

"I'm gonna—"

"Enough!" Peter shouted from the office doorway. "Just get out of here, Eric."

Eric stood eye to eye with Grant, reading his anger and bluster. He laughed. *Oh, yeah, I hate you. I properly hate you.*

"Yeah, you'd better walk away!" Grant called after him as Eric made his way toward the gates. "I'll see you around, though, Eric!"

"I fucking hope so," Eric said under his breath, and his shadow heart seemed to squeeze extra hard in agreement.

"THANK YOU FOR coming, Laurel. I hope to see you again soon," David said as the young woman with a pixie haircut and big, blue eyes, smiled and handed him the Bible in her hands.

"I hope so too," she replied, pulling her coat tight as she headed for the double doors and the rain outside. *The brass on some people today,* Jhardine thought.

"Are you telling Eric today?" the vicar asked Jhardine in between parishioners and Bibles. It'd been a lovely service, so calming and peaceful. Sadly, all things end.

"Can't leave it any longer, I suppose."

"I think that's for the best, Jhardine." He smiled, but it seemed forced. The vicar had been looking peaky lately, she thought. He was stretching himself thin, running all the outreach and community groups. *All the stuff I used to do.*

"Actually, I was hoping to ask you for your help?"

"Help? I can't imagine how I can, but of course."

"Well, would you mind being there with me, David?"

"Oh, ah. It's such a private thing." He sat down on the pew next to where she stood, running his hands over the stack of Bibles he'd collected.

"I don't want you to give him any counselling or owt like that. He'd hate that." The vicar laughed. "Well, he would, wouldn't he?" she said. "No, I just need someone there to make sure I go through with it, you know? Because as soon he gets one of his faces on, you know that hurt little boy look, I just can't. And I need to. I know I do."

"Yes, I understand, I'll...." David held up his hands. "How can I refuse you in your time of need?" he said, smiling. Was he aware he sounded like a very stuffy greeting card? "And I should ask you something, Jhardine. Something I've been meaning to say for a while."

"Oh heck, is this about what I said to Ina, because I didn't know she could hear me, you know, what with her hearing aid always being off or up so high it squeaks. And to be fair, those flowers had seen better days."

"No, no, none of that," he protested. "And to be honest, I was glad someone told her. The other day she brought in nettles. Honest to goodness nettles. And for a baptism. No, it's just, I was wondering if I might I take you for a drink one night?"

Her tongue fell dumb in her mouth.

"We've been dancing around it for a long while, haven't we?" he went on. "But I don't think I can any longer. Your illness has got me thinking."

"That I could die," Jhardine said. "Yeah, I've thought about using that with the Lottery people, too. Not for the jackpot, obviously, but you know, one of them grants. That would be—"

"You're rambling," he said, soft and kind. She laughed. "See, we have a good time, you and me. And I just meant, well, we don't know what will happen in the future. I don't want to regret not, erm, giving this a go."

"That's lovely, honestly. But I don't know, David," she said. "I'm flattered, really I am. And I've thought about it."

"But...?"

"Well, where do I start?" she said, teasing her fingers through her hair. "I've not been with someone for so long. I wouldn't even know where to begin."

"It begins with friendship," David said, his hand reaching out for hers. "I think our society greatly undervalues what that means. Friends. Were it to become romantic I would very much like that, but I understand that this is a terribly difficult time for you,."

"It's not just that, though. When Eric's dad left, I don't know, he took a part of me with him. And I know people say that and it used to make me want to shove a loo brush down my throat and give my insides a good clean, but I do feel that way, and I think I've only really started to, you know, face up to it recently. So...."

"Please understand, I'm not asking for anything from you. I just want to be there for you, especially in these next few months when you'll need to rely on—"

"And then there's Eric," she said, talking over him. "I mean, the next few months are going to be bad enough as it is. Imagine finding out that I've gone and got him a prospective new dad." She fiddled with the strap on her purse. Oh hell, she *had* become one of *those* women. "I'm sorry, you've just made a lovely gesture and I'm being dead negative about it, but it's, well, a lot to think about, you know?"

Understanding returned to his eyes. "Yes, of course, I can imagine...." He shook his head. "No I can't. I can't imagine what you are going through. But I can at least understand that you must be feeling, what's the word, er, overwhelmed." The vicar stood. "I quite understand and I'm very sorry. I shouldn't have brought it up," he said, and he was keeping his distance now. "I will be there tonight though, if you still need me?"

Of course I need you, she wanted to say, but all she could do was nod, mumble a time and say her goodbyes.

ALISTAIR TURNED THE suds-heavy rag in the cup, listening to the water in the bowl slosh and the crows outside the caravan caw their loudest. They were restless, but he couldn't blame them for that, could he?

"I've tried to see Marishka, give her what for, but she's not letting me into the warehouse. She did it on purpose. Those umbra, she'd blooded them. Made them do exactly what she wanted. And what they wanted was to rip me apart. It's not on, so it isn't!"

"I know, you've said."

"And there's something else. It got me thinking." Alistair put the cup down on the metal sheet of the draining board and squeezed out the rag in his hands. "That umbra of Tim. It's not right. It's just...not *right*."

"Well, that's nice and clear," Eric coughed, rubbing at his prematurely lined forehead.

"You're being dry again. Hurtful, it is," Alistair said, only half kidding.

"Sorry, just a really shitty day at work."

"What happened?" Alistair turned to face Eric. By the way he was squinting it looked like he was still having the headaches. Alistair just hoped that this would be the only price his shadow heart made him pay.

"Got fired, didn't I?" Eric sat forward. "And that git, Grant. I can't believe that he got away with it. I just...." Eric shrugged. "And then there's the Tim umbra. I mean, I can't figure it out either. It wants me dead, obviously, but going by what it did to Marishka, it doesn't want anyone else hurting me either. I don't get it."

"And that's another thing," Alistair mused. "How did it manage to do such a number on her? Marishka, I mean. Going by what you said, she was pretty badly beaten up. Can't remember the last time that happened."

"Evil old cow deserved everything she got, if you ask me."

"She's not evil," Alistair said. "At least, not in the traditional sense."

"I have a tooth missing and a badly bruised face that says otherwise."

"Well, she *is* unfeeling, that I'll grant you. The perfect Lilithian Bearer. Only one thing matters, and that is carrying out what the Sisters want. If that means beating you until tender, she'll do it and she'll never say sorry for it."

"Lovely, but why are you telling *me* this?"

"Because it would be wasted energy hating her too, so it would. You'll never make her care and you'll never beat her. She's only shown you a fraction of her power."

"Oh, believe me, I know. That thing where she compels you with the cyphers, that was a nice surprise."

"Ah, she used one on you?" Eric hadn't mentioned that before and, in truth, Alistair hadn't expected it. Marishka must have really wanted to see Eric's abilities if she was prepared to use up one of the three oath bindings.

"Yeah. And it hurt like hell. Then the umbra turned up and, well...." He screwed up his face. "Anyway, if she's so damned powerful, why can't she do it? Why can't she take out the umbra? It was right there."

This topic excited Alistair a bit. It was a fair question, wasn't it? And he'd been mulling it back and forth now for a good while. "I think the Sisters are putting a lot of stock in your power. Well, in you. And she wants to test you, see if they're right."

"And in the meantime people are dying." Eric's mouth tightened until it became a thin little line. He stood. "No, I've had enough," he said. "I want it to end. Now."

"What? What do you mean now?"

"I'm going to go to it instead of waiting for it to come to me," Eric said, grabbing up his coat.

"You know where it'll be? You've worked it out?"

"No, but it appeared to me in the fields by the bridge near the primary school, you know? I'll start there."

"Wait," Alistair called. "Little Bird, you're not ready. You don't know how to use your powers. Eric. Eric!" Alistair grabbed Eric's shoulder. "Eric, you're still tired from the fight the other day and even if you weren't, you don't stand a chance right now. It *will* kill you—"

"The umbra could kill someone else!" Eric shook off Alistair's hold. "Wearing his face. Tim's face. I can't. I *won't*." He headed for the door.

"It's not your fault, this." That made Eric stop. "I know you think, somehow, that you killed Tim, but that's not what happened."

"You don't know anything about me or my life, so don't pretend to understand."

"I do know, actually," Alistair said. "I...." He should have told Eric this before. He should have, but everything happened so fast and there's never a good time to tell someone you might know them better than they know themselves. Apart from, apparently, when it can really piss people off. "When I heal people I see them. I see...everything."

There was hot anger in Eric's eyes. He seemed to want to say his piece, but nothing would come.

"I saw," Alistair started. "I felt how you loved him. How you love your mum. I know you ache from not knowing your dad. And I know...." He had to say it. He'd not meant to find the thought, but now that he'd tugged that thread he couldn't stop himself. "I know how you were ready to die."

"Stop."

"You think I made a mistake, don't you. Saving you back then?"

Eric raised his face toward the ceiling. "If I wasn't around with this thing in my chest maybe, I don't know, maybe Tim wouldn't have got killed."

"You know that's not true. Your friend was already cruising some dark lanes all on his own. Besides, even if that was true it makes the fault mine, not yours. I broke the habit of my life. I saved you."

"Then why did you? Eh?" Eric shouted. "Save me, I mean. Why? Why couldn't you just pass me by like you did all those other people?"

"I...." He wrestled with it. He ran it over his tongue like wine. He crushed it under foot like a snail shell. "I looked at you and you reminded me of her."

"Her?" Then knowing slowly reached out for memory and the realisation twisted Eric's lips. "Your...your daughter?"

Alistair put his back to the fridge, letting it take his weight. "It was...."

Her hand reaching out to him, the blue of the ocean surrounding her as she fell, as she sank away.

Eric in his hospital bed, the blue light of the machines making a rupture in time.

"I get it," Eric nodded. Then he laughed. "You know for a minute I actually thought...." He laughed again. "God."

"What?"

"It doesn't matter. I have an umbra to kill."

"Eric, tell me."

"No—"

"Eric!"

"I dunno, I...." He sighed. "I had it in my head that maybe it was something about me. That you thought I was, I dunno...."

"Well, it was about you," Alistair said.

"You just said—"

"That might have been the spark, but I didn't have to go through with it. I could have turned away. I wanted to." Alistair felt that, for so long, they'd been picking off petals from a flower. Finally, they were getting close to the filament. "I wanted to walk away from you and your strange heart but when I looked at you in that hospital bed and, when I touched you, when I knew you; I thought about the goodness in you, and all the life that you would miss, and for one moment, one second in all my selfish days I managed to put aside everything I hated about my unending life, and I realised that I would give anything to be able to give you my power. And that's what made me able to heal you. Do you see? I'd never tried before and because I.... Oh...."

Oh, I wanted to give you my power. And what if, in a way, I did? That there was a mighty powerful thought. He'd heard something once, something from the clerics about a theory about umbras and shadow hearts being connected, but he'd been dying at the time, several times over in fact, and everything was fuzzy. He scanned around at the books at his feet. Maybe he could resurrect that thought, but it would have to wait: Eric was shifting for the door again and if Alistair didn't go with him he was sure to get himself killed.

"When we were close the other day," Eric said. "I thought that was the beginning of something, but since...." He caught Alistair's gaze. "And I know I'm to blame. I pulled away. But...."

"Does this help?" Alistair, seeing a way to solve two problems in one, let his hands settle on Eric's shoulders and then slid them down his sides so when they came to rest he had his hands on Eric's hips, and he gently pulled Eric to him. They stayed like that a good while, Alistair holding and Eric letting himself be held. "If you want to face that monster I'm coming with you."

"But Marishka," Eric protested. "She said I had to kill it on my own."

"She didn't say I couldn't heal you though. Not a word about that."

"Okay, fine, let's just get it done. Then Mum will be cured and—"

"Then war."

A cold fear flattened out Eric's lips, making his gaze hard and his chin jut. "Then war," he said as he pulled away.

"All right, you got your shades?"

"Yeah, I—" A chime. Eric took out his mobile phone and read. "It's my mum. She says she, er, wants me to go home. That it's important."

"I'll come with then," Alistair said, in no way being subtle about the fact he didn't really trust Eric not to go on a walkabout. "Then we can go down to the bridge after. Probably better off going out in the dark anyway, and... ." Eric was already out the door, doing a fair speed-walk for the edge of the quarry. "I'll just talk to myself then, shall I?" Alistair huffed.

SHE DANCED. SHE turned and spun, her wedding gown's gorgeous silk flowing around her as she waltzed around her Jobcentre office. In the moonlight Dee was alone to dream, to hear the wedding bells ring. Her big day was almost here. She ranged in time with the music that filled her head, until she had done a full turn of her office and, exhausted, let herself sag against the door frame.

She had no appointments tomorrow, and so she was free to take her time redressing the mannequin, returning the beauty she felt when wearing the dress to its dormant, waiting state. Soon, though, her perfect day would arrive. Perfect day, perfect bride. *Perfect.*

Flushed from the dance and weak from hunger, Dee perched on her desk and sat a spell. Preparations for the wedding were almost through now. The Lavender Hall and its double dance floor with on-site beer garden was booked, the dress was of course bought—though nowhere near paid for—and the wedding invites were all sent. Only a few responses yet, but there was still time.

The day will be perfect, she reassured herself while rubbing at her gurgling stomach. Perfect. The setting will be magical, the weather balmy, and the groom will love her. *He will finally say he loves me.* Well, he'd have to. She'd written it into his wedding vows.

A harpoon of pain sailed through her stomach, and Dee winced. A fat gurgle of stomach acid became a whine. Her body was trying to trick her into eating again, the canny thing. She wasn't falling for its buttery ploys this time though. Not when her diet was, finally, going so well.

Folding open the door to the small cupboard at the back of the room which she had cleared so as to install a full length mirror, Dee beheld her reflection.

A pearl of moonlight shining through the window by her shoulder added a blue tinge to her very obvious angles, so that it seemed she was made of blank cuts of chalk. Dee looked to her wedding gown. Its symmetry was beautiful. Off the shoulder and tapering to a cinched waist, then billowing out in eddy after eddy of fabric. Wearing it, she looked as though she was spun from the clouds themselves. But when she looked at her body now, at its angles, she still looked wrong. By some cosmic joke she was both too fat and too thin.

I need to be even stricter with my diet, she resolved. That will be the answer. Still, this didn't cloud her good mood.

Kneeling on the floor she slid a small black box out from under her desk. Nestled inside, among the loving folds of tissue paper, was the snowfall of her wedding veil. As she removed it from the box the crystals woven into the fine mesh gave a flare, sending out tiny diamonds of light across the walls, illuminating the dark. The material was thick, a rich Alaskan white and, when she wore it, it was hard to see the world outside. But that was the idea. When, at the altar, Trevor finally pulled back the fabric, she would be revealed to the world as someone new. As a better, purer version of herself; the deep sadness in her would die and, with the placing of a ring on her finger, the life she had always chased would be bound to her forever. It would be hers at last, and Dee would be happy.

She carefully laid the veil down over her desk and held to the chair a moment as yet another wave of dizziness swabbed her. Her eyes caught on the mirror. She thought she saw....

She turned, but there was no one there.

"Mum?"

"I'm in here," his mum called from the living room.

"Right, I'll just be a minute."

"I'll wait for you in your bedroom," Alistair said as he walked up the stairs.

"All right, cheers."

Eric, deep breath and all that, pushed open the living room door. The first thing he noticed was that the vicar was sat on the sofa. Neither he nor Eric's mum looked particularly happy.

"W-what's going on?" Eric said.

"Come in, love, please," his mum said.

There was a tray of biscuits on the coffee table. Ginger biscuits. Normally, she'd have scoffed the lot by now. And there was a cup of tea in Eric's favourite mug. Untouched and, by the look of it, stone cold but, still, waiting for him. These were bad omens indeed. "Mum?" He looked from his frazzled looking mother—in her nightgown no less—to the priest. "Okay, you're both freaking me the fuck out—sorry, Vicar—so, what's up?"

"Please, Eric, just sit down."

He did. An ache of silence stretched. "Jhardine?" prompted the vicar.

"Yes," Eric's mum nodded, her hands grasping her knees. "Eric, I have something to tell you. Something that's not very nice."

Eric's view of "not very nice" had changed a great deal in recent months. How bad could this really be?

Jhardine looked to the vicar.

"You can do this," the vicar encouraged. "Ask God for the strength."

Normally, Eric would have rolled his eyes. Now though, the words felt like a sudden flurry of hail. His pointed eyebrows drew close for warmth, for protection. "Mum?"

Jhardine nodded along. "Yeah. Yes. Well, you know I went to the doctors and I had to go and have tests and all that? Well, they've told me...." She sighed. "Eric, they've told me that I have...oh, I can never remember the proper name for it. Long story short, though, it's a, well, a tumour."

He looked to the priest, then back to his mum. "What k-kind of a tumour?"

"Oh, erm, it's not the kind that spreads, apparently. So that's good. It's in my head, in case you hadn't guessed."

"In which region?" he said. Even if benign, there was more than one way a tumour could kill.

"I don't know, Eric."

"How can you not know? Didn't you ask?"

"Eric," the vicar said in his quiet, calm voice. "There'll be time enough to talk about that later."

Eric sat, feeling his cheeks grow hotter. "Yeah, course. Sorry."

"Oh, he's just doing what he always does," Jhardine said, waving away Eric's indelicacy. "You're trying to find out about stuff, aren't you, love?"

Eric shook his head and ran his hands over his face. "Is it operable?"

"It'll be radiation first. It's quite big, they reckon, and they need to shrink it. I start with the treatment on Monday."

"Right. Okay. Well, I'll go with you. Just tell me when and I'll be there."

She smiled and reached out for his hands. Her fingers felt so delicate as they laced with his. "I'm going to be okay," she said.

"Of course, yeah. Yes," he said, though it wasn't a fact. He couldn't know that. Except if he could find the Tim umbra and kill it. Then Marishka could find a cure. Eric looked to the faint symbols on the back of his hand. He just had to kill the umbra. *Simple.*

He lowered himself down onto his knees before her, taking her hands in his. "Whatever happens, Mum, I'll be here for you. I promise. Everything you need, I will take care of you."

"I know, love."

"We all will," the priest said. "Be here for you, I mean." He reached into his pocket and took out a white envelope. "This is a card from all our regular attendees at the church."

"Oh, thank you, David. That's so kind of you."

"Yeah, that is," Eric agreed.

"Really, it was nothing. All the people that signed just wanted you to know that they will help, any way they can."

"Have you told Sandra?" Eric said, relaying the thought as it occurred to him. "What about Nan?"

"I still need to tell your nan, but I did tell Sandra, yeah. I was hoping to have her stay for a bit, you know, to take the pressure off us both. But she's busy. You know how she is."

"Self-centred?" Eric said, and then shook his head. "Sorry. I didn't mean—"

"Yeah you did." She looked up at the vicar. "And, forgive me, but Eric's right, she's a right bitch."

For some strange reason, Eric found himself laughing. Then his mum started, and they held each other and laughed.

"I'm going to beat this," she whispered to Eric. And he wanted to believe that. He really did.

"LET ME GO, Al!"

"I can't. Not while you're like this. You'll get yourself killed." Getting Eric back in his room had required Alistair to sling the swearing and hollering lad over his shoulders. Alistair had just been lucky he'd heard the front door go.

"It's my choice."

"When you're in your right mind, sure. But right now you're not exactly cogent."

Eric took a run at the door. Just before impact the door let off a spark of black which sent Eric stumbling across the room. The lock was holding firm, but so was Eric's stubborn streak. Eric bent over, face turning an odd bruised red, and he shrieked: "Let me out, let me out, let me out!"

"No." Alistair tried his best to look caring and empathetic. He wasn't used to all this people nonsense and, he feared, it was starting to show. "Listen, Eric, we'll find a way to pin the umbra down. I'll—"

"You'll what? We both know that Blood won't settle for you holding that thing while I cut its throat. It's meant to be a proper fight, and I don't have the gumption for it. The best I can hope to do is somehow take the bloody thing with me. I'm thinking a fire. An explosion."

"What?"

"You heard me. Chemical fires are easy to cook up. Now let me go while I've still got the balls to do this."

"Were you imagining that you going up in flames would be a persuasive argument?" Alistair asked, and then he swore. After a solid minute of being stunned by Alistair's sarcasm, Eric turned and punched the wall. "Eric, stop." Eric punched the same spot again, skinning his knuckles deep. Alistair's first instinct was to heal Eric up, but that would only provoke him. Instead, he tried to defuse the situation. "I could try healing your mum again."

"What'd be the point? You said you can't, so you can't."

"I've not tried on a full shadow heart. Maybe one concentrated burst, you know, it might find a way through the voiding."

Eric looked hopeful. "Could that work?"

Alistair winced. "I don't think so or I'd have done it already, but it might be worth a shot, I mean—"

"You're bullshitting me. I can't believe you of all people would...." Eric rested his head against the wall. "I want to be alone. If you're not going to let me out of here then at least piss off."

Alistair straightened out his clothes. "No."

"What do you mean no?"

"Exactly that, because I'm a bit tired of your shitty attitude," Alistair said. "It occurs to me you need to hear something."

"And what's that? You going to tell me you can wave your arms, do a bit of shadow forming and make this all go away? Because unless you can, I don't want to hear it, okay?"

"Will you just shut your hole for five seconds," Alistair bit back. "Before I met you my life was one unending battle. Kill an umbra, kill another. Die over and over. And then I healed you, and I didn't even know I could do that, but I did it. For one brief moment my life had a purpose. I could give it purpose, and—"

"Well, that's a nice story—"

"Don't you dare belittle that. Not even for a second, because it matters. To me, your life matters more than anything because it means I'm not completely a...a monster."

That earned Alistair a sideways glance. "What are you going on about? A monster?"

"Listen, Eric, I've done things in my past that I can't ever take back. Before I got this heart, I mean, I... ." Tongue between his teeth, he shook his head. "The heart was a kind of punishment for what I'd done. See, it means I'm bound. I have to live with what I did and I have to live with it forever."

Eric picked up a shoe and threw it at the door. The shoe bounced back with a sizzle. "Why are you telling me this?" Eric said, picking up the other shoe and throwing it.

"Because when I found out I could heal you, and when I realised that I cared enough to want to, that was the moment I started to feel...not better about what I'd done. Never that. But that there was still some good in me. That I was still capable of something in this world beyond just endless, pointless fighting."

Alistair ran his hands down the sides of his waistcoat, wiping away the sweat that had gathered on his palms. He felt sick, talking this close to the flame of his past, but he needed Eric to understand.

"So, what, I should have hope? Is that it?" Eric gave a vicious laugh. "That's hollow and rubbish. Your situation is completely different."

"Why can't you understand what I'm saying to you? Why do you have to have an answer for everything? For once, can't you just let yourself actually feel something, and—"

"You think I don't feel things?" Eric spat. "My mum is probably dying and there is nothing I can do to stop it because I can't kill that sodding umbra by myself."

"That's just it, you're not by yourself!"

"But it has to be me that does it, Marishka said! And I've never been strong enough, not for that, not for Tim, not for whatever it is that's between us, and God not even for Mum. Do you understand? And even when I was dying, yeah, people couldn't wait to get away from me. And...I can't...I keep trying to hold everything together but every day...it all slips further and further away from me, and I can't...." Eric's throat corded. "I...." He gulped down air. "I can't. I.... I...." His fingers clawed, his lips turning into a snarl. "Useless, fucking me!" He kicked the chair at his desk, sending it rolling across the room. "I am *never* good enough."

"To me you are," Alistair said, but Eric didn't hear.

"I am never strong enough. Never clever enough. I am, I'll tell you what I am: I am useless!" Eric's shadow became a tangle of vines that spread across the floor, sweeping this way, that.

"Eric...."

"No, don't touch me."

"Eric, you need to keep your calm. Your shadow heart—"

Eric's shadow spun about his feet, and with its increasing pace a gale began to build in the room.

"I hurt everyone. It's what I do," Eric said. "It's what I do. It's who I am!"

"You need to settle down, Little Bird," Alistair said, reaching out a hand.

"I said don't come near me!"

A tendril of shadow cracked across Alistair's face, making Alistair stagger back. He held that cheek, grimacing against the pain. Blood leaked through, thick and fast.

"I'm so sorry. Oh God. I'm...." Eric looked away. "See! Everything I touch turns to shit!"

"I'm okay," Alistair said, wiping at the blood. "See, watch." Thumb rubbed across his cheek and the wound closed itself up. "You can't drive me away, Eric. There's nothing that you can do that would—"

"No, you need to leave me," Eric whispered. "Leave me now before...." His shadow reared up and like one massive wave came pouring down on the room's chest of drawers. The wood cleaved in two. Still, Alistair thought he saw a tiny gap in Eric's hurt, a way under the skin.

"Leave you now, before what, Eric?"

"What?"

"You said, I should leave you before...before something happens, yeah? What is it?"

"I don't know," Eric said.

"Yes, you do. The heart knows, and it's trying to keep you from having to say it. But you need to because—"

"No, I don't, I...." The shadow reared up again and crashed against the door. Alistair's cypher lock sputtered. Whatever juice Eric was packing tonight, it was mighty potent. "Please, just—"

"What is it, Eric? Before what?"

"No!"

"Come on, Little Bird!"

"Before I love you!" Eric's shadow bubbled and rolled like a great sea, and as one body it pushed outward, sending Alistair back against the wall and pinning him there. "Before I love you enough to hate you, because I hate...*God, I hate....*" Eric sagged, collapsing to his knees. He was shaking, and for a moment he looked like a little boy again.

"Say it," Alistair wheezed, the pressure of the shadow making it hard to breathe.

"I hate that I didn't get to have a childhood."

Alistair, violet fire starting in his eyes, lifted himself off the wall, digging in his feet.

"I hate that I don't get to be loved."

Alistair took a step forward against the tide. Another.

"I hate that I don't have a dad. That I'm losing my mum."

Closer.

"That no matter how hard I try, all there is in the end is death and loss, and I hate it. I hate it. I—"

"Eric, let me...." Alistair stepped closer. A vine of shadow sliced his arm.

Eric looked up at Alistair then, and shades were running from his eyes as thick black tears. "Oh God, I'm sorry, I, I don't know what I'm doing. I—"

"It's fine. Already healing, see." Alistair thrust himself forward, closing the gap between them. He was about to put his arms around Eric when Eric's shadow lurched under Alistair's feet and sent him to the floor.

"I'm sorry, I can't stop this. I...."

Alistair's power flared, and the violet light made the shadow retreat.

"Take my hand, Eric," Alistair said, reaching out for him. "It has to be you who does this. I can't end this by force."

"I could hurt you. I could—"

"I think we've established that you can and that it doesn't matter. I'm still here. Take my hand."

Eric mopped at his face. He saw the black of his tears. "W-what's happening to me?"

"It's not healthy for shadow formers to repress stuff. It tends to come out sooner or later, and in the most inconvenient of ways. Now take my hand!"

Eric dithered.

"Eric!"

Eric's fingers closed around Alistair's wrist.

"Your heart's having a bit of a panic," Alistair said, pulling Eric toward him as the wind lashed, as the waves rolled and made kindling of the room's furniture, rattling the windows and cracking the walls. "Come here. Come on." He pulled Eric in close until, like a child, Eric was pressed into Alistair's shoulder. Finally, Eric's shadow disbanded and the gale in the room died.

When everything was still, Alistair made Eric face him. He wiped the black shades off the young man's face. "You look really gross, Little Bird. Like, I'm feeling unclean just touching you,"

Eric laughed.

"Any chance you can, like, heal the room? Otherwise, I won't have to worry about the umbra," Eric sniffed. "Mum will kill me all on her own."

Alistair stroked Eric's hair. "I'll see what I can do."

JHARDINE DIDN'T KNOW how it had happened, really. Her and the vicar—David, she had to start calling him David—they'd been on the couch watching television. Then she'd looked over at him and just thought she couldn't possibly face going to bed alone, not after telling Eric everything. So she'd reached over and kissed David and, at some point after, they'd made their way to the bedroom and their clothes had sort of all just fallen off.

Oh hell, those orange curtains are filthy. Fancy having sex next to filthy orange curtains. A sound behind her. She turned over to see that the vicar was already awake—and sickeningly immaculate looking. His hair lay perfectly flat against his head, and there wasn't a crease or line of drool to be seen. He was also reading one of her filthy books she got from the charity shop. He looked over at her, a disapproving pull to his jaw.

"Oh, I'm so sorry. I—"

"It's simply reprehensible, Jhardine, that I'd never thought to try that." He pointed to a passage in the book, which involved a dowager and a far-too-young but just-old-enough-to-be-legal Mormon stable boy, and she giggled at the joke. Then she hissed. Her head hurt terribly.

"Are you okay?"

"Oh, it's nowt, Vicar."

"Please don't call me that. It feels a bit kinky when we're between the sheets." This made Jhardine laugh again. "And, you're sure you're okay?"

"Yeah, I'm fine. It just sometimes takes me a while to get going in the mornings, you know?"

"Yes, yes, of course," he said, rubbing her shoulders. Forget the saucy book, she'd bagged a vicar. She couldn't wait to tell her mother. It'd finish her off good and proper. "I tell you what," David said. "I'll get Pat to cover my appointments and I will spend the whole day with you. I would feel awful to have such a wonderful night and then leave you."

"Really, there's no need," Jhardine said, despite really wanting him to stay.

"No, I insist."

"Well, if you're sure you don't mind." Then her smile faded. She thought they better have the talk then. "About last night."

He turned over, one of his broad and hairy forearms threading underneath her pillow. "If you don't want what happened last night to ever happen again, Jhardine, I quite understand. I have to admit, I feel a bit ashamed of myself that I didn't have more restraint."

"No, that's not what I was going to say." Jhardine got up from the bed and pottered over to the dressing table. She opened the bottom drawer and took out her bottle of pills, the most recent stop-gap designed to lessen her symptoms. She hesitated. "David, we didn't...." *Time to be a big girl, Jhardine.* "I don't really remember much. It were a bit of a blur. A good blur, but.... Well, we didn't use any, erm, *precautions* last night, did we?"

"Yes, I noticed that too." He smiled, and then he said, "I can't have children, Jhardine."

"Oh."

"I never have been able to. The fish, you see, they don't swim."

"I'm sorry, I didn't mean to bring it up."

"Don't fret over it. I never have. Not really."

Jhardine moved back to the bed and ran a hand over his arm. He kissed her, his lips finding their place in the groove of hers. "David," she started. Why was this so hard to say? "You're not with me because you, erm, feel sorry for me, are you? Because I couldn't take that, I—"

David looked fierce. "I would never patronise you in that way, and I am hurt that you think I would."

"No, I didn't mean it like that. I just meant...." She lay her head down on his chest. "I suppose I meant, this is going to make it harder for you, if the worst happens and I—"

"Don't you worry about me," David said. "I've loved you since the moment I laid eyes on you that day when you were moving in."

"No you didn't."

"Yes I did. I'd not long arrived here myself and I was feeling rather sorry I'd bothered. My car had been set on fire outside of the church."

"Oh, that's just a friendly hello round here."

"I realise that now. Anyway, the day I saw you I happened to be out on a walk. I'd just been to Mr Singh's and was coming back through the subway. You were unloading the car. I remember because your mother was with you, shouting that you were taking too long and you, well, you shouted right back at her."

"Oh, no," Jhardine put a hand over her face.

"You were a revelation," he chuckled and kissed the crown of her head. "Do you remember what I said to you that day?"

She racked her brains. "I think you said about wanting to help."

"I did."

"And I said no, because," she pondered, "I said something awful about Mum then, didn't I? Oh Gawd."

"You called her the She-Devil in Teal, if I'm not mistaken."

Jhardine snorted. "She is, you know. Oh, and I suppose you'll have to meet her eventually. I mean, not to assume that this is a longterm thing, but—"

"Whenever you're ready," he said, like they had all the time in the world. "I knew I loved you that first day. And I love you now."

He laid his forehead against hers. She wanted to say it back to him. She wanted it to be true. She *really* did. "I'm so lucky to have you." Even if he heard the difference, he was kind enough not to make an issue of it. "Not to hurry on but, I have to pop in to work today to sort a few things out," she said. "I'm going to keep up with the paperwork from home, and I might go in some days when I'm feeling strong. But there's a lot to sort out."

"I'll come with you." He held her tighter. "We're in this together now."

She laughed, reaching for her hair brush. "To the bitter end."

He smiled. "The good thing about the Faith is that there is no bitter end, is there?" He ran a hand down her naked back. "We need never worry about anything again."

"Except being late," Jhardine said.

THE CAFÉ JHARDINE ran wasn't exactly Dee's type of establishment: she'd always considered herself above cheap and cheerful. But, walking into the warm air of the CC's interior, feeling the rattle of soft voices as people chatted over their meals, and smelling the grease of a fry-up wafting like news of the Second Coming, she decided she could endure it. Let it never be said that Dee was not a woman of the people.

She made her way toward the counter, wobbling on her high heels until one foot went down badly and she almost fell. Tania's tattooed sack of meat, Lance, was there to catch her. The smell of weed wafting from his denim jacket was enough to take her from lightheaded to stratospheric.

"You all right, Dee?"

"Yes, sorry. Tripped over my own feet," she smiled.

"I'm always doing that. Mind you, one of mine's false so...." He pursed his lips. "You don't look so well."

"Well, I said I'm fine, didn't I?" she bit off as she took her place in line. When, eventually, she reached the front of the queue she was in no mind for any friendly claptrap.

"Hi there. Sorry for your wait, how can I—"

"I'll have a salad," Dee snapped.

Tania, with a lolly sticking out of her mouth, repeated the order back: "Okay, chips and salad."

"No, just a salad, thank you."

"It comes with chips."

Dee stiffened. "But I don't want them."

"But it comes with chips. Just have the chips."

"I'll leave them."

"Doesn't matter to me. They're only chips."

"Then why are you insisting—"

"Because it comes with chips. Salad and chips. See on the menu. Doesn't say just salad, does it?"

"Fine! I'll have the buggering salad and chips!"

Tania moved the lolly back to the other side of her mouth. "Would you like something to drink?"

"Milk. I will have a glass of skimmed—"

"We only do full fat—"

"Water! I'll have water then."

Tania removed the lolly. She punched a button on the till. Another button. "Sparkling water or still?"

Dee threw the money down on the counter and went to sit at the nearest table. There, she tried to find a spot of calm in a world that was now dancing around her head.

I'll just have a nibble at the salad. Barely any calories in that. Just enough to get me through the day. She said this like a mantra, a meditation. All the while, her stomach clenched and unclenched with a rapid pulse. Just a week and a half now and she would be married. Trevor would be her husband. For better, for worse. She just had to be disciplined, and then life would be wonderful and everything she had always wanted would fall into place. It was a simple matter of self-control.

When her salad and chips appeared, all on one plate and so chip-abundant it could reasonably be wondered if there were any potatoes left this side of the Humber, Dee was rendered speechless.

"Enjoy," said Tania in a flat tone.

The smell of the chips was tantalising. No. Dee wouldn't wobble, not now. She took up a crescent of celery, scraped off the goop of mayonnaise as best she could, and began to nibble. If she just ate her salad slowly, the chips would grow cold. Then they would be less appetising. Yes, she could do this. She'd made an art out of making one meal last hours. She had endurance on her side. Chew. Chew. Don't let it sit. Chew. Finer, finer. Soon it disappeared on her tongue like a melting bit of frost. She would reward herself with another, measured bite. All the while, her eyes were on the chips and how they were scattered through the salad like little nuggets of gold. A food she was too strong to eat, she reassured herself.

She'd been nibbling at the same leaf of lettuce for almost five minutes when Tania returned. "Forgot to put the salt and vinegar on."

The pop of vinegar as it left the tapered bulb of the bottle top, the scratch and settle as the salt pelted the chips, and the smell. Oh, Holy Ghost, the smell!

"I'm sorry about earlier," Dee said as she sat, mesmerised by the food. "I'm a bit tense today."

"Don't think owt of it. You've got your wedding soon, right?"

"Yes," Dee looked up. Conversation was good. Distracting. "I noticed you haven't replied to my invite."

"Invite? I've not had one."

"What do you mean? No, no, you must have. Trevor was supposed to mail them weeks ago." She stopped. "I've not had any replies at all except for the ones I gave out by hand."

"Well, you know what the postal service is like. Probably they've got jammed in one of the machines, or—"

"No," Dee said, picking up a chip and pushing it into her mouth. "It's him. It's Trevor, that hideous, hairy sea lion of a man."

"Steady on, Dee."

She reached out and picked up her fork and began shovelling food into her mouth. She felt her body start to relax as the nourishment slid down into her stomach, but the relief lasted only seconds. A pressure in her head began to build. Her stomach clenched again. After weeks of being starved, her body couldn't handle this sudden influx. She began to gag.

"I need the loo. Which way? Which way!"

"Just down there." Tania pointed.

Dee pelted through the café and threw herself at the bathroom door. Inside, she reached the dingy sink just in time and coughed and spluttered as she vomited up all the food she'd eaten. She ran the tap, cupping her hands and stealing a small sip of vile tasting, and what she soon realised was dirty, blackish water. Her hands were shaking, and finally she couldn't deny what she knew to be true: something was dangerously wrong. Her fingers were almost skeletal, the joints of her wrists painful when moved. This wasn't control anymore. It was all wrong. And why was she doing this to herself over Trevor, the most awful man she had ever met?

"You deserve this," she whispered, remembering what Eric had told her not long back. "You're marrying him because deep down you think what people have been saying is right. He's all you can get, and he's all you deserve."

This epiphany washed over her, and for the first time in such a long time, Dee forgot about food. She forgot about controlling what she ate and how she exercised, and instead she thought something that was very alien to her, a soft whispering voice that came from the deepest part of her mind: *I deserve better. I am a good person, and I don't deserve to hurt like this.*

She would get help, she thought. She would call off the wedding and she would find a therapist and then, when she was coping better, she would find a partner who really, truly, would honour her with their care. She could do this. *In fact, no time like the present.* She turned, ready to march out of the door and home to Trevor to tell him to get out. And that she was keeping the dress!

A shadow appeared over the door. A shadow so dense that it caught her eye. A man, six feet tall at least and wide like a barge with flesh hanging from his face, stepped out from that shadow. Not a man, she realised, but a monster. Dee tried to scream but before she could even open her mouth, the monster's giant hand clamped around her head and threw her to the floor, holding her there.

"It's your fault," the dead man hissed, maggots cascading from its mouth and scattering over her blouse. "You left me."

"DEE!" ERIC YELLED as he sat bolt upright. "Al, get up. Get up! The umbra, it's attacking Dee. We've got to do something!" The vision in Eric's left eye dilated again, and Eric could see Dee on the ground. She was screaming as the umbra's knife-like fingers sliced into her gaunt cheeks and peeled off strip after strip of flesh. She was shouting, crying, but no one would come to help her: the umbra's influence would suffocate her cries. "Oh, God."

Alistair's hands clamped around Eric's arms, and Eric was brought back to the bedroom. "Eric? Listen to me, you have to focus." He pushed a shade sweet into Eric's mouth. "Chew," he commanded. "Now, somehow, the thing is connected to your powers. You have to find out where they are."

"There's so much blood. I—"

"Dee's life could depend on it. Come on, Eric."

"I, yeah, yeah okay." Eric closed his eyes and concentrated. Suddenly he was there with the monster as it lifted its arm to hit Dee again.

"No, I can't. He's hurting her."

"Stay with her Eric. It might be the only chance she has."

The arm descended at Dee's chest. There was a sickening crunch. It pulled back again, readying for another blow.

"No! Stop!" Eric yelled, and the most curious thing happened. The umbra's arm hovered above Dee, the fist refusing to fall. Dee kicked out hard and slammed a foot into the umbra's stomach. The umbra staggered back, and Eric felt the hit. The umbra was winded, and so was Eric. "Tania," Dee wheezed. "Lance. Someone, help me!" she cried, reaching for the handle, but she slipped and fell hard against the sink.

The Tim umbra lumbered forward. "You left me to die!" it chanted. "You left me. You deserve—"

The vision cut out, plunging Eric into darkness. Eric opened his eyes, blinking. The black in his left eye remained. "I can't see. I can't—"

"What?" Alistair said. "What do you mean?"

"My left eye, it's, I'm blind in it. I can't...." Panic rose, but he capped it. This was no time to go to pieces. "It doesn't matter. I think it's the café. Where Dee is I mean. She was crying for Tania, so they're probably at Mum's café, erm, CC's. You know where that is, right?"

"Yes," Alistair said, dragging Eric toward the door. "Now let's go."

"No. You have to get there, Al. I'm not fast enough and Dee's really hurt. She needs you to heal her before it's too late."

"All right then, we'll take a different route." Alistair jumped up on to Eric's bed and threw open the window.

"What are you doing?"

"Come here."

"But—"

Alistair gave that pleading look he'd had the night before, right after Eric had hit him with his shadow. "Trust me."

Eric, despite all better judgement and his persistent sense of self-preservation, clambered over the bed to take Alistair's hand. Tethered there, Alistair swung his own body out the window and onto the narrow ledge. "What the hell are you doing? I'm going to fall. Al! Al!"

Alistair's arm clamped around Eric's waist, pulling him up and in so that Eric's back was pressed hard against Alistair's chest. Alistair's entire body tensed as they hung there on the exterior wall suspended just by Alistair's grip on the window frame. Violet fire wrapped around Alistair's legs, lighting up the window ledge. "Hold on tight!" Alistair said, and he leapt. A sudden, unremitting rush of cold and they were heading up into the air with a speed that made Eric's eyes sting. Up and out they went, over one street, the next, until they began to lose forward momentum. The rooftops started racing closer as they fell, and then seconds before the moment of impact Alistair tilted forward and brought his feet slamming down, sinking deep into the roof and dislodging a whole swathe of red roof tiles.

"It's on Blezzard Street, right?"

"What, the café? Yeah."

Alistair crouched. A wave of violet fire shot up Alistair's legs.

"No, no, not again. Please, not...."

He jumped.

"I'm gonna hurl!"

"IF YOU WOULDN'T mind clearing Table Seven for me, Ruth, I'd love you forever," Jhardine said, doffing her padded orange coat which David took for her. It made her smile. *Such a gentleman.*

"Not a problem, Jhardine love. You sit yourself down—but not there!" Jhardine hovered. She'd been about to perch at Four. "I've just cleaned it. Wouldn't want you getting that stuff all over your clothes," Ruth explained with a big, placating smile.

"Oh, thanks, chick." Jhardine gleamed. "Shall we go over in the corner?" was her question to David.

"Yes. I've always liked that table the best. You get a lovely view of the street."

"You mean that ruddy skip? I've told them about that but they won't move it. I'm going to have to...." Jhardine stopped. She couldn't help but giggle.

"What?" David asked.

"I just realised, I don't have to sort it out, do I? I've got other stuff to worry about."

"Oh, don't, Jhardine."

"No, it's not me being morbid," she said. "In a way, it's really nice. I mean, all that stuff that would have been important—it just isn't anymore."

"I...suppose," David said, though he didn't seem all that convinced. "Perspective, and all that."

"I don't know what she's playing at!" Tania said, looking down at a nearly full plate of salad and chips sat lonely on the table in front of her.

"Who's that?"

"Bloody Dione. Her from the Jobcentre. You know her don't you?" Tania crunched on the end of a lollipop stick.

"Aye." Jhardine nodded. "I know, Christian charity and all that, but she can be a bit of work, David."

"A bit of work?" Tania huffed. "She had a right go at me over the salad because it comes with chips—"

"She didn't want chips?"

"Didn't want the chips, no."

"Well, what kind of sense is that?"

"Exactly. Who just eats salad? So I said that to her, I said, 'Just have the chips.' Then I came over and was putting salt and vinegar on for her. Didn't have to but I remembered what you said about making an effort with the difficult customers, you know?"

"Aye, that was good of you, Tania."

"Right, well, then she just freaks out and runs into the bathroom. She's not been out since."

"When was this?"

"About twenty minutes ago."

"Oh, heck. Have you tried to go in?"

"Yeah, but she's locked the door. I can't find the spare key and she's not answering."

"Here, I wonder if she's pregnant!" Jhardine clapped. "It's her wedding day soon. Happen they're planning for a quick delivery after?"

"Perhaps someone should, you know, try to get in there," David said in his most concerned tones. "What if she's having some difficulties? I—"

Then everything went mad. CC's front door vaulted open with a rattle. Then a huge bang and the toilet door blew in, splintering like it had been kicked. People shrieked. Jhardine stood but David pulled her to him, wrapping a protective arm around her. She wriggled away, making a mental note to have a talk to him about *that.*

Barry threw open the kitchen hatch, his greasy face made even more shiny by his spell in the kitchen. "What the chuff is going on out here?" he said, panic eradicating all of his false Oxford sensibilities.

"I have no idea, I—" Her voice cut out as she saw Eric stood in the bathroom doorway. "Where the chuffing hell did you come from? And what's going on?"

"Mum, get everyone out. I'll explain later."

"Eric? But...."

"Please, Mum!"

The tone of his voice said this was no prank. "All right, you heard him," Jhardine shouted. "Everyone out! Come on. You! You can finish that pastie outside! Sounds like we might have a little gas leak. No need to panic, just make your way out. You too, Barry."

"May I remind you that—"

"No, you may not. Now, out!"

DEE LAY IN the middle of the bathroom, a husk of a human being. Flesh hung from her swollen face in strips, while a dark aura of blood pooled under hear head. Her eyes were bloodied too, her pupils vastly dilated. That was the worst of it. That the Tim umbra had somehow managed to make Dee look less human and more like, well, an umbra herself.

Eric had a hand over his mouth as he watched Alistair work. "Come on, come on, come on."

Alistair clamped his hands over her chest, then her arm, then her leg. The electricity wouldn't come though.

"You can't do it, can you?" Eric whispered.

"There's something wrong. My powers...." Alistair shook his head. "I've barely got any shades. I used them getting here. I should have...but I didn't think."

"You mean she's going to die?"

"No, I can keep her alive. If I concentrate, I can keep her breathing by syncing my renewal to her, just to keep her heart going, the blood pumping, hold her wounds together, but that's about all I can do." Alistair's face was screwed up, his lips pulled back from his teeth. "Damn it! I always keep a supply on me, but with not going back to the caravan last night. Wait, do you have any shades in you?"

"No, no, the umbra took them all and my jacket's back at the house."

"Ah! How could I be so stupid!"

"It's not your fault. It's mine. I should have kept some on me, I—"

"No, no, it's not. I'm always saying to you, aren't I, keep a good shade supply, and what do I do?"

Eric put his hand on Alistair's shoulder. Alistair was shaking with effort, sweat beading on his forehead like tiny blisters. He couldn't last long.

"Doesn't help that there are some sick shades in her," Alistair said.

That hit Eric like a punch to the face. "I didn't...." Alistair clocked him with a cold stare. "The other day she, erm, almost collapsed. I gave her some of the old shade sweets I had in my jacket. Just a couple. It was all I had and I didn't think...." He was already shaking his head in apology. "Could it have, you know, drawn the umbra to her?"

To Eric's relief, Alistair only rolled his vision down to focus on Dee again. "It wasn't a good idea, but purified shades aren't as dangerous, and if they were from the last batch, they were nearly a week old. They wouldn't have done anything to her except give her some wild dreams, and maybe even made her feel a bit better about herself," he huffed. "No, it's this place, Eric. There are shades everywhere. People are just ripe to be turned. I've, well, I've never seen anything like it in all my long life. Not this bad."

"What are you saying?"

Alistair's eyes caught on Dee, as though reading something Eric couldn't find in her badly folded limbs, her raking breath. "I'm saying we need to get her to that there hospital of yours, and soon."

Eric didn't argue. "I'll get the ambulance," he said, and hit his left shoulder on the door frame. "Shit."

"You all right?" he heard Alistair call.

"Yeah, just can't see out my left eye still."

Jhardine, her curly hair scraped back from her face by a hastily applied yellow bobble, met Eric as he walked out into the café proper.

"Mum, what did I tell you? Yeah? Stay outside."

"Is it Dee? What's happened?"

He sighed. *Can't get rid of her. Never could.* "She's hurt. My friend's with her. Please, no, don't go in there! I don't want you to get ill from this!" Eric pulled his mum back from the doorway. "Mum, she's alive but she's not going to last much longer. Where's your phone? I need to ring an ambulance."

Phone retrieved from her coat pocket, she dialled and handed it over to Eric.

"Yeah, erm, ambulance, please."

"Eric, how did you get here? How did you know to help her?"

Eric struggled to find an answer. He searched to make sense of everything he knew and how he could tell her. Then he thought of Alistair, in that room, desperately holding on to Dee's life. "You have your miracles, Mum," Eric said, noticing a grey fox slip through CC's doorway, "and I have mine."

"OH, ERIC, WHAT the bloody hell was I thinking?" Jhardine puffed. *Take the stairs, I says. It will be healthier, I says.*

"I don't know," Eric said, following as they climbed toward the third floor of the hospital.

Jhardine almost slipped as they reached the top step, cursing the always polished floors.

"Are you all right?" he said, his concerned face, his doe eyes.

Is this what I've got to look forward to over the next year, then?

"I'm bloody fine," she said, catching her breath. Maybe giving up the cigarettes would be a good idea after all. "She was such a bonny girl. Dee, I mean," Jhardine said, thinking out loud. "I hope they catch the bugger what did it to her. Shame you didn't see anyone," she said.

"Like I told you, just passing the door weren't I, and heard her shout. Guy had already got out through that little window."

"No," Jhardine said. "You weren't, I mean, you didn't come with us though, did you? Me and David." She rubbed at her forehead. There was such a weird fog about the whole morning, and for some reason she kept thinking about a scraggly looking grey dog.

"I was already there, remember?" Eric said. "Tania'd cooked me a breakfast while I waited for you."

"Aye, yeah. Yeah." Things seemed clearer. "Oh God, these tablets I'm on are doing a right number on me today."

She opened the door out to the long corridor that led toward the ward. *I'll be in here soon enough, won't I?* Oh, that unnerved her a bit. The thought of gradually getting sicker even as the doctors tried to make her well. She thought of Eric, remembering how he'd looked during what was meant to be his final days. He seemed to have just been all body parts and no spark; all that she had called her child slowly evaporating. She didn't want to be that. A massive brain haemorrhage. A fall down those lethal stairs. Hell, even being blown up when she tried plugging in a hairdryer. That would be better. Quick. Clean. Simple. Maybe she needed to make a plan for if the worst should happen?

"Why the bloody hell didn't she shout for help?" said a male voice as they turned the corridor. *This must be Trevor.* Jhardine grimaced. The heavy burden of Trevor's manifest overeating gave his midsection a blimp-like audacity as he drifted back and forth between the walls of the narrow corridor outside a room in which Dee was invested, sleeping. The vicar—David, she corrected—was stood outside, his hands clasped, apparently praying. "I always knew she were a dumb cow, but this takes the Michael, this really does. Can't have her walking down the aisle looking like a Frankenstein, can I?"

"Frankenstein was—" Eric started.

"I wouldn't bother," Jhardine cut him off. And then to Dee's groom-to-be: "You've got some brass, you do."

Trevor lifted his round glasses as though to blur out what he found offensive. "Excuse me?"

"Blaming her, that's what. Happen he hit her from behind or, you know, the poor love was too terrified to say owt."

Nurse Lesley happened by, the drift of her hair and droop of her eyelids saying she was in no mood. "What's going on here?"

"He's Dee's feller. The reason why she's in here."

"Me? Oh no, you can't blame this on me. She's always been a nut!"

"No, you've given her a complex. If she'd been feeling stronger, happen she'd have been able to fight the sod off."

"Right, well, I don't want any trouble," Nurse Lesley said, and then in a more quiet tone reserved only for Jhardine, "I recommend going for his herniated scrotum." Then she walked away.

"Now, now, let's not get carried away," David began as he rejoined the group. Jhardine shot him a glare and he didn't so much clam up as fold down on himself.

"You'll get used to that look," Eric said to David. She'd not thought about the fact there would now be two men in her life. That was a lot of male habits to have to correct.

"You're disgusting," Jhardine said, turning her attention back to Trevor.

"Oh, fattist now are we?"

"I'm not talking about how you look on the outside. Who gives a damn about that? I'm talking about how shitty your insides are. You reek of it."

"You're one to talk, you flaming loon! Going on about how God saved your son. Like he'd fucking bother!"

"Here, what've I done?" Eric barked.

"Right, I've had enough of this," Tania said, emerging from over by the vending machine, a packet of crisps in hand. She walked right up to Trevor, kneed him in the groin, then sat down on a nearby chair. She opened her prawn cocktail crisps while Trevor rolled on the floor at her feet, moaning and swearing. The rest of the assorted gang looked between Trevor, now looking like a putrid raspberry, and Tania who was noshing on her latest snack. "What?" she asked. "He was being loud. This is a hospital. He should show some respect."

"Violence, er, solves nothing," David said, though it was more a recitation than a criticism. He went over to Trevor to offer him a hand. Trevor knocked it away.

"Mad! The lot of you! Well, I've had enough. Enough!" He clambered to his feet. "I'm off back down to Devon. It's like the fricking Dark Ages up here."

"Here, what about Dee?" Jhardine shouted.

"Sod her, sod you, and sod this stinking place!" He lumbered down the corridor, turning the corner and gone.

"Oh, what a bloody drama queen," Jhardine commented. "We were only having a polite word."

She clocked Eric looking about.

"What you being shifty for?"

"I, er, need the bathroom Mum. I'll be back in a few."

"All right, love." She watched Eric walk off.

"I hope you don't think I was taking sides," David said to her.

"No, I understand. You're a man of the cloth. You have to be good."

"I really do," David said, making Jhardine laugh with his sincere face, and then he turned away from her. "Before I forget, Tania," he said, "Have you ever considered women's rugby? I know someone who organises a team based not far from here."

"To tell you the truth David, yes. I have."

"Jhardine! There you are!" Ruth stepped out of the lift, her bright red handbag swinging. *Had she gone home and changed?* Jhardine couldn't remember. "Christ, it was murder parking. And now I've lost Stanley. I'm sure he'll turn up somewhere. How is Dee?"

STANLEY PUFFED ON his cigarette. Jesus, he'd needed a breather from Ruth. The cow never stopped wittering on. He couldn't wait to see her face when he served her the divorce papers, took his money and left. It was going to make all those hours of fiddling with that sodding cameraphone worth it when he captured those tears, that was for sure. He threw the cigarette down on the ground and stubbed it out. Ever the caretaker, he reached down and picked the stub up, throwing it in one of the small green bins that dotted the hospital's car park. He hated people who littered.

Stanley turned to go inside, but a stray thought made him stop. He slipped a hand into his coat pocket and took out a metal chain. As jewellery went, it was fairly unremarkable, but the blood on it made it special. He smiled. This was his ticket to another life. A stolen life, but a new one all the same that would be disease free and a chance to do everything he never got to do the first time around. He brought the chain to his lips and kissed it. "You little beauty," he smiled. Just a few more days now and he could leave all this behind.

He pocketed the chain and set off across the car park. He was a few hundred yards from the visitor's entrance when something black stepped out in front of him and sat down in his path. At first he thought it was a dog, but quickly revised that opinion. A fox—and a very unimpressed one at that.

"Get out of here, you mangy...."

Its fur prickled, and then burst like a fire igniting. Before he could so much as gasp, the dark rushed over Stanley and the world disappeared.

"THERE YOU ARE!" Eric grumbled, pushing his way into the store cupboard. "You're lucky I can find you."

Alistair was stood shirtless, smears of blood over his face and chest.

"Well, how did you find me?" he said, riffling through what looked like a large waste bin on wheels.

"Felt you, didn't I?" Eric said. "Or your shadow forming at least. Here. I went home to get these in case you needed them." He handed over two bags of shade sweets.

"Marvellous that," Alistair said, shoving a handful of sweets into his mouth. "I held her together long enough to get her on the operating table, then I had to fall to pieces. She get through okay?"

"Apparently. Stable, they say."

"Good. And how's that eye of yours?"

Eric switched his focus and peered at Alistair through the blur of his left side. "Vision's coming back. Slowly."

"Good. That would be—"

"The price. I figured. Can I look forward to going deaf at some point? Or maybe becoming a tetraplegic if, you know, I start being able to like touch stuff when they're far away?"

Alistair looked a tad mournful at that. "I don't honestly know. The price can be, well, severe, so it's a possibility."

"Right," Eric breathed, trying not to let that weigh him down. "I take it you regenerated into a corpse again?"

"A patient what they'd lost, actually. Could have done without having to pull my own ribcage back together, but never mind." Alistair pulled a white shirt with navy stripes at the shoulders from a nearby clothes basket. On it were splatters of some vile human secretion, but a violet pulse and it was renewed. He slipped on the shirt. Eric had to admit, he looked quite fetching. "It's a nice get up, ain't it? I might have to put it in my weekly rotation—"

"What is it with you and clothes?"

Alistair gave a saucy grin that somehow reached all the way into his silver hair, making it flash. "I have a thing for uniforms," he said.

"You're disturbing. Like, I think you can't get weirder and then you do."

"I've always been a high achiever in that regard. Now, we should get on." A hand on his shoulder stopped him.

"We didn't really get chance to talk about last night, did we?" Eric said.

"I suppose we didn't, no. We should probably—"

"Though, maybe, we don't need to talk."

"Oh." Alistair's expression tightened. "Right. Okay. Understood."

"Don't get huffy," Eric teased. "I meant you're frustrating, and annoying, and—"

"You forgot handsome and witty and—"

"—you're barely one of those those things. But you are, possibly, sort of not that bad. Person-wise." Alistair gave a short laugh. "And last night I properly, legitimately fell to pieces, didn't I? And I hurt you and you forgave me. Last night, with you—"

"You don't have to say—"

"It made the best out of the worst night of my life," Eric said. "You did. And I can't, oh fuck, this is embarrassing, but, yeah, I can't thank you enough."

Alistair let his thumb trail Eric's cheek, that sweet silence filling them up. "You don't have to thank me, Eric."

"I do. I really, really do." But now wasn't the time. "Here's the thing though. Here's the, well, *the* thing." Eric turned away, rubbing at his mouth, like massaging his lips might make this easier to say. "It's about the Tim umbra."

"Right, okay."

"Well, I thought maybe that it was going after people that Tim didn't like, right? Or that he had a grudge against. The attack on his dad. The girl from the subway. That sort of made sense. But then it turned up with Marishka, and Tim didn't know her. And it keeps hunting me, saying it's my fault, right. And that's what Tim's dad—the umbra he, you know, became—also said. Right?"

"You shouldn't pay that much attention to an umbra."

"Yeah, but what if it was telling the truth? See, the attack on Dee. Tim never met her either. Not even once. But, the last time I saw her I remember properly...." Eric shook his head. "We fell out. And now I'm wondering...."

"You're—" Alistair's forehead wrinkled. "You're saying its attacking folk *you* don't like."

"Not just don't like. Jesus, it'd be busy if it did. No, people that I'm, you know, angry with. Really angry."

"But why would it do that?" Alistair crossed his arms. "What could it gain?"

"That's what I can't figure out either. Like, shouldn't it be going after my mum or the people I care about?"

Alistair nodded. "That would normally be how umbras work. Although, it says about punishing you." Alistair seemed to consider this. "It could be that it wants to make you suffer by, in a weird way, making it your fault that these people are getting hurt." There was a moment of silence, then Alistair piped up, "Not that it is. Your fault, I mean. You weren't to know—"

"You don't have to spare my feelings," Eric said. Since he'd first thought he might be responsible, looking down at what was left of Dee, he'd felt the tingle of guilt running through him. He'd have to deal with that, but later. He didn't have time to indulge himself now. "I just need to make sure it doesn't happen again, right?"

"Well, that's easy. Just don't get angry with anyone else."

Eric shook his head. "That ship sailed a while ago."

"You what?"

"It's too late for that. With Tim dying, and...well, you try being in a hospital bed for a good part of your life and you not feel a bit of resentment. I mean, you felt it, Alistair. You felt what's in me. You know how hateful I am."

Alistair had. Eric could see it on his face, that look like Eric was tainted. Then Alistair pulled him closer. "You're not a monster, Eric."

"Didn't say I was, but I'm not exactly good, am I?"

Alistair ignored that. "You're saying that because you hate these folk, it's punishing you."

"I don't know exactly, but—"

"But, no, that woman at the subway. You never met her. Sally. Why would you hate her?"

"I hated anyone Tim might have...." Eric swallowed. "And if she was the one that ended up getting him killed...."

"Oh," Alistair said. "About Tim. Look, I'm not trying to start a fight, but he doesn't sound like he was.... What?"

Eric couldn't help the bold smile that spread over his face. "That's it! You're a fricking genius."

"Well, it's not the first time I've heard that, so it isn't, but do you mind clueing me in as to why I'm a genius?"

"You said it: I start a fight." Eric dug into his pockets.

"You've lost me."

Eric paced. "If, right, the theory holds up, it should be that if I get angry enough with someone, then the umbra will come. It did when I was fighting Marishka. I was so frustrated and scared, and then she said something about me being a victim and that, well, that got to me. That chuffing pushes my buttons. Don't like hearing the truth, do I? Never have. Oh and I'm starting to ramble like you do. Oh, hell. And anyway, she ordered me to use my power and I guess the umbra felt the rise in my shades, and it came."

"You're gambling a lot on this, though, Eric."

"It doesn't matter," Eric said, putting his mobile phone to his ear. "If I'm wrong it won't matter, yeah? We'll just end up pestering someone. But if I'm right, we can end this. I can get the umbra to appear and fight it. Get this over with."

"Simple as," Alistair said, surprising Eric by not putting up a fight. Then again, Dee was evidence enough that this needed to end, and soon. "Who are you phoning?"

"There's only one person in recent memory who has royally pissed me off enough to warrant being bludgeoned to death." The phone rang, and rang, before a cocky male voice coughed a hello.

"Hi, Grant, how are you?"

CHAPTER FOURTEEN
THE LAST SET

MARC TOLBRIDGE STEPPED out of his car and stretched. The fabric of his clothes complained, cutting into his huge arms. When you reached Marc's size, closing in on close to two hundred and thirty pounds in the off-season, it was hard to find any decent clothes to fit. He enjoyed that fact, though. A bit of a thrill, wasn't it? To be a giant in a world full of small people.

He opened the car boot and unzipped one of his two sports bags. Thank God Spartans had reopened! He'd been having to go to the health club at the other side of Willingsley. It didn't have weights over forty kilograms and it didn't let you take selfies, so it was hardly worth the petrol turning up.

His wristwatch beeped. Time for his pre-workout drink; a carefully timed liquid jolt to ensure his mind would be razor sharp in the gym. Marc prided himself on being a natural bodybuilder. He would never touch steroids of any kind, growth hormones or the rest. But a bit of caffeine and a few legal stimulants were just fine—and this new drink was spectacular. He'd made up about seven different shakers full of the stuff and packed them in the car boot for when he needed them, and he took the first out now. The dark taint was a result of the powder his friend Dwain had given him. It tasted so bitter it was difficult to swallow, but the benefits were worth it. Marc'd added over ten pounds of muscle to his frame since taking his first sip. The drink made him so focused that he could train for six hours straight and barely feel tired. Now, a part of him knew that wasn't normal. How could it be? Logic said not, but he didn't want to believe it. And so he didn't.

"All right, Fit Fam!" he said to his mobile phone as he set about recording a quick intro to his latest fitness social-media post. "I'm about to hit you up with some epic shoulders and squats, because you know how I like to keep you guessing! So let's get inside and see the crew, all right?"

He ended the recording with a cheeky arm flex. Then, phone away, he took a sip of his drink, wincing against its cat-scratch taste. Another. Another. It got easier with every mouthful and he could already feel the mind-muscle connection deepening. He was a beast. A machine.

A monster.

"YOU'RE SURE THIS Grant lad will be here?" Alistair enquired as they walked through Spartan Gym's electronic doors.

"Yeah." Eric nodded. Truth be told though, he was barely listening. He'd not been inside the gym since the days just before he'd found out Tim had died, and the thought of it now made his guts want to come up and say hello. The gym's pulsing up-tempo music, that was still playing despite the late hour, certainly wasn't helping matters, and nor was the fact that, save for shade sweets, Eric hadn't eaten in over a day. "I wish we could have done this someplace else though. I mean, there's still going to be folk about, even at this time. They could get hurt."

"Well, I'll put a lock here," Alistair said, already gesturing over the threshold. "That'll stop more people coming in. And I reckon cornering Grant in the changing rooms is your best bet. We'll be able to keep the umbra contained when it does come out to play."

"Sounds as good a plan as any," Eric muttered as they walked to the silver turnstile gate. He slapped his gym card to the red laser reader on top, and it clicked to acknowledge he could enter. Alistair, unnoticed by the retired boxer behind the desk who had her feet up and was watching a raucous talk show on the telly, jumped over the turnstile with one quick leap.

"You got those shade sweets?" Al asked. Eric nodded, tapping his stuffed coat pockets. "Right." Alistair looked around surreptitiously, though of course he needn't have bothered. With his hand on Eric's shoulder, the pair were practically invisible. "Just in case them sweets aren't opportune, here is something a bit special," Alistair said, handing over a small bottle of what looked like orange juice. "I've fused some shades into that. Liquid doesn't hold on to shades as long but it's easier to swallow, and you can make 'em more potent. Happen in case you need a quick hit without the chewing, that's what you should go to." His violet eyes were full of concern. It seemed he hated the thought of Eric fighting the umbra. Him and Eric both, then. "And this," Alistair said, pulling a knife from his inside coat pocket. "Is one of my favourite creations. I call it a swan blade." The bone knife had a fat handle that tapered to a flat needle-point. Along its length and branching off from its sides were several jagged branches, larger at the base and smaller nearer the tip. It really did look like a long, lethal feather, and though it wouldn't be much good for stabbing, Eric imagined that for gutting someone it'd do the job a treat. "It's weighted so that it should be light. Don't think it won't cut, though. Way back when, it was the kind of blade I carried when I...." Alistair's eyes flashed. "Well, it served me well." Alistair gave the blade over, laying it across Eric's flat palm with amusing reverence.

"Thanks," Eric said, but he was only half there now. Something had occurred to him. They'd left the hospital in such a hurry to get to Alistair's caravan and get tooled up that he'd not even told his mum he was going. The last thing he'd said to her was that he was going to the bogs and, if he died, that would be the last time they'd spoken. They'd gone full circle then, hadn't they? "I know we've got to get on, but...." He'd done the preparing to die bit before, but this felt different. There was so much left undone. There was so much to live for now, because he'd been wrong last night. Even if people and things and life were all always slipping away, it didn't mean he couldn't try to keep them. It didn't mean it wasn't worth fighting to hold on just a little longer.

"I'll do everything I can to make sure you don't get killed, Little Bird."

"I know that, and you chuffing better," Eric said, painfully serious. "But you said yourself, didn't you, that you can't heal the dead? If it happens—"

"It won't."

"But if it does, then I need you to...I need you to promise...."

Alistair put his hand on Eric's shoulder. "I'll look after your mum. And I'll find a way to heal her. You have my word."

Relief. Small, but needed. "Thank you," Eric smiled. "And the umbra?"

"I'll take care of it."

"Good, cheers."

"Not a problem, so it isn't. Now, let's crack on, aye?" Alistair said, sounding more confident than he looked. "I haven't had anything to eat yet and I hear your ma does a good fry up at that café of hers."

"Quick as we can, then," Eric agreed.

"He's coming," Alistair called, holding open the changing room door. He'd put a lock on the threshold to keep people out, and then they'd played the waiting game. "I'm going to keep my eye on what's going on out here. Call when you need me."

Eric got up from the wooden benches, cracking his fingers and limbering up. The room was a pleasant enough black and yellow tiled affair, matching rows of wooden lockers lining the walls, and a row of sinks on the opposite wall to the door. Eric wondered how much of his own blood would stain this place by the time they were through. *That's right, Eric, think positive, mate.*

Grant, red faced and wearing a tight vest, came ambling into the room. He stopped when he saw Eric. "Oh, what the fuck? I said I didn't want to talk to you, didn't I?"

You could just strip off, if you'd like, Eric thought. *No, focus. Monsters.*

"I know what you said," Eric glared, "but it weren't my fault what happened at that library, and I don't think it's right that I was fired."

"Not my problem, mate!" Grant opened a locker on Eric's right and started digging through. The heavy smell of feet wafted Eric's way.

"I saved your arse a bunch of times. I could have ratted you out to Peter but I didn't," Eric said. "You owe me."

Grant took out a can of deodorant and sprayed one armpit, then the other. The thick stink didn't cover up the lingering scent of feet so much as join with it to make a noxious super-smell. "I owe you nowt, you nonce."

Ah, I knew you had it in you, Grant. Eric angled his head, sticking his tongue into his cheek. *This is why you're here. Let it come. Let it come.*

"Nobody at Radley's really liked you. They just do what I tell them," Grant said, lifting his vest and rubbing the sweat off his face. "Mind you, I hear you come from a frigging lunatic family anyway. That mum of yours, telling everyone you were saved. Praise Jesus!" he shouted, putting his hands in the air. "What a nut job."

Eric prepared himself for the cold wash of anger. He balled his fists. He readied the curl of his lips. But, quite astonishingly, the anger didn't come.

Why aren't I getting mad? Eric mused. *Is this personal growth? Is it neurotic to wonder that? Oh fuck,* he groaned to himself. *I'm happy, aren't I? Alistair's made me chuffing happy. Oh, well, that's just bloody marvellous, that is!*

It was time to go on the offensive, then. "You, Grant, right, are a bully." Not a great start. Could do better. "And the fact that you're even classed as a manager is proper hilarious to me. You couldn't manage your way into a nunnery, and your little plan to take over at Radley's was about as subtle as a nuclear warhead." Grant's eye twitched. Eric took that as a good sign. "I'm sorry, was that too cerebral for you? Do you need a simpler analogy for your tiny amount of working brain cells to get what I am saying?" Eric grazed Grant's eyebrows with his own. "It was an absolute joke that I should be labouring underneath you, King of the Morons, every single day—"

"Nobody talks to me like that!"

"Really, because I just did. What are you going to do about it, breeze-block head? Eh?"

The sense of Grant's fingers clenching. A golden red flash encircling Grant's hand. The punch hit Eric square in the nose and Eric reeled back a few steps, nudging one of the wooden benches with his leg.

He glanced around expectantly, but the tug of the Tim umbra didn't come. All Eric had for his troubles was a bloody nose. *Playing hardball, eh? If at first you don't succeed*: "I'm sorry, were you trying to hit me, darling, or kiss me?"

"I'm going to batter you!"

"Oh, promises, promises, Grant!"

Another punch. Eric staggered back. His shadow heart contracted, but it was out of annoyance rather than fear. The heart wanted Eric to fight back.

"I should give you a proper hiding," Grant smiled through lips made thin and ugly. "Show you what it's like to be a real man."

"Have you seen one about?" Eric asked, stemming the flow from his bleeding nose and straightening up. "Because all I see is a pathetic little boy."

"I swear to God, I'm going to knock seven shades of—"

"Well, fucking do it then! Or are you all talk? Come on, Grant, fill your boots. Hit me!"

The punch to Eric's stomach made him double over and slump to the ground. A kick to his legs, then one to the chest. It was the boot to the face, though, that did it. Eric's shadow rose up and slammed into Grant, knocking him off his feet and into the lockers at the other side of the room. Eric turned himself over inch by inch, spitting out blood. A shade sweet swallowed down, and the pain in his chest and his nose began to ease. Grant, still on the ground, was wide of eye and slightly sick looking.

"You're not the only one who can fight, mate," Eric croaked. "I just do it a bit different than most, that's all."

"Fucking freak!" Grant scrambled to his feet and ran from the changing room, pushing Alistair out of the way.

"Where's he off to?" Alistair asked.

"To change his underwear, I'm guessing."

Alistair's lips curved for a smile. "You just used your powers, didn't you?"

"Yeah, why?" Eric said, picking himself up off the ground. "You're not going to give me a lecture are you, because I didn't mean to, I—"

"No, just something strange is happening in there," Alistair said, thumb pointing through the changing room door to the gym proper. "And I've got a feeling they're connected."

"Wait, what do you mean strange?"

"It's better I show you."

Alistair led Eric across the gym, skirting the stationary bikes where a few young mums were busy sweating away the day's stress. There weren't many folk in at this hour, only the really dedicated and, if the skinny teenager over by the pull-up bar was anything to go by, the desperate. "I want you to take a look at someone."

"Tell me the truth," Eric said. "Has Grant messed up my good looks?"

Alistair gave Eric an appraising look. "I can honestly say you look no worse than you ever have."

"You just won't stop with the compliments, will you?" Eric said, rubbing at the bridge of his nose. It had stopped bleeding. Not for the first time, he thought Alistair's mere presence seemed to have its own healing effect.

"I can't see shade infection until it's percolating, but I reckon that you might be able to," Alistair said. "Look," he pointed. Among the shining iron and steel, on a large square of blue mats in front of a long wall of mirrors, stood a group of men who were obviously well acquainted with the gym: they had the size and the area map of veins across their arms, necks and, one man, across his forehead, to prove it. But as big as they were, they couldn't compare to the man currently working a pair of massive dumbbells. A curling wave of blond hair up top, a chest that was so vascular it made Eric a wee bit queasy, and a back so wide it could be used as a lifeboat; the man grunted and hissed as he worked at raising his arms out to the side, taking each dumbbell up into the air and then back, his bulging shoulders cording and reddening with every pump. He repeated this three times, six, eight.

"Yeah!" one of his friends said.

"Go on, Marc!" another, who was recording proceedings on his phone, encouraged.

Eric's sight augmented on its own, letting his left eye find its focus. The burst of sensation made him start.

"Shit," he exhaled. From head to toe, the bodybuilder's veins were running black and sickly. It was like looking at Eric's own shadow heart, except this gave off a distinct wave of menace. "He's, hell, he's riddled with it."

"That's what I was worried about. Kindling, just waiting for a spark. The lack of shadow forming here's probably saved him so far, but as soon as you used your powers in there, the shades started to wake up so that even I could get a sense of it. And now look." As if on cue, the black in the man's veins took on a hot red, and then the darkness in the man grew darker still. "Turn your attention away from him, Little Bird. Quick."

Eric did as he was told, letting his focus dissipate. "What do we do?" Eric asked.

Marc replaced the weights on the rack, but he showed no sign of fatigue. His friends slapped him on the back, and they began to chatter amongst themselves and to the camera.

"Me trying to detox him with the violet fire won't work," Alistair said. "It would require shadow forming, and that'll set him off, so it will. Our best bet is getting rid of some of the shades in his system first, take him down to a level where they can't mutate him, and then I can purge him. Thing is, I can't undo what's done."

"You, you mean he'll always be altered? Like, changed by the shades?"

"Aye. Thing to do now is stop it before it gets any worse."

"Right, well, how do I help, then?"

Alistair took hold of Eric's shoulder and steered him toward the edge of the mats.

"I need you to keep an eye on him while I draw the shades out. If there's any sign of him changing, you have to let me know. You'll also have to look out for me. Once the heart's aphrons are exposed, I'll be vulnerable. Shadow hearts can take in shades direct but we don't do it because the hearts don't much enjoy it and it lays our powers low. In fact, it can kill off a shadow heart. But—"

"Not yours, I get it," Eric said. He centred his gaze on the bodybuilder, letting the man's huge frame take over all that he could see. Despite trying to hold back from probing with his senses, Eric could still feel the shape of the man, could even detect his increasing warmth and the excitement of the shades in his body. Alistair was right, Marc was on the edge.

"Nah, more weight than that!" Marc said from inside the metal cage of the nearby squat rack. His friends began adding plates to the barbell Marc was preparing to take on his shoulders. "It's all about form, and going all out on these last sets," he told the camera.

"Here we go," said Alistair as he rolled the fingers on his right hand and reached out. Then, with his other hand he cradled the space over his shadow heart. A burning violet glow bloomed. Not unusual, this, but then something rather more unsettling happened. Black, probing tubes reached out from the mire, snaking and grasping for the air. When a fair tangle had emerged, they surged out, almost like the arms of a squid, and crossed the distance between Alistair and the hulking man.

Just as Marc was preparing for his squat, legs set firm, feet planted, back slightly arched but not yet having taken the weight, the black tentacles—aphrons, Alistair had called them—grazed Marc's stomach and then shot into his gut.

"Gah!" Marc doubled over, falling to the floor in front of the weight wrack.

"You all right, mate?"

Moments passed as the hungry tubes slid deeper.

"Yeah, just, just a cramp, I think" he said.

"It's okay," Alistair soothed as he saw Eric's hesitance. "That's to be expected. He'll just feel some discomfort. Like a bad meal, that's all. You need to watch him though, because this will—"

"Al, it's like the shades in him are starting to boil."

"Don't worry, I've got a chunk of them now." The aphrons slid free of Marc's gut with an audible slop. The tendrils, which were coated with sickly green shades, curled back toward Alistair's shadow heart, where they crammed those shades into the furnace burning in Alistair's chest. Every poisonous shade stoked the fire and lit Alistair's face with gorgeous purples.

Marc, who had been trying to regain his feet, slumped to the floor again. His gaze locked onto Eric. "What are you doing to me?" he called out to them, just as the aphrons reared up and slid beneath his shoulder-blades. "Ah!"

"Marc? Mate?" said a short and somewhat portly member of the group. "Who are you talking to?"

"Them," Marc said, pointing. Again, he tried to stand but found his thick legs wouldn't support him.

Eric grabbed hold of Alistair, hoping that whatever it was about Al that made him invisible would get to work now.

"There's no one there," said the bodybuilder's friend with the cameraphone.

"They're right there!"

"He can see us," Eric said.

"It's just the effect of the shades. They're not changing him, though, are they?"

"How would I know?" Eric asked.

"They'd start fusing to his limbs, or maybe congregating somewhere in the meat of him. His stomach or his head or...."

"Then, no. They're just being dragged out by those aphron things—which, by the way, creepiness to a factor of ten."

Marc, though, hadn't got the memo about them helping and he lurched forward across the matted space between them. "Stop!" he begged.

"I need a few minutes more," Alistair growled. "Distract him."

"What? How?"

"Think, Eric. You're supposed to be good at that."

With nothing else to do, Eric stepped into the bodybuilder's path. "Listen, mate, we're not wanting to hurt you. We're trying to help. You've been having this stuff, haven't you? Mineral?"

The man winced. "My, my workout drink. I—"

"Yeah, well, it's got some funky shit in it that was gonna make you sick, but we're fixing that. You'll be fine—"

"No, no, you're doing this. You and him!"

The man reared up and shoved Eric to the side, lunging for Alistair.

"No!" Eric shouted, and with that he felt his shadow heart empty. The world seemed to slow, time dilating.

"You left me!" the Tim umbra, huge and rotting, said as it curled from a cloud of black smoke that rose between Alistair and the bodybuilder. Wasting no time at all, the umbra reached out and closed a giant fist around Marc's head.

"No!" Eric yelled, catching the monster's arm and trying to pry it away. "Al!"

"I can't," Alistair said, winding in the aphrons, but the process was too slow.

"Let me go! Let me go!" Marc yelled, battering at the creature.

"No, don't do this," Eric begged, trying to pry the creature's fingers off Marc's face. "Don't do this! Please!"

Marc screamed as the Tim monster squeezed. Squeezed.

"No!"

The hideous crunch and pop, the burst of blood that oozed from between the umbra's hand. Then it released the man and let what was left fall to the ground. Eric dare not even look.

"Fuck!" shouted one of Marc's friends. As one, the troop backed away and ran.

"You forgot me," the umbra said to Eric. "And now you will—

"Hi, I don't think we've been properly introduced," Alistair said, slapping a hand to the umbra's chest and letting the violet fire surge. The umbra rocketed back into a weight rack, scattering metal plates across the floor. Screams went up around the gym, but Eric ignored them. Instead he concentrated on shoving a handful of shade sweets into his mouth and pulling free the swan blade he'd been hiding in his coat.

The umbra turned to smoke, then recollected to stand just a few feet away. Its chest heaved, and with every step it left writhing maggots on the ground.

"You must be a special blend, umbra," Alistair said, a spear already across his shoulders, waiting. "There's no way you're above wild class, not yet, but that fire barely grazed you, so it did," he said, angling the spear in an accusatory manner. "I'll fair enjoy getting a taste of your shades."

Eric wasn't listening. He was preoccupied with a very pressing question: *Why'd it come now but not before?*

Someone screaming stole his attention away. Over on the yoga mats a woman in blue shorts and a thin white vest, in the midst of a downward facing dog pose no less, pitched over onto her side, let out a wail and with an awful rip her back heaved and split open in one long seam, bursting like an overripe berry.

Folding up and out of her there came two, four, then eight twitching stalks of white legs that scraped and scrabbled for purchase on the mats. The creature's head, replete with twelve differently sized blue bulbs for eyes, emerged next, then at last came its body; a long length that curved round into a lethal hooked tail baring the woman's face. The fat nubs of the creature's foremost legs broke apart into sinister claws which it clacked while hissing in hungry pleasure.

Screams rattled Eric's ears.

"They can see it," Eric shouted.

"I'd noticed!" Alistair walked back a few paces, eyes always on the Tim umbra. "Glamour's broken. This is bad."

"You left me to die," the Tim monster yelled. "We were best friends. I loved you and you left me! I was alone. Afraid!"

That brought Eric up short. He looked at the Tim umbra, and in one turn his mind finally saw the shape of the problem and its answer. *My medium is my shadow. My power is to see. To feel. But what about what's already there? What about what I felt, deep down? What if it's not attacking people because it's trying to get to me. What if....*

"Prepare yourself! This is going to get bad," Alistair shouted, before running at the umbra again. He aimed the spear at the umbra's side but before he'd even let the spear go the umbra sank into the ground, vanishing in wisps of black. "What the?" Alistair said as he skidded to a stop. "Can you see it?"

"No, I'm...." Eric held up a shade sweet as he chewed another mouth full. His shadow heart filled and Eric let loose a sensory flare. "There's another umbra."

"Where?"

"I can't—"

"Eric! Where!"

Eric stopped fighting the sensations and instead tried to listen to his shadow heart. "There." He pointed. One of Marc's friends, now alone in front of the mirrors, dropped the phone he'd been recording everything on. The man shook, muscles lurching and pulsing, and his eyes bulged in their sockets.

Eric said it before Alistair did. "It's too late. It's gone too far." And, sadly, he was right. With spraying blood and a gurgling scream, the man went to pieces. Insects like big woodlice forged of the man's own muscles ripped out of his skin, burrowing out from his stomach and legs, and soon a few intestines and the powder of broken bones was all that was left of the beta male.

"That's...rank. Oh, crap!" As one of the creatures scuttled by his feet Eric saw that on their backs, each wore an image of the man's scream. "This is mental, I...." Another flare. "There's another near the door."

"The Tim umbra must have done it," Alistair said, grabbing at Eric's wrist and leading him to crouch behind a row of vacant rowing machines. "Oh, this is not going well, so it isn't."

"You think?"

Alistair cupped a hand over his own shadow heart. "Marishka, I need you here. Now."

One of the muscle lice, unseen until now, leapt from around the corner, pincers trained on Eric's throat. An arm of smouldering shades shot out from a nearby white pillar, grabbing the monster and crushing it, followed by the rest of the Tim umbra's hulking form. "After all I had given to you. After everything I tried to do for you. You left me to die alone!"

"I didn't leave you. I wasn't...I wasn't there...." The umbra was deathly close and swinging. "Fuck," Eric said, the single syllable almost a squeak.

An arm hooked under Eric's shoulder and Alistair leapt, pulling Eric up high into the air. They landed on a metal strut that ran the length of the gym's ceiling, Alistair picking a spot close to a vertical beam where Eric could wrap his arms for balance.

"Marishka," Alistair shouted, touching his shadow heart. "Get your leathery arse over here."

From this dizzying height, Eric could see the chaos and carnage that had taken over the gym. People were running every which way as the muscle lice and the scorpion woman ran through the crowds, picking people off with their teeth and claws. Another man over by the door was retching. Eric chewed a shade sweet to replenish his supply and augmented his sight again. Tangles of weeds poured out of the poor man's mouth, then double-headed vines pushed out through the man's eyes, spreading an awful milky fluid down his face.

Eric pulled back his senses, one hand over his mouth to keep back the moan that he could feel brewing. Now he knew it without a doubt: "It's all my fault."

"I'll give you one thing, Jingoro," Marishka said as her feet touched down on the beam with perfect grace, her veils shifting around her as her transport flies settled into their dormant state as the cape at her back. "I thought you were being a bit dramatic, but I suppose not."

Alistair scowled. "It's manic in here, so it is. The umbra of his dead friend keeps showing up, I had to fight it, and that set off all this." Alistair popped a shade sweet in his mouth, set fire to another bone spear and threw it, harpooning one of the lice creatures and a now out-of-order rowing machine. "Marishka, if they get out...the city is chock full of these dark shades. The entire place will begin to turn. It's...." He clocked the expression on her face. "But you know that, don't you?" And then another question came in bright and clear. "How exactly did Finder die?"

Marishka smiled. "Now what about that umbra, Eric?" she said, putting an arm around Eric's shoulders. "Time is running out."

What was up with the lad? Alistair wondered. No backtalk. No quick wit. It was like all the air had gone right out of him.

"Class this," she said, waving a hand over the bloody scene, "as an incentive, Eric. You have to face the umbra, or no one is getting out of here alive."

She was up to something, Alistair was sure. He had to distract her until he could figure out what it was. "Marishka, this has happened before, hasn't it?" he said, slinging another spear. The silence, though, lasted a little too long. He looked at Eric. "What's going on between you two?"

"I'm right, aren't I?" Eric said to Marishka, ignoring Alistair's question entirely. "H-how long have you known?"

Marishka clucked her tongue. "I suspected it for a long time. I've been watching you, Eric. But when that *thing* appeared in the library cellar, that was when I had my proof. How long have you known?"

"I didn't. Well, I didn't know enough to question whether it really was an umbra or not."

"What do you mean?" Alistair barked. "Of course it's an umbra."

Marishka looked at Eric with an understanding, almost a sympathy, that Alistair had not seen in a long time. "Then you know how to beat it, don't you?"

"What in the Verse are you two talking about?"

"Th-th-this," Eric said, taking a glug of the shade-infused juice Alistair had given him. Then he stepped off the metal beam and fell hurtling toward the floor.

"Eric!"

The Tim umbra coalesced beneath Eric, caught him and in the same quick move threw him against the wall, where the lad crumpled up on himself, coughing.

Alistair let himself tip over the edge of the beam and then, overclocking his muscles with the violet fire, slammed his legs into that metal so that he shot toward the umbra. He collided with it, sending them both rolling across the ground. Before Alistair could right himself the umbra had its hands around his neck, squeezing, robbing him of breath. It was strong, but Alistair had the advantage. He opened his mouth and belched a plume of fire. The monster reared back. The flame might not kill it, but the umbra really didn't seem to like the attempt. Alistair used the advantage to leap up and over the umbra, landing on its other side not far from Eric. The lad had picked up the swan blade, but he was twitching in fear, and something else. Something worse.

"What's going on?"

"C-c-can you use that fire to make sure that it can't get out?" Eric asked.

"Eric, now's not the time. The other umbras—" Just to illustrate the point a hissing muscle louse leapt for them, its metallic legs ready to clamp around Alistair's face and hollow him out. A click and the thing exploded in midair.

"Don't you worry about them, or any of these umbras," Marishka called down. "I have the danger in hand," and just to illustrate the point she shot out her arm and a ribbon of flies spun toward the door where the dreadful plant umbra, now fully formed and almost reptilian, hissed. The flies landed on the creature and as one detonated, blowing it into twelve dozen pieces.

"Why do you think you can beat him now when you couldn't before?" Alistair asked Eric, eyes always on the monster.

"Because I know how it was made." The Tim umbra threw a punch. Alistair caught it, twisted up in the air and flipped the creature onto its back. A deep swing with his leg and Alistair kicked the umbra, sending it rolling end over end across the floor. When it came to a stop Alistair was there, standing over its chest. He brought his arm down, his fist breaking through its ribcage with a deep crack.

"You betrayed me," the umbra yelled, seemingly unaffected by the fact Alistair was elbow-deep in its chest cavity. "Damn." Sadly, its hands weren't as insubstantial as its insides and it grabbed hold of Alistair and threw him. Alistair twisted in the air to land on his feet, skidding into the exercise bikes and getting himself caught among their frames. *Not my finest landing.*

"Al," Eric said, walking toward the umbra. "Do it."

"Eric?"

"Please," Eric started, and Alistair knew what was coming next. "Trust me."

He stood. "I hope you know what you're doing."

"Never have before," Eric said, but there was none of his usual humour now.

Cringing against his every instinct, Alistair flexed his arms and slammed his fists against the ground. In motes like feathers, violet fire surged out. The light circled the monster, penning it in, and when the umbra approached the inner circle's wall it flared and the umbra reared back. Confident it wouldn't cross that perimeter Eric stepped within the circle, and Alistair allowed the fire to rise and the circle close.

THE MONSTER LOOKED down at Eric, its eyes now burning black and so deep they seemed endless. "Look what this has done to you," Eric said, his voice thick with sadness. "What I've done to you."

"You forgot me," the Tim creature said and it lunged.

Eric brought the knife slashing through the air. It passed straight through the monster, but it had the effect of interrupting its charge. "No," Eric said. "Never." The monster began circling. Eric could feel the danger. It wanted to kill him. It hated him. Hated him for what he had done. "If anything, for the first time I think I know exactly who you are," Eric sniffed and, though it took all his courage, he threw down the knife. "You're me."

"You left me to die. I was on my own. In agony."

"No. That wasn't your story. That was never your story."

"I loved you!" the creature screamed, and it arms stretched impossibly until its sinewy hands closed around Eric's throat, its razor-sharp fingers dragging blood out of Eric's back and shoulders, its palms pressing his windpipe until Eric couldn't breathe.

"Kill me," Eric gasped "and we both die."

ALISTAIR SET HIS feet. He raised his hands, and from his back there burst a skeletal set of wings. He flexed those new appendages and the wings set ablaze with violet energy, pulsing and dark. "Eric!"

"Alistair," Marishka called as she landed next to him. "You'd dare show yourself to him?"

"It doesn't matter if he knows what I am. I can't let him die." Alistair readied himself to break his bonds, to let the true fury of the fire in him pour, but then Marishka's gloved hand closed around his arm and he knew he would never even get the chance. "No. Please!"

"By the Law of First Binding, I forbid you to interfere."

"No!" But though he struggled to fight the command, to keep his power running, a symbol seethed to life on his forehead and the violet fire dimmed before going out entirely. Bare now, his skeletal wings withered and turned to dust. "He's dying," he cried, throwing off Marishka's hand.

"But not dead yet," she said, and the note of confidence threw him; it made him look at the situation anew.

Behind the curtain of power that kept them confined, the Tim umbra stood, even larger and more menacing than before, a true colossus now, and in its clenched fist Eric hung like a rag doll. There was no way Eric could fight it. The little trick of throwing his shadow, it wouldn't work. The thing was too strong.

"No, he's going to die," Alistair repeated and prepared to enter the ring. Before he could take even one step he felt the blood in his veins turn cold and solid. He would move no more.

"Keep yourself awake, Jingoro," Marishka whispered. "Burn that violet fire. But watch, because you have vastly underestimated your Little Bird. He is far more accomplished than either of us could have guessed."

Alistair, with his chest ablaze, was forced to do exactly as she said. He would watch. He would watch Eric die. He wanted to scream. To cry out, but he couldn't so much as wiggle the end of his fingers.

Long seconds stretched of the umbra throttling Eric, shaking him, raging about the ring screaming, and then the umbra stopped. Seconds throbbed, and its fist twitched. Then its fingers unclenched and Eric dropped to the ground.

More silence. More time.

Alistair, with everything he had in him, tried to scream. It came out a whisper, but there nonetheless. "Eric?"

ERIC, SON, TIME *to wake up.*

Eric dragged in a breath. Another. He was right then. *Good news, that.*

"You deserted me! You should have stayed at my side! You all should have. I was alone—"

"In that hospital bed," Eric coughed, finishing for the monster. He knew this script well. It was his own, after all. "Alone when I needed to say goodbye and I had—"

"No one. I mattered that little. And I loved—"

"Tim, so much," Eric said. "But it was unfair. Whatever Tim felt for me, I always asked for more. And he tried, he really did. But he was damaged, and I didn't see it. I didn't want to see it because I needed someone. I needed a guardian. I needed someone perfect. So when he left me that night, that dark, awful night—"

"I hate you," the Tim monster bellowed.

"I hated him. And I hated—"

"This world! And I hate that—"

"Mum is sick and one day, one bloody awful day I will have to say goodbye to everyone and everything I love and that, in the end, everything and everyone will—"

"Come to dust," the monster said.

Silence claimed the room. Such impossible silence. Eric looked around. The gym had been emptied. The umbras were gone. The room was a gory wreck. "But," Eric said through bloody lips, "not today." He tried to stand, felt his legs almost give, but no. He reached out for a metal pole, a barbell he realised, and used that to raise himself up. The monster glowered at him. It raised its fist. "No." Eric said, and just like that the umbra lowered its hand. "I know who Tim was now. He wasn't perfect. Not even close. But I believe, even though I can never know for sure, that if he could have stayed with me that night—"

"I would have," the monster whispered.

"And I believe he was sorry. That's why he trained so hard. That's why he said—"

"I want to be strong enough," the Tim creature echoed. "I want to be good enough. For you."

"And maybe that's me making shit up to comfort myself, but perhaps that's okay too." Eric reached out his hand, his fingers hungry to touch a face now long gone. The Tim monster's features blurred. When they resolved again, it was Tim as Eric had remembered him. The Tim from Eric's drawing and that too perfect face, those lovely indigo eyes. A horrible, unworthy fiction. "Just how I hope you know," Eric said, letting his hand graze Tim's chin.

"That if I could have been there for you when you needed me," the creature droned.

"I would have done anything. I mean, I have bled for you." Eric took back his hand. "I can't keep at it. Bleeding. I can't. Look what I've done. This heart made you to protect me, but my hate, my anger, made you into something awful." Eric closed his eyes. When he opened them again, he was smiling, a big, bold smile. "We did the best we could, mate, and we got a fucking lot wrong, but I have so many good memories. So many. And I won't forget. Not a second. Not a one. So thank you. And...." Eric wanted to look away. He wanted to make this easier, but, *No, don't you dare.* "Goodbye."

Tim smiled, holding up a hand as if to take Eric with him into whatever vanishing point the dead will lapse, but Eric stepped away. Then the creature began to fade like a cloud had passed over its sun, until it became nothing more than a shadow. Eric turned his back on it, and it slipped into place at Eric's feet.

THAT WAS THE last of the bins taken care of, then, Jhardine ticked off on her fingers. Good, she needed to put her feet up. Felt like she'd done a marathon, what with the hospital and everything. *Poor Dee,* she thought as she shuffled down the landing, and then she stopped. *What was that?* Then again: a flicker of light crossed the stair wall. Jhardine turned. That same light shone on the door frame of Eric's room. Jhardine, hand on the wall like she was working her way through a maze, crept close.

"Oh chuffing hell!" She raced to the bathroom and ran the tap. Dumping the toothbrushes out of the glass on the sink, she got a dose of water and then ran for Eric's room again. There, on Eric's tip of a desk, something was on fire. She threw the water and, in typical Jhardine style, missed entirely. "Oh, sodding, bloody, chuffing," she panicked. And then, of its own accord, the fire went out.

Jhardine's face turned mardy. This wasn't normal, and she had no patience for *not normal,* not today at least. She stepped closer, closer still, and reached out a hesitant hand. She picked at what appeared to be a fairly crispy bit of paper. It wasn't warm, but its edges were singed. She lifted it up. In the moonlight, Jhardine could see a very faint image. Yes, it was definitely the picture of Eric and Tim, except faded now, and there were queer symbols where there hadn't been before. In fact, they dotted every inch of the page. She'd seen them before, she was sure. She'd seen them....

In a bathroom at the hospital. They were on the wall, creeping like frost, that night Eric was supposed to die.

Before she could wonder what they were doing on a piece of paper in Eric's room, Jhardine ripped the page and scrunched up each leaf. She put first one half and then the other in her mouth, chewing and swallowing them down.

When this was done, she clapped her hands. "Right, time to tell Mum about banging a vicar," she said with no small amount of glee and she left the room having completely forgotten the fire, the paper, and the odd bout of mastication.

"YOUR HEART TOOK the idea of shadow forming a tad literally," Marishka said to Eric. She ran a hand down Alistair's back and the man's stiff arms relaxed, his posture slackening as though the string that had been pulling tight in him had just been cut.

"You did well, Little Bird." He closed the gap and pulled Eric into a hug.

As always, Eric felt the heat of Alistair's power lapping at him, mending his scars.

"If you don't mind," Marishka said and Alistair let Eric go. The woman offered her metal hand to Eric. "I was looking for more than power," she said as he let that arm hang. She looked amused and took her hand back. "I was looking for intelligence. And for a will to survive. These are qualities that the Sisters honour. But I had to know that you could overcome this mess you had created for yourself."

"Does that mean I can join, and that you'll help my mum?" Eric asked. It was really the only thing that mattered now. Well, that and.... He glanced at Alistair, then away.

"I think there's one other little matter to which we should attend." Marishka cupped her shadow heart. "Dianna, if you please."

A gout of black energy erupted a few paces from where they stood, and from it fell a man. A familiar man. "Stanley?" He looked pasty and cold, and as he stood he seemed unsteady, as though not having used his legs in a while. "What's he doing here?"

"Stanley?" Marishka said.

"I gave you freaks what you wanted, and you said I could have the cure."

"I'm afraid you mean the other freaks." Marishka smiled. "Empty your pockets, there's a good boy," she said.

"You can bugger off. I—"

His voice cut off with a flex of Marishka's hand. His eyes widened and fair threatened to pop out of his head as his left hand trembled and travelled toward his jacket pocket. From it he took out a metal chain.

"What's that?" Alistair said, but Eric knew instantly.

He snatched it from Stanley's grasp. "This is Tim's. I got him this. Where did you get it?"

Stanley looked at him.

"Answer," Marishka said, and Stanley roared in pain.

"All right, all right. I got it off him. The night I...." He looked to Marishka, seeming to finally understand that pain would be the answer for his not cooperating. So he straightened himself out in the way that Yorkshire folk have, and he tried for dignity. "The night I cut your little boyfriend up and supped his blood. I was so glad I happened on him. Off his head he was, so tanked up on that Mineral filth. Even big as he was, it were child's play. Used that chain to steer him into the car. Pulled on it like it was reigns."

Eric's fingers traced the ghost of hurt he'd felt on his own throat. "Why?"

"I'm old and I've done nothing with my life while you little shits parade around here wasting yours. And then *he* came to me."

"Who?" Marishka pressed.

"The man with the face made of wax," Stanley finished. "And he showed me the way."

Marishka and Alistair exchanged a look, but Eric only had eyes for Stanley. "You killed Tim so you could keep living?"

"I did," he said, and he actually looked proud of himself. "And I'll do it again when it needs renewing ten years from now."

"You assume that we'll let you live," Marishka said. She picked the swan blade off the ground where Eric had dropped it and held it out for him. "No one would blame you, and indeed, by the laws as set out by the Sisters, he is yours to punish as you see fit."

Eric took the knife.

"Think careful, Little Bird," Alistair said. "This is a different kind of killing. You can't take vengeance back."

"I know," Eric said, and pushed the blade to the nape of Stanley's neck.

"Now, come on, Eric, I—"

"Shut up," Eric snarled.

"But I—"

"Shut it or so help me, I will pour my shadow down your throat and make it take form. Explode you from the inside. See if you survive that, you cock." He turned to Marishka. "Is there a way to wipe his memory of the shadow forming?"

"The foxes can, but why?"

"We have courts here what deal with this. He should be arrested. He should be put away."

"You could end it now," Marishka said, as though speaking to a child. "You have the power, you just said it yourself."

"But I don't have the right. And if I killed him, cold blood and all that, it'd make me just as bad as him," Eric said, throwing the knife down on the floor once more.

Marishka nodded. "I will make the arrangements. But first, there is something I would like to know, dear Stanley."

"You can go diddle," he said, but he seemed unnerved. The thought of spending his remaining time in prison clearly wasn't sitting well.

"The Waxling. Have you seen his face?"

A smile broke out on Stanley's face. "Oh, aye." He laughed.

"Tell me."

"No."

"Tell me!" Marishka flexed her metal fingers and Stanley screamed. He screamed and screamed, then threw back his head and began to choke.

"Marishka?" Alistair asked.

"I...." Marishka was puzzled. "I'm not doing it. I—"

Wax bubbled up out of Stanley's mouth, thick globs of it that solidified to plug his airway. He collapsed to his knees, clawing at his own neck, and then his head turned a sharp angle and something snapped. He slumped, dead.

"I guess Ruth'll get to go on that cruise after all," Eric said.

Marishka huffed. "It seems Wax would like to stay hidden a little longer. Shame."

"Never mind that," Eric said, not caring that this was probably breaking the rules of what one should do after someone died. "Have I done it? Have I passed your test?"

Marishka looked pleased. "In fact, you did quite well. I was surprised. So, you have done enough to earn a place among our initiates."

Eric's mouth opened, then it closed. Then it opened again. "What?" He could hardly believe his ears. "What do you mean, initiates? I thought—"

He heard Alistair groan, but Marishka only laughed. "Did you think that you were in our ranks just by clearing up this little mess? You flatter yourself."

Where's a fucking huge shadow giant when you need it?

"But," Marishka said, "the initiation process will be swift. I have a few other candidates in this area. I will come to you in a few weeks, and we will begin."

"But—"

"I'm not done." Marishka's eyes flashed. "As a courtesy, I will start the search for a cure for your mother at once."

Alistair clapped a hand on Eric's shoulder and whispered, "I'd take it. It's the best you're going to get."

"Fine," Eric said. "Yeah, cheers." His disappointment and anger were obvious but he couldn't risk throwing an epic tantrum. Well, not in front of Marishka anyway. "W-what are you going to do about all the dead?" Eric looked around at the severed limbs and headless torsos that littered the room.

"We'll have to use the foxlings, I fear," she said, picking her way across the gym's ruined floor. The banged-up drinks machine in the corner gave a loud groan and collapsed in on itself. "Though it might have been prudent to cancel your membership before the fight, Eric," she said.

EPILOGUE
UNFINISHED BUSINESS

IRENE HARDINE WAS FEEDING her face with a huge slab of chocolate cake. She figured, given that radiation therapy would start making her feel ill any day now and she wouldn't want to eat, she might as well gobble down whatever the hell she wanted while she still could. So, for her next treat, she was eyeing the quiche she'd brought to share. Eric, she reasoned, was getting dangerously close to being chubby. This was more a service to him, then, really. "There's a good side to everything, Eric," she'd told him as she bit through the quiche's pastry base and felt the cool egg and cheese blend to form a cloying, delicious paste. "You know, I reckon," she said around a mouthful, "that this is probably going to be the last good bit of weather we have this year."

"We're talking about the weather, Mum," Eric said, swinging his legs over the edge of the railway bridge. "Something's gone desperately wrong."

"No, it's just that you're so boring I can't think of owt else to talk about," she said and then cackled, which wasn't easy to do around a doorstop-size lump of food. "Here. I've been meaning to say, though, thank you for being right with the vicar being round so much. You've probably figured out—"

"That you've been rogering each other." Eric nodded.

"Oh, Eric, you do have a way with words." She laughed again.

"It's okay, though," he said. "I mean, theologically speaking me and the dear old vic might not get along, but...he makes you happy. I reckon that you deserve that. More than deserve it, actually. I—"

"Oh God, you're a drama queen!" she said. "Here, hand over that flask will you, love?" Eric did, and she shoved it under her jumper. "It feels like my tits are gonna break off it's that nippy. And I can't be having that. Not now that there's someone to appreciate them."

"Aw, Mum, that's rank. I don't want to know what you and him get up to." Eric's face took on an inquisitive twist. "Is he dirty? Like, really dirty? I don't know why but I just think he has one of them faces what says he would be."

"I can't say owt. You know me, Eric, height of discretion." Another mouthful, and then: "I do need some new knee pads though. Worn right through all my best trousers."

"Oh, hell." Eric buried his head in his hands.

Jhardine cackled some more.

Yes, life could be scary, but today was a good day and she'd decided to hold on to those for as long as she could.

ERIC PICKED AT his pickled onion-flavoured crisps, watching the clouds racing across the sky. He was reaching for another swig of tea when his shadow heart prickled. He kept a constant, small supply of shades burning now, just in case there were umbras or the like near. It also meant that the symptoms of the heart's power, the auras, errant tastes and strange smells, would occasionally bother him. Things were getting better there, though. He'd found a bit more control. He could tell, for example, that the tingle wasn't danger but down to Alistair being nearby. The scent of rose water was what clued him in, and that darkness that Eric couldn't name. "Mum, I need to take a whizz."

"Oh, you dirty thing, can't take you anywhere," she said, rolling her eyes. "Well, make sure you do it well away from me. I don't want splashback, or trickle down for that matter. These are new clothes, you know?"

"Duly noted," Eric said, walking around the bridge and down the track.

Alistair was waiting for him just a few meters after the bend in the path. He wore a dark charcoal-grey suit, those huge black boots he was so fond of, and black epaulettes and a black bow-tie. A bit fancy, but pleasant to behold all the same.

"You all right there, Little Bird?" he asked by way of a greeting.

"Aye," Eric said. It had been a week since the Spartans fight and, after Alistair had helped Eric home, they'd not seen each other since. No falling out, just an understanding that some space was needed. "What about you?"

Alistair smiled. "Not too bad. I have something for you."

"Oh?"

"From Marishka."

"Oh." A chill ran through him. "War time already, is it?"

"No." Alistair held up a clear, fluted bottle that contained a red-violet liquid that seemed to glow. "Technically, it's for your mum. The first in a line of treatments. It won't cure, but we're trying to weaken the voiding. It'll also fortify her. Keep her healthy while your doctors do their job."

"B-but..." Eric said, "I thought shadow forming wouldn't work because she's voided?"

"Difference between actively using our powers on her and her taking in something that's been engineered by cyphering. You'll understand when Marishka starts training you. It's her department rather than mine."

Eric stared at the bottle. He stared and stared. God, he couldn't even put a price on this. "I don't know what to...I mean, *thank you.*"

"Well, it's not—"

"A cure, I know, you said. But still." He couldn't stop the grin. "The colour. The, the violet. Did you?"

"Me and Marishka's hearts are, er, let's just say they have a history. They work well together, so they do. Marishka's blood is poisonous, and she can create all sorts of banes but, if you add my healing fire to it, well, we can create medicines." Eric held the bottle tighter. "We'll keep working on a cure. Marishka's put out a call to other healers. We think a cyphered healing on your mum might be the way we'll finally beat this, but we'll need to work out precisely which hearts we'll need and how we'll connect our powers. And of course, I'm doing what I can. I'm looking for the bugger what voided your mum. They have the power to take it away, so...." Alistair's unlined face became serious. "But Marishka's firm. She wants that shadow heart of yours on our side. You have to keep up your end of the deal."

"I'm not going to go back on my word. Especially not now." Eric couldn't help the flash of memories. All those people in the gym. The blood on the floor. The screams. "People got hurt and died because I couldn't control my power. I'll never forget that. Not them at Spartans. Not Dee, not any of it."

Alistair didn't try to console him, and he was grateful to not be patronised. All this was an unfortunate fact: it *was* Eric's fault, whether he'd meant it to happen or not. He would have to hold that inside for the rest of his life.

"That Dee, her with the, the face," Alistair pointed a vague finger. "I was thinking I could go round and heal her. Get her back to fighting shape, you know?"

"That's nice, but you can't. I mean she's not there at the hospital. She's gone missing." He'd heard a few days ago from his mum that Dee had just up and left the hospital not long after she came round from the surgeries, no word to anyone as to why and no clue left behind as to where she might have gone.

"That's a damn shame, that is," Alistair said, and he looked genuinely aggrieved. "So, what are you going to do while you wait for Marishka to come round for you?"

"I hadn't given it much thought, really. Just being there for Mum, you know?"

"Sure. Well, what about letting me train you?" Alistair said. "I might not have much of the book learning stuff, but I'm a good fighter."

"That won't piss Marishka off? Before, she said...."

"I think that was more about the creature you made rather than anything else. Anyway, I'll talk her round."

"Well, yeah, then. That'd be good."

"Good," Alistair echoed. He glanced around, and then he stepped closer. "You happen to know if any of Marishka's flies are about?"

Eric closed his eyes and probed the air with his powers. If her spies were there, he couldn't feel them. "Go on."

"Okay." Alistair took in a deep breath. "Here's the thing: she's going to want to examine your heart. She'll get Reader to do it, but you have to make sure he doesn't."

"What, why?"

The wind picked up and threw a glitter of cold rain their way. Eric heard his mum give an annoyed squeal. "Because your heart is, well, not special exactly, but different." Alistair smiled. "Really different."

"What do you mean?"

"I had a hunch, something what came to me the other day, before the fight at the gym. I think that your heart...."

"What is it?"

"Eric, I think that your heart is—"

"Eric? Where the flipping heck are you?"

"Crap, I've got to go, but what were you saying?"

Alistair seemed to consider for a moment, but then shook his head. "No, it doesn't matter. I mean it does but maybe the less you know, the better. I don't want to put you in any more danger than you have to be in. Just think on what I said about Reader, yeah, because I don't know when it will happen but it *will* happen, you know?"

"Okay, yeah, I'll try my best not to let him get a hold of me."

"And if he does, use your powers, try to keep your heart active, it confuses what signals he gets."

"Yeah, sure."

"Good," said Alistair. And he seemed to want to say more, but:

"Eric!"

"Christ, yeah, I'm coming," Eric shouted back. Then to Alistair he said, "If you hadn't guessed, that's Mum, so I've got to...."

Alistair nodded. "Oh, I was thinking I might swing by tonight if, that is, you don't mind?"

"No, that's fine. We can start training, then."

"Yeah, or, you know, whatever." Alistair gave a flirty smirk.

Eric grinned. "Right, I will catch you tonight, sunshine." He tramped away a few paces then stopped. He walked back. "I, er, forgot something."

"You did?" Alistair looked confused. "I—"

Eric cut Alistair off with a bruising kiss. Their fingers laced, their breath came fast, and for the first time in his life, Eric felt the beating of another man's heart.

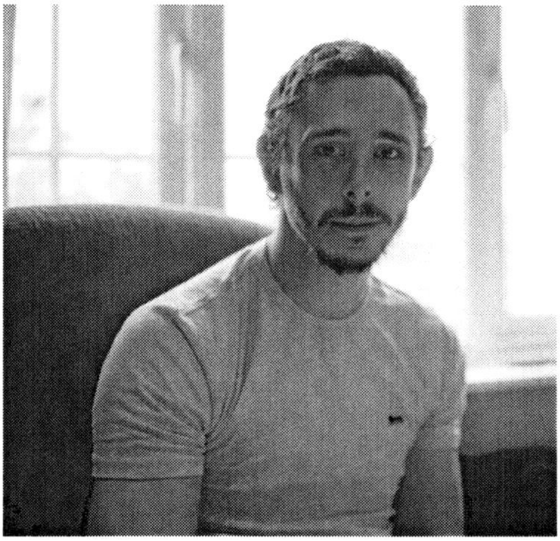

STEVEN B. WILLIAMS is a thirty-year-old tie-wearing, tea-swilling, curly-haired writer and poet from West Yorkshire, England. When not working on dark fantasy he can be found scribbling about queer rights and mental health, cooking up a vegan feast, running charity races, or generally cooing over his cats. His short stories have appeared in zines such as *Lots of Planets Have a North*, and he is co-writer on the forthcoming webseries *The Misadventures of Delilah James*.

CPSIA information can be obtained
at www.ICGtesting.com
Printed in the USA
LVOW08s1112300117
522599LV00002B/309/P

9 781590 212622